CW01082934

DEADLY DEED

ARIZONA HOMICIDE FILES BOOK 2

RENA WINTERS

PREFACE

This book is based on an actual homicide incident that took place in the 1950s in Arizona.

Gene McLain, nicknamed "Bulldog" and the "Man of Murder," was an investigative reporter employed by a national Hearst newspaper who wrote about and solved major crimes.

In the 1950s, computers were not used in police work; there was no internet, cell phones, boom boxes, MTV, seat belts, air bags, VHS, CDs, DVDs, or DNA testing. None of the technology we take for granted today was available. There was only the teletype, and law enforcement agencies were not connected.

Television was brand new, and the nation was amazed at black and white images that seemed to come out of thin air. There was no air conditioning in vehicles, and air conditioning in new homes was just coming to the marketplace.

There was no Miranda-Escobedo law. So, when you were arrested, you forfeited your rights, and the police and sheriff departments could get confessions any way they wanted.

We did have crime, and that's what this is all about. The world of homicide and the mean streets, Gene McLain's world. He not only wrote award-winning stories about crimes, but in many cases, he also solved them.

CHAPTER ONE

JUNE 1, 1953, 4 PM
CUSTOM TAILOR SHOP
PHOENIX, ARIZONA

WALTER BRENNAN REMEMBERS CHECKING HIS WRISTWATCH ON JUNE 1st at 4:05 pm. The Phoenix valley sun shined with a vengeance; minimal traffic occupied the streets, and an outside thermometer boasted a stifling 109 degrees. Walter would join his family for a 6 pm train headed to his home in San Francisco, a beautiful city cooled by the morning fog. In the meantime, Walter escaped to Val Tchaikovsky's air-conditioned tailor salon, where the lyrical stream of a Mozart sonata filled the air. There was a side joke that Val Tchaikovsky, born in Moscow, disliked most Russian composers but insisted on playing Mozart over and over and over. In fact, Brennan recognized Mozart's Sonata in "C" playing as he walked into Val's salon.

Two snowbirds remained in Phoenix—Jerry Goldman, a sixty-year-old retired banker from Denver, Colorado, and Fred McIntosh, a sixty-five-year-old stockbroker from New York. Jerry and Fred were having the final alterations to summer suits they had ordered from Tchaikovsky. In his mid-thirties and known as Rick, a third man was in the fitting room and had removed his pants, preparing to dress in his newly-purchased suit.

The fourth, whose identity was unknown, paced up and down a long rack of lightweight sports jackets suitable for the summer months. This man and Mr. Tchaikovsky were in the middle of a verbal confrontation. As the music moved into the recapitulation movement of Mozart's Piano Sonata, the sound of a .45 automatic ripped through the air.

The first bullet hit Tchaikovsky in the stomach just above his shiny belt buckle. Tchaikovsky threw his hands into the air, attempting to ward off any more incoming bullets. The second shot entered high in the center of his chest, turning his shirt into a bloody rag, and the final bullet entered the left side of the chest. All three shots left gaping exit wounds in Tchaikovsky's back.

"That fixes you, you son-of-a-bitch," yelled the gunman. Tchaikovsky fell backward, blood quickly pooling around his head. "If any of you move, you're dead," the gunman added as he backed toward the velvet drape separating the front and the back of the shop.

He pushed the door open where he ran into the Perkins sisters, both taking souvenir photos at the time. The gunman disappeared down the alley while the third man known as Rick quickly dressed and exited through the front of the shop.

CHAPTER TWO

JUNE 2, 11 AM
GLOBE, ARIZONA

IT'S A HOT, DUSTY DAY IN THE SUMMER OF 1953, PROBABLY AROUND 110 degrees, and I am driving to Globe, Arizona, at the request of my editor, Ralph "Specs" Bornheim, at the Arizona Republic. You must be crazy, Gene McLain, to take this two-hour, 87-mile drive from Phoenix in the middle of the summer, I think to myself—a bad habit I have, speaking to myself in the third person, that is. Specs smells a story since he read the wire service about a homeless man being found alongside U.S. Highway 60 just outside of Globe. So, here I am sweating like hell—even with the windows down—instead of having a tall, cool drink in one of Phoenix's local bars, listening to the local gossip and looking for a story.

Globe has been called "one the friendliest towns in the west." Everyone is your friend, and people don't wear politics on their sleeves. It's a small old copper mining town that has not seen any new development since its inception around 1875. Its main street,

Broad Street, is still narrow and lined with the original structures from the mining days.

I seek out the local sheriff and inquire about the murdered homeless man found a few days before on the side of the road. The sheriff informs me that murders simply do not occur in Globe, there's just a tiny resident population, and people get along. He directs me to the medical examiner's office, who is also the only local doctor in Globe. I arrive at the medical examiner's office to find an elderly gentleman working over the body of what appears to be the homeless man.

"I am Gene McLain of the Arizona Republic in Phoenix, and I am here to cover the story behind your homeless man and why he turned up on the roadside."

The medical examiner is not friendly. I take a seat, intending to wait until he can answer some questions, and pull out my notebook.

"This is not a library. You can't take up residence here. Leave your card on the desk, and I will contact you when I have completed the autopsy," was the gruff reply from the medical examiner.

I look closer at the body, and it seems to me that he might be an Indian from the San Carlos Apache Indian Reservation, which is just a few miles up the road. It's hard to tell. The body is covered with dirt, shredded clothing, long hair, and a beard.

"Possibly an Indian, huh?" and I make a note to look into that possibility further.

The reply is harsher this time,

"I will call your paper when the autopsy is complete."

Well, so much for the friendliest town in the west. It's been a long drive for nothing. I walk down Broad Street and chat with a few of the locals, but none of them have any idea who the murdered victim might be. This is going nowhere. I stop at the local eating establishment and order a cold Coke. The locals stare—definitely not friendly to a stranger from out of town.

I take a drive out to the San Carlos Apache Indian Reservation and speak to several local Indians hanging out in front of a run-down store. They laugh at my question about any local Indians who have turned up missing.

They say, "Indians go missing every day, wander off the reservation never to return. Some get roaring drunk and return a few days later after they've sobered up and run out of money to spend in town."

They don't put names to the individuals they are referencing, and the conversation seems to have dried up, so why am I standing in the heat like an idiot. The Indians sit down, and the conversation is over.

I return to my old jalopy, roll the windows down, and start the long drive back to Phoenix. At least evening is approaching, and there seems to be a slight breeze coming up. The drive home should be more pleasant.

CHAPTER THREE

JUNE 3, 8 PM
PHOENIX, ARIZONA

MY WIFE BLONDIE HAS PUT SIX-YEAR-OLD JERRY AND EIGHT-YEAR-old Larry to bed, and my dinner is waiting cold in the refrigerator. She is listening to the sounds of the radio, dancing around the living room as Teresa Brewer sings "Till I Waltz Again With You," which now permeates the downstairs of the house.

As she hears me coming through the house, she flips the radio off and stops dancing to greet me. I make a mental note that I need to take my wife dancing more, although I am not much on the dance floor. We head into the kitchen, and she turns the oven on, placing my cold dinner on the rack to heat, which will take a few minutes. She sits down at the table and obviously wants to talk.

"Have you heard the news? You know the murder of the local tailor, Mr. Tachaikovsky. You've been by his shop, I don't know, maybe you have even been inside?"

I know who she is referencing, but I have never been in his tailor shop. His clothes are too expensive for my taste. Besides, I like Hawaiian shirts or loose shirts to wear outside my pants to hide the pistol tucked inside the waistband. I am not a suit kind of guy, which doesn't exactly please Blondie. She sees cops all day long with uniforms or the detectives and the lawyers with suits. She thinks I am a bit of a slob, but I prefer to be comfortable.

Blondie pulls dinner out of the oven and proceeds to tell me about the killing of the tailor. "He was killed in cold blood, right in front of several people. No reason. No motive. Seems several witnesses heard him arguing with a young man—five to be exact, who identified the killer."

I assure her that with that many witnesses, it won't be long until the sheriff makes an arrest.

At that moment, I hear our youngest son hollering from upstairs for his mother to read him a story. She gets up from the table and proceeds upstairs. I finish my reheated dinner in solitude. It's been quite a day. Tomorrow I will talk with the cops about the tailor's murder and see what information can be had to follow up. For now, it's off to a cool shower and bed.

CHAPTER FOUR

JUNE 4, 9 AM
ARIZONA REPUBLIC NEWSPAPER
PHOENIX, ARIZONA

I WALK THROUGH THE ARIZONA REPUBLIC WITH COFFEE IN HAND, looking for Specs. I pick up my messages, hoping there is one from Globe, but there isn't. The ME is really slow in doing his job. Everything moves slower in Globe. Specs doesn't have any new information to add to what Blondie has already told me about the tailor's murder, except the police have some kid they think is the killer, a Bob Davis. I return a few calls, make some calls, jot down notes, and decide to wander over to the police station for more information.

Chief Deputy Harry Morse speaks up as I approach, saying, "Well, here comes Bulldog," and the guys he's talking with turn around.

"You know why I'm here? I want the names of the witnesses in the Tchaikovsky killing and any information you may have regarding the killer. Have you got him yet? Seems with all the witnesses you must have an identification."

The guys all laugh. It's only been forty-eight hours, and they feel confident that the kid they have in custody is the killer. Right now, sitting in the Chief's office is the killer, and when you ask my old friend, the Chief, for an interview with him, he nods as if it's almost routine.

"Okay to go in now?"

"OK, sure, Gene. Go ahead. He has calmed down."

"Calmed down? Why, was the trip from Chicago rough when you brought him back?"

"It's always tough when young punks like that know that we've got them cold. He is a funny kind of kid, funny kid, jumpy, you know. So go on in and see what you think."

"I won't take long."

"My name's McLain, Bob, Gene McLain from the Arizona Republic. Do you want to talk?

"About what?"

"You know, what I've been doing this morning."

"What?"

"When my paper got word that they were bringing you back, I started looking up the people in town who knew you. Just talking to them and making notes."

"I don't know anybody in Phoenix."

"Sure you do. Alex Fergus said that you stayed at his rooming house for a while. Here, see."

"What did he say?"

"Not very much. You have a rough time back home, kid?"

"You mean reform school? Partly."

"What did your teacher back home mean? She told me on the phone that she remembered that you were afraid of the dark."

"My teacher? Ms. Hodges. Boy, you did a lot of talking."

"That's my job. Are you afraid of the dark?"

"Me, look Mr. … McLain. I guess, in a way, I have always been afraid of something. Sometimes it's okay, like when the grass is getting green, and the sky's all blue, but then it's dark and cold, and nobody cares. Real scared like a little kid. Ah, forget it. It don't make sense."

"Are you scared now, Bob?"

"Sure I am. That guy that brought me back, he says that I killed Mr. Tchaikovsky."

"Did you?"

"No … Do you have to go?"

"Now, look at me, Bob. Listen to me, listen to me real hard. Alright. Three witnesses pulled your mug out of the file. Three good, decent, honest people who swear you went into that tailor shop and killed Val Tchaikovsky."

"But I didn't."

"Do you expect me to hear you say that you did? Now look, you knew the place. You worked there once, and you needed dough."

"Sure I did."

"Listen, there is more. Right after the murder, you fled, kid. Do you know what that means?"

"Sure."

"And finally, you've got a record for armed robbery. Go ahead, add it up yourself."

"I didn't kill him."

"No, why not? Where were you on the 24th?"

"I told them I was in El Paso. I hitchhiked with a friend."

"El Paso is 500 miles away. Can you prove that you were there? Where in El Paso? Did anyone see you?"

"I talked to this guy in a tourist cabin."

"You haven't told me anything yet."

"I am trying to. I didn't kill anybody, Mr. McLain. I got to keep saying it. Don't you understand? Does anybody believe me? Do you?

"Alright, Bob, I need my head examined. I will go along on a hunch. I will try to help."

"I tell you, I never killed anybody."

"Look, son, the cops in this town play square with me. I play that way too. If I come up with something against you, I give it to them. It works both ways, kid. That is the only way I want it. Okay? Okay. Let's go to work now."

You listen to this boy, Gene McLain. You see what Chief Morse meant. A funny kind of kid—nervous, jumpy—and I wonder if my hunch is all wrong, but somehow when I look at Bob Davis, I go on trying. I go back to Chief Morse and try again.

"I am not making a big pitch for the kid, but all I say is that if the kid did hitchhike to El Paso, let's talk to the boy that was with him."

The Chief says, "We did. The FBI picked him up the same time that we landed Davis."

"What did he say? Was he with Davis in El Paso?"

"In Chicago, they told the boy that Davis was in trouble, and they didn't hold him. There was no reason to. By the time that we got there, the boy was gone. Makes sense, doesn't it? You don't hang around when your buddy is up for a murder rap, not when you know that they have him cold. Sorry to punch holes, Gene, but this one is cold."

CHAPTER FIVE

JUNE 4, 6 PM
MCLAIN HOME—CAMELBACK AREA

I GO HOME THAT NIGHT THINKING MAYBE THERE ISN'T A STORY HERE. Perhaps the kid *is* guilty. All evening through dinner, I only half-listen to the boys chattering about their school day, and to Blondie, I seem distracted.

Once the kids are in bed, she comes back downstairs and wants to know what the trouble is. I try to explain about a young kid being held for the murder of the tailor and the fact that he keeps saying he is not guilty to anyone that will listen.

The trouble is that the police captain and his crew are not listening. They believe they have him dead to rights. He has a motive—money—and opportunity, in that he knew the tailor. And once he is placed in a lineup, they are sure he fits the witnesses' description, and he will be identified.

After my first meeting with him, I am not so sure he is the right person. A person of interest, yes, but maybe not the right person.

My gut is doing funny things, like when there is something really wrong.

CHAPTER SIX

PHOENIX POLICE DEPARTMENT
ENCANTO BLVD.

On the second day of incarceration for Davis, the police bring in Davis to face the witnesses in a lineup.

I sit there listening to one witness after another. *It doesn't look good, Gene McClain. You can't feel sunk now.*

"I was right there on the sidewalk right in front of Mr. Tchaikovsky's store. That's the man, alright. That's him, right there."

"Me and young Bob were friends, sure. Him and this other young lad came to my room the day Mr. Tchaikovsky was killed and changed all their clothes. Yes, sir, and told me to be sure and burn them," Alex Fergus remembered.

"I heard the shot in my barroom next door, so naturally, I ran into Mr. Tchaikovsky's shop to see what the trouble was, and I bent over him and saw that he was bleeding profusely. And Mr. Goldman, a client in the shop, was bending over him and said, 'Was that the guy who did it? The one who was trying on a sports jacket,' and Tchaikovsky looked at him, and says,

"Yes, that's him."

Now Goldman looks at the lineup of men and says, "That's him right there."

Gene, you are faced now with a nod from the grave but still hopeless as it seems you go back to the boy.. Why maybe because somehow, deep down inside of you, you want to believe him.

You go back to the jail to see the kid.

"Hello, Bob."

"Hello, Mr. McLain. I was just looking out the window."

"Oh, anything special, hm?"

"Funny how green it is. Back home now, this time of year, everything is all brown and cold. You were there when all those people said I killed him."

"I was there."

"Sorry, Mr. McLain. They're wrong. They are all wrong. All of them."

"You don't seem very excited about it, Bob."

"I just have to keep saying it to you. I don't know how or anything, but they made a mistake. I didn't kill anybody. They are all wrong."

"What was the name of the tourist cabin in El Paso, Bob?"

"The Bluebird. I kind of know the guy that runs it."

"Oh, he saw you on the 24th?"

"Sure. I said I was there, didn't I?"

"What's his name?"

"Ah, Bill Gorham, no wait a minute, Jim Gorham.

Well, make up your mind, son."

"I got mixed up for a minute. His name is Jim Gorham. Well, what's the matter, don't you believe me?"

"Take it, easy kid. Jim Gorham, huh? I'll see what I can do."

I go back to my office and sit there silently, wondering if the kid really is innocent or is he just stringing me along. Better check out this Jim Gorham, though, just to see if he remembers anything.

CHAPTER SEVEN

I START OUT THE MORNING WITH THE INTENT TO FOLLOW UP ON Davis's lead—this Jim Gorham guy—when the phone rings. It's the ME's office from Globe.

Yes, he has completed the autopsy, and yes, the man was stabbed several times in the upper chest region, which caused his death. Most of the dirt and the bruising was caused when the body was tossed from a vehicle at a fairly high speed. The amazing thing is that the corpse turns out to be much younger than the body represented. He is a young man about thirty-two, thirty-three years old. The dirty clothing, the beard, the long hair, and the weathered face made him look much older. The ME says he probably spent a great deal of time outdoors, possibly herding sheep or cattle, or he just loved being outside in the sun. Nobody has reported a young man missing, so probably no family to speak of. He put up a rather good fight, as there are marks on his hands, knuckles, etc. His features identify him as an Apache, probably from the San Carlos Apache Indian Reservation or the Salt River Canyon area of Arizona.

Now that the coroner has cleaned him up, I ask that they take a picture and mail it to me at the Arizona Republic. I plan on running a story about the mysterious murder and the discovery of the highway corpse in Globe, using the picture. Perhaps someone will see it and identify him.

The doctor says, "Okay, expect it in a few days."

Already I am thinking about the story "The Highway Corpse" in quiet Globe, Arizona, where nothing out of the ordinary ever happens "in the friendliest town in the west."

I go over to the police department to see if Chief Morse has any additional information on the kid.

"You sure are spending a lot of time on this Davis thing?

"Well, what's a reporter got? Time. Well, and maybe hunches."

"Hmm, with hunches like that, it's a good thing you don't play the horses," says Phil Rivera, a uniformed police officer, over his coffee cup.

"The District Attorney is all set to ask for first degree."

I turn my attention back to Chief Morse. "I know. Do me a favor?"

"Sure, if I can."

"Run a check on a hotel owner in El Paso. A guy named Jim Gorham, runs a tourist cabin called the Bluebird."

"Check for what?"

"See if he was with Davis in El Paso the day of the murder, the 24th."

"Ah, Gene, I want to be fair, you know …" the Chief pauses.

"A routine check, Harry. You know it won't be much bother."

"Look, Gene, I don't have to tell you how I operate. The way I look at it is a good cop has two jobs. He helps put the guilty in jail, sure, but his job is just as much to protect the innocent too."

"I know that."

"Nobody is railroading this boy, Gene. If you think we ought to check this guy in El Paso, okay, we'll check him. That's no bother at all."

A call goes into the El Paso authorities. *You sweat it out, Gene McLain.* I wait for them to find Gorham if there is a gentleman named Gorham. I wait to see what he will say. *You hang on to your hunch, Gene.*

And then it comes.

"Mr. McLain, I thought that you were alone."

"I have something to tell you, Bob."

Chief Morse has come along on this visit and speaks up.

"They have set a date for your trial, Davis. The District Attorney is going to charge murder in the first degree."

"But you said they found my friend in El Paso, Jim Gorham?"

"They did."

"Well then, didn't he tell you that I was there."

"He thinks that you were in El Paso around the 18th, not the 24th."

"The l8th, but I was there on the 24th."

"Gorham doesn't know that for sure, Bob. All he can remember is that you were in El Paso around the 18th, which leaves you plenty of time to get back here and knock off Tchaikovsky." Chief Morse speaks up, "Gorham is no alibi at all. You do understand that?"

"I understand."

"Well, son."

"First-degree murder, that's the gas chamber? Or life imprisonment? Is that right? Suppose I plead guilty to second-degree murder? What is the punishment for that?"

You get a hunch about a suspected killer, Gene McLain. Then, one by one, three witnesses blow your hunch to bits. You hear one of them tell how a dying man nodded his head, and you know that nod from the grave can consume all that you believe. The story blows up in your face, Gene. Blows up when he wants to make a deal.

"Why shouldn't I plead guilty, Mr. McLain? Second degree means they can't give me the gas chamber."

"Because innocent men don't try to make deals. Don't you see that?"

"They do if they are licked. When it's dark and cold."

"You still stick to your story that you were in El Paso the day of the murder?"

"I told you I was with Jim Gorham."

"And you didn't kill Mr. Tchaikovsky?"

"I didn't kill anybody."

"Then why did you offer to plead guilty. Why kid? Why?"

"You remember the first day you talked to me."

"Yeah, I do."

"You asked me if I was scared? I'm scared now, Mr. McLain."

"Well, I don't know why kid, but I believe you."

"You are the only one that does."

"You're telling me."

Leaving the jail more perplexed than ever before, my gut tells me the kid is telling the truth, but none of the evidence points that way. He is a goner for sure. What more can be done?

CHAPTER EIGHT

JUNE 5, 6 PM
MCLAIN HOME

ALL THAT DAY AND INTO THE EVENING, MY MIND KEEPS DRIFTING back to Bob Davis. The way he looked at me as if I were God and could make the police department find out the truth and get him out of jail.

He's just a scared kid. Won't admit it, but he is scared. He is trying to stay tough and hang in there—for what, he doesn't know.

I am constantly troubled by something about this case but can't put my finger on it. Seems as though the police department has it all wrapped up—neat and clean. The only thing left to do is prosecute him, convict him, and sentence him.

There must be something more that I can do.

All that evening at home, I am troubled by that thought—even into story time for the kids. I read them a story about a bear who invades Goldilock's home and destroys everything. They want to know when the bear will be brought to justice. How do you identify which bear? That is the problem.

Even in the kids' books, I seem to be trying to find the answer for Davis. How to identify if he is the right person.

I toss and turn most of the night. Even get up and walk downstairs to get a glass of water and sit for a while in my recliner. My mind is racing. What more can be done to help this kid?

Then it hits me.

CHAPTER NINE

JUNE 6, 10 AM
PHOENIX POLICE DEPARTMENT

YOU GOT A CRAZY IDEA, GENE McLAIN. I GO BACK THE NEXT DAY TO see the kid.

"Did you ever hear of a lie detector, Bob?"

"Yeah, I read about it."

"Would you be willing to take a lie detector test? Now, think before you answer. If you're lying, that machine will know it."

"Well, I'll do anything that you say. If you want me to take a test, sure, I'll do it."

"Alright, Chief Morse must be getting sick of me, but I will try. That's all that I can do, Bob. Try."

My hunch worsens, or maybe it's just my hope. Chief Morse agrees to the lie detector test, and as a special favor to me, Dr. Morrison agrees to conduct it. So, I sit there, tense, listening to a boy battle a machine for his life.

"You live in Massachusetts?"

"No, I mean use to. Now, I don't live anywhere."

"Try and confine your answers to yes or no. Are you twenty-five years old?"

"Yes."

"Do you own a gun?"

"No, well … I did. I had an air rifle once."

"Do you own a sports jacket?"

"Yes ... I did once, anyway, once a long time ago."

"Would you like to own a sports jacket now?"

"Oh, sure I would, anybody would."

"Can you drive a car?"

"Sure, I could a long time ago, maybe not now. Maybe now I couldn't."

"On the afternoon of the 24th, were you in Mr. Tchaikovsky's tailor shop?"

"No, not then, before. I worked for him … a couple of days for him."

"Have you ever been to El Paso?"

"El Paso? Sure. There is a motel there, a tourist cabin, you know, green grass …."

I'm no expert, not when it comes to determining the results of a lie detector test, but I know even before Dr. Morrison explains that it's the result Chief Morse wanted.

Dr. Morrison clarifies, "Some courts will admit it as evidence, and some won't. If you need me at the trial, I will be glad to appear. I don't think the DA will need it. The whole thing was Gene's idea."

"I had that agreement with Dr. Morrison that if the test turned out wrong, Chief. you were entitled to use it if you wanted."

"It certainly turned out wrong for Davis." Chief Morse said.

"Frankly, it couldn't have been worse. Lying all the way through?" I looked at Dr. Morrison.

"The results were identical to those you would expect if a man were lying, yes." The doctor confirmed.

"By the way you answered the question, Doctor, do you mean he could get these same results if he weren't lying?"

"In special cases, yes, it is possible. Not probable, you understand, but it is possible."

"What? Just what kind of special case, Doctor?"

"Well, if the subject is highly erratic, emotionally unstable, what might be described as an upset personality. Someone like that taking the test could produce answers that indicated he is lying, even if he were telling the truth."

"Even if he was telling the truth."

"Gene, you are beating your head against a brick wall, don't."

"I am sorry, Chief. I have to, but I don't know why."

"There isn't one single fact about him that gives you any right to believe in Davis."

"I know. I know that, and yet I still do."

CHAPTER TEN

JUNE 6, 12 NOON
ARIZONA REPUBLIC NEWSPAPER

I AM SLOW ARRIVING AT THE OFFICE; I STOPPED AT THE POLICE station first. Specs is frantic, trying to reach me.

"Gene! Gene, there is another highway murder in Globe."

He wants me to drive back up there today, but I don't like the idea. It's hotter than hell, and I have a lot to do here in Phoenix. I tell him I will make some calls.

On the phone with the sheriff of Globe, trying to get details seems like a thankless effort. I get simple answers to questions, "Yes, no, and maybe."

Yes, another body was found alongside the highway. No, there has not been an identification yet. Maybe another Indian, but he couldn't tell, as the body was too damaged. He isn't talkative.

I call the ME for more details.

"The body is another Indian, a young man. Seems there's an epidemic all of a sudden." Two murders in Globe. Epidemic!

They should spend some time in Phoenix with the gangs, Mexican gangs. Largo Hall, who heads the south side gang, and his buddies are viscous. Every day we have a murder, mostly Mexicans. Street violence is escalating daily on the south side of Phoenix. Chief Morse has gone out on a limb and said, "His cops will clean up the south side of Phoenix."

This means that for the foreseeable future, things are going to get rough in town on street punks.

The medical examiner says, "The body has stab wounds, just like the first victim who they have now identified as John Ravenshead."

There seems to be a war against Indians all of a sudden. They have lived quietly next door to the reservation for many years and never experienced the problems going on now. The medical examiner says, "That this new victim's—Jimmy Purple Hills—wrist is very swollen like something has been torn off his arm, perhaps a bracelet. He also put up a strong fight. His knuckles are badly bruised, and his face shows marks of being hit several times. This Indian did not have traces of alcohol in his system, which is quite rare. Someone probably thought he was just another drunk Indian. He really put up a fight. His attacker, or attackers, probably would have some marks, bruises, scratches, and indications of a struggle on their body. The sheriff is looking around town at the local population to see if anyone he meets seems to have indications of a fight."

Not much happens in quiet Globe, so it should not be difficult to spot someone with scratches and bruises.

I make a note to follow up with the sheriff in a couple of days to see if there has been any progress in "The Highway Murders," now plural. I hammer out another column on the typewriter about the second murder in Globe, put it on Specs's desk, and leave for the day.

A good reporter finds stories outside of his office desk, not sitting around waiting for the phone to ring.

CHAPTER ELEVEN

JUNE 7, 10 AM
PHOENIX POLICE DEPARTMENT

I WANDER BACK TO THE DETENTION AREA AND MEET WITH DAVIS once more.

"Come over here by the window, Bob. You can see the lawn."

"Yeah, I know. I have been watching that tree out there … it changes shape all the time, you know."

"Yeah, sure as it is green. Let's go back to El Paso again."

"Sure, if you want to. Mr. McLain."

"Now that motel is called the 'Bluebird,' right? And Jim Gorham owns it?"

"We have been through that a hundred times."

We have nothing else to do, kid. Now, the day of the 24th, the day that you say you were in that motel in El Paso. Did you see Gorham that day? That was Wednesday. Remember, we figured it out."

"I know, that was the day that he had Joan with him."

"Joan? Joan who?"

"I don't know. Joan, a nice girl, kind of red hair, short."

"Wait a minute, this is important. You met this Joan at the motel, right?"

"I told you Jim brought her around. They were going to get married. Yeah, that's it. Saturday, they were going to get married."

"Him and Miss Joan? You saw them together. They both saw you?"

"Sure. Oh, I am sorry that I forgot that. Is it important?"

"Important, anything is important, anything at all."

I leave the kid thinking that this may be an important bit of news and drive directly to the Chief's house.

"Yes, Gene, come in, or you will drown on a night like this. It's raining hard."

"Well, I thought you would be here at home, Chief. This won't take a minute. I just saw Davis again."

"You're a glutton for punishment. I'll say that."

"Look, Davis met a girl at that motel in El Paso, a girl named Joan. She is an alibi for him."

"What makes you think that?"

"The girl was going to marry Jim Gorham, you know the guy that owns the motel. The guy who can't be sure when he saw Davis, but maybe the girl is sure. Now listen, this girl was supposed to get married the Saturday after the 24th, three days later, you see, so that is a big week in her life. She will remember things, women are like that. Now, if she saw Davis on Wednesday before she got married, met him, and talked to him, she might remember."

"Is that what you came out in all the rain for?"

"Well, somebody has got to go to El Paso, find this Joan and ask her."

"The somebody being me, I suppose."

"Well, that would be official."

"El Paso? You know a trip like that, there and back is close to twelve hundred miles."

"Davis is pretty close too."

"Yeah, yeah, he is. I don't know what you do to me, McLain, I swear I don't."

I know the Chief, or probably one of his detectives, will make the trip. I know that he is that kind of a cop, and now through the next weeks and the long nights, all I can do is wait and hope. I don't know when he will go or send one of his detectives, so all I can do is wait. And I hope that they can find this Joan, the redhead in El Paso. I remind myself again that if I play fair with the police around here, and they will play fair with me.

CHAPTER TWELVE

JUNE 7, 7 PM
MCLAIN HOME

AT HOME, BLONDIE KNOWS THAT SOMETHING IS NOT QUITE RIGHT. I explain the situation that I'm waiting to hear from the police that this girl "Joan" exists and that she remembers Davis being in El Paso on the 24th.

Blondie understands my concern, but she still wants me to take the kids to the park on Saturday and spend some time with them. They miss their father. Yeah, yeah, I know, but another young kid's life is at stake—and that seems to occupy all my thoughts and time right now.

As I lay in bed this night, I realize that Blondie has a point. I don't seem to spend much time with our kids. Maybe we should plan a vacation. Just some time away where we can all be together.

My kids need me too.

Tomorrow I'll think about something fun that we can all do together.

CHAPTER THIRTEEN

JUNE 7, MIDNIGHT
MCLAIN HOUSE

I KEEP HAVING A FUNNY THOUGHT ABOUT THE MURDERED INDIANS IN Globe. I hear the ME telling me the last victim's arm was badly bruised and that there was no alcohol in his system. Suppose whoever attacked him thought this was just another drunk Indian, and we will roll him for a few bucks. Doesn't seem reason enough to fight so hard. Maybe he was wearing a nice silver and turquoise bracelet, or perhaps that red stone, red jasper, they use. One of those big things that the Indians make on the reservation and sell. It might even have been a gift from a girlfriend or family member, which is why he fought so hard to keep it.

Suppose they are attacking the Indians for their jewelry. They're all wearing some jewelry, necklaces, bracelets, rings, or such. They make them on the reservation and sell them to visitors in town. Some of the Indians even take a bus trip or drive in an old car down into Phoenix and sell their handmade items to the jewelry stores in

Phoenix and Scottsdale. The tourists that visit Phoenix each winter grab up the Indian jewelry. They love the look of the custom pieces and especially like showing them off back home in the east. Maybe it's not the money, but the jewelry that the killer or killers are looking for. I'll have to make another trip to Globe to the reservation now that we have a name for each of the victims and see if they liked to wear nice jewelry, or perhaps they created the jewelry they were wearing.

Surely, one of the Indians locally will remember what they designed or were wearing, especially if they were large, extra nice pieces. Just a thought that I have to follow. Why else would they fight and kill two young Indians? The victims fought hard but didn't have much in clothing or probably money on them. What was it that made them victims? Just hate crimes? Probably not—Globe has lived alongside the reservation for years and never had a problem. Everyone accepts the Indians in town, knows that they are harmless. They just get drunk and then return home to the reservation in a few days.

These strange thoughts keep rolling around my brain all evening, preventing me from sleeping soundly. Finally, I get up around midnight and sit in the recliner in the living room, turning the radio on to listen to music. Nat King Cole sings "Pretend," Frankie Laine sings "I Believe," and I finally drift off with Eddie Fisher and "I'm Walking Behind You." Tomorrow is another day, and I never know what it might bring.

CHAPTER FOURTEEN

JUNE 8, 9:30 AM
ARIZONA REPUBLIC NEWSPAPER

IT'S MORNING, AND WITH MY SECOND CUP OF COFFEE FROM ACROSS the street in hand, I hit the newspaper room and my desk. There are a couple of calls to return and a few new leads to follow.

Another murder on the south side, but the cops have arrested a Mexican kid, Randy Gonzales, who claims he was home with his mother all evening. I will follow up on this as the mothers are usually so scared of their sons that they will say anything to keep peace at home. Out of love or fright, they lie for their delinquent children, perpetuating the crime on the streets of south Phoenix.

Many are illegal, terrified of being sent back to Mexico where they can't earn a living as housekeepers, cooks, gardeners, drivers, etc., leaving them with no way to support their large families, several children, and a useless drunk father laying around.

The only way the Phoenix police are going to clean up the south side is to actually catch the kids committing the crimes and lock them up, giving them long sentences. Perhaps this will instill fear in the youth gangs, enough that the murders, rapes, robberies, and vandalism will stop at least for a while.

Some of the Phoenix police just want to shoot them and ask questions later. They claim that will also stop the crime sprees. The sheriff's department runs pretty much autonomous and has been known to beat confessions out of criminals.

I drive out to the south side of Camelback Road and hunt for the house where the arrested kid lives. His sister opens the door, and I explain that I am from the Arizona Republic and that I am there to see their mother. She explains that her mother does not speak English. Great! This is going to be difficult. I ask the daughter to translate, which she agrees to do. I explain I am a reporter from the newspaper and want to know about her son's arrest for a gang killing.

The mother starts yelling to her daughter that her son is a good boy and would not kill anyone. He takes care of his sister and mother, even works sometimes. Yeah, it's the same story each time. The mother does not know where the boy goes or who his friends are. He brings home a little money, so she thinks that he works for it. Doesn't know where he works. Probably steals the money or sells items that he steals for cash. To her, he is a good boy. Helps his family out. This has been a wasted morning, getting me nowhere, and a trip to the south side, which I really don't like.

I drive back into town and stop at the Legal Eagle coffee shop for lunch. Mary O, the owner, greets me with her Irish brogue, "Top of the morning!" and "How is your day going?"

My day is not going. I know that the detectives will have a hard time getting the mother to say anything against her son. This will be another one of those cases that remain unsolved. Another young Mexican kid, probably illegal, on the streets is found murdered. No one seems to pay much attention, no one is missing him, so little is done. The police think another criminal is off the streets, and no family is screaming for justice if that is possible.

So, it slips into the unsolved boxes of cases in the back room downtown at the police station. One of these days, I should spend time looking through those boxes and perhaps come up with clues that might solve some unsolved cases. The police department is too short-handed to assign officers to review cold cases. Once they go into the cold case boxes, they are usually just stored unless some-thing, some clue, drops into their hands, and they reopen the case, which is most unlikely.

In your head, you see the box "Cold Case #21 and the date—Young Mexican Gang Kid Murdered—being stored on the shelf at the police station, probably next to others with similar markings. No one seems to be looking for this kid. Just another hoodlum off the streets.

Maybe there is something more that I can at least do for the one kid that claims he is innocent. I go back across the street to the jail and see Davis once more.

"Pretty good town, Phoenix. If I got, that is, if I get out of this, then what? Oh, I could stay here and get a job. Maybe stay right here and stop wandering around all the time."

"I think that would be a good idea, Bob."

"Look, can I ask you something, Mr. McLain."

"We might as well talk, Bob. We may have a long wait."

"Those witnesses that said it was me, why?"

"Well, look, Bob, people are human. And people can make a mistake, especially if they're excited."

"I can understand old man Ferguson. We did tell him to burn our clothes, but I can't understand the other two witnesses, the bartender and the woman on the street. They weren't even in the shop at the time of the shooting. I sure can't. They were so sure it was me."

"Before you were picked up in Chicago before you were even suspected, these people were shown photographs of people convicted of armed robbery."

"They picked out my picture?"

"That is right. Let's say whoever shot Tchaikovsky looked like you, not too much, but a little, okay? The word goes out to pick you up in Chicago, right. Now in the meantime, the witnesses go on staring at your picture. A couple of days later, who do they see in the office? You. And what happens. They identified you because, by that time, your face was familiar to them. They honestly thought they saw you in Tchaikovsky's store."

"Hey, Bulldog, Ralph Bornheim is on the phone looking for you. I thought you might be in here."

What the hell does Specs want now?

"Well, kid, I have to go for now. See you soon."

Yeah, Mr. McLain."

I grab the phone from the cop, "Hello, what's so important that you are looking for me at the jail?"

"Two gang kids just stole a gold statue from St. Mary's Catholic Church and beat up the priest. Get over to St. Joseph's Hospital and talk with Father Nicolai. That's if he's able to speak with you."

CHAPTER FIFTEEN

ST. JOSEPH HOSPITAL
PHOENIX, ARIZONA

At the hospital, I locate the room of Father Nicolai and see a figure in the bed swathed in white bandages with only the eyes showing. The kids must have beat him up pretty bad. I tell the Father that I am Gene McLain of the Arizona Republic newspaper and want to talk with him about the robbery. He doesn't seem very interested. I ask if he knew the kids. He shakes his head slowly from side to side, which I take to mean that he doesn't. I ask how many of them entered the church. He raises a hand with three fingers. I ask if he can identify them. He slowly shakes his head again. This is going nowhere. I ask about the gold statue, trying to get some identification.

"Was it a statue of Mother Mary?" More slow movement from side to side.

Guess not.

"Was it a statue of one of the saints?"

The head moves slightly up and down, and the eyes blink. How am I going to get an explanation of which saint?

Probably not today.

Where the hell can kids sell a statue of a saint which everyone will identify with as coming from a Catholic Church? These street youths don't think very far ahead. How are they going to unload this statue? It's too identifiable.

CHAPTER SIXTEEN

JUNE 8TH, 4:30 PM
ARIZONA REPUBLIC NEWSPAPER

I RETURN BACK TO THE PAPER AND PASS BEN IN THE COMPOSING room, telling him I will shortly have a hot story for him to run. He says he will wait for my return.

Sitting at my desk, I start pounding out the Catholic Church story headlined "Who Would Steal From St. Mary's?" This is one of the most horrendous crimes that has hit our city. Young gang members rob and steal a gold statue of a saint from St. Mary's Catholic Church on Camelback. They maliciously beat Father Nicolai, the long residing priest of the church, who happened to hear a noise in the church and interrupted them tearing down the statue—I wish I could name the Saint, but that will have to wait for tomorrow's newspaper when I can re-interview the good Father and hopefully he will be able to describe the statue in detail. It will be virtually impossible for these kids to unload the statue of the saint as it will be immediately identifiable. What are the youth of the streets of Phoenix thinking? How are they raised that a crime of this nature is okay? Someone must know something. Speak up and turn these kids over to the police as soon as possible. Hopefully, the two-foot statue can be recovered and placed back in the church. This is sacrilege! The people of Phoenix have to step up and stop these kinds of crimes. Turn the kids in. Parents, speak with your children and see if they have any knowledge of this crime. Father Nicolai and St. Mary's Catholic Church of Phoenix need your help at this time.

I deliver the article to Specs, who glances at it and says, "Take it down to Ben to run as soon as possible."

When the morning paper hits the street, everyone reads, "Who Would Steal From St. Mary's?"

My story is the headline article, and people are aghast. Everyone in Phoenix is talking about this crime. It has crossed the line of acceptable behavior for our kids.

As soon as I get home that evening, Blondie rushes to me and gives me a great big kiss and hugs me for a little longer than usual. I ask what the problem is, and she replies, "I am so glad our boys are good boys and would never consider doing something like the theft of the statue of the saint."

I ask her to talk with them and see if there is any gossip at school about the story and who might be involved. They may just hear something and can contribute to crime-solving in Phoenix. She says that she will in the morning at breakfast.

At breakfast, I will be gone early so will miss them and the conversation. My days start early so that I can hit the coffee shop and get caught up on the local gossip going around. The Legal Eagle and Mary O keep me pretty well informed. God Bless her Irish outgoing nature and the ability to talk with everyone and keep up on everything going on locally.

CHAPTER SEVENTEEN

JUNE 9, 8 AM
LEGAL EAGLE CAFE

I SIT NEXT TO ONE OF THE LOCALS AT THE LEGAL EAGLE, HOPING TO hear something of interest. All they want to talk about is the church robbery. Why? What kind of kids would do this? What the hell are they going to do with a gold statue? Use it as a statue in one of their broken-down building hangouts?

I listen as they talk and don't mentally agree with them. I can't believe three young kids would go to that much trouble to tear a statue off its base, lug a very heavy gold statue out the door of the church, and load it into a vehicle just to have a statue for their club-house. Also, beating up the priest will bring certain penalties if caught. Why would they take this chance? Not just to place a statue in a clubhouse. Yeah, I have to make another trip to the hospital to talk with the priest and find out exactly which statue was stolen. I need a name. Maybe there is a connection to that specific saint.

I wander over to the police station and talk to some of the cops that are hanging out. Run into uniformed officers Jimmy Lynch and Phil Rivera just bringing in a kid from the south side. After booking and locking him up, I ask them if they were able to get any information from him about the theft from St. Mary's.

"No."

"The kid said that he didn't know anything about it and wondered why someone would want a heavy statue."

They picked him up for fighting with another kid in an empty lot, causing a crowd to gather. The other kid went to the hospital in an ambulance. Neither of the Mexican kids would say why they were fighting, probably over a girl.

I get in my car and drive over to St. Joseph's Hospital. Maybe I can talk with the kid that is injured, as he may be more cooperative. Also, I will look up the good Father while I'm there.

Johnny Hernandez is pretty well beaten up. Obviously, the other kid was the better boxer. *Maybe we should get him released and train him to box professionally. Arizona could use a good lightweight contender.* Just a thought.

Johnny Hernandez's nose is broken, and his face looks like mincemeat, red and raw. He is not the chatty type, or at least at this moment when the doctor is finishing setting his nose and bandaging his face. They wheel him out into the hall alongside an empty corner in the emergency room. He is handcuffed to the bed, so he is not going anywhere.

The other residents of the hall look at him with disgust. Most are there because they are sick, coughing, in physical pain, or suffering old age problems. They don't like the look of the kid, are not happy to be in the emergency room, and certainly are not happy that treatment takes so long and that they have to wait with numbers to be called in the hallway of St. Joseph's Hospital.

I walk over and introduce myself, "Gene McLain of the Arizona Republic, and I would like to talk with you about the fight in the empty lot."

He gives me a cold stare and turns away. I keep talking, hoping that something I say may sink in.

"Look, kid, you are going to be booked for fighting and

disturbing the peace and probably resisting an officer. You might as well tell your side of the story."

"Drop dead, reporter" is his only comment.

I try once again. "Why don't you tell me what you heard on the streets about the robbery from St. Mary's Church. You know, the good saint?"

He turns over and looks at me.

"I don't know nothing about any good saint. What are you, crazy?"

Well, at least he is talking.

"You know, the one taken from St. Mary's Church, where they beat the priest."

"My boys would never do anything like that."

"And why not?"

"The old priest was nice. He would always talk to us if we ran into him. You know, about getting off the streets and doing something with our lives and coming to church with our family. Some of the kids even go to church with their mothers on Sunday. Why would anyone hurt the priest?"

"Well, it seems he heard the kids stealing the statue and tried to interrupt the theft."

"Probably tried to grab one of them, and one of the others whacked him in the head with something pretty hard. Maybe a gun."

"Are you sure you haven't heard any talk on the streets about the robbery?"

"Naw, nothing."

"Well, I will leave you my card if you hear anything once you get released. Okay? That is, if you get released."

I walk back into the regular part of the hospital to try and locate the priest. Need to see him while I'm here because I hate hospitals. So depressing.

The receptionist in the front of the general hospital gives me the room number and directions to the elevator. I take the elevator up to the third floor and hunt for room 324. I enter the room to find one of the younger priests sitting with the good Father. He immediately stands and greets me. Yes, I know who he is. I sometimes attend church with my family, although many times they have to go alone to services.

The priest has read the newspaper article and thanks me profusely for running such a good story. There is a great need to find these thieves and get the statue back into the church. The good Father nods his head and mumbles something unintelligible. I ask the young priest in attendance which statue is missing, and he says, "Saint Francis of Assisi. It stands about two feet tall, made from gold, and was in the small alcove chapel area of the church."

"Is there any particular reason that this saint should go missing?"

None that he knows of. Just that it was located closer to the door than some of the other saints in the quiet alcove, and maybe that was the reason. Quick access and removal."

He may have a point. This young priest is pretty smart and should have a promising future with St. Mary's Church, especially now that the Father may not be able to handle as many of the duties as he did before, at least for a while.

I send best wishes for the older priest's health and make a speedy exit to depart. I have too much to do to hang around sitting and praying all day; not my thing.

CHAPTER EIGHTEEN

JUNE 9, 12 NOON
ARIZONA REPUBLIC NEWSPAPER

As I get in the car, I mumble enough religion for one day. I cruise back to my office, hoping that there is a call from the Chief about whatever they can locate in El Paso. Yeah, there's a call. Not good news, though. Jim Gorham, the motel owner, and his new bride have just taken off for a much-delayed honeymoon and won't be back in El Paso for a couple of weeks. This means the officer that is there will come home and then return later.

No one seems to know where they have decided to go. There was talk about an extended camping trip somewhere in the mountains, also talk about going to Dallas, and some conversation about going to Santa Fe. No one knows for sure where they went. They have left Jim's parents in charge of the motel for two to three weeks while taking off for their honeymoon trip. After the wedding, it took them a while to save up enough cash to talk about a honeymoon somewhere, giving them time to consider several places.

The Captain inquired if Jim Gorham would be checking in with the parents. They seemed to indicate probably not, as they were familiar with running the motel and had originally owned it before their son acquired it. He knew they would do a good job and really needed to get away for some quiet time. They would contact the officer if they heard from Jim and try to get a location where the couple would be.

Chief Morse decided to have Detective Steinberg return to Phoenix until they could try and locate Jim Gorham and Joan. They would have to determine where they are, decide if the Phoenix police department should put up the money for another trip, try for a phone conversation, or return to El Paso when they were home and interview both of them. Probably the last option is the best, but that means Bob Davis will just have to wait longer. He is not going anywhere anyway. His trial is a ways off and, if necessary, could be postponed by the DA if required. Also means probably Detective Steinberg will make another trip to El Paso, which doesn't exactly thrill him, but it may be necessary.

CHAPTER NINETEEN

JUNE 10TH, 7:30 AM
MC LAIN HOME

I wake up this morning with the full intent of going to the office and then realize it's Saturday. Blondie's not home, the kids are watching cartoons, and I will have to get my own breakfast—and maybe the kids' breakfasts.

"Hey kids, have you eaten breakfast?" They don't hear me over the loud voices of the cartoon characters. I walk into the living room and see that Huckleberry Hound is on the television, and they are totally absorbed.

"Hey, have you kids eaten?" They nod yes before mother left.

So, back to the kitchen, where I pull down a box of Shredded Wheat, empty a couple of rectangles into the bowl, break them apart, and pour the milk. The coffee pot on the stove is still hot, so I pour a cup and sit down to eat my breakfast.

Blondie probably expects that I will take the kids to the park today so that they will be exhausted by evening, and we can hire a babysitter and go out for dinner. After all, it is Saturday, and I haven't been home much. I know that her birthday is coming and that would be a nice thing to do. But just as I am completing this thought process and thinking about a good restaurant for dinner and making a reservation—like maybe the famous steakhouse on Camelback "Durant's"—the damn phone rings.

It's Mrs. Roper next door. I call her the "Pekinese," for which Blondie gets upset with me. Mrs. Roper has reddish-blonde hair piled high up on her head, and she has a small frame. I don't know why, but she reminds me of a Pekinese dog, small and flitting about. She is charming and a friendly neighbor to have. She must be clairvoyant, as I was also just wondering how I might get some time today to work. She says she talked with Blondie earlier in the week, and Blondie told her she would have to work this Saturday. So, she called to see if our boys would like to join her and her son to go shopping, have lunch, and see a movie. I ask the boys, and they jump with joy, so I send them upstairs to shower and dress properly for an outing. I tell Mrs. Roper they are thrilled and will be ready in half an hour. I am happy that she can take them today as I have work to do.

She responds, "Yes, I want you to concentrate on catching those boys who stole the statue from St. Mary's Catholic Church. It's such a horrible thing for them to do." She is Catholic and says a blessing, almost inaudibly. I ask her if she would talk with her son to see if he hears anything, and she agrees to do so. The school network sometimes brings great results. Kids like to gossip as well as old folks. It's worth a try.

There are no leads on the church case, as the good Father can't remember very much about the theft. He entered the church and grabbed one of the boys from behind by the collar of his shirt, and the next thing, everything went black. He remembers coming to with an ambulance worker leaning over him and his young assistant priest standing over him, as well as one of the lady church workers.

One of the other boys must have hit him on the head on the side toward his face with something very hard, and he immediately dropped to the floor, bleeding profusely, and blacked out. There seemed to be blood everywhere. He was having trouble focusing his eyes. He kept drifting in and out of consciousness. He never had a chance to see the other boys up close. He thinks that two were Mexican and one was a white kid, but he was not sure of that.

Not much of a description to work with. It could be any of a hundred kids on the south side. This criminal case is going nowhere fast. We need a break. Perhaps some kid will talk, or a mother will turn her son in when she overhears him talking about the statue. *Naw, Gene, you know that is not very likely to happen.*

More than likely, a local policeman will pick up one of the south side youths for a petty crime, and to save his skin and not serve prison time, he will talk about what he knows about the church robbery. We have to wish for one crime, one scared kid, to solve the other greater crime.

CHAPTER TWENTY

JUNE 10, 9 AM
MCLAIN HOME

THE DOORBELL RINGS, AND THE PEKINESE IS HERE TO PICK UP THE boys who simultaneously come flying down the stairs and hit the front door just as I am about to open it. They jerk the door open and race out, hollering "goodbye" as they head for Mrs. Roper's car. She mumbles something about 6 pm as a drop-off time, and Blondie should be home by then, and goodbye, Mr. McLain.

Still thinking a lot about the highway murders and the possibility that Indian jewelry might be involved, I decide to drive over to Scottsdale and walk the tourist shopping area where multiple shops sell Indian jewelry. Perhaps they have names of the Indians who make the jewelry and market to them, and if any of them happen to come from Globe to make their sales.

I stroll down Scottsdale Avenue and then stop and walk into a fancy-looking shop with lots of Indian jewelry in the window. A gentleman asks if he can help me. I ask for the owner. He excuses himself and exits to the rear of the store. So, I wander around looking at the cases. Shortly the owner, a jovial, overweight Jewish man, appears.

"Can I help you?"

I introduce myself, "Gene McLain of the Arizona Republic," and begin asking questions about his Indian pieces.

He immediately wants to take some unique pieces out of the case, showing me their quality silver and turquoise settings. He is very proud of his pieces. Says he only buys the best. I try to explain I am not purchasing, although the thought crosses my mind that it would make a good birthday gift for Blondie, that is until he tells me the prices. I work for a living. I can't drop $50, $100, and up for a bracelet. The tourists must be crazy. I know that he is not paying the Indians who handmake the jewelry anything near that price. He is stealing them from the Indians and raking in a huge profit for himself.

"Ah, free enterprise."

The owner looks startled at my statement. His face displays disappointment when I tell him I am investigating a jewelry theft ring and not in the market to purchase something. He immediately puts the most expensive silver pieces back in the glass case. I ask him for the names of the Indian jewelry makers and possibly an address or phone for them. He looks confused and says they stop by occasionally and sell him their wares. They don't leave names or any info, barely talk to him—just place their pieces on the counter in the back, wait to see what he will purchase and accept whatever money is forthcoming. I ask him if he can identify the Indians. Are they from up near Globe and the Indian Reservation there? He doesn't know and is not very cooperative now that he knows I am not purchasing anything.

I notice that some of the Indian design pieces with turquoise and red jasper in another case are set in gold, which is new. I didn't know the Indians worked in gold or even had access to gold to set their stones. I ask specifically about those pieces—the bracelets, earrings, and necklace sets. He says some middle-aged guy brings him these pieces claiming that he does the workmanship himself. He does have a card with his name and phone. He will go and look for it. Again, he places the pieces back in the case so as not to leave me there handling the merchandise. This guy has been around.

The card says "Handcrafted Gold Designs by Jimmy Doe" with a phone that lists an area code. This is not a Phoenix number but somewhere in Arizona. I ask the proprietor how often this "Jimmy Doe" comes to his shop. He indicates about once every two months. Does he know if he is driving and what kind of car?

The owner looks at me like I am crazy, "What do you think? I stand around, looking out the windows all day. I spend most of my time in my office in the back."

"Well, do you pay this guy with a check?"

"These people don't want checks, probably don't have accounts anywhere. They want cash, which is what I provide."

I take the card and wander on down the street, stopping at another of the upscale jewelry stores only to hear much the same story. The Indians come in with their jewelry wrapped in cloth or paper sacks and lay it out for the owners or managers to peruse. Once they have decided what they want to purchase, the Indians hold out their hands, expecting cash.

They all know Jimmy Doe, but not all the stores handle his merchandise as it is more upscale, so they must charge more. Usually, though, their customers don't seem inclined to want to spend that much money. It may also be that they expect Indian design jewelry to be in silver settings.

"I don't' know, but the gold doesn't move as quick, but there is a market for it," says one owner.

I am out the front door and look up the street. It's getting hot. The temperate is rising into the triple digits, and the sidewalks are beginning to radiate heat waves. I spot the Pink Pony just up the street. I dart into the bar out of the heat of the day and have a cool one. Sitting at the bar looking at all the sketches of the rich and famous in Scottsdale. The walls are covered with pictures of socialites, politicians, successful businessmen, and beautiful women. As I look closer, some are infamous. There are pictures of a famous couple, the murdered husband and wife hanging side by side, and farther down the wall, hangs the picture of the lady's police detective lover. I remember this case because it went down unsolved.

Power and connections can do a lot in a small wealthy town like Cadillac Scottsdale. The wealthy that come out from the east each year leave their expensive light-colored Cadillac convertibles in the garages of their houses in Scottsdale. They only drive them when they are in town for the winter months. Back home, they probably have black town cars and drivers, but in Phoenix, they all want to get a fabulous tan during the winter months to sport back home upon their return.

The bar is quiet in the early afternoon, although it is packed at night with the elite of Scottsdale. I make small talk with the bartender, who can't shed any light on any of my outstanding cases. He is a world removed from the south side clientele and the problems there and doesn't deal with the Indians because the owner doesn't want them in the place. They are hustled out quickly and usually don't return, knowing that they are not welcome where the tourists go.

I step out into the pulsing heat of the afternoon and look for my car. Roll the windows down and quickly get moving to circulate the air a bit. It's hot inside the vehicle.

I stop by Blondie's desk at the police department. Say hello to Lieutenant Vale, who has just brought in another Mexican kid for something from the south side. The police department is keeping its word. They are rounding up as many as they can, hoping to find the answer to the church theft and also quiet down the problems on the south side of Phoenix, which is drawing too much attention for the Police Chief.

I ask Blondie where she would like to go for dinner so that I can make a reservation.

"How about Durant's Steakhouse or maybe the Arizona Manor where we could hear Bobby C play some of the new songs that are so popular on the radio?"

"Gene, that's a great idea, but I don't know how late I will have to work and how tired I will be when I get off. Let's just wait until I get home, and then we will see if we can get a babysitter for the evening and if I feel like an evening out."

I explained the Pekinese came and picked the boys up for the afternoon and would bring them back about 6 pm.

"Yes, I know. We discussed it earlier in the week when I ran into her on the street. She's a genuinely nice lady, Mrs. Roper, and you shouldn't call her that. One day you'll forget and call her that to her face, which will be most embarrassing."

"Yeah, yeah, I know. Anyway, goodbye, sweetie. I'll see you at home later."

CHAPTER TWENTY-ONE

JUNE 10 – 2 PM
ARIZONA REPUBLIC NEWSPAPER

I WANDER INTO THE OFFICE. IT'S SATURDAY AND PRETTY QUIET. A few people are working, Ben is downstairs at his job, but all the management is out. I put my feet up on the desk and recline back in the wooden chair. I take a chance and call the sheriff in Globe to see if there are any leads on the highway murders. He answers his phone, so he is working at his office.

No, he has not been able to locate anyone that looks like they have been in a fight recently. Globe is the friendliest town in America.

"Yeah, save the speech, sheriff. You do have two unsolved murders, so maybe not so friendly to everyone."

He says, "He will keep me informed," and I hang up.

There's nothing new on the Bob Davis case. The Chief would let me know the results of his officer's trip to El Paso, so obviously, they have not been able to locate Mr. and Mrs. Gorham.

The Phoenix police are rounding up Mexican kids from the south side as quickly as possible, hoping to find a snitch with information about the St. Mary's robbery. Father Nicolai is still in the hospital and recovering very slowly. Seems his memory has also been affected. The assistant young priest has been doing all his duties, and I hear that the ladies of Phoenix really like his Sunday sermons. Guess he has stepped up to the job. At least the ladies like him. He is good-looking and very pleasant.

I look at the clock on my desk—it's 3 pm, and not much happening here.

I drive back home. It's been a long, hot day.

At home, I flip the radio on and listen to Tony Bennett sing "Rags to Riches" and Perry Como "Say You're Mine Again" as I drift off in the recliner for a short nap before Blondie and the kids come home.

CHAPTER TWENTY-TWO

JUNE 12TH, 8:30 AM
ARIZONA REPUBLIC NEWSPAPER

IT'S MONDAY MORNING, AND SPECS HAS CALLED HIS WEEKLY meeting to update everyone on what is going on. Actually, nothing new is going on.

Pam Rushman has been given the assignment to interview one of the local politicians running for office. She is scared and thrilled to get the opportunity and keeps telling me how she wants to do hard news. Specs is never going to send a woman to do homicide or crime investigations. He is old-fashioned and doesn't think a woman can handle that type of story. Still, after much persuasion on her part, he lets her go and do political interviews connected to the upcoming race in Arizona. For the time being, she seems to be happy with the assignments and isn't pestering him daily for something more than the social entertainment news.

Specs wants to know what is happening with the missing church statue at St. Mary's. I have to be honest and say the police are rounding up the street gang kids and hoping one of them will spill the beans about the statue or at least give them a lead to go on. So far, nothing. Can't put together in my mind why gang kids would want a two-foot plus gold statue that must weigh a ton. Where can they hide it? Where can they put it, and why do they want it? St. Francis of Assisi is known as the Patron Saint of Italy and later became associated with animals and nature and the environment. Did the kids take it to put it in a park or garden somewhere? What the hell do 13- and 14-year-old kids want with this statue? Specs says to keep digging until I uncover something. The governor is putting pressure on the paper's owner, David Sacks, to get his reporters to turn up something. The governor and the mayor are also putting pressure on Chief Deputy Harry Morse for results.

There was the body of a dead homeless man, around sixty years old, who was found behind Goldwater's Department store. The medical examiner in Phoenix determined he died of natural causes from living on the street. Unable to locate any family, so he will be buried in potter's field for the indigent. No story there.

Otherwise, it was a quiet weekend, and the meeting is over.

My desk has a couple of phone messages to be returned, and I need to try again to contact that Jimmy Doe to see if that leads anywhere.

Pam stops by my desk to thank me for putting in a good word for her with Specs. I did mention to him that I thought she could do more at the paper. She thinks I am the reason that she now has the new political assignment. I know that she really wants to do crime stories, but I don't think that will be possible. Who knows, she might meet a politician she likes and eventually get married, have kids, and quit reporting. That is what usually happens to the young ladies. They come and go at the newspaper—just the old dogs like me who hang in there.

CHAPTER TWENTY-THREE

JUNE 12, 10 AM
ARIZONA REPUBLIC NEWSPAPER

FINALLY, I CATCH UP WITH JIMMY DOE BY PHONE. SAYS HE DOES make gold and turquoise jewelry and certainly would like to show some pieces that he has for sale. I sense he wants to make a sale, thinks that I am a potential prize client. We agree to meet at the Arizona Manor for a drink, and he will bring his work.

He is an old guy, gray-haired, probably late fifties. Comes in with a paper bag in which he has several pieces wrapped in black velvet. Wow! They show great. Beautiful workmanship. I ask where he does his work. He indicates that he rents a space at the back of a warehouse with a small smelting area set up for the gold and silver. He is quite a craftsman, been making jewelry all his life. Funny that he has not achieved greater success. Seems down on his luck. Wonder what his problem is.

He explains, "I acquire the stones from local Indians who call me, and when possible, four times a year, I make trips to various Arizona Indian reservations to see what they have for sale.

"Have you been to the San Carlos Apache Indian Reservation lately?"

"No, I've been too busy to leave town," he says, then explains that when he makes the trip, he likes to stay in Globe overnight and come back the next day.

Once he senses I am not buying anything, he seems in a hurry to depart. I forget to ask him where he stays in Globe, a hotel with friends, or somewhere else. There really isn't much selection in town.

There is something odd about this guy. He is too old and feeble to beat up the husky young Indians, so he definitely is not my "Highway Murderer."

I sit, finish my drink, and ponder what it is about this meeting that went the wrong way. Wait a minute, he could have connections in Globe that provide him with jewelry and stones stolen from murdered Indians. He may know more than he wants to say, and that's why he left in a hurry. He didn't actually say where his workshop was located and seemed nervous once he realized I was a reporter and not there to purchase something.

I dash out of the Arizona Manor to see if I can locate his car before he leaves the lot. Want to make a note about what he is driving for future reference. Hell, he is already gone. Gone baby gone. I had a great deal of trouble reaching him by phone, and now that he knows I am not a buyer, he will probably not answer the damn phone.

CHAPTER TWENTY-FOUR

JUNE 13, 9 AM
PHOENIX POLICE DEPARTMENT

THERE IS ANOTHER GASSING AT THE FLORENCE PRISON THAT SPECS wants me to cover. I hate making the drive but have to do it. I am sure Warden Franks is already cranking up the peach juice in the jitterbug room for his next prisoner. He likes lowering the jailhouse population numbers.

I ask Pam Rushman if she wants to attend another one with me, as I hate driving alone. She immediately declines, remembering the previous horrible experience. I will go early and maybe stop and have a steak dinner at the Ranch House on the way. They prepare great New York steaks cooked over an open pit with mesquite branches that add flavor, making the trip worthwhile.

Of course, I will have to write an article about the event. What the hell can you write. They all plead innocent, rarely talk, don't look at the crowd in the adjoining room, not wanting to make eye contact with family or friends. Some spend their last day's special dinner before entering the gas chamber with family and end up crying a lot and not eating their special-ordered meal.

They should have had those thoughts before murdering their girlfriends or committing a bank robbery and shooting the guard in the process. Most criminals going to the gas chamber are hardened individuals and are fully aware of the consequences of their actions. They just don't believe that their actions will catch up with them. They think they are smarter and can get away with anything.

Well, tomorrow is decided. Off to Florence for another one.

Today I have the afternoon, so I make another trip back to St. Mary's Catholic Church to see the young priest. See if he has heard any gossip from his parishioners about the robbery and who might be responsible. Hopefully, there has not been another attempt at removing the other statues.

The young priest, Father Dave, says, "After each service at the coffee gathering, the conversation centers around the young thieves. Nothing of consequence has come from these conversations, just very unhappy churchgoers."

They don't understand why anyone would do something like that, especially hurting the senior priest, who has not returned to his duties. His recovery has been very slow, and he spends much of his time in his quarters. The good father says, "Even the youngsters in the church classes don't understand how this could happen in a religious setting." Father Dave states, "the church lady who discovered Father Nicolai is very traumatized and doesn't want to be alone in the church anymore. She has never seen so much blood before. I ask Father Dave to give my best wishes to Father Nicolai, and if he hears anything, let me know as soon as possible. I then depart.

I stop by the Legal Eagle on the way home for a piece of home-made apple pie. It's the best in town, very tart and delicious with coffee. Mary O is bright and shiny as always. Upbeat and laughing with the customers. When she stops by to take my order, I ask if she has any interesting news to share. She shakes her head from side to side and says she only has some gossip about love affairs going on in town, nothing important about robbery or murder.

I change my order and request that she give me a "to go" box with two slices of apple pie. I will take it home, and Blondie and I can enjoy our coffee and pie after dinner when the kids are in bed. Tomorrow night I will be late getting back from Florence, and dinner will be on the road. I am trying to spend more time with the kids per Blondie's request. Get home early enough to read them a story or talk about their day at school. I know that she is right, but it is difficult.

CHAPTER TWENTY-FIVE

JUNE 14, 9 AM
ARIZONA STATE PRISON—FLORENCE, ARIZONA

YESTERDAY WAS A LONG GRINDING DAY. WENT TO THE JAIL IN Phoenix to see if any leads have turned up on the missing statue case or any contact made with Bob Davis's absent motel owner, only to discover that there is nothing new to report.

Then I drive down to Florence for the execution. On the way, my radio is blaring some of the new songs making the top 100 hit list. Perry Como singing "No Other Love," The Hilltoppers with "P.S. I Love You," and Tony Bennett singing "Rags to Riches" are a few of the hits that I sing along with as I can remember the words. So many of the new songs I am not familiar with, but a few I do know as Blondie frequently plays the radio at home.

Everything went off as expected. There were very few family members or visiting individuals at the gassing. A priest, a lawman, and an elderly gent, possibly a relative. This guy, Joey Dean, was a toughened criminal convicted of murder and robbery. The general public was not sympathetic to his case. Most believed that he was guilty of the crimes committed, as some of the take was found in his apartment, which he could not adequately explain. When the conviction came down, no one was surprised at the sentence.

The execution went off as well as expected. On the drive back, I stop for dinner at the Ranch House and enjoy my all-day antici- pated mesquite-smoked steak and baked potato, loaded with every- thing. I know it's not on my diet, and Blondie probably would disapprove, but what the hell. You have to live a little, which is why I order a bottle of Dos Equis beer to wash it all down. Janie, the wait- ress, remembers me from previous visits.

"Hello, Mr. McLain. How goes the newspaper business?"

"I am always looking for a good story. Got any?"

"Not much happens around here. A few fender benders, and maybe someone runs off with the local mechanic's wife. That's all."

Doesn't sound like much of a story there. These things happen every day."

She wanders off to place my order, and I pick up a copy of the local newspaper lying on the chair by my table. I start to read when I realize that it's yesterday's paper. The beer arrives, and it's cold and tasty, so I put the paper aside.

Yes, I have made this trip several times to Florence, not my favorite excursion.

Arriving home late with everyone already in bed, I hit the shower and join them.

Oh yeah, just remembered tomorrow, Wednesday, is Blondie's actual birthday. I think she is going to be forty-six? I have to confirm that. I just don't remember things like that, which does not endear me to her. She always remembers my birthday and the kids. She is an angel. My angel—and I am incredibly lucky to have her. The guys at the paper don't understand how a guy with my mug won her. Just my Irish charm, I guess.

I think I will make a trip back to Scottsdale tomorrow and talk with some other jewelry shop owners about their sources for stones and maybe purchase something small for Blondie for her birthday, perhaps a turquoise ring.

CHAPTER TWENTY-SIX

I CHECK OUT MY DESK AT THE PAPER FIRST THING WEDNESDAY morning. There are calls to return - one from Walter Brennan, one of the witnesses in the Val Tchaikovsky murder. The message is written by the secretary and states, "He is screaming he doesn't understand what is going on with the Phoenix police department." It then continues. They won't return his calls, and nothing seems to be getting done with the murder of the tailor. He understands they have a suspect in jail, but that is all anyone will tell him. He came down from San Francisco specially to do the lineup identification and no further contact from anyone. He was expecting to be contacted by the DA's office when Bob Davis comes to trial. So far, no word, and he doesn't read anything about the murder in the San Francisco papers. What the hell is going on down there? The police won't answer his questions. "Perhaps Gene McLain, the hot shot reporter for the Arizona Republic, will return his call." All followed by a telephone number.

A big murder case takes over the headlines and the front pages for a week, maybe two, then if the killer is not captured right away, it fades to page three or page five. After that, it moves to the second section and at last fades away. When the killer is captured, the whole process begins again.

Behind the scenes, the attorneys for the state and the attorneys for the defense are working long hours, round the clock. Stories are not placed about what is going on behind the scenes. We know that the police department is working to find the one guy and gal that might be able to provide an alibi for Bob Davis; otherwise, he goes to trial soon for the murder of the tailor, and with the eye witnesses and the tailor's dying words, his chances of beating the crime are very small. Probably be sentenced to death unless he opts to confess, plead guilty, and the judge could possibly sentence him to life. Neither option is great for this kid.

I return the call to Mr. Brennan, explaining the situation and asking for his patience in this matter. He is not a patient man. As head of a large corporation in San Francisco, he is used to getting his requests responded to. This one will just have to go forward at its own pace.

"Mr. McLain, I demand that you keep me informed of the situation there. This is disrupting my life as I don't know when I will have to make another trip to Phoenix for the trial, and I am trying to run my business here."

"Mr. Brennan, this is disrupting Bob Davis's life also. The police department must take its time and check out every possible lead before they prosecute him. They want to be sure that they have the killer and not an innocent kid."

"Everyone there the day of the lineup identified the one guy. What is the problem? Why the holdup? By the way, where was the muscle man in shorts the day of the line-up?" The police have not been able to locate him. Probably a well-paid "companion" or even a bodyguard to someone in the mob brought from the east to spend the winter with someone wealthy for protection. They will never find him.

"Well, the law takes its time and moves slow. I am sure they are doing everything possible to either prosecute the kid or find him not responsible for the crime. Also, they are managing many other cases that take place daily."

"Well, Mr. Tchaikovsky was an innocent victim. Something should be done as quickly as possible."

"I will be in touch if there is any progress that you should be aware of. Thanks for the call, Mr. Brennan."

I don't have time for these kinds of conversations. Rich and powerful people don't understand why they just can't force situations. This is one of those situations that I am glad is taking time. Still have that gut feeling that Bobby Davis may just be a victim of circumstances, even in the face of evidence that makes him look guilty.

I will stop by the Legal Eagle for a cup of coffee and sandwich, then off to Scottsdale.

Jo Oakes, the waitress, says "Hi," as she pours my coffee and asks what type of sandwich today.

"Corn beef on rye" is my reply. "Any hot tips for me today, Jo?"

"Only that it is scorching. 120 degrees is what the temperature is supposed to be, according to the announcer on the radio station playing. Business is slow. People are not moving around much. Glad to see that you are working."

"I am always working. That's my problem."

She sets down my sandwich with fries, and I begin eating. One of the cops from across the street comes in and sits a stool away from me.

Officer Jimmy Lynch says, "They are sure getting pressure from the high ups to get answers on the gold statue case. They keep dragging gang members from the south side in, but no one has answers, or they are not talking, which is strange since each of the competing gangs usually likes to snitch info on other opposing gang members."

They are roughing up the south side rabble looking for clues.

These kids are tough with baseball bats and knives. Some even have guns. The cops are tougher and hit back harder.

I tell him, "There are no rumors on the street either that I have been able to find. Will keep searching."

I finish my coffee and head to Scottsdale.

CHAPTER TWENTY-SEVEN

JUNE 15, 11:30 AM
SCOTTSDALE TOURIST SHOPPING – 5TH AVENUE

THE SCOTTSDALE STREETS ARE HOT. VERY LITTLE SHADE. I TRY A side street where there are also shops. I walk into this one place and look around. The clerk approaches and asks if he can be of help.

"Yes, I would like to see some of the gold and turquoise rings for sale."

He pulls out a tray, and I begin looking. I notice in the tray next to the rings are small charms. There is a gold and turquoise charm of an angel. I ask the clerk if I can see that one. He pulls it out and lays it on a cloth, bringing a gold chain along to put it on. Yes, that would be perfect. Now the price—$55 for the charm and $35 for the gold chain. Wow! Perhaps I should take another look at the rings.

I turn my attention to the other tray, but nothing seems to hit me like the angel. Well, my angel is worth it. There goes last week's paycheck that I was hanging on to for a special weekend event and maybe dinner out. With Blondie's schedule and mine, getting a weekend or even a night out is difficult, and also, the kids have homework schedules, ball games, etc. I think she would really like the angel and would be willing to give up a weekend event or dinner for this keepsake. I tell the clerk to wrap it up in a fancy box and hand over the money.

While he is wrapping, I inquire where they get their jewelry from. The same response, "From Indians that wander through periodically and show their wares, and from an old guy who brings in the gold pieces." That was pricey information that didn't amount to anything new, and it just cost me almost 100 bucks!

I stop by the Pink Pony bar while I am in Scottsdale once again and ask the same questions, getting the same responses. I have a cold Coke, throw the bull around with the bartender, and cool off. The place is empty at this time in the afternoon. After an hour, I head home to the kids and Blondie. I'll get the kids to sign the card, and after dinner, we will give her the gift.

CHAPTER TWENTY-EIGHT

JUNE 15, 5 PM
MC LAIN HOME

Blondie is baking a cake when I arrive in the kitchen, probably making her famous upside-down pineapple cake which is her favorite. The aroma of dinner is wafting through the house. Smells like a roast of some kind, probably with vegetables and potatoes. The kids are working on homework upstairs, but I interrupt and have them sign the card for her birthday, saying we have a wonderful surprise for her.

I wander into the living room and play the radio. Joni James, a new young hot singer, is giving her rendition of "Your Cheating Heart," which is a big hit. Blondie calls out that dinner is ready, and I rush to wash up. The kids and I hit the door at the same time.

After dinner, the kids are getting antsy, and so am I. As Blondie gets the coffee pot off the stove, I slip the wrapped box in front of her place at the table. When she turns around to pour my coffee, she sees the box. Her eyes light up, showing she is surprised. The kids are jumping up and down and hollering for her to open the box. She says we must wait until she cuts the cake and serves it. The boys gobble down their pieces of cake and anxiously wait for her to open her present. I sit there, hoping that I have made the right choice. I don't usually buy her jewelry, except our wedding rings, which are matching gold bands.

Blondie carefully unwraps the gold ribbon and the blue paper holding the small velvet box. As she opens it, her eyes light up, and I explain that she is my angel for always. Tears well up in her beautiful eyes, and she starts to cry.

The boys ask if she likes the present, and she barely stammers out that she is delighted and overwhelmed. She comes around the table and gives me a long kiss, with her wet cheeks brushing mine, which holds the promise of more things to come later.

Now it's time for the boys reading program and book reports, which she needs to oversee. As they set up books and paper on the cleaned-off dinner table, I start to wash the dishes. Blondie says no, she will do them, but I remind her this is her birthday, and no, she will not do dishes, housework, or anything except help the boys with their reading summer assignments. Then they are to go off to bed, and we will spend the evening together with the television or listening to one of Bobby C's records. Ever since she had met him at the Arizona Manor playing, she has started to collect his records. She really likes his voice. So, I make a mental note to take her out more often. It seems our lives are both so hectic that getting time together is an absolute priority. Guess we'll just have to schedule it into our busy lives.

We turn out the lights and move upstairs to the bedroom. This evening holds lots of promise.

Blondie slowly undresses, revealing her well-rounded curves, slips into a black silk gown, and sits down to brush her platinum blond hair. Quite a vision for these tired bones. In a few minutes, she slips into bed beside me, and my angel proceeds to climb on top of my body, pressing her body to mine and taking me to heaven.

CHAPTER TWENTY-NINE

JUNE 16, 9 AM
ARIZONA REPUBLIC NEWSPAPER

SOMETHING HAS GOT TO SHAKE UP THE STATUE THEFT CASE. THE heat is really on from upstairs at the paper. David Sacks, the owner, calls a meeting with all the staff. He wants results—"Now."

"What the hell is happening on the streets? Why are there no leads to follow? You guys are not doing your jobs. The Mayor and the Chief of Police are my friends, and they want answers. They're doing their jobs, but the people of this newspaper need to do more."

"I agree and volunteer to write another headline article hoping to stir up results." I have been thinking about this anyway and now am prompted to do so. We need to shake things up. The cops are not getting anywhere hauling in kids off the street. Perhaps another strong story aimed at the parents and adults of the community will cause results.

I visit Father Nicolai once again to see how he is doing. He is not doing well. When the boy smashed in the side of his head and his face, it not only caused some broken bones but caused trauma to his head and brain. He seems very slow to respond to questions and moves and walks much slower than before. I recall seeing him give powerful sermons in church on Sunday mornings. Today, he seems old and frail, can't walk far, has trouble standing for an extended time, and his speech pattern is extremely slow. Also, there appears to be memory loss regarding the accident and many previous events.

I want to write an article about how this one action, by one boy, has changed the destiny of St. Mary's Church and certainly has affected the life of its outstanding leader, once a pillar in the community.

He was also a champion of the youth in the district, always willing to help the kids. He created many events at the church to get the kids to attend—baseball tournaments among the youth in the area, dances for the teens, music recitals for the gifted, and book reading sessions for the young. So many events throughout the years to help protect kids from the streets and keep them out of trouble. He succeeded with many and was genuinely loved in the neighborhood and within the church community. The public, the people need to know what has really happened here. How one act of violence has destroyed an entire community.

"One Life Matters" is my headline for the Sunday issue of the paper.

Specs has Ben put the story on the front page.

"One Life Matters" is the story of our beloved priest, Father Nicolai Vicovavich, who built St. Mary's Church into one of Phoenix's best cathedrals of worship. He single-handedly conducted services every Sunday morning and Friday night and arranged special events for the local kids in the neighbor such as baseball games, teen dances, youth reading sessions, etc. And why did he do this? To keep the kids in the surrounding area off the streets and out of trouble. Your kids.

But trouble found Father Nikolai. One of the neighborhood boys brought a couple of friends and stole the gold statue of St. Francis of Assisi. While they were dismantling it from the base, the good father heard a noise in the church and went to investigate. As he approached the outer alcove where the statue was located, near the church's front door, he spied three youths working diligently to remove the statue from its base. As he approached quietly, one of the boys turned and saw him. Using the hammer he held in his hand, he repeatedly hit the good father in the head and on the side of his face, causing severe damage. He even kept slamming the hammer into his head, hitting him viciously, as he fell to the ground. Pools of blood surrounded the unconscious and dazed priest. The boys then turned their attention once again to the statue, finally removing it from its base and managing to lift it down. This is one heavy object. How they did this, we really don't know. Three young boys are stronger than they appear, apparently. They were not concerned about anyone else being in the church because they were unaware that Father Nicolai had recently requested assistance, and a young priest Father Dave was working with him. However, Father Dave was out making church calls to the parishioners on that particular afternoon. Perhaps they did know. They were not in any hurry, as they slowly removed the statue carefully and managed to carry it, or with the use of a collapsible cart, deliver it to their waiting vehicle and depart without being seen by anyone.

Of course, leaving Father Nicolai bleeding profusely in the inner chamber alcove of St. Mary's Church. It was only luck that one of the church ladies who help clean and set up the flowers for services happened to stop by and immediately called the ambulance and the police.

Father Nicolai is not recovering well and may not be able to return to his duties at St. Mary's. Someone is responsible for this. Someone needs to pay the price for the crime that they have committed and be accountable for what they have done to one of Phoenix's outstanding citizens.

Won't you help find the thieves? Most importantly, won't you help find the statue? St. Mary's needs its Saint returned now. To the good people of Phoenix, we ask that you inform the newspaper or the police of any leads, information, or gossip that you hear about this crime. There is a large reward for tips resulting in the arrest and prosecution of these criminals. If they are underage kids, which we believe they are, who put them up to this crime? That is the person responsible, and they need to be located. Citizens of the city of Phoenix, we need your help. Call the Arizona Republic or the Police Department anonymously and leave your information.

Ben runs the story on Sunday as the headline article as Specs has requested.

The phones start ringing at the newspaper on Sunday as soon as the paper hits the streets. Perhaps it's the reward aspect, or maybe people just want to help. The phones are also repeatedly ringing at the police station.

Monday should provide multiple leads to follow and hopefully some results.

I don't want David Sachs on my case. I know that he has been pressuring Specs and some of the other management for results. Hell, David has to understand, we all want results.

CHAPTER THIRTY

SATURDAY, JUNE 18, 9 AM
MCLAIN HOME

IT'S THE WEEKEND, AND I SHOULD BE ABLE TO RELAX AT HOME. TAKE the kids to the park and maybe schedule a dinner out with Blondie. Wonderful thoughts. Unfortunately, I can't turn off my brain which is racing with the idea that time is running out for the Davis kid. No one seems to be doing much of anything to help his situation. They are all so sure he did it. I am not that sure, which is what is bothering me daily and causing sleepless nights.

Also, I really need to spend some time putting notes together on the church robbery. Who the hell would do that? Steal a church statue, an icon? And the vicious attack on the priest when they were interrupted during the removal of the statue. Father Nicolai is in serious trouble and needs all our help. A really good man deserves better from his community and friends.

The boys want to go to a baseball game at the park. I agree to drive them and sit and wait.

I can make notes while I am in the stands, presumably watching the game with them. If I keep them supplied with hot dogs and sodas, they will never notice I am not into the game.

I want to find a seat in the shade as the summer days in Phoenix are brutal. The kids don't seem to mind it, but as I get older, I sure do.

CHAPTER THIRTY-ONE

JUNE 18, 6 PM
MCLAIN HOME

SATURDAY EVENING, BLONDIE RETURNS HOME FROM WORK AND brings dinner, Mexican food. She has stopped by one of her favorite spots and picked up dinner for everyone.

The kids love the tacos, and I enjoy the enchiladas, especially the chicken and cheese. Blondie also has a salad which we all share on our plates. The boys stuff themselves with tacos and then go off to watch TV. After all, this is Saturday, and they don't have to read books.

Blondie and I sit, still eating. The carnitas, enchiladas, quesadillas are all fantastic and make a great dinner surprise. We all enjoy Mexican food, and Phoenix has several authentic Mexican restaurants. All of which are good. There is one particular small place near where Blondie works that all the cops frequent, producing outstanding food. That is where she has stopped this evening to pick up dinner.

I holler to the kids that it's ice cream time and ask do they want a dish in the living room while watching TV. Of course, the answer is a resounding, "Yes."

I scoop out a couple of balls of ice cream into plastic dishes for the kids to eat while watching television. I, of course, want a large scoop of ice cream, my favorite being strawberry, which Blondie has purchased. She declines ice cream saying that she is full; however, I know that she is trying to watch her weight and thinks that I should do the same. However, I am not going to give up ice cream for dessert after such a great dinner. Mexican food and ice cream. What could be better?

Tomorrow, Sunday, we will go to church, maybe St. Mary's, and hear the new priest. Then home and change clothes for an afternoon of baseball at the park and a picnic. I note that Blondie has made fried chicken, which is now residing in the refrigerator waiting for Sunday. I am sure she has potato salad somewhere in the works.

CHAPTER THIRTY-TWO

JUNE 20 – 9:30 AM
ARIZONA REPUBLIC NEWSPAPER

Monday morning finds me sitting at my desk with a stack of messages to return. First, I think it's time for another call to the sheriff in Globe. Has he located anyone in town that he thinks may have been in a fistfight or a fight for their life? Although, I don't believe the two dead Indians started the brawl. One was too drunk to want to fight, and the other put up a really great fight. However, he was not drunk and obviously didn't like being assaulted and wasn't going down easy.

A young girl in the sheriff's office answers the phone. The sheriff is busy. Wonder what the hell he is busy doing in Globe. Sleepy, lazy town of Globe. I ask that he call me back. She takes the number, but I'm not so sure that she will relay the message. She sounded disinterested—Globe, the friendliest town in the west.

Better start returning some of the calls from the Sunday "One Life Matters" article. One call after another, people are really concerned and want to bring the criminals to justice. After I talk awhile, I find out they really don't have any pertinent information to share, just deeply concerned and want something done. Yeah, we all do. Thanks for calling. On to the next caller. This story repeats itself over again for the rest of the day. Yes, they all want justice but have nothing important to add to what is already known.

Then, as the calls drag on, the afternoon wears thin, and the coffee cup keeps getting refilled to stay alert, there is one caller that seems different. This one is from a Mexican mother who says she overheard her son talking with his friends. He seemed really scared. The boy said someone in his group had assaulted a priest, and the priest may die. When she attempted to question them more about what she overheard, everyone clammed up, including her son.

He said, "She misunderstood."

He said, "Her English is not good, and she thought they were talking about a priest when actually they were discussing something else."

After seeing the headline story in the paper on Sunday and talking with her next-door neighbor, she is not so sure that she misunderstood the conversation. She does not go to that church, so she wasn't familiar with the incident until seeing the story and trying to decipher the English words, which is why she discussed it with her neighbor, who reads English better.

She says her son, Miguel, hangs around with a neighborhood gang. She thinks he gets into trouble with his friends but has never been caught. Lies to her constantly about where he is going and, in general, is a problem. She is really concerned because she has a younger son who she does not want to be in the gang as he grows up. The older boy is not a good influence. She said she overheard the boys talking about being arrested for injuring a priest. Some old guy gave them money to bring him gold jewelry. Since they were stealing from family and friends, they now had an outlet for the stolen jewelry. They didn't ask why he wanted it. So, from time to time, after robbing a few homes, the leader would call a phone number, and the old guy would meet them and take the pieces of jewelry and pay them cash. The gang leader, being very enterprising, thought a gold statue from the church would bring in a great deal of money.

The mother, Marguerita, does not want me to come to the house. She is afraid that her son will see me. I have a feeling about this call. I agree to meet her tomorrow at the local mercantile in her neighborhood. She doesn't have a car and doesn't drive. Her son has a car and gets around all over town. I ask what kind of car. She doesn't know. Maybe a white Chevy, old.

I continue to make the rest of the calls, but my heart isn't in it. I think I may have hit pay dirt with Marguerita and can't wait until tomorrow to meet her. I wanted to meet today, but she is working as a housekeeper for someone. She is using their phone, as she doesn't have one.

I complete the rest of the calls with nothing viable coming from them. Tomorrow is another day and maybe a fruitful one.

So, I check with the police station, and they are flooded with calls and trying to return them. Several of the cops have stayed in at the station today to return the calls. Mostly they are taking names and trying to get general information. So far, nothing significant except that now they know that the local community is very angry with the police for not solving this crime. They get callers ranting and raving about the inefficiency of the police.

It's probably not a good day for me to show up at the police station since my article prompted the phones to ring.

CHAPTER THIRTY-THREE

JUNE 21, 9 AM
MERCANTILE, SOUTH PHOENIX

Tuesday morning, I am anxious to meet with Marguerita. I pass on breakfast at home, stop at the Legal Eagle and grab a muffin and coffee. Jo Ann, Mary O's assistant waitress, senses I'm in a hurry and rushes my coffee and heated muffin. I thank her and race back to my car, driving south to the mercantile.

I arrive at the little coffee bar located inside the market and wait. Finally, I see an elderly lady, maybe not so old, only tired, walking through the front door. Marguerita wanders toward the coffee bar, and I jump up to meet her.

"Hi. I am Gene McLain. We talked on the phone yesterday. Can I get you a cup of coffee?"

She sits, says "no," and just looks at me for a long time. No conversation. Finally, I remind her she called me yesterday, and we talked about her son being in a gang.

"Yes, the boy is a problem."

I gently remind her about the newspaper article and the conversation she overheard between her son and his friends. She seems reluctant to discuss this. I am not sure how much English she really understands, which is why I wanted to meet with her before suggesting she talk with the police.

"You heard them saying something about being arrested and a priest."

"My son said, 'I misunderstood the English,'" the woman said. "After my neighbor translated the article from the paper, I was concerned. How could young boys do something like that? Could my son be involved in something like that? Sadly, I have to say, Yes."

She keeps talking about her son. He is busy running around with this wild gang and their girls, always needing money. Somehow he comes up with it even when I say no, I don't have it. I don't know where he gets it.

We talk a while longer, and she names his friends Jesus and Julio. I ask her where we can find these kids, and she says, "They hang out at the local pinball machine cafe near the theatre." Jesus and Julio, she thinks, are older than her boy. Her son is just sixteen and already a problem. She thinks the other boys may be eighteen. She has not met their families. The boys just hang out together.

I gently suggest to her that we should go to the police station and report what she knows. She panics,

"Police? No, no."

I get the feeling she may be illegal and terrified of the police. I manage to get her home address and suggest she return home and not say anything about our conversation to anyone.

She leaves in a hurry, probably glad to be away from me and the entire subject.

I drive over to the police station, which is still receiving an unusual volume of telephone calls, and get mean looks when I approach, not the usual friendly ones.

"Hi, Bulldog."

I ask for the Chief who is busy with someone at this time. I think I hear the mayor yelling in the Chief's office. Finally, I locate Captain Reed, who is kind enough to take a minute from his paperwork to listen to my story. He shakes his head and says he will follow up and have a couple of the street cops pick up these kids. Maybe they can scare them into talking. He immediately hits his phone—I don't know how he doesn't break it into pieces—and orders the front desk to put out a call to pick up the kids, Jesus, Julio, and Marguerita's son, Miguel.

I ask, "When you have them, will you give me a call?"

"Yeah, yeah McLain," and he goes back to the paperwork on the desk.

I sense this conversation is over.

"So long," as I depart.

CHAPTER THIRTY-FOUR

JUNE 22, 9:30 AM
ARIZONA REPUBLIC NEWSPAPER

WEDNESDAY GOES BY UNEVENTFULLY. I SIT IN MY OFFICE MOST OF the day and try and dream up different angles that I can use for the church robbery story. Since it is not being solved quickly, I need to keep the story in the public eye.

I still can't figure out why anyone, let alone kids, would want a statue of Father Assisi.

Daily, I try and give the Phoenix readers a blow-by-blow description of what the police department is doing to find the criminals. Also, I try and keep them updated on Father Nicolai's progress. The Phoenix people love him and want to know, hopefully, that he is improving. I try and give a daily update in my column. Unfortunately, not much to report there. He really is not doing well, and progress will be slow.

Blondie is late coming home tonight. She has called the office to indicate that I should stop and have dinner. The Pekinese is going to have the boys over to her house and fix them something to eat.

As I leave the office, I am not in the mood to stop and eat and chat with someone. I decide to go directly home and find something from a can that I can fix quickly. I certainly am not a cook. That is a skill that I never learned at home or later on my own. I will open a can or stop and pick up something on the way home. My favorite spot is Tom's Sandwich Shop in the alley behind the police station, and all the cops frequent his place. He makes the best ham sand-wiches in town. Sometimes, he has to brush the flies off the ham hanging in the shop, but no one ever seems to mind, and no one ever gets sick. He will bring your coffee with his thumb in the cup, but cops are tough. His personality is gregarious, and everyone loves him. Mostly because his prices are fair, and every now and then, he will give a cop a free sandwich. He appreciates their service, which, unfortunately, not all the restaurant owners in Phoenix do. They should, though.

His ham and cheese, which he has several varieties of cheese in block form, are always exceptional. Tell him what you like once, and he always remembers and will give you generous slices of meat and cheese on special homemade bread that is baked by his wife. He is a prince of a guy. With only a small shop in the alley, he seems to do well. The people that know about it are the ones that really matter. Almost all the police department personnel frequent him, along with the personnel from the legal office buildings surrounding the area.

CHAPTER THIRTY-FIVE

JUNE 23, 9:30 AM
ARIZONA REPUBLIC NEWSPAPER

THURSDAY IS HOT, EVEN FOR PHOENIX. APPROXIMATELY 120 degrees during the day. This is a record for this time of year, or at least that is what the weathermen are saying. I think they just want us to feel better. Pretty hot and sweaty. Uncomfortable weather. I stay close to my desk all day, really not wanting to venture out in the heat. I have had my share of hot weather. Let some of the young reporters go out in the heat to find their stories that they hope will make them star reporters.

I hit the telephones instead, a great invention, and make my contacts on most days now. Saves a lot of gas which has gotten expensive. Also, my old car is hot, so I don't look forward to running all over town just to hear gossip.

After a call to the police department, I learn Captain Reed is out, so no update there on Bob Davis. The desk officer is afraid to give out any information to a reporter. He doesn't really know me to know that I would be cautious about obtaining my information. I will have to call back later in the day or perhaps tomorrow.

I keep working the phones and make calls around town. Talk with a bartender that thinks he may have a tip on the church situation. He thinks a transient that had drinks at his bar and got loaded was talking about the robbery. Hell, everyone in Phoenix is talking about this robbery. It's such a weird case. I tell him I will stop by on my way home, and we can chat. Don't get the feeling that there is anything there of value. I do have a funny feeling about Marguerita though, she may have stumbled on something valuable by overhearing her son talk.

I stop by the Arizona Biltmore Hotel bar as promised and talk over a beer with the day bartender. Who says this guy just walked in and started drinking. Probably a drunk tourist. He wanted to talk about the church robbery with the bartender. As I said, everyone in Phoenix is talking about this case, so that is not a rare conversation. No details are given by the bartender that could lead to any verifiable information of importance in this case.

I talk with the cocktail waitress as she walks back into the bar from the patio area where she has just served gin fizzes to a couple by the pool. She is a flashy redhead dressed in a skimpy fitted one-piece shorts outfit amply showing her boobs. She makes quite an impression. She's a looker. I ask her if she has heard any gossip or conversation regarding the church robbery.

She replies that everyone is talking about it. The only Mexicans she sees are the wealthy business owners in Phoenix that come into the hotel. They are the ones that can afford the Arizona Biltmore. No leads there.

Thanking the bartender again for the free beer, I depart toward home. It's always good to humor these bartenders as they are excellent sources of information from time to time.

CHAPTER THIRTY-SIX

JUNE 24, 8:30 AM
ARIZONA REPUBLIC NEWSPAPER

On Friday, we have another meeting with Specs in the office. He once again conveys how angry the upper-level management of the newspaper is with our performance. They do not believe that we are doing enough.

"Where the hell are the old newshounds of years gone by?"

Why do I feel that he is looking directly at me?

Yes, I'm one of the older reporters that have been around for a while, but I still bring in good stories from time to time, and he knows it. Also, I am one of the few reporters that have won awards for outstanding reporting for the Arizona Republic. Still, he looks directly at me, expecting me to say something. I don't say a word. I'm as frustrated as everyone else is with the church story.

After a long pause, thankfully, Pam rescues me by asking Specs about one of the political events coming up. Did he want her to attend and take notes? His attention is diverted, and we move on with the meeting.

Chuck, one of the young reporters, says he has been talking with a southside gang member, but they are not indicating that they know anything about St. Mary's. It doesn't make sense. Gang members usually do street crime, not something with a church. Some gang members even go to that church with their mothers and have attended some special events, like the dances. They will go anywhere to meet young girls.

Speaking of dancing—it's Friday night—maybe Blondie and I will go over to the Arizona Manor and listen and dance to Bobby C for a while later in the evening. Hopefully, she can arrange a babysitter, and we can get out for a time together. Doesn't happen very often as we are both so busy with jobs and kids and the like.

CHAPTER THIRTY-SEVEN

JUNE 25, 9:30 AM
MCLAIN HOME

It's Saturday morning, and I can sleep a little later, especially after being out late last night. We enjoyed the music and had a good time which happens only rarely anymore in our lives.

The house seems quiet, and I stagger out of bed about 9:30 AM, which is very late for me. Coffee is in the pot on the stove, which I turn the heat to, washing my face and hands in the sink. I pull down a bowl for my favorite cereal and sit and wait for the coffee to get hot.

I see a note from Blondie on the fridge, which reads the kids are at the neighbor's house, playing with their son. Blondie has gone to work and should be home about 4 pm.

As I eat breakfast, I glance at the Saturday morning paper which Blondie has laid out for me on the table. The news seems to center around the forthcoming political campaign. Each of the candidates running for governor is vying for space in the paper to get their pictures and campaign rhetoric out. Everyone wants to do good things for the state of Arizona. Once they're elected, their agendas seem to change so that they're doing good things for themselves, not the state.

I glance at the sports page. Baseball is in full swing during these summer months. Then I happen upon the movie page. The hot new movie is "Shane" starring Alan Ladd, Jean Arthur, Van Heflin, and Brandon de Wilde. As I read about the story, it seems like a great western picture the entire family might like. In my mind, I plan when Blondie gets home to go out for hamburgers at the new concept place that just opened, a fast-food restaurant with things called Golden Arches at Indian School Road and Central, and a movie. McDonald's has just opened their first franchised restaurant, which happens to be in Phoenix. She will like that.

I settle into the home desk and look over the bills. Always seems there is more money going out than either Blondie and I make together. The boys are growing like weeds and need new clothes and shoes. I try for a moment to think about how they will be able to go to college. Guess they will have to get scholarships or work their way through. Thank goodness Blondie puts a lot of emphasis on their education and makes them read and do their homework every night when school is in session. Hopefully, they will continue to be good kids, but you never know.

My mind wanders. Marguerita is probably a good mother also, perhaps too tired from her day job to pay much attention to her son Miguel and doesn't really know where he goes or with whom. Her son has fallen into bad company and now portrays that image, but she is not a bad mother. Trying her best to do what is right.

Hopefully, our boys don't have the same experience because Blondie and I work long, unpredictable hours due to our jobs. However, Blondie has managed to find suitable substitutes for the kids, good babysitters and good neighbors who step up to help. There is something to be said for this lower-income neighborhood. We are all in the same boat, and neighbors and families try to help each other and look out for each other's kids, houses, cars, and such.

My mind drifts to the young kid sitting in the Phoenix jail

waiting and hoping someone will find the answer that sets him free. Most of the police department personnel think that he is guilty of the murder of the tailor. Probably the prosecutors share that same opinion. They are convinced because of the number of in-person identifications that pointed him out as the killer. The tailor had class. He loved classical music—Mozart, Chopin, Beethoven, Bach, and Ravel were all part of his collection. Wonder what will happen to the collection now? I must try and find a classical radio station that can expose the kids to this great music. If we don't show them, they will never listen to it on their own. Perhaps they will even express an interest in playing an instrument.

I pick up the phone and check with Captain Reed, but they have not located the young newlyweds yet. They must be really spending time off the grid, in bed, because no one can locate them. Wonder if they are camping somewhere in the mountainous areas around Mt. Lemon outside Tucson? That would be a cheap honeymoon and, indeed, take them out of communication for a while. I'll have to suggest that to Captain Reed the next time I'm over at the police department, not that he will send a police officer into the mountains to locate them. We will just have to wait for their return to question them.

I finish the bill paying and turn the radio on to hear the latest news. Nothing earth-shaking, speaking of that, Phoenix had a mild earthquake recorded. I relax and drift briefly in my recliner.

Blondie comes bouncing through the door, and I give her a kiss and my suggestion regarding dinner. She is all for it. She is tired from her day. She freshens up her Tangee lipstick and says, let's go round up the kids and head for the hamburgers, the new place the cops are raving about, McDonald's, as she missed lunch working today.

McDonald's is an instant hit with the kids and the rest of the family also. We all have a good time with hamburgers and fries and look forward to attending the movie down the street.

CHAPTER THIRTY-EIGHT

SUNDAY, JUNE 26, 8:30 AM
MCLAIN HOME

IT'S SUNDAY, AND WE ALL PREPARE FOR CHURCH. THE KIDS THROW A fit because they want to watch one of their favorite cartoon shows. But it's off to church we go. Father Nicolai is still nowhere in attendance. His recovery is taking an awfully long time. The young priest does an excellent job of the sermon and conducting the service. As we leave, I ask about Father Nicolai.

He says, "The good father has had some memory loss from the blow to his head and is slowly recovering."

I guessed as much since he has not been participating in the services. Actually, the assault resulting from the confrontation may finish his career and retire due to the injury. Just too difficult for the senior father to gather his thoughts and recite sayings from the Bible, too difficult to come back.

I had promised the kids I would take them to the park and pitch a few baseballs for them to hit this afternoon. Blondie has things to do at the house, housework. So, after church, we change our clothes and head for the baseball field. The boys are getting surprisingly good at hitting my feeble attempts at pitching. This leaves me running around the field trying to catch their fly balls. I'm beginning to realize that my legs are not as young as they once were and don't respond as quickly as they once did. To say nothing of the fact that tomorrow at work, I will have sore muscles in both my arms and legs from today but can't let the kids know it.

CHAPTER THIRTY-NINE

JUNE 27, 9 AM
MARICOPA COUNTY COURT HOUSE, 125 W.
WASHINGTON, PHOENIX

BOB DAVIS GOES ON TRIAL. THE DATE HAS FINALLY ARRIVED. THE courthouse is packed with the local gentry. Almost everyone knew the tailor or knew about him. He had an excellent reputation in Phoenix for creating great-looking summer suits, sports coats, and slacks. The ladies liked his alteration expertise and attention to detail. I think they also liked his foreign flattery and manner.

The prosecutor hammers away at the fact that Bob Davis failed the lie detector test and that several eyewitnesses have definitely identified him, and that the kid can't establish a good alibi regarding his whereabouts at the time of the murder. He's very convincing.

Davis's court-appointed attorney really does not have a defense for the kid. He is probably busy with other higher-profile cases than this one, and the fact that so many witnesses are against him makes it difficult to find a reason that he is not guilty. The kid is actually considering a plea deal, taking a lesser charge, to avoid the death penalty. This fact makes his attorney actually think that he probably is guilty of the murder of the tailor. Unfortunately, the kid doesn't decide quickly on the plea deal proposed by the prosecutor, and the jury returns. He is sentenced to death row, awaiting his turn at the gas chamber. Everyone seems happy it is over, that is, everyone except Bob Davis.

I leave the courtroom depressed. I really believe deep down that this kid is innocent, yet nothing can be done to establish his alibi. They still have not located the honeymooners, so no explanation for his whereabouts.

A few days later, I drive out to the big house in Florence, Arizona, and sit down with Bob Davis. He is not communicating very much. Only wants to talk about his childhood home and growing up poor. He believes that is why he was convicted—that he is poor, moved around a lot, and really didn't have a permanent job.

I tried once again to explain to him that the reason the jury found him guilty had nothing to do with his background, his being poor white trash as he calls himself, but the fact that he could not establish his whereabouts at the time of the murder. They believed he was in Phoenix and certainly could have done it. They all thought that he needed money, which was the motive for the killing. Several of the eyewitnesses were really convincing. Walter Brennan, Jerry Goldman, and Fred McIntosh all found a way to be present at the trail, even though they had to travel long distances to do so. Even though they had to take time from their businesses, golf games, etc., they found a way to be there. The murder must have made a strong and lasting impression on each of them to give up their time and travel to this trial.

The drive back to Phoenix is long, and I'm not in the mood to stop and eat, so I drive straight back.

There's a black cloud that seems to be following me all the way home. I ask myself, "Am I losing my touch?" Pieces just don't seem to be coming together this time. No other news on the young couple, no more word from the ME in Globe or, for that matter, from the sheriff up there. Father Nicolai is not recovering, and the juveniles picked up for questioning have not provided any pertinent information.

Tonight, before I go to bed, I will go down a scotch and try and sleep soundly, which I need. The morning will bring a new day and perhaps some better news.

CHAPTER FORTY

JUNE 28, 7:30 AM
MCLAIN HOME

IT'S RAINING HARD THIS MORNING WHEN I GET UP. I TURN THE RADIO on and listen to the weather report of heavy flooding on the Phoenix and Scottsdale roads. I know that some of the roads are impassable when it rains. The hard desert ground does not absorb the fast, quick flow from heavy storms passing over. Streets become treacherous very quickly, and flash flooding occurs in some areas, stranding cars. Parts of Scottsdale's downtown areas can even flood. The Safari Hotel in Scottsdale has flooded before.

There are about 105,000 people that reside in the city of Phoenix and thousands more in surrounding communities such as Scottsdale, Mesa, Paradise Valley, and Carefree. The 1950's growth has been spurred on by advances in air conditioning, which allowed both homes and businesses to offset the extreme heat experienced in Phoenix and the surrounding areas during its long summers. There has been a drastic growth of homes following World War II in the greater Phoenix area. When the floods come, and they do, people don't know how to drive and try and make their way through heavy water on the streets only to get their cars washed away and sometimes endangering their lives.

This is going to be a long day with accidents and flooding occurring all over Phoenix and Scottsdale. I wish that I could just stay home, but I have to go to the newspaper and check on messages and any hot stories that Specs wants me to be following. Glad I will not be driving out of town today. I flip the radio on in my car and hear, "Heavy rains swamping the Phoenix metro area this morning, leaving some roads flooded and impassable. The National Weather Service is relaying reports from trained spotters who say nearly an inch of rain has fallen in a half-hour—more than enough to cause major flooding problems in the desert city—near North l6th Street and Thomas Road just northeast of downtown Phoenix. There are several reports of flooded roads and washes, especially near Scottsdale and areas to the west.

No wonder it's slow going this morning to downtown Phoenix and the Arizona Republic. Cars are backed up on the roads and only able to drive in one of the lanes in the high crown area of the roadway, which is not flooded like the edges of the streets. When I get into the newsroom, the phones are ringing like crazy, with people complaining about the rain, high water on the roads, and some shops and businesses being flooded. They all want to know when it will stop and when Phoenix politicians will do something about it.

Well, Phoenix has been appropriating money to build flood channels, and they have been doing at least one a year for some time. Where they build the canal, water is contained, but other areas flood over. It's going to be a long project to complete. The town of Scottsdale has just incorporated in 1951 and is trying to raise enough funds to handle the flood issue.

No one's looking for me at the office, so I head over to the Legal Eagle to see if Mary O has any updates on local scandals. She is pleasant and cheery as usual, and the coffee shop is bustling this morning. Other places may be fighting water, but the Legal Eagle is dry and hopping. She is too busy to stop and chat but says she hasn't heard any tasty tidbits of scandal that she cares to repeat to me that I would find interesting.

A couple of cops from the department across the street are having coffee and breakfast in a booth, so I wander over and say hello.

"Hi, Bulldog."

"Sit and shoot the shit with us."

I am looking for information from them regarding the Mexican kids and the church robbery. They have interviewed one of the kids but can't hold him, as they do not have any real evidence, just hearsay. I was afraid of that, knowing that Marguerita would not come forward and talk with the police and that she just heard her son talking and she doesn't really understand English well. All reasons they can't hold the juvenile without evidence or a confession which he definitely is not going to give up. They plan to keep an eye on him and his friends, hoping to see or hear something that can be helpful.

The Black and Mexican communities remain largely sequestered on the south side of town. The color lines are so rigid that no one north of Van Buren Street would rent to them, and the police try to keep them in their own neighborhoods. The kids do not talk to the cops unless it happens to be a Mexican cop. The police force has just hired two. The Chief has finally gotten smart and realizes that they will have to have officers that speak Spanish if they want inside information. The department will have to wait until they get feedback from the two new cops.

The streets are getting worse, traffic accidents everywhere, and crime has taken a holiday. No one wants to be out in this weather.

I give Blondie a call to see if she is okay and has arrived at work without any problems. She says everything is fine in her department and she will see me later.

CHAPTER FORTY-ONE

JUNE 28, 6 PM
MCLAIN HOME

At the end of the day, I arrive home to see Blondie and the kids putting up a couple of buckets where drops of water are falling from the ceiling. Blondie asks that I call the landlord and explain the situation. She has just gotten home and is trying to deal with it. I try to reach our landlord but to no avail. He is probably not answering the phone at this time because he also owns several low-rent apartments that may be having problems today.

I talk with the kids and see how their day went. Unfortunately, the school building also has leaks in several rooms, so most of their day was spent in the auditorium. They had two teachers that taught an American history class with lots of questions from the kids, which filled the day.

Dinner is an impromptu event—macaroni and cheese and cold cuts. The kids are thrilled. This is their kind of dinner. Blondie is tired, and so am I, so we just partake of the food, mostly quietly.

The kids go off to do some reading and baths and then bed. Blondie and I sit looking at each other and make small talk. With the rains, the telephone on her desk at work has been busy ringing all day with complaints from people. She did have one call for assistance.

A car had been washed over the embankment into a flood channel and was sinking. She made a couple of calls and sent the nearest cops to their assistance. They managed to pull the elderly couple to safety, but the car was lost, rushing down the waterway into the flood channel. It will turn up in the desert in a few days when the wash dries up again, ruined, only to be junked.

We talk briefly about the church robbery investigation, which doesn't seem to be going anywhere. She indicates the heat is on at the top level from the Mayor and Governor to the Chief of Police to get this public outrage of a case solved.

I mentioned to Blondie that Father Nicolai will not be able to return to the church in all probability. She is very sad but indicated the police department is not aware of this issue. It would only make matters worse daily. She suggests that I not write about it or let anyone know that I have inside information about the good father at this time.

The strong hot coffee is not keeping our eyes open. Blondie's eyes are slowly closing, and mine are almost closed. So, we head to the bedroom and await another day tomorrow. I will continue in the morning trying to reach the landlord and give him my tale of woe.

CHAPTER FORTY-TWO

JUNE 29, 8:30 AM
ARIZONA REPUBLIC NEWSPAPER

THE DRIVE INTO THE OFFICE IS AT LEAST DRY, AND WARM SUNSHINE floods the car's windows, but there is a lot of refuse along the roadway that will need to be cleaned up in the next few days now that the storm is over.

I look at my messages and then make my first call to the landlord to answer my obligation to Blondie and the kids.

I wish I could say that he was very responsive, but he says, "I will look into it as soon as possible."

"What the hell does that mean."

"As soon as I have time. I am dealing with other units and apartments and homes also."

I guess that is the best that I will do with this guy, so I hang up and proceed with my day.

As I look at the first message, Specs calls me into his office. There is news to report. They have identified the homeless itinerant found behind Goldwater's department store. His name is Jimmy Doe.

Also, the medical examiner has restated the cause of death from natural causes to a possible homicide. There appears to be a tiny puncture wound, a stab mark, from some type of tool just above his heart which may have caused his heart to stop. Also, there is some doubt that he died behind the Goldwater's department store location. The medical examiner says the body had been moved after death occurred.

I stand there stunned at the name. Specs is looking at me strangely.

"Did you know this guy, McLain?"

"Yeah, I met with him once."

"Well, spit it out. What was the occasion?"

"I was looking for a unique piece of jewelry for Blondie's birthday, and one of the store owners along Scottsdale Boulevard showed me a gold and turquoise necklace that was beautiful but beyond my price range. The owner recommended I contact this guy because he makes beautiful gold and turquoise jewelry, and perhaps he would give me a reasonable price for a bit of advertising.

"I did meet with him once at a local bar and saw some of his jewelry. When I inquired regarding where he got his turquoise and other stones, as they were especially nice, he clammed up and said, 'Do you want to purchase anything?'

"When I hesitated, he took off, running from the bar. I quickly paid the bar tab and followed him out to the parking lot, only to discover he had jumped into a vehicle and was racing out of the lot. I couldn't identify the vehicle, too far away and moving too fast. My thought was he might somehow be tied to the dead Indians up in Globe. The Indians from the reservation slightly north of Globe.

"Most of those Indians make turquoise and other silver jewelry and harvest stones from their reservation area. Although Jimmy Doe was known along Scottsdale Boulevard for his beautiful gold and turquoise settings.

"I am sure he had space, probably somewhere in the warehouse district, where he melted his gold and created the designer settings that were so popular with the Scottsdale jewelers. They indicated they always pay the Indians and anyone selling to them at wholesale prices in cash. That is what the individuals want, and the prices sure work for the jewelry store owners. They then mark up the jewelry and sell at a substantial profit. The visiting easterners on vacation don't seem to mind paying for the items they want."

I tell Specs, "I will spend time trying to locate the dead jeweler's workshop."

Meanwhile, many thoughts are rolling around in my head. Is there a connection to the Globe murders? Seems farfetched but possible. Is there a connection to the missing gold statue from St. Mary's? No one would be crazy enough to melt down a religious icon, would they? That is, no one unless they were desperate for money or to fulfill an obligation. I am sure there would be some kind of religious curse on your life for melting down a famous religious statue like St. Francis of Assisi. Maybe there is. Perhaps that is why he is dead. More likely, someone is scared and afraid that he would talk about where he purchased his supplies and didn't want them to discover his sources.

In the afternoon, I plan to drive the warehouse district and make some inquiries. Someone should be aware of his jewelry-making setup. Surely someone would take notice of this old guy and his workshop.

Pam stops by my desk and inquires about what type of jewelry I had purchased for Blondie., then adds she wishes someone would buy her pretty things.

She seems lonely. I guess working the political scene has not turned up any possible suitors to her liking. She is young. She has to give it time. I explain I purchased a piece from one of the stores in Scottsdale. She says she can't wait to see it when Blondie wears it. I am not sure when she and Blondie will see each other but nod in agreement.

CHAPTER FORTY-THREE

JUNE 29, 3 PM
PHOENIX SOUTH SIDE DISTRICT WAREHOUSES

IT'S LATE AFTERNOON, AND I AM CRUISING AROUND IN THE warehouse district as some of the workers seem to be leaving for the day. I stop the car and roll down the window as two approach.

"I'm Gene McLain, a reporter for the Arizona Republic, and would like to ask you guys a few questions. Can you spare a minute?"

They stop, startled, look at each other and say, "Yeah."

"I'm looking for a workshop that may be in one of these warehouses where an elderly guy melts gold and silver to make expensive jewelry. Do you know where that might be?"

They look confused, "Hey, guy, you are in the wrong place. Everything here is warehouses, stocked full of boxes. Seriously doubt anyone would be making jewelry here."

They move along. Not helpful.

I stop another man approaching along the street. Ask the same questions. He is a little more responsive and says, "Maybe you should check out the warehouses down along the border to the south side of the Mexican district. They store all kinds of things there, and the owners are not very particular. They even sometimes store "hot items." The Mexicans working there would not ask questions as most are illegal and just want to have a job."

This seems plausible, and I thank him for being helpful and move along. I stop a couple of more workers, but nothing productive comes from the conversations.

It's now getting late in the day, and the sun is starting to set. I really don't want to ride around asking questions in the dark on the south side at night. It can be dangerous. The gangs are at work all hours of the nighttime. This will have to wait for another day.

Turning the old vehicle toward home and dinner, I can't wait to see what Blondie has cooked up for tonight's dinner. Yes, I'm hungry. I am always hungry, unfortunately, so are the kids as they are growing taller. I am just growing sideways. Blondie just nods and watches as I fill my plate a second time around. She never says anything, but I know that she thinks I am overweight, and probably she's correct, but I am too old to change. I give her credit as she never says anything about it.

CHAPTER FORTY-FOUR

JUNE 30, 10 AM
LEGAL EAGLE CAFE

I RUN BY THE OFFICE TO PICK UP MESSAGES, NOTHING STARTLING, then head over to the Legal Eagle for coffee and a sweet roll. Blondie doesn't have them at home as she thinks they are too fattening for the boys and me. Probably also for her. She knows that I frequently stop at the Legal Eagle for information and almost always have something to eat. She knows that I am not deprived of sweets. Mary O takes very good care of me in that department.

It's quiet today, maybe a little later in the morning than usual. Mary O sits downs to chat briefly before serving up the hot sweet roll and coffee. She says the clientele is sure talking a lot about the church robbery. They want justice done. Can't understand why the police department of Phoenix can't find the statue and arrest the perpetrators.

That's a question that we all would like answered. I feel deeply sorry for Father Nicolai. Just wasn't his day. Having to retire early and not being able to do his traditional functions, I am sure, is very frustrating for him. The police department is also frustrated with no leads and no answers.

I decide to take a swing by the south side warehouse district—driving along run-down warehouses, not many people on the street in the early afternoon. I spot a Mexican just leaving one of the warehouses and stop him to question him.

"Do you speak English? That is my first question.

The answer, "Yes, Senor, a little bit."

I try and explain that I am a reporter with the Arizona Republic, and I am looking for an elderly man who makes jewelry. Probably has a workshop in one of the warehouses locally.

Not sure how much he understands. He just nods his head.

"Si Senor. Aqui."

I grasp that he means here. I ask, "Which building?"

He points an arthritic hand with curled fingers to the building located just to the right of where I am standing. Can I really be having such good luck? I thank him and offer a couple of bucks for his help. He takes the two dollars and quickly moves down the street, acting as if he hopes no one sees him.

I enter the large, unlocked warehouse. In the front section are rows and rows of boxes, which look like machine parts. Toward the back of the building, I see what looks like an office area. I approach the back cautiously, not sure what to expect. I peer through the door, which has a small glass window near the top of the door. It's not an office but looks like a workshop. I notice that there is a small circular pit area with some kind of kiln. This could be what I am looking for. The place looks trashed. The door is locked. Pressing hard, extremely hard, too hard, the door opens to reveal a trashed room with worktables, picks, and tools spread everywhere. I notice some small turquoise stones scattered on the floor, as well as a spot of blood. I think this is Jimmy Doe's work area.

I back out of the room, not touching anything except the door, which I pull closed. I leave the warehouse and start driving my car to locate the nearest telephone to call Captain Reed. Driving down the street, I spot Officer Vail walking and checking the buildings to ensure they are locked. I stop and tell him that he needs to call the Captain and have them come and investigate the warehouse just up the street as I believe that I have found Jimmy Doe's jewelry workshop. He heads for a phone and then will come and meet me at the location. I head back up the street, hoping to not run into anyone. A couple of Mexican workers are leaving the building next door but don't seem to notice me sitting in my car waiting for Officer Vail.

He appears shortly, and we both enter the warehouse and move toward the back of the building where the shop is located. He presses on the door and says it seems to have been forced. I don't comment, not wanting to get involved, just wanting the story. We look around, and he also spots a small pool of blood. Another cop arrives and goes to the patrol car to call for backup to check out what might be a crime scene.

As the other cops arrive, I say my hellos and goodbyes, leaving quickly. I am convinced that this is the crime scene for the murder of Jimmy Doe. Also, this is the location where he worked on making his gold pieces with precious stones. This is definitely his workspace. Thinking back about some of the tools I saw scattered around, any one of the picks with handles could easily be the murder weapon.

The medical examiner said, "A small puncture hole probably killed Jimmy Doe."

The real question is, "Why?"

CHAPTER FORTY-FIVE

JUNE 30, – 6 PM
MCLAIN HOME

THAT QUESTION FOLLOWS ME INTO THE EVENING HOURS AT HOME. Hard to shake the thought. "Why would Jimmy Doe be murdered?"

Blondie puts dinner on the table. We all eat, the kids and I until we are stuffed. She sends the boys upstairs to complete their reading assignments. She then cleans the table and makes a bit of small talk as she washes the dishes. I sit there idly thinking, not about what she is saying, but about "Why kill Jimmy Doe?"

Finally, she turns and says she is finished and is going into the living room to watch television as I am a poor communicator this evening. She knows something is on my mind. She is one smart lady and knows I will discuss it with her when I formulate my ideas in my own mind. At this point, images and thoughts are just running around in my head. Nothing is very clear, nothing substantial to cling to—just a haze of thoughts.

CHAPTER FORTY-SIX

JULY 1, 8:30 AM
PHOENIX POLICE DEPARTMENT

THE NEXT DAY I TAKE A TRIP OVER TO THE POLICE STATION AND WAIT to see Captain Reed. I want answers. Did I locate the actual murder scene of Jimmy Doe? Is this where he designed and crafted his handmade gold and silver pieces? And the real question I want answered. Is this where he was murdered? Can you tell me by whom?

Captain Reed looks up from his desk as I bombard him with my questions.

"Hold on, Gene. I will try and answer some of your questions. Yes, we believe this is the right location. Probably is where he was murdered. Why? We don't know. Do you have the answer, smart guy?"

"No, not yet. I was really interested in some of the small tools with sharp-pointed blades. Could one of them be the murder weapon?"

"Yes, possibly. They will have to be checked out by the lab before we can say for sure. The tools are the types that are used in making jewelry designs and molds. We also found some hand-drawn sketches of pieces he was working on."

As soon as the owners along Scottsdale Boulevard find out he is dead, the pieces that they have in their collections will skyrocket in price. Always more valuable once the artist is deceased. Could it be the motive to kill him? However, they will not be able to acquire additional pieces from him. It's not too likely that one of them is the killer, but you never know.

The Captain did disclose something of valuable interest. They found a small plate with the name St. Francis Assisi engraved on it. Could it have come from the base of the statue?

Can't wait to get out of the station and drive to the church. I must take a real good look at the remaining statues. Do they have a plate engraved with the saints' names on each of them?

Could Jimmy Doe have melted down the gold statue to use the gold for jewelry pieces? Where would he have acquired the statue? From whom? He certainly was not one of the kids that Father Nicolai described as young Mexicans, possibly gang members, that committed the crime. Now, they would be motivated to kill him and be crazy with fear that he might talk because they really don't trust older people.

Jimmy Doe would never talk. It was not to his benefit to do so. He liked being known as a weird recluse. Yet, he was highly creative with his jewelry. The solitude gave him time to design special pieces. The Mexicans working in the warehouse didn't bother him. They really didn't know what he was doing in the back. The landlord never came around, so he had the perfect spot to work and not be disturbed.

Someone found his shop and punctured his heart with a tool from behind. Probably snuck up on him as he was working, bent over a mold. Being old, he never heard them until it was too late. Then they ransacked his work area. What were they looking for? They loaded his body up in a vehicle and dropped him off behind Goldwater's department store.

Must remember to ask Captain Reed if he thinks that more than one person was involved in the killing. Also, I want to find Miguel, Marguerita's son and question him. I make mental notes of things to do early tomorrow.

CHAPTER FORTY-SEVEN

JULY 1, 9:30 PM
ST MARY'S CHURCH

On the way into the office, I drive by St. Mary's. I am sure the young priest will be up and working. He now has a challenging workload to handle each day. I knock on the door of the rectory, and a woman housekeeper opens the door. I ask if Father Dave is available. She indicates to come in, and she will find him.

In a couple of minutes, he appears, looking bright and energetic.

"What can I do for you today?

"I ask to see the church area where the statue was removed, and could I examine a couple of the other statues."

"Sure, come along, and I will open the church. We never used to lock the doors, but since this last incident with Father Nicolai, I decided to lock the doors at night. We don't want any other statues stolen or any other damage to the church."

I understand his reasoning and follow behind him. We enter the church, and he points to the alcove where the statue was removed. I go and thoroughly investigate the base area. It looks as if something was pried up from the plaster base area where it resided—the actual statue was set on a wood base with the nameplate attached. I walk around the church and view a couple of the other statues, some larger, some the same size, and each has a wood base with a nameplate.

When they ransacked Jimmy Doe's workshop, they forgot about the nameplate. The kids probably didn't even notice that there was one. They were looking for the gold, hopefully melted down into smaller pieces, and any large stones that they could resell later plus cash.

I thanked the good father and asked that he give my well-wishes to Father Nicolai. Father Dave said Father Nicolai putters around the garden area of the church working most days. Has no interest in conducting services or being actively involved with the daily duties.

It about noon, and I decide to take a drive through the south side of town. Perhaps I can locate Miguel and have a little talk. I pass the movie theater and look into the game store cafe where the pinball machines are located. I don't see Miguel, lots of other kids, but not Miguel. As I drive up the street, I see Miguel hanging out with two other boys. They are just parting, and Miguel takes off in the direction of his home. I slowly follow him for a little while. Then I pull alongside and identify myself. I explain I have talked with his mother.

He grumbles, "Yes, I'm aware. Leave my mother alone."

I ask if he would like a ride. His head shakes no.

We slowly keep moving down the sidewalk. I, with the window rolled down and asking questions, and he, shuffling along, now and then looking up toward me. Answers are not forthcoming.

Finally, I say, "I know that Largo Sanchez is no longer in control of the south side gang."

He has moved on. Either arrested or just moved from the south side somewhere else. Chicky Hernandez is now the formidable threat leading the guys on the south side of Phoenix. Does Miguel know him? He looks up abruptly as though I have just hit him. He does know him, that is for sure.

"What are your other friends up to? Jesus, for instance."

Miguel is not talking, but I am sure that he knows something, maybe even involved in the theft and murder.

I am going to suggest that Captain Reed bring Miguel in for questioning. Being the younger of the three boys who hang out together, he will perhaps be scared and talk. I can't picture Miguel being the killer or even hitting the priest on the head, but he might have been involved with the others.

"Miguel, if you know something, you should protect yourself and tell the police."

At this point, he takes off running, and I am reaching an intersection with traffic coming the other way. I must stop. He disappears down the street with flashing speed.

He doesn't realize that I know where he lives. I have checked out Marguerita and her sons.

CHAPTER FORTY-EIGHT

THE PAPER IS BUZZING THIS MORNING. THERE HAS BEEN ANOTHER crime committed on the south side of Phoenix. A man and wife have been robbed and beaten and left on the street. Apparently, they were visiting some people. When they left at approximately 10:30 pm and approached their car, three teenagers came at them with a gun, demanding money and jewelry. The man resisted and was beaten to the ground and hit with a gun, a baseball bat, and some kind of club. The wife was screaming at the sight of her husband's blood and would not stop. They beat her into submission and quiet. Removing her jewelry, the man's wristwatch, and wallet. The kids fled down the street, leaving the couple on the sidewalk bleeding and unconscious. They are now both in the hospital, unable to talk, and their condition is considered extremely serious.

As the morning paper hits the street with this headline story, the phones start ringing in the office. The people of Phoenix are outraged. This violence must stop. What's wrong with the police department? Why can't they clean up the south side? After taking a few of these calls, I am prompted to go over to the Chief's office and divulge what information I have regarding Chicky Hernandez and his gang.

I suggest to the Chief that they should bring in Miguel for questioning. I think that he might crack under pressure. I don't believe he is a bad kid, just in with the wrong gang. Since Miguel is sixteen and considered a juvenile, his sentence would be lighter than the older boys, eighteen and over. The police investigator might scare him enough to gain considerable information about the south side gang. Also, about the church robbery.

Chief Morse agrees and says he will look into it. I ask if I can be present when they interview Miguel since we have had some conversation, such as it was. He says he will call.

I run into Officer Vail as I leave the police department and inquire about the ongoing investigation of Jimmy Doe's death. He says they still have not received the information back from the lab, but it does look like one of the tools used for jewelry making could have been the instrument used to cause his death. I thank him for the information and move along. The police department sure moves slowly in investigations. I assumed that was the case the day I saw the workshop. They are just now putting it together. No mention of the plaque with the Saint's name. Have they figured out that Jimmy Doe melted down the statue of gold? I doubt it. The bigger question is, how did he get the statue? Did his having the statue cause his death? And who the hell stole the statue from the church?

The following day the Chief calls my office and leaves a message. They have arrested Miguel and are sweating him.

I rush over to the police station with mixed emotions. I know that they cannot really sweat a teenager and give him too bad a time, yet they have to scare the hell out of this kid to get answers. When I arrive, there are two detectives in the room with Miguel, and he is looking sick. He is handcuffed and slumping in the chair. I ask if I can go in.

Sure, the Chief says, "See if you can get anything out of him."

"Hello, Miguel. Remember me?"

"Yeah, Mr. McLain"

"Miguel, I bet your mother is pretty worried about where you are right now. She will be looking for you to come home from school."

"Mr. McLain, they won't let me go. Say that I am being arrested for the theft from the church of a statue, plus the murder of some guy named Doe."

"Well, kid, you better tell them what they want to know, or you will be going off to jail."

"If I talk, the gang will kill me."

"If you don't talk, the police will lock you up and throw away the key."

"They can't do that. I didn't do nothing. Just heard them talking."

"Well, if you want to save yourself, you had better talk."

Detective Owens says, "Quit wasting our time, kid. We have plenty of work to do."

"Okay. When I was together with my friends from the gang at the pool hall, they talked about a big cash deal. Some old guy approached them about stealing a gold statue. He would pay them good if they could deliver it. A few days later, three of the guys seemed to have plenty of cash. Then the newspaper story, and my mother was upset with my friends. I wasn't part of the deal, but I did hear them talking. Chicky Hernandez is tough and brutal. If he finds out I am even here, he will beat me up or have me killed."

"I need names, kid."

"Here are a paper and pencil, write them down and where we can find these guys."

We watch Miguel scribble on the paper.

"Meanwhile, go home and don't talk to anybody. Don't mention being here. Got it, kid." I say.

CHAPTER FORTY-NINE

JULY 2, 9 AM
ARIZONA REPUBLIC NEWSPAPER

THE NEXT MORNING AS I APPROACH MY DESK, THE PHONE IS RINGING. It's Captain Reed.

"We got two of the punks last night. They are residing in our lock-up. Going to question them this morning. Thought you would like to know."

I rush over to the police department to watch the detectives take turns with these two hardened gang members. Getting no response. Finally, they are out of patience, and one of the cops puts his hands on Jesus and threatens to kick the shit out of him.

Jesus is not cracking but says, "Why us? Did that kid Miguel give you our names? Slimy bastard. He is one of us also. Just as dirty."

Captain Reed reaches for the phone and says to the operator,

"Have Officer Vail bring in Miguel again for questioning."

Marguerita is not going to be happy today.

Especially if one of the victims from the recent street robbery regains consciousness and can identify these guys.

I leave the police station and take a swing past St. Joseph's hospital to see if the victims have regained consciousness.

"Yes, the nurse says, the wife is just awake. She doesn't know yet how bad her husband is."

I approach the room, identify myself, and ask if she is up to answering a couple of questions.

"Have the police been to see you yet?"

"No."

"I am sure they will be around to ask questions."

"Hopefully, they can find these guys. They were really rough on us. My husband gave them his wallet, but when they reached for his watch, he fought back. That is when they started beating him, and I screamed, and they hit me also. The watch was a gift I had given him for our twenty-fifth anniversary. He loved it."

She relaxed back into the pillows, and I sensed she was very tired—time to depart.

"Oh, one more question. Did you hear any names? Did they call each other by a name?"

"As I was falling, I think I heard someone say, Jesus, you really hit her hard." And then, 'Shut up, Miguel. You idiot.'"

Marguerita is really, really not going to be happy when she hears her son was involved in at least one of the robberies and maybe more. Poor lady. Even though she works so hard, there is no money for a lawyer. So, Miguel will have a public defender.

I will go and see him again in jail. I will explain that he will be charged with a crime, but because he is a juvenile and turns state's evidence against the other gang members, he will serve a limited amount of time in a juvenile facility. I hope the kid has smartened up and realizes that this is his only hope for a future outside of jail by the time he reaches twenty-one.

CHAPTER FIFTY

JULY 3, 9 AM
ARIZONA REPUBLIC NEWSPAPER

THIS GUY JIMMY DOE SEEMS TO HAVE A LOT OF CONTACTS. I wonder if he was also making deals with some of the Indians. Like in Globe? You wouldn't think a guy like that with such talent as a jeweler would also be such a criminal. Have to look into his background to run a story in the paper. Wonder where his money went? Booze, drugs, must investigate that also for the story. Maybe his killers weren't looking for gold and stones but cash. Since he sold his pieces designed in gold at pretty high prices, maybe it was cash they were looking for when they trashed his workshop. He has become an interesting character now that he is dead.

Apparently, he approached someone in the gang with the idea of stealing the gold statue. Pretty ingenious if you ask me. Who the hell would suspect an elderly man, a bum, of being the mastermind behind a gang heist. I am sure Chicky Hernandez did not need encouragement and readily agreed to use his guys for the church heist since he was already robbing people on the south side streets of Phoenix.

The church heist seemed easy, and yes, of course, his guys could do it. He figured that no one would be around. The church doors were always open, so it should be very easy to lift a statue. He probably didn't anticipate the actual weight of the statue or that it might be mounted to a base. Hell, he had probably never been in the church before he decided to case the job. He doesn't strike me as the church-going type. He certainly didn't anticipate running into Father Nikolai.

At the office, I arrange through a friend to acquire a copy of the arrest files for Jimmy Doe. Seems he does have a lengthy criminal record. Certainly not an upstanding citizen of Phoenix. He has been around but mostly flying under the radar of the police department until now. Small stuff, loitering, DUI, assaulting another person, and such.

Headline for my story about Jimmy Doe "Bum Mastermind of Church Heist." How one elderly guy got one of Phoenix's most notorious gangs to commit the church robbery, and everything went wrong. That is except they managed to steal the statue and get paid a handsome sum. The Phoenix police department has in custody three gang members that they feel are involved in the church robbery. One a juvenile, and two just eighteen and nineteen years of age. Finally, closure to a horrific crime that terrified the good people of Phoenix. However, there is a catch. The gang did not come up with this idea. Instead, they were influenced by an elderly jewelry designer looking for a cheap source of gold to use in his jewelry designs.

Jimmy Doe was murdered for his efforts in setting up the robbery. The gang members were probably looking for his cash stash when they ransacked his workshop and killed the elderly man, possibly afraid that he would get drunk and talk, disclosing the gang connection to the crime. Then they dumped his body behind Goldwater's department store, and he became the itinerant, unidentified deceased body.

The Phoenix coroner amended the autopsy and finally identified him as Jimmy Doe days later. Also, as having died under suspicious circumstances. The police department then set to work, trying to find his living and working space. But unfortunately, the gang had already located him and disposed of him, trashing his place and leaving very little evidence.

I file my story with Specs, who nods approval, and I take it down to Ben in the basement for the typesetting. The story should be the headline of the next morning's Arizona Republic.

CHAPTER FIFTY-ONE

JULY 4th HOLIDAY
MCLAIN HOME

IN THE MORNING, WE WATCH A COUPLE OF THE FOURTH OF JULY celebration parades featured on television. Then in the early afternoon, we go to the park to toss a few baseballs around. The boys are growing up and becoming better hitters, which means I am chasing the ball around more. It should be good for slimming the waistline, which Blondie would really like me to do.

Blondie is home slimming her waistline by cleaning the house.

Late afternoon we fire up the backyard grill and roast hamburgers and hot dogs.

Everyone is exhausted by evening, and the boys go to bed early. Blondie and I sit watching TV, the Lucy Show, and then an episode of Dragnet. By the end of the show, our eyes are slipping shut, so we head to bed early.

CHAPTER FIFTY-TWO

JUNE 5, 9 AM
GLOBE, ARIZONA

TODAY IS COOLER IN PHOENIX, SO I DECIDE TO TAKE ANOTHER DRIVE to Globe. This time with Jimmy Doe's picture to see if I can find anyone there that knows him.

I check in with the sheriff, who doesn't recognize him and has no leads to follow. This means I will walk the main street and ask some of the shop owners if they know him. If that doesn't work, then on to the reservation to try communicating with some of the Indians.

I walk the two blocks of the main street, talking to people. No one recognizes Jimmy Doe nor gives any information. Once again, I stop at the local eatery. A couple of guys are at the counter, and one of the tables is occupied. I walk up to the table and show the picture. No response. The two guys at the counter are truck drivers and just going through town, so no leads there.

I sit at a table and wait for service, which seems to take a long time. They are not really friendly here in the "friendliest town in the west." A blonde bimbo with hair piled high on her head arrives with pad and pencil in hand, nodding that I should say something. I order a piece of apple pie topped with ice cream—Blondie would not approve—but it sure looks good. Coffee, black, and a bit of conversation. She looks up from the pad after writing "conversation." I know that this is not the town scholar.

"What?"

"I am looking for anyone who might recognize this man?" holding up the picture of Jimmy Doe.

She glances at the picture and says, "Lots of old men come into the coffee shop. How do I expect her to remember this one?"

"Well, for starters, he might be showing gold and turquoise jewelry for sale?"

"No, no one like that has been here in Globe."

"He might ask if you know of any Indians that sell turquoise or red jasper stones or work in that kind of silver jewelry."

"There was a guy a long time ago that came by and inquired if I could point him in the direction where some Indian silversmiths were selling their wares. I told him to try the reservation north of town. That's all I know."

"Thanks."

It could have been anyone asking about Indian wares. She really didn't remember seeing this particular guy.

I finish the pie and depart. I take a leisurely drive out to the reservation, park, and walk around like I know what I am looking for. Ha!

Talking with any Indians I pass on the street and showing my picture, it's difficult to determine if they recognize him or not. They show no facial emotion, no expression—just tired and worn-out looks. Then, finally, hit a guy that says two young male Indians work in that kind of jewelry, but one has been missing from the reservation for some time. He points me in the direction of a teepee set up at the end of a dirt road in the reservation. I wander down and find a guy working in silver on a turquoise bracelet. An incredibly beautiful piece. He says he is making it for his sister, who has lost her husband. He disappeared one day and never returned to the reservation. He had made a bracelet just like it for his sister to give to her husband on their first anniversary. He never took it off.

A beautiful piece with heavy silver work encircling a large turquoise stone of irregular shape with red jasper carved balls encrusted all around the turquoise. A very large, heavy piece. Spectacular in design. He said the bracelet he made for his sister had an inscription written on the inside—her name and date of their marriage. I asked him if he had ever met Jimmy Doe. He said an old man came around the reservation once or twice a year and purchased stones but rarely silver pieces. He was looking for unusual stones. Whatever the Indians could locate. The old guy had a couple of healthy young Indians with him on his visits to safeguard the jewelry and maybe his cash. He thought they all lived in Globe or somewhere outside of Globe.

I tried to get a description of the young Indians who traveled with Jimmy Doe. His description was vague, just that they seemed to be young and healthy. Not much to go on. Whoever attacked the Indians in Globe were young and strong. To outsiders, all the Indians looked the same, only young or old. I drove back through Globe and stopped to talk with the sheriff, giving him the description of the two young Indians who traveled with Jimmy Doe. I let him know that perhaps they didn't live in town but out in the peripheral area. He thanked me for the information but didn't feel it was much to go on. I didn't either. There had not been any other incidents of Indians being attacked and left alongside the road, so the sheriff was not pushing too hard to locate the original perpetrators. Things move slowly in Globe.

Frustrated, I said goodbye and started my long drive home to Phoenix. About halfway back, I had a flat tire and had to stop and change the tire myself, as there was nothing close by. I really didn't want to walk a long distance since I was unsure where I was heading and what I might find.

So, I opened the car's trunk and pulled out the patched spare tire and a jack. It has been a while since I had to do something like this. Kneel down in the dust of the road, jack the car up, and hope that it holds while I pull the tire off after taking off the lugs. I really have to pull hard. The tire has not been off in a while. Rest a bit and put the spare on. Tighten the lugs and throw the old flat tire in the trunk. Close the trunk and sit in the car a while, catching my breath. Attempt to dust off my trousers and shoes. I start the engine once again and head for home—what a day.

I do have a lead to follow, though. I will make another circle through some of the shops in Scottsdale. If Jimmy was involved somehow in killing the two Indians in Globe, perhaps the one for his bracelet, he might just have sold it to a store owner in Scottsdale for resale. If it was as nice as the Indian craftsman said in his reservation teepee and looked like the sketch that he made for me, I doubt that Jimmy would have removed the stones from this bracelet. After all, he was a jeweler and did admire outstanding workmanship.

I arrive home very late, dirty and tired. The family is all in bed. Blondie stirs a little as I put the light on to undress and head for the shower. I am filthy, and I don't want to climb in bed all dirty with the world's most beautiful woman.

When I do come to bed, she rolls over and mumbles something, and then continues to sleep. So much for being clean.

CHAPTER FIFTY-THREE

JULY 6, 9 AM
ARIZONA REPUBLIC NEWSPAPER

Guess what! Captain Reed calls and says the honeymooners are returning to El Paso. He just got a call from the boy's mother. They should be back around the end of the week and be available to talk. The captain will send an officer to El Paso to meet with them, but it will take a couple of days for him to arrive there and set up the meeting. Finally, something is moving in the Bob Davis case.

Specs holds his weekly meeting. Boring! Nothing exciting to report. Phoenix is hot in July, and not much happens. The City is afraid of another monsoon hitting and flooding everything. They are just starting to dig out of the flood debris that has backed up and cleaned up the streets. They must wait for another election to get additional funds on the bill for the people of Phoenix to approve increasing the budget to build more canals to handle the floodwaters. If another monsoon comes before that, there will again be mass flooding and damage. Not a cheerful thought. I don't want to write a story about that.

No murders this last week. Everything is quiet for the moment. Even the gangs have settled down or are scared, so they are not committing any street robberies, which were prolific before a couple of weeks ago. Perhaps the police department has put the fear of God in them or maybe it's only temporary.

I am looking out the window when I hear my name called.

"Yeah, Specs."

I realize that he doesn't like being called that. He prefers Mr. Bornheim or Ralph to the employees. I wasn't thinking. My mind was wandering on this hot day, and I try to recover by saying,

"Yes, Ralph, what can I do for you?"

"Try and pay attention, McLain."

"Yes, sir."

"What is happening with the Bob Davis case? Is he just waiting for the death penalty to be delivered?"

I inform him that Captain Reed is sending an officer again to El Paso to interview the motel owner and his wife. They are just returning from a long, secluded honeymoon where they were not available. In the next couple of days, they will return home, and the Phoenix police will be there to meet them and ask questions.

He also wants to know about the Globe "Highway Murders" since I have been out of the office again and on the road to Globe. He received my mileage, gas slips, and the tire repair bill on his desk.

"What the hell are you doing in Globe again?"

I try to explain the theory that Jimmy Doe may have had someone working with him and that person or persons could be the one committing the murders in Globe. Perhaps the murders are occurring over jewelry or stones from the area.

Specs doesn't seem interested in the idea that murder was committed over stones.

He moves on to other subjects, grilling some of the other news people present.

Back to daydreaming, mind drifting out the window. Going to be a long, hot day.

CHAPTER FIFTY-FOUR

JULY 7, 10:30 AM
ARIZONA REPUBLIC NEWSPAPER

After leaving the morning meeting with Specs, I wander out onto the hot sidewalk of Phoenix and consider how I might drum up a good story for this week's Sunday headline. Deciding to stroll down Phoenix's main street, I stop to talk with a few people as I amble along in the heat. Finally, I come to Durant's Steakhouse and decide to go in for a tall cool Dos Equis. It's just lunchtime, and they are preparing for the large crowd that appears every day. I am not hungry, so I head to the bar for a tall cool one.

As I sit there, looking out over the dining room, I see the good people of Phoenix, the hard-working office personnel, the laborers, and others come in for a quick lunch special. There, sitting in the back booth, is one of Phoenix's top wrestlers. He has won his last several bouts with newcomers and seems to be enjoying his celebrity. Durant's restaurant probably picks up his meals for lunch and dinner to just have him hanging around. I spot the owner who is talking to him feverishly.

Durant's likes to have the sports guys hang out. Draws a large crowd of guys who drink and eat often and shoot the bull with the athletes. Several football players and boxers hang around Durant's. I'm sure they are encouraged to do so with free drinks, food, and introductions to local girls. Also, probably some backroom betting takes place. If the athletes hang out, they give some interesting information regarding the odds on their fights, team members, and such. Betting goes on here quietly; it does exist.

Durant's has always been the place in town where the mob hangs out as well. Mob boss Giorgino Scorsese, Don of the Capello crime family, often dines at Durant's. Usually with several of his henchmen. Athletes and crime figures as a good combination for winning bets. There is always an array of beautiful girls that hang around Durant's in the evening. Some are supplied by the restaurant, and some just come to be where the athletes and gangsters hang out, hoping to land a generous guy for the night.

I make small talk with the bartender. Ask if he has any interesting stories to tell that I might use for the paper. Most of his stuff centers around the girls that the athletes pick up. They hang around his bar, and occasionally he makes out okay also. If it is a slow night, they might let him hit on them for the evening. He refuses to pay but tells them he will set them up with some good spenders, mob guys, athletes, which he does do. The guys tip him generously for the introductions. He does not take any money from the girls, so they like him. He's a good Joe. Not like their usual pimps or boyfriends who push their services and want a percentage of the evening take and sometimes take all their money—the cost of a working girl. We pay taxes and complain, and they pay pimps and complain.

As we sit talking, a hot blonde named Josie comes in and sits at the bar at the end. Good Joe nods and points her out. Am I interested? No, not interested that way, but I would like to talk with her to see if she knows anything about the jeweler's demise. Joe makes the introduction, and I slide down the bar, offering to buy her a drink.

She says it's too early to drink hard liquor as it will be a long night. She will take a Coke. We sit idly chatting about the weather—it's hot, the summer in Phoenix, and on.

Finally, I get around to asking her if she has any information on the jeweler who was murdered recently downtown. She said she read the news story but didn't know him. She did hear some of the mob guys talking about how he seemed to be a pretty smart guy getting the gangs to do his robbing for him. She doesn't think any of the mob guys were behind his hit. He probably worked alone. He seemed to be a loner.

Josie says she will talk with her roommate, Grace, who will be working later tonight. She asks if I will be around.

I tell her no, but I give her my card and ask that Grace give me a call if she has any information that she thinks I should know. I finish my tall one, pay the bartender for Josie and my drinks, and say goodbye, heading off down the hot pavement. I must be crazy since it would have been much easier to stay inside Durant's and share stories with Josie and the bartender, sitting in a cool atmosphere.

Not my thing, hanging out in bars and picking up broads. Oh yes, I have had my share in my youth but never liked to pay for something that can be had for free.

Bobby C, the pianist, once said that he never pays for broads. They just hang around the piano bar. He told me to come over and have a drink any night, and he will introduce me to some of the girls. By the way, I just heard that Bobby C has his own television show now at KPHO. An afternoon hour special where he plays games, plays the piano, and introduces some special guests when they visit Phoenix. This guy is working all the time. I make a mental note to talk with him. He may have some interesting information on the jeweler. He plays at the Arizona Manor, which is close to where they found the body. Slim connection, but you never know.

I walk back to my office in the heat of the afternoon. Tired, hot, and sweaty. On the way, I pass KPHO, which is housed in the Hotel Westward Ho. KPHO is Phoenix's first television station and is a CBS affiliate, but has the other three—ABC, NBC, and the

Dumont Network—also affiliated since they are the only television station open in Phoenix at this time. A crazy guy named Johnny Mullin had a futurist idea and raised money to open KPHO in early 1949. By 1953, the station is well established and going strong. Wonder if Bobby is working this afternoon? Too hot and dirty to stop and see him now, but I will make a note to drop by the club some evening soon. Maybe bring Blondie for a night out and a few drinks and a dance or two.

CHAPTER FIFTY-FIVE

JULY 8, 10 AM
ARIZONA REPUBLIC NEWSPAPER

THE BIG STORY IN 1953 WAS THAT DESEGREGATION CAME TO THE Phoenix schools. Actually, it happened here rather quietly and without a great deal of fanfare compared to what happened down south. The schools just quietly did it.

I wrote a couple of stories about how desegregation was coming as segregation had been declared unconstitutional. No one paid much attention—very little comment from the public regarding these articles.

Arizona has had a large population of Mexicans for many years, and mostly they get along well with the other citizens of the valley. If they want to work, they have to be hired by white landowners to pick crops or do domestic work in the houses of the wealthy in Phoenix. The cantaloupe fields and other fruit and vegetable land crops are picked mainly by Mexicans. The only problem areas were with the young Mexican gangs on the south side. They were a problem that was ongoing in Phoenix. The police were constantly trying to calm their activities down. Stop the street muggings and the robberies. The Phoenix police would use force if necessary to try and keep things quiet on the south side.

The Black population of Phoenix was small and insignificant, so introducing them into all-white schools did not change the dynamics much. The kids all seemed to adjust, and there were no school protests or fights here.

The Arizona Republic had recently debuted a new section to the newspaper entitled "Arizona Days and Ways," a Sunday supplement. Occasionally I would submit articles on something new in the Phoenix valley. My articles on desegregation went relatively unnoticed when they appeared in the supplement.

Recently I wrote an article for this new section about McDonald's with their Golden Arches being new in Phoenix, which is the first in a franchised format hamburger restaurant opening in the nation. Actually, the food is quite good. The kids, Blondie, and I sure enjoy it. Reasonable for a family outing, quick service, clean, and kid oriented. What more could you ask for in a meal with the family?

The new section covered stories about new buildings and new businesses opening in Phoenix. The area is exploding with population. New homes everywhere. Mostly they're single-story ranch-style homes with a modern design. Many of the homes have multiple windows, now that air conditioning has come to the valley. Homes can have more windows and still never be hot in the summer months.

The new section has taken off, and Pamela Rushman is also writing a fashion column that pleases her to no end. Political stories happen mostly only when it's time for elections, so the fashion column and the society page keep her busy year-round. Specs is happy as he feels she can cover the fashion angle and maybe stop pressing him for the harder news stories. He just can't come to grips with a woman doing hard news. He is old fashioned and will not change.

I am sure he has a problem with Blondie being a cop. She is a darn good cop. She takes all the assignments even when they are dangerous. I hold my breath, but I won't stop her from pursuing her career. She never suggests that I work shorter hours or take less risky assignments, so I won't do that to her. She always told me right from the start that she wanted to be a cop. She does not look like a cop. She looks like an actress— like she should be on television. She is petite, curvy, and good-looking. She is a tough one, though. That is why they use her sometimes in undercover work. Wouldn't hesitate to shoot if necessary. She and I have been at the firing range, and she is a dead shot, better than I am.

Women are capable of doing anything if they set their minds to it. Specs is wrong to hold Pamela back on soft news. One day she will get tired of it and probably leave the paper. I believe that Specs thinks she will get married and have kids and quit being a reporter. He may be wrong on that issue. She seems determined to have a career. I am sure she is aware that Specs has moved up the copy boy to writing assignments, and I am sure she feels slighted. The other reporters would work with her, but Specs won't give her any tough assignments.

Even old Ben in the basement likes her and gives her advice from time to time on her articles. She has improved considerably since coming to the paper.

Specs has got to get with it. Women are coming on stronger every day. They are gaining power in government and business everywhere. Not all ladies want to stay home and bake cookies. Some want to make something of their lives. If guys like Specs don't see it and give them a chance at their careers, they will eventually move on to look for success elsewhere.

I wonder what he thinks of Blondie being a cop. She never wanted to do anything else and made it quite clear when I proposed to her that she intended to remain a cop. She loves her career and wouldn't consider giving it up for anything, even marriage. I, being an understanding guy, said she can do whatever she wants to do. I didn't understand how many nights I would worry about her being on a case or how many times our jobs would overlap, and we would have to find babysitters for the kids. But I had made her that prom-ise, and I won't go back on it for the world, although I worry about her every day that she works. The police chief often would send her on undercover cases because she didn't look like a cop and was bright and smart. Yeah, I worry all the time, but I love her too.

CHAPTER FIFTY-SIX

JULY 14, 9 AM
PHOENIX POLICE DEPARTMENT

BECAUSE I FEEL SORRY FOR MARGUERITA, I DECIDE TO TAKE another swing by the jail and try and talk some sense into Miguel.

I wave to Captain Reed and ask the desk clerk if I can see Miguel once again.

He says, "Take a seat, and we will bring him up to a room."

"Miguel, have you thought about what I told you about turning state's evidence and receiving a lighter sentence because you are under the age of eighteen. You would serve your sentence in a juvenile facility, which is quite a bit nicer than the adult jailhouse.

"Yeah, my court-appointed lawyer said the same thing."

"Well, what is your decision?"

"Yes, I guess I will. Seems like the best thing to do. My mother is frantic with the whole situation. Her English is no good, and she has relied on me to help when needed. My younger brother is still young and not helpful at this point.

146

"Sorry to hear that. She will have to make do. You will go away for some time for sure."

"If I turn state's evidence and give the captain the information that he wants about the gang, it will mark me though. They will probably try to kill me."

"You will be safer in juvenile facilities."

"Nowhere is safe if these guys want you."

"If you are ready to talk, I will call the captain now."

"Yeah, sure, go ahead."

I signal for the attendant cop to get a cop on duty and bring him in with paper and pencil or a recorder. Instead, he arrives with a young cop who will take notes.

I stay and listen for a while. Miguel knows a great deal about the inner workings of the gang and Chicky Hernandez.

He says, "Chicky Hernandez has connections with a Los Angeles gang."

"Los Angeles gang, are you sure, kid?" The interview cop wakes up.

This is news to both the cop and me. We didn't realize that the LA gangs had moved into the Phoenix area. That puts a new spin on what is going on the south side of Phoenix. No wonder the street robberies and store thefts have increased. They did slow down for a while, right after the police department cracked down on them. Then Largo Sanchez disappeared, and Chicky appeared to be running the Phoenix gang. I wonder if Largo moved on to the LA gang? Or did they eliminate him? Only Chicky probably knows, and he's not talking. This is a hard-hitting street guy who will never talk. He has seen trouble before. Probably even served time in his youth. Must make a mental note to review his police file. If the LA gang sent him to Phoenix to step up crime here, you can believe he knows what he is doing. Also, he is nineteen and has been around the streets for years.

Miguel rattles on about street heists, storefront shop robberies, and more that have occurred over the past two years since he has been heavily involved in the Phoenix gang. He does not mention murder. I wonder if he was present when they murdered Jimmy

Doe? Or Largo, for that matter. The older guys may not have used him on those occasions, fearing that he was too young to handle the situations and might talk and spill the beans about what was going on. They did have that right, but he may not know about the murders, only the rumors. Hell, that will make the cop's jobs harder. The two older guys are hardened gang members and not likely to talk to cops.

I will talk with the captain about getting access to each of them and give it a shot to see if they will open up with me. Probably not, but worth a try.

Since my mind is wandering while Miguel is blabbering, I decide to go to Captain Reed's office and see if he will approve my idea of talking with the other gang members.

I approach his office to hear him yelling at one of the cops for being too physical with an inmate. Do I hear the name Jesus? Christ, now he will never talk. I slow my walk and wait until the cop leaves his office.

"Hi, Captain."

"What the hell do you want now, McLain?"

"If this is not a good time, I can come back later."

"Spit it out, Bulldog."

"Well, I thought, if you agreed, I would like to take a turn at the two other gang members you are holding. Since these guys are streetwise, I doubt they will talk to cops. Thought maybe they would be more likely to talk with yours truly. What do you think?"

"I doubt Jesus will talk with anyone now. My cop interviewing him just had a go-round with him, and he slipped and banged his face. The jail nurse is looking at him now."

"How about the other guy?"

"Come back tomorrow. I'll see what I can do."

I mention to him that Miguel has agreed to spill information on his friends in the gang and is doing so as we speak. Hopefully, the prosecutor will take that information into consideration when trying his case. Also, the fact that he is a minor and should go to juvie instead of jail.

He nods and mumbles, "Thanks."

148

CHAPTER FIFTY-SEVEN

JULY 20, 9 AM
ARIZONA REPUBLIC NEWSPAPER

Yesterday was a good day. I got Miguel to make a statement that will probably help his case and reduce his time as he is a juvenile. Sure hope so, for Marguerita's shake.

After having coffee at my desk and cleaning up phone calls and papers hanging around, I decide to wander down the street to the jail. Can't wait to talk with Julio, the third kid that the cops picked up for the church heist and the street robbery.

I walk into the station with a wave to the desk officer and ask them to bring up Julio, the Mexican kid in the church theft.

"Sit down and take your turn," the heavy-set guy behind the desk barks.

"Okay, hold your water. I'll wait."

In a few minutes, he waves at me to go into one of the holding rooms where they have brought up Julio. He doesn't look so good. I wonder if they questioned him also as well as Jesus.

"How's it going, kid?"

He doesn't even bother to look up. Well, I'll try again.

"I'm Gene McLain, a reporter from the Arizona Republic, and it would be good for your case if you told the truth about the church robbery and the recent street heists."

Nothing.

"I thought maybe because I am not a cop, you might want to talk with me. By the way, are the cops treating you okay?"

He gives me a grunting sound and looks up. I notice the black eye.

"I see time in jail is not going well?"

"I've done worse."

"Kid, have you been in jail in Los Angeles before on other charges?"

"Yeah, why?"

"What were the charges? You know you can tell me. I can research the files and find out if you don't anyway."

"One felony count of robbery, several misdemeanors for a variety of dishonor issues."

"You mean, like bullying? Starting fights?"

Yeah, when another gang member dishonors you, you fight. Or you fight to show your girlfriend you care about her."

"That's an interesting custom in the Mexican community. Does that go on with all the gangs? When you are dishonored, do you use knives and guns?"

"Sure, how else are we to protect ourselves?"

"Okay, I get it. You've been in trouble before. How did you get involved with the other two guys and do the church robbery?"

He now looks down and becomes incredibly quiet.

"Do you want to talk about the church thing or maybe about the robbery of the older couple on the street recently that put both of them in the hospital for a small amount of cash and a wristwatch?"

"I got nothing to say."

He signals for the jail keeper to take him back to his cell.

I point out to him that there are several serious charges against him, and it would be in his best interest to talk to me. Let the public hear his side of the story.

He slams the door as he leaves. This guy is not going to talk—will go to jail, not saying a word.

District Attorney William O'Neill is going to love this case. He definitely will throw the book at this hard-core kid. A long sentence, several years of a hard time. This kid has been there before. Maybe inside is better than his life on the streets. Florence is a hard time prison with a tough warden, Warden Franks, who takes no shit. Not like the California prison system.

Some kids you can help, but some kids are too far gone.

CHAPTER FIFTY-EIGHT

AUGUST 2
PAYSON, ARIZONA

August and September are monsoon season in Arizona. Heavy rains in the mountains bring flash floods to the low lands. Several dry wash beds outside of the city become filled with water at this time of year. Some of the small outlying communities use the river pools of water for swimming and daytime outings.

Each year people drown. They will be enjoying a quiet day with the kids, picnicking, swimming, and generally having fun, when suddenly they hear a roar, and a wall of water comes down the riverbed washing everything in sight downstream.

Yesterday, this happened again in Payson, a town to the northeast. Several family members drowned as they struggled to swim through the heavy tide of the river. Young children who traveled two miles downstream didn't have a chance to fight the surge of water and debris being washed down the mountain. Their tiny arms and legs could not fight against the heavy water surge carrying them away.

Every few years, flash floods come, and people just don't want to believe it can happen. In an instant, cars, trucks, small items, picnic tables, and people are washed away, never to be seen again.

Now the sheriff's officers are looking downstream for two young children and their mother. All of them were wading or swimming in the river when the flash flood hit. The husband was reading a magazine at the edge of the river on a rock when all hell broke loose. Unfortunately, although he was a good swimmer, he could not reach his family in time to save them. This day will create a lasting memory for him—his entire family taken away.

It's too late now to drive up there and try to get pictures. The riverbed will have returned to just a small stream, and everything will look as it did before, a small amount of water running through a dry bed area. Everything will be the same except for the tragic memories of the family members who were lost in this flash flood.

Tomorrow I will write a story about the dangers of flash flooding in the state. Newcomers especially are not aware of the dangers of flash floods and are not aware of the intense heat in Arizona. They regularly leave kids and pets in their cars while running into a store for just a moment. They don't realize that moment, which can be a few minutes, can bring the interior of a vehicle well into 140 degrees of baking heat. Young children and animals cannot withstand the intense heat and go into a coma. Many do not recover and later die.

An article about the summer dangers in Arizona might not be a bad idea. Hopefully, save some lives. It's never wrong to be reminded of the constant issues that the police department faces daily, especially during the summer and fall months. Blondie would especially be pleased if I write an article about flash floods.

She says, "Most people just don't understand how dangerous flash flooding can be here." Having received emergency calls for help, she has heard and understands the anguish in parents' voices when their kids are missing.

Tomorrow's headline—Flash Flood Washes Family Away.

CHAPTER FIFTY-NINE

AUGUST 3, 9:30 AM
ARIZONA REPUBLIC NEWSPAPER

CAPTAIN REED CALLS THIS MORNING AND SAYS HE HAS GOOD NEWS. I sure could use good news after spending time at the typewriter writing the story about the family being washed away. What a tragedy. Yes, I could use good news.

He says that his officer, Detective Steinberg, in El Paso has located the honeymooners and is scheduling them for interviews at the El Paso police station in the next couple of days. Then he will be returning with all the details of the information and written statements notarized by both parties.

From the preliminary conversation with the girl, he indicates that she does remember Bob Davis and is willing to provide information and a statement.

Tomorrow or the next day, we will have the statements from both of them. Another day to get them typed up and notarized. Then the officer will start his drive home back to Phoenix, which will take another day and a half. Finally, in a week or so, we should have the information.

At last, something is moving forward in this case. I know that Bob Davis has given up ever being free again. He sits in the Florence jailhouse, waiting for the day of his execution. Time hangs very heavy. He is depressed and once has tried to kill himself while he has been there. Fortunately, he was found hanging. One of the other inmates in a cell across from him alerted the guard, and they took him down in time to save his life. The other inmate thought he was too young to die that way. Bob Davis thought, what the hell is the difference, hanging or execution.

I will not tell him about this just yet, just in case there is some unforeseen problem that could occur. Also, I don't really know what the information contains, just hoping for the best for Bob Davis.

CHAPTER SIXTY

AUGUST 3, 6 PM
MCLAIN HOME

At home tonight, I tell Blondie about the officer taking their statements in El Paso and that we will all know the real truth in a week or so. She is pleased and hopeful that it favors Bobby's release.

She reminds me that even if the evidence is in his favor, it will take several days, maybe as long as two weeks, to get everyone to sign off on it. That is to get Bob Davis released from prison. Justice moves slow not only when they are convicting you, but also when they are releasing inmates.

She asked me if I have told Bob Davis about this.

"No, I want to make sure that it is something that will help his case. He is so depressed right now that he even tried to take his own life. I don't want to get his hopes up and then dash them again for some reason. He is young and impressionable. We will just have to wait for the facts before jumping to conclusions. We have waited all these long months now. Another few days, weeks won't matter."

Blondie agrees.

She is off to help the kids get ready for bed. I sit in the recliner in the living room and turn on the television just in time to hear the news.

They have found the bodies of the mother and her two daughters almost four miles downstream from where the family was picnicking in northern Arizona. There is a picture of the distraught husband and other family members. Some stupid news guy in this small northern Arizona town is pushing a microphone in the guy's face and wants him to make a comment. What can he say at a time like this? He is gracious. Thanks the local sheriff's deputies for all their help and concern and for not giving up on finding the bodies. He then chokes up and turns away from the camera.

I drift in and out of consciousness. I am more tired than I realized. It's been a long day. I do hear the weather forecaster say that for tomorrow there's no rain. That's good. Very good.

I manage to pull myself up from this amazingly comfortable chair and stagger upstairs just as Blondie is coming down. I mumble that I am tired and going to bed early. She understands.

CHAPTER SIXTY-ONE

AUGUST 4, 9:30 AM
ARIZONA REPUBLIC NEWSPAPER

AT MY DESK THE NEXT MORNING, I HAVE A TELEPHONE conversation with Assistant District Attorney Lee Winters about the Mexican kids in the south side gang that the police department is going to charge. She says that Jesus and Julio will not divulge any information. The only real evidence that they have is the written confession and statement from Miguel. Lee Winters is an intelligent attorney and will keep digging to find more evidence. I am also sure she will insist on a lineup with Julio, Jesus, and Miguel, including other guys for the older couple who were robbed to view. Depending on their statements, the case could look a lot better for the prosecution.

I ask her kindly if she will try to go easy on Miguel as he is underage and most likely was not the brains of the gang. In her conversations with the kid, she said that he was probably easily influenced by the older kids in his neighborhood. As for the other two gang members, they are putting the case against them together, which will probably take several weeks, and fully intend to try them as adults as they are over eighteen. Both of these guys are hardened criminals with no regrets for their actions and refuse to cooperate with the police at this time. She is looking into their criminal records both in Arizona and California to see if there are any outstanding warrants or other pending charges.

The attitude of Julio and Jesus is that they want to bring charges against the Phoenix police department for brutality against them while they are being held in jail. We both know that is not going anywhere in today's world. The old-timers sometimes use force to entice criminals to make confessions. The broken wood chairs in the interrogation rooms testify to the use of force. However, none of the officers, including the police chief, will ever admit to using force to acquire confessions. Prisoners slipped or fell when being transported from their cells or other inmates brawled with them. That is what accounts for the bruises and black eyes.

Lee is a nice lady, and I know she will help Miguel if possible. She will also throw the book at the other two guys, as will District Attorney William O'Neill.

Specs says they will hold a funeral for the flash flood family in Payson, and do I want to attend. Not really. I don't want to make that long drive and suggest that he give it to one of the younger news guys. They will jump at the chance to get out of the office and take a drive that allows them to stay overnight in northern Arizona. Most of them are single and enjoy being out of town for a couple of days. I just want to go home to my wife and kids every night. I'm grateful to be able to do that. I always work long hours, so I am not interested in making trips that last overnight somewhere in Arizona. I am away from home a lot as it is.

CHAPTER SIXTY-TWO

AUGUST 10, 11AM
ARIZONA REPUBLIC NEWSPAPER

THIS MORNING AS I SIT AT MY DESK AT THE PAPER, MY MIND DRIFTS to the officer doing the investigation in El Paso. I sure hope that he is thorough in his questioning of the honeymoon couple. Bob Davis's life and future depend on what he finds out from them. Hope that he is detailed and takes lots of notes to be typed up later, or even records the interviews, which would be better. I am sure the captain sent an experienced officer, heard it was Detective Lou Steinberg, to El Paso as so much rests on his findings.

Another couple of days, and we will have some answers, hopefully.

The phone rings, and it's the medical examiner from Payson with the names of the drowning victims. I will include their names and the funeral information in today's column of the Arizona Republic. They may have family or friends in the Phoenix area. One never knows.

Marie Atchison, wife and mother; Sara Lee Atchison, age twelve; and Mary Lee Atchison, age ten, are the family members that drowned in the flash flood incident in Payson.

I would like to make a trip out to Scottsdale Boulevard today and stop and see the jewelry shop owners along the avenue once again. This time inquiring if they have purchased a beautifully hand-crafted silver and turquoise bracelet with an inscription on the inside. That is, if the jeweler, after purchasing it, noticed the inscription and didn't file it off or re-silver it. I hope that is not the case.

Driving out to Scottsdale, it is a hot and muggy, humid day. It's a weekday, so only tourists are on the streets shopping and not many of them in mid-day, Too hot. That means the shopkeepers will have time to chat with me, which is a good thing. Sometimes they are so busy with customers they don't want to be interrupted by a reporter asking questions.

I walk into the first shop, "The Indian Jewelry Co-op," and ask for the owner or manager. A polite middle-aged man approaches and recognizes me as having been in the shop before. He thinks I have returned to purchase an item.

"Can I help you, sir?"

I flash my reporter's badge, and instantly he remembers we have met before.

"What can I do for you today?"

"I am looking for a specific piece of jewelry. An Indian made a silver bracelet with turquoise and red jasper stones.

He laughs, "A quarter of my jewelry case fits that description."

"No, this particular piece has an inscription, a date, a name, and place on the inside of the bracelet. It was specially made as an anniversary piece of jewelry. Have you received an item from an Indian seller or perhaps a white elderly man that would fit that description?"

"No, I have not seen any item with an inscription. I would be very wary of purchasing something like that, as it might be stolen. Is that not correct?"

"Yes, but this particular piece is exceptionally beautifully crafted, and you could probably resell it for a significant profit.

"No, I have not seen anything like that."

"Well, thanks for your time. If it turns up, give me a call," I say and leave my card again, hoping beyond hope to hear from him."

I head next door to a smaller, more exclusive shop where the sign reads "Fine Indian Jewelry," hoping that this may be more informative.

Pretty much the same result. No, they have not seen anything like I am describing or like the hand-drawn picture the reservation Indian had made for me.

Five stores down the street, and I enter a small corner shop with fine Indian clothing and a small selection of upscale Indian jewelry.

A nice lady in her mid-forties comes forward to wait on me. I explain who I am and the situation.

"Yes, she did have an elderly white man come into the shop several weeks ago with fine gold and turquoise pieces, as well as some exceptional silver pieces. She purchased some items from him as his prices were reasonable, and she knew she could make a profit with the items.

There was an especially fine silver and turquoise piece with red stones and superb heavy silver craftsmanship. In fact, she still has it in the back of the store as she was contemplating keeping it for herself. She disappears through a curtain and returns a few minutes later.

She hands me a bracelet that looks exactly like the one that I am looking for. I turn it over, but there is no inscription. However, upon reviewing it closer, it seems as if someone has done something to the back of the piece. Perhaps re-silvered it to cover an inscription.

I inform her I have to take a picture of the piece and ask that she definitely not sell it. It may be evidence in a murder case.

She says she will not sell it as she was going to keep it for herself anyway.

I get the pictures and her full name and address for future reference.

This means that Jimmy Doe did steal the piece from a dead Indian in Globe, or someone he hired did the deed. It wound up in his possession. He probably did the silver repair work on the back as it was professionally done to hide the inscription. He then sold it to the shop owner along with other upscale specialty pieces.

She had his card in her possession and remembered that he infrequently would come around with nice gold and turquoise pieces he wanted to sell. In fact, she almost always bought pieces from him for her upscale clientele, usually out-of-towners.

She stated that she had not seen him in a while. She wondered where he was as her supply of pieces was getting low."

I think about how the sheriff is doing in locating two tough young thugs who murdered Indians twice for their money and jewelry, which they then sold off to Jimmy Doe on his trips north. We may never know who they are, as their mentor Jimmy will not be making trips north again in the future. They have lost their money source and outlet to sell merchandise. They may lay very low for a while, and it will be hard to find them.

Maybe the friendliest town in the west will suddenly become friendlier for the Indians trekking into town from the reservation.

I want to have coffee with Captain Reed and discuss my theory about the Jimmy Doe connection. I will be seeing him in a couple of days anyway when he calls saying that Detective Steinberg has returned from El Paso.

I want to be there when he comes into the station with the information on Bobby Davis. The captain may get busy and delay his call to me. I will call him and see if I can move things along.

CHAPTER SIXTY-THREE

AUGUST 14, 9:30 AM
PHOENIX POLICE DEPARTMENT

Today's the day that Detective Steinberg should return from El Paso with the notarized statements of Mr. and Mrs. Gorham. Can't wait to see them and hear his discovery of information.

After coffee this morning at the Legal Eagle, I walk on over to the police station.

"Is Captain Reed in yet this morning?"

"What the hell, does your day start at 10? Our day starts at 8 and runs long. You have a cushy job, Bulldog."

Little do they know the hours I spend digging up information and making contacts.

"Yeah, the captain is here."

"Would it be possible for you to tell him I'm here and waiting?"

He buzzes the phone, and the captain answers.

"Send McLain back. It's a good day."

I stroll back to the captain's office and see Detective Steinberg across the desk from him talking.

"It certainly took long enough to locate the honeymooners. They must have been having a real good time. They camped out at Mt. Lemon. Went fishing, horseback riding, hiking, and whatever else young lovers do. They managed to disappear for a while from their regular lives. When they finally returned, I set up interviews at the local El Paso police station where their statements were recorded and later typed up, and they signed and notarized them."

Geez, don't keep us in suspense any longer.

"What did they have to say?" McLain and Captain Reed say in unison.

"Just read the statements."

As I read, my heart is jumping up and down. The girl, Joan, remembers specifically the date she met Bob Davis with her fiancé. She was going that afternoon for a fitting of her wedding dress. She thought he was a nice guy. They talked about weddings and how someday he hoped to find the right girl. She told him how thrilled she was to be getting married the following Saturday, and if he was in town, he should come to the wedding and the reception. It would be a big deal here in the small town as her family and her fiancé's family knew almost everybody of importance in town.

Joan remembers Bob Davis saying that he would be gone by Saturday, but thanks for the invite anyway.

She specifically remembers the day because it was the day of the last fitting for her wedding gown. How could she forget that? She also recalled that her mother purchased her white satin shoes at the bridal shop that day to go with her dress. She still has the receipt from the shoes at home and could locate it if necessary.

Detective Steinberg says he will check with the bridal shop and get a copy from them. Also, he wants to verify her story that she did go to the shop for a fitting on the 24th. The day she met and spoke with Bob.

Jim Gorham, her fiancé, was a little vaguer as he was working and taking care of the front office when they chatted. His attention was diverted with phone calls and people coming into the office for coffee and a sweet roll. He definitely remembers talking with Bob Davis but couldn't swear to the actual day. He knows it was right around that time, though.

Detective Steinberg says he drove all night to get back to Phoenix with the statements as he feels sure they will clear Bob Davis.

"It's over. I found the girl. Talked with her an entire day, and her details did not change. I made real sure. I know how important this is Captain, Bulldog. She definitely was with him in El Paso on the 24th, the day of the murder. The shopkeeper confirmed her fitting and the purchase of the shoes. I have a copy of the actual receipt if you want it. She is a good witness too. I made sure of that. She even remembered that tattoo on Bob's arm.

The captain says he will get the paperwork going to clear Bobby and release him. It will take time, probably a couple of weeks. Just as Blondie has predicted.

"McLain, tomorrow do you want to drive down to Florence with me and tell Bob Davis?

"Sure, Captain. What time do we leave? Can't wait."

I will pick you up at the Legal Eagle at nine o'clock, and we'll head to Florence and tell Bob the good news. He won't believe it after all this time.

CHAPTER SIXTY-FOUR

AUGUST 15 9 AM
LEGAL EAGLE CAFE

THE GOOD CAPTAIN IS RIGHT ON TIME. HE PICKS ME UP IN FRONT OF the Legal Eagle at 9 am sharp. I have had my coffee and doughnut and purchased one for the captain to munch on the drive down to the state prison.

He thanks me and eats and drinks as he drives at a high rate of speed on the open highway heading to Florence. Who's going to arrest a cop? A captain in Arizona, to be exact, for speeding. There is no marked speed limit on the highway, so whatever is considered safe is acceptable. He finds driving at eighty acceptable. Glad I finished my coffee and doughnut before getting into the car. Wouldn't want to spill it on his seats.

As we wait for the prison guards to bring Bob Davis to a holding room, I can hardly contain my excitement. I am up, pacing the floor, and I wonder how he will accept the news.

Captain Reed starts by explaining that he has sent Detective

Steinberg to El Paso for the second time to locate the honeymooners who were presumed to return to their home and their jobs in the next few days.

When they returned, they explained how they had enjoyed the outdoors of Mount Lemon, camping, hiking, and riding. All the time being unavailable for the local police department to find them and question them. Detective Steinberg arranged for interviews to be done, recorded, and finally, statements typed up and notarized, answering all the questions that both police departments had.

The girl had a definite memory of meeting you on the 24th as she was having the last fitting of her wedding dress that day. Also, her mother purchased satin shoes for her to wear with her dress at the shop. We have the receipt and verified with the shop owner that she was there on the 24th. She also remembers seeing your tattoo on your arm. She remembers asking you to attend their wedding on Saturday, and you saying you will be gone from El Paso by Saturday but thanks.

Bob stammers, "You mean … I'm…."

"You are going to go free, Bob. The paperwork is now in the process of being drawn up and signed and should be delivered to Florence in no more than eight to ten days now. We haven't a case against you."

"Gosh, I don't know what to say…."

"Say it to Gene McLain. You sure knocked a lot of my hard work right out the window."

"I'm sorry, Captain."

"Sorry, I am not. Making sure a man goes free when he is supposed to be is part of what I am here for. Come to think about it, Gene. That is the part that you make possible."

All charges against Bob Davis were subsequently dropped, and he was scheduled for release.

CHAPTER SIXTY-FIVE

AUGUST 30, 12 NOON
ARIZONA STATE PRISON—FLORENCE

ON THE DAY OF BOB'S RELEASE, GENE McLAIN WENT DOWN TO Florence to drive him back to Phoenix.

He asks Bob, "What are you going to do now?"

He states that he would like to remain in Phoenix, thinks that it is a pretty nice town with possible job opportunities as it is growing so fast.

I tell him my friend, Mary O at the Legal Eagle, is looking for a dishwasher. It may be a way to start his new life in Phoenix. I know it's not much of a job, but a start with money coming in regularly.

He takes the job upon meeting Mary O and is on his way to becoming a valuable and respected member of the community.

I check on him every few days to see how he is doing.

Mary O says he is a hard worker, and she plans to have him do some bussing of the dirty dishes. In time, she will move him to wait tables. She wants more time off to spend with her family. She works constantly.

Bob sticks with the job and becomes a waiter at the Legal Eagle. All the cops, lawyers, and administrative people coming in there from the police station, the courthouse, and peripheral administrative offices know his story and give him good tips and want to see him make something of his life.

In time he meets a local girl, Evelyn, and they start dating. Eventually, they get married and have a new baby on the way.

The past is past.

CHAPTER SIXTY-SIX

SEPTEMBER 1, 9 AM
ARIZONA REPUBLIC NEWSPAPER

I RETURN TO MY DAILY LIFE AS A NEWS REPORTER AND MOVE forward with my hunch about Jimmy Doe and the bracelet and a couple of young thugs in Globe robbing Indians. I share the information with the captain once again, who says he will investigate it, but the murders in Globe are the responsibility of the local sheriff there.

The case of the church robbery is still pending a court date. It has dragged on for months and perhaps months more before it comes to court, and a final decision comes down. The Phoenix police department is developing more evidence as time goes by.

I'll have to dig up some new stories for the paper. Maybe review some of those cold cases.

This evening at home, I get some distressing news from Blondie.

Blondie is going undercover for a couple of weeks. This means the boys will go and stay with their grandmother for the time that Blondie is away. They look forward to these visits, as does Grandma.

The house will be quiet for me, and I will be worried until she is home again.

I like blondes—one particular blonde, Blondie, my wife.

CHAPTER SIXTY-SEVEN

POSTSCRIPT
PHOENIX BANK OF AMERICA

FIVE YEARS LATER, IN A SHOOT-OUT DURING A BANK ROBBERY IN Phoenix, a man lies dying on the floor of the bank.

He is an exact look-alike for young Bob Davis.

McLain rushes over to him as he lays dying and asks him about the tailor killing five years earlier. "What do you know?"

He gets the real story of how this guy killed the tailor, and some other kid almost went to the gas chamber for the crime.

He was the real killer. He laughs and wants the world to know. He is one tough guy.

Not so tough as the blood gurgles up into his throat and out his mouth, drooling down his shirt as he lay choking and dying from the cop's bullet. The money from the bank heist sprawled around him. The news photographer taking pictures, and the cops standing around not rushing to help him. Yes, an ambulance is on the way, but no one rushes to help this tough guy.

EPILOGUE

AFTER THE FINAL STORY WAS TOLD IN GENE McLAIN'S NEWSPAPER article, he won the Story of the Year award, the Big Story award, and was nominated for the Pulitzer Prize for his work on this case.

It was broadcast over the radio on "The Big Story" and won him the Pell Mell award.

Dear reader,

We hope you enjoyed reading *Deadly Deed*. Please take a moment to leave a review, even if it's a short one. Your opinion is important to us.

Discover more books by Rena Winters at https://www.nextchapter. pub/authors/rena-winters

Want to know when one of our books is free or discounted? Join the newsletter at http://eepurl.com/bqqB3H

Best regards,
Rena Winters and the Next Chapter Team

ABOUT THE AUTHOR

Multi-talented Rena Winters has enjoyed an outstanding career in the entertainment industry as a writer, talent, producer, production executive, and as a major TV and Motion Picture executive.

Her writing ability won the coveted Angel Award for the "outstanding family TV special, "**How to Change Your Life,**" which she co-hosted with Robert Stack. She wrote the two hour script (and co-produced) for "**My Little Corner of the World**," winner of the Freedoms Foundation and American Family Heritage awards.

Feature films include "**The Boys Next Door**," "**KGB, the Secret War**," "**Charlie Chan & the Curse of the Dragon Queen**" and "**Avenging Angel**."

Her producing credits include "**The Juliet Prowse Spectacular**" for 20th Century Fox, "**Sinatra - Las Vegas Style**" and "**Peter Marshall - One More Time**," which produced a best selling soundtrack album.

As Executive Vice President, she headed the entire USA operation for the international entertainment giant, Sepp-Inter, producers of TV Series, TV Specials, Feature Films and all areas of merchandising for their animated entities including "**The Smurfs**," "**Flipper,**" "**Seabert**," "**The Snorks**" and "**Foofur**" (all Emmy Award winners) plus "**After School Specials**" for CBS-TV.

Author of the bestselling book "**Smurfs: The Inside Story of the Little Blue Characters**" currently available on Amazon and Kindle and in all book stores.

Contributing author to an anthology of patriots and heroes, "**I Pledge Allegiance**," sponsored by the Wednesday Warriors Writers group currently on Amazon and Kindle.

Latest book – "**Target One"** A story about how terrorism escalates in America. Winner 2nd Place Best Fiction 2018 by the Public Safety Writers Association.

Rena is a contributing writer to the "**summerlinww.blogspot.com**" as a member of the Summerlin Writers and Poets Group.She is also a contributing writer to WTTmagazine@ gmail.com. She is a former writer/reporter for "**thenowreport.vegas**," an online newspaper.

Rena Winters was voted one of "50 Great Writers You Should Be Reading - 2017and 2018" by The Authors Show.com.

At the College of Southern Nevada, Rena is an adjunct instructor teaching Creative Writing courses. She makes her home in Las Vegas, Nevada and works in her spare time as an editor and ghostwriter.

Lightning Source UK Ltd.
Milton Keynes UK
UKHW012141170921
390772UK00001B/129

9 781006 523410

Trail of Fire

Siân Westbury, on a sketching holiday in Crete, slipped easily into a camping partnership with handsome Scandinavian Per, and was content to follow where his archæological interests led—until a car plunged in flames down a mountainside. There were curious details about the dead man thrown clear of the wreckage. Was there also something curious about Per's reaction? But in a matter of days the arrogant young Anglo-Swede was also to die mysteriously when leaked camping gas exploded at an isolated farm.

As his family gathered and the police stepped in, it was Siân who came under suspicion. Yet as she learned more and more about the Wennbergs, she grew convinced that the trail led back far beyond her meeting with Per; back to an earlier death when a Youth Hostel burned down in Cumbria—and there too Per had been on holiday . . .

CLARE CURZON

Trail of Fire

COLLINS, 8 GRAFTON STREET, LONDON W1

William Collins Sons & Co. Ltd
London · Glasgow · Sydney · Auckland
Toronto · Johannesburg

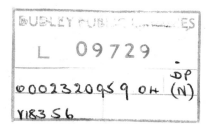

DUBLEY PUBLIC LIBRARIES

L 09729

0002320959 OH (N)

YI83 56

First published 1987
© Clare Curzon 1987

British Library Cataloguing in Publication Data

Curzon, Clare
    Trail of fire.—(Crime Club)
    I. Title
    823'.914[F]   PR6053.U7

    ISBN 0 00 232095 9

Photoset in Linotron Baskerville by
Rowland Phototypesetting Ltd
Bury St Edmunds, Suffolk
Printed in Great Britain by
William Collins Sons & Co. Ltd, Glasgow

CONTENTS

Part One

SIÂN'S STORY

CHAPTER 1

I sat back, raised my chin and let the wind of our passage slick sweat from my glistening face. Instant chill. I was burning all through but deliciously cool on the surface, like a reverse Baked Alaska.

We were running downhill now with the sun still high as we zigzagged into the ravine towards the eastern coastline of Crete, slathering and sliding when the tyres failed to hold, the metalled road having run out just after Zakros proper.

Per was driving too fast, much as he would tackle a scree descent on foot, riding the miniature avalanche which his heavy body set in motion, surfing down the loose rocks, his long Scandinavian legs, burnt teaky brown, working like pistons, weight on the heels.

My own descents were instinctively different. If I could transfer tough hide soles from feet to backside I'd rather luge down on that. Per had a way of waiting pointedly at some stable point below, grinning inside his curly blond beard and relishing the inequality of the sexes. I may have held my own in the mixed Fencing Club at university, but I'll admit that female shoulders, forearms and thighs aren't designed for male Olympics. I can't complain, though. I made a free choice in teaming up with the husky Goliath, which is why, cringing inside at the crazy speed, I sat tight then, sweated and said nothing.

The map had shown no proper road from here on: merely a purple shading with a few dots down to the solid blue where the Eastern Med met what the Greeks call the Libyan

Sea. 'Kato Zakros' was printed small in black over it, 'kato' meaning 'lower'.

There was no real village down there; just a huddle of four tavernas competing for trade from anyone who made this unlikely journey to yet another Minoan site. This excavation was directed on and off by a Professor Platon, variously rumoured to be a nonagenarian, long dead, or petrified and temporarily removed for restoration. There were easier alternatives for tourists, and the few who came were mainly indefatigable Germans. Locals from Zakros itself would come down occasionally by donkey or supply truck to sit and stare at the lapping water. Parties of quiet, dark-eyed children appeared from nowhere to paddle on the rocky beach. The Tourist Police made irregular inspections and presumably even okayed the primitive sanitation, having advertised their intention in advance.

If I am to write down all the whys and hows of everything that happened, I must admit that it was to avoid such an inspection that we'd gone inland that morning, not having a camping permit for here and it might have been an occasion when they'd deny us the blind-eye treatment. In matters of international relations Per's recklessness stopped short and professional caution took over. His role then was that of his imposed career, the Swedish Diplomatic Service. (Imposed by family tradition. Per himself had wanted to become an archæologist.)

All I knew about his background then was what he'd told me over the past week. We'd met at the car hire place when I was drumming up courage to present my new licence and pretend I knew what I wanted. I stood and watched Per make purée of the mechanic, diving inside the engine, kicking tyres, bouncing on the back springs. He was magnificently contemptuous about things like distributor heads and battery leads. 'Look, corrosion!' he shouted, and the bemused Greek spread his hands helplessly at the English words fired at him.

The bearded giant turned quickly and nearly knocked into me. 'Sorry,' I said and stepped back. He barely looked at me but nodded. 'Nip in and rev it up, will you?' And he disappeared again under the bonnet.

The car man shrugged, past caring, so I did as I was told, got in, switched on, flooded the carburettor. I was thinking that as a return favour this genned-up customer might pick out a foolproof car for me, something modest and manageable, easy on fuel.

It was, understandably, a Volvo he was interested in, a real freak among all the Skodas and Fiats and Renaults on show. When he'd put on his disgusted act, started to mooch off and then let himself be persuaded back with a lower price, he eventually signed the papers and took possession.

I was still sitting behind the wheel, fascinated. He suddenly grinned at me with a wide slice of white teeth. 'Have a drink while they fill it?' he asked, nodding to the taverna opposite.

Talk to strange men a nice girl didn't, of course, but he spoke good English and he shouted orders, which to me made him a normal sort of man. My father would have acted exactly the same, with the difference that Daddy wasn't still half way through his twenties and dazzlingly handsome. Per didn't use a seductive approach, so there was no need to bat him off. Mine was quite simply a craven case of gut surrender because he was so vital, so much larger than life. Perhaps because I already felt inadequate, I fell for what seemed a heaven-sent chance to join forces, share expenses, fit my botanical interest in with his archæological ones. We both intended to cover the whole island and it didn't matter to me what order I took it in. And then there was the experience thing. Per had plenty, I hadn't.

He seemed only mildly surprised that I'd arrived on Crete alone and I really believe he'd no idea how the reality of it had slugged me between the eyes after the busy contriving and semi-deception I'd used to get to that stage. I had kept pushing myself one step farther out of stubborn refusal to let all my plans fall through when Marcia, poor idiot, broke her femur out riding. I did mention at home that she'd had a fall and was better now. And I continued with my travel plans, still prefacing them with 'we'. I even managed to divert my stepmother from escort duty to the air terminal.

If Marcia lay low at her home in Dorset there should be no trouble on the home front. Any backwash there might be—as I realized when the plane journey provided my first break from hectic replanning—was going to be all mine, and would start when I set foot on Cretan soil. Being quite alone was one thing. Making sure I stayed that way would be another. People tend to be so friendly.

Having Per alongside—a Marcia-substitute-plus—seemed a sensible idea. There'd be a price to it, but I thought I might even like that. There had been a college boy one vacation when I'd stayed at my cousin's. And Per was older, bound to be more sure of himself. I suppose in a way I was flattered. I thought I knew more or less how it would be. I went into it with my eyes wide open. But perhaps a little too starry . . .

The Volvo squealed on a hairpin bend. The rear drifted and I kept my face to the burnished sky, focused on a hawk suspended motionless, denied myself sight both of the precipice and the rock-face looming over us. Then the hawk dropped away like a stone and my eyes followed its fall. A new bend intervened and there was the dark sea in a deep vee ahead. The bird had disappeared but something flashed and caught my eye. 'There's a fire!' I called to Per above the engine's growl and the tyres' complaints. 'Ahead, at two o'clock and below. Something's burning.'

He slowed to look. 'Can't stop here. Probably trash. Madness in this heat. See later.'

We continued, zigzagging towards the sea. Two bends later the fire was brighter, close now below. 'It's a hut, I think. I can see a window. Oh no, it's—' Even as I spoke the squarish frame toppled, gushing flames, hung suspended, then fell out into space, down to an invisible level below.

'A car,' Per said, and at last braked to a stop. In the sudden hush as he cut the engine there seemed to be a distant hum.

'We must climb down,' I said. 'There may be—'

He caressed his golden beard. 'Pointless, I think. Poor

bugaroo, whoever. We'll phone from Kato Zakros, have the appropriate service called out.'

'But shouldn't we at least look?' I didn't wait for an answer. I was already across the dusty road, kneeling at the edge, my fingers twisted tight among the wiry grass stems as I leaned over to see. Per came and hunkered beside me, field-glasses to his eyes. He shrugged, started to lower them and then stiffened. Looked again. Grunted. 'Ugh!'

I took the glasses from him, adjusted the focal length, ran them over the panorama of tumbled rocks and found the alien thing, sand-coloured too but less angular, lumpishly sprawled. 'There *is* somebody. He must have jumped, or been thrown clear.'

Per took back the glasses. 'Not moving.'

'All the same—'

He found an overhang of cliff to leave the Volvo under, not exactly on the straight but towards the sort of corner Greeks invariably take on the outer rim because of danger from a rockfall above. From our gear he selected a rope for over one shoulder and a small pick wrapped in sacking which he fitted to his belt. For me it was going to be a toes-fingertips-and-teeth operation.

Eventually we reached the man. What had lately been a young man, little more than a boy. He was really broken up, his clothes torn, the swarthy skin of his face laced with blood, eyes staring. As Per had said, no hope. Despite that, I reached out and tried to straighten the bare arm so pathetically askew. Its skin, like his clothing, looked scorched but was cold to the touch.

'Poor bugaroo,' Per said again. 'We leave him here, go back and report. The car seems to be burning itself out. No bushes near it to catch fire.'

'There's something in his hand, Per.'

He moved back, bent and prised open the fingers which, unlike the flaccid slackness of the broken arm, were tightly crimped about a small object. 'What is—?' I began, then was distracted by a dancing spot of light beside my feet which travelled up Per's body. My eyes followed its path.

11

He was buttoning the left breast pocket of his bush shirt, frowning, seeming unaware of the light.

It could only be sunlight glancing off a moving reflector. Another car descending the rough track? Per seemed to recover himself, wheeled and stared back at the way we'd come.

'No, lower down,' I said pointing. 'Your Volvo's all right. It's something five hundred yards farther on.'

'Look,' Per offered, pointing south, 'you go across to that loop of road. No need for both of us to climb back the hard way. I'll drive down and pick you up. Can you make it on your own?' (Scornful implication. When had I ever leaned on him? Hill-walking just took me a little longer than Scandinavian Wonderman, that's all.)

'I'll be there,' I promised and started off. When I looked back he was standing in contemplation of the dead man at his feet. Then I went round an overhang and had to concentrate on the route.

When he picked me up some twenty minutes later from my roadside patch of shade he was merely a little more glistening, not breathless or put out. But thoughtful. The encounter with death had shaken us both. We didn't speak any more on the descent, and Per drove with untypical caution. At Kato Zakros he went through to Nikos's family room to use the phone. Informing the emergency services.

While we waited for The Authorities we tackled lunch— smoky *souvlaki* charred by Nikos while he listened grim-faced to our tale, and a Greek salad with *feta*. I couldn't take the meat and supplemented the oily salad with an orange from my pack.

I had expected a police invasion, but as we were sitting screened from the road by the vined canopy of the taverna garden, their sole representative was upon us without warning. Of medium height and wearing a sergeant's stripes on his slate-blue uniform, he was almost perfunctory in his questions, took no notes, gazed out the meanwhile over the hazy sea.

'You will write all this,' he said in English at the end of

12

our story. 'The two of you. Separately.' Then for the first time his eyes met mine.

Some people carry their country in their eyes. Per is like that. I can sometimes look right through the cold blue stare and see glaciers, frozen fields, forests of firs. So it was with the policeman. He carried Crete. It was all there in the wide, dark glance—the burning seriousness, the exuberance, the impatience, the chaos, the simple ethic, the distance from us strangers. He was total islander, and he did not trust us one inch.

He sent me for writing things, detaining Per with the movement of a finger. I felt the resultant vibes, ice-cold diplomatic, emanating from the bearded giant at the little white-painted table. He sat straight, big bare knees wide, and heavy bootsoles flat against the earth floor. He could have risen in a single lithe movement and flattened the other like a fly. And with, I think, as little emotion. But he chose not to, did the correct thing, as if it figured in the Book of Protocol.

At either side of the same round metal table we wrote our brief statements out, while it wobbled with the alternating pressure of our elbows. Nikos did not dare to come and fix it level with a wedge because now the sergeant was thoughtfully regarding the taverna itself, taking stock while still sitting with one ankle resting on the other knee.

He put our papers together like an exam invigilator, without reading them through. Where they were signed and dated he added an initial. 'There will be other questions,' he said flatly. 'Come to us up in Zakros Town tomorrow, at noon.'

Noon. Drinks time, leading via lunch into siesta. The temperature would be in the upper nineties at least. He intended literally to grill us. Coming back this morning I should have kept my gaze on the sky, ignored the flame, practised Per's diplomatic detachment, then we'd have stayed free of all this.

We followed to watch the policeman get into his car. He was alone, his colleagues presumably still busy on the mountainside collecting the remains, examining the road for marks, measuring. Or did they bother so much here? Crash barriers on precipices seemed to remain unmended. Later someone other than officials would mark bereavement with a little white shrine on the spot. Who would do this for the scorched young man I'd touched that morning, sightless eyes fixed on the sky and broken like a celluloid doll?

'Per,' I asked, 'does Nikos have any idea *who*—?'

He glanced at me. 'Why should he?'

'The car either came up from Kato Zakros or was on its way down here. The dead man looked like a local.'

'You can't say that.' His voice was high and singsong. Very Swedish just then. That usually meant it was on auto-pilot, with Per's mind elsewhere. I held my tongue and let my own mind orbit likewise. It had, by now, quite a lot to work on.

For almost a week we had succumbed to the siesta habit, and on that day for some reason it wouldn't wait for us to get the tent fixed up again. We simply walked up the deserted excavations with our sand mats under our arms and spread ourselves below a canopy that shaded the current but abandoned workings. I fell asleep lulled by the monotonous tickings of giant grasshoppers and mesmerized by the nodding of a yellow poppy on the rocky wall beside me.

When I awoke Per was away on the western slope setting up his camera tripod to take full benefit of sharp shadows from the afternoon sun. The stone colours were so beautiful, gold to rose-red under frowning ranges of grey-purple mountain. I rolled our mats and removed myself to the beach for a swim.

My skin dried quickly under the sun, so when I'd fetched fresh shorts and shirt from my pack in the Volvo I was ready for the next work session. Just like any other day. Only, when I had my sketch-pad open, the blank white paper didn't exercise its normal function, didn't connect with the *Anacamptis pyramidalis* blowing on the hillside. Instead I found myself staring at the empty page until something quite different insisted on emerging: another crimson flowering on a rocky crag. A grotesque pattern of broken bone and blood.

14

I let it happen, let the picture build up under my pencil where it traced out the lines of the body as it lay before I'd touched it. Then I turned over the page and on the next blank space I drew from memory the dead young man's face.

It was a strange, brief reliving of shock and revulsion, experienced more vividly the second time, a morbid act perhaps, but in recording the horror I had somehow freed myself of its hold. I felt a relief I hadn't known since we started the downhill run that morning.

Afterwards I sketched the *Anacamptis* and took a single perfect bloom for pressing. Then higher up, between two ridges in the high-stepped rock formation, I came across three specimens I'd not yet seen on Crete. The island is a wonderful place for botany, though May and not July is the ideal time. I don't pick the more spectacular finds, just capture them on paper, and when time runs short I use my Jap camera for close-up stills. But at heart I'm a puritan and equate value with effort. The shutter's click is too instant, too easy. I'd rather work myself to a frenzy, then I don't feel the art is diminished. To Per, of course, I'm a primitive, preferring magic to science. And a frightful *kid*. He never misses a chance to point out my shortcomings. I have to watch my enthusiasms, act cool, cut out any mention of college, remember to say 'my father' instead of 'Daddy'. He almost makes me feel guilty about the three or four years I lag behind him.

Nikos had fish for us that night, or his womenfolk had. He had disappeared, gone off perhaps on his motor scooter. I haven't decided which of the three shy, overweight, brown-skinned women is his wife. Perhaps they share him. Or they could equally well be his sisters, all four having the same marked Cretan characteristics. Of an evening they would sing and dance while he performed frantically on a miniature fiddle. He had two cronies, one playing the single reed pipe and the other a sort of simplified bagpipe. Assured of an audience and unlimited *ouzo*, their concerts were liable to go on until three in the morning, the locally accepted hour at which guests are assumed to be adequately entertained.

We were spared that this night. I stretched my few Greek words to compliment the women on the meal. They giggled a bit and apologized that it was white and not red fish, which didn't matter because the sauce it was cooked in was rich and aromatic. I should have liked to join them later under the vine as they worked at their embroidery and lace, but I sensed Per's restlessness and followed him out on to the darkened beach.

He stood thigh-deep in the water and brooded, unbelievably handsome with more than a hint of Valhalla about him. Just when I'd decided that communication was over for the day except for love-making, he waded back and said sternly, 'Tomorrow at Zakros they will ask all sorts of questions. Least said, soonest mended, eh?'

'Just as you like,' I agreed.

He was rough with me that night, coming to bed after I'd fallen asleep and waking me. I started to resist and he had to prove how much stronger he was. Afterwards he fell asleep from exhaustion and I was left restless and resentful. The pity was that he could seem so warm, even caring. At first I'd taken it as more than skin-deep. I was fed up with myself too. For some reason I just couldn't fall for him the way I'd thought I would.

We had a route roughly agreed for the next ten days, but I'd half decided to break up our double act before the time was up. All I needed was a little more practice at driving on the right-hand side of the road, and then probably I'd take off.

CHAPTER 2

After breakfast next morning, without explanation, Per went into his camp-striking routine. I looked up from his shaving mirror where I was doing my make-up—only mascara, but I can't face the waking world sandy-lashed. I had applied the full Cleopatra treatment, glanced up to see that he was disgruntled at my not sharing in the toil, and forestalled his complaint. 'We're leaving, then? Have you done all you wanted down here?'

He frowned, crouching to beat out a guy-peg sideways with a rock. 'I could use another two days, but the police will only waste my time if we stay on now. There will be endless questions, fuss by the man's relations, the inquest and funeral. We must insist on moving on today or we'll be caught up in it all. I may come back later when it's gone quiet again.'

He didn't consult my requirements. He considered botany an inferior science, perhaps even imagined flowers of all types grew abundantly wherever he chose to stop. Actually I knew he would never have given real thought to the question at all. Well, I admire professionalism, and concentration does require some degree of blinkered vision. Or so I told myself. Increasingly often. Until there seemed just a touch of desperation in the self-reminder.

'Get the gear stowed, Siân,' he ordered. 'I'm going along to settle up with Nikos.'

I did as he required, probably making a less neat job of it because I hadn't his height for swinging up the heavy stuff. It had to stay where it landed, with minor bundles stuffed between to hold the whole load steady. Anyway, everything went in or on top without obscuring the view in Per's driving mirror, so I at least was satisfied.

Just as I finished, Per came striding back impatient to be on the road, so I had to content myself with a distant wave to Nikos's three women who had grouped themselves at the taverna door to indulge in a more theatrical farewell. I hoped they would understand that I'd be mad to make a stand over equal rights at the start of what could prove a pretty deadly day.

The old mountain road showed no evidence of the previous day's accident. Any difference I noticed was in ourselves, that we weren't communicating, not even on the level of pointing out marks of interest on the route. I should have welcomed diversionary prattle then to keep my mind off deepening misgivings, but with Per the shutters had come clanging down and I was out in the cold. At Zakros he announced unnecessarily that we were an hour early for our appointment with the police.

Instead of making for a taverna terrace with some welcoming shade, Per peeled a couple of notes off the wad in his billfold and held them out to me. 'Get a tidy dress. Look womanly.'

'I have money,' I said coldly, infuriated because I was already tidy. And I am a woman. No one could overlook the fact despite the tailored shorts and sports shirt.

'No need to waste your own money,' Per lorded it. 'Regard this as wardrobe issue.'

I suppose he had reason on his side. If he thought the occasion demanded feminine attire, he could have it that way. He could have the dress back too when our ways parted.

'We meet back here,' he stated, nodding my dismissal.

It was pleasant to be wandering alone among the open-fronted shops. Zakros has nothing special about it, a stereotyped Cretan small town with the ubiquitous unfinished look of buildings half way either to completion or to demolition when suddenly deserted by the workers. Crete is one of those islands where they even seem to be constructing new ruins. As a result there is always a film of dust over everything, including the wares exposed for sale in the streets. I shook the dull grey grit off one or two beautifully worked blouses and scanned the dresses on hangers which hung like overlapping scales of butter-muslin and pastel lawn all over the house fronts. I had one lifted down on a pole from almost roof level, and half a dozen black-clad women came to help overwhelm any sales resistance I might offer. But I liked it. It was ivory-coloured cheesecloth, cut straight with short trumpet sleeves. The inescapable embroidery was genuinely hand-sewn in harebell blue. I saw no real reason to offer less than the asking price but tourists are expected to haggle. They were happy to let me have it for three hundred drax less. I asked who had made it and they called a girl of about my own age, maybe less, from a back room. She was plump and very pretty, rather embarrassed by my admiration for her work. I asked to put it on then and there, so she took me through a cane-and-bead curtain to a small space that looked out on a sunny courtyard bright with geraniums and roses. While I changed I asked questions in my imperfect Greek and she told me shyly that half the price would go to her dowry and the rest to the women of the shop. She was to be married next February to her dear Manolis who by then would have a house of his own and some land. They were going to grow apricots and olives, and one day they would build a hotel.

'Lucky you,' I said falsely. 'I hope you have lots of sons, and a daughter to help you look after them all.'

That pleased her. 'My sister,' she confided, 'lives in London. Her husband has a taverna and I go next month to help them and learn better English. Then Manolis will be proud when I come back rich.'

Perhaps because I felt guilty about her share of the lost 300 drax, or because I was sorry for her being in London alone, I admitted I lived there too and wrote down my phone number for her. But I didn't for a moment imagine she would ever make use of it. I guess my patronizing role must have run away with me.

When she complimented me on my spoken Greek, I explained how I'd picked it up in school holidays, years back, when Daddy was technical representative for a British electronics firm and working on the mainland near Athens. I had a basic vocabulary but indifferent grammar and I never seemed to get the genders right. The main thing was that I could make myself understood.

I had to go and show myself off to the women of the shop, and they made an exuberant fuss of how well the dress suited my red hair, what beautiful skin I had and so on. I was afraid they would all insist on flocking back to the Square with me to make quite certain that Per was equally delighted with my transformation. Fortunately two elderly American ladies hove into view just then and my new friends' mercenary instincts proved strong enough for them to let me go.

When I reached the Square I saw that the Volvo had been moved. Per wasn't to be seen, and the bonnet, when I

19

put my hand on it, was hotter than I expected in view of the deep shade under the eucalyptus trees.

I had been waiting no more than two or three minutes when Per came bouncing along on new crêpe soles. He wore a grey silk shirt with a blue cravat and immaculately tailored silver slacks. His flaxen hair shone and his beard bristled with bonhomie. He looked every inch the Nordic god, and he was flaunting his most charming manners.

I knew then the answer to my question of the past few days: what on earth had attracted me to him so fatally over our drinks after the car hire. The façade was stunning, and when he could be bothered to do the social thing you felt cocooned in caring warmth. You began to suspect you might be as wonderful as he implied you were.

Solicitous now, he laid the flattery on thick, twirling me round. 'Perfect colour with your tan,' he said, 'and that glorious copper hair. What lucky policemen Zakros will have today.'

Well, he was certainly putting on a show for them. I wondered was it important then to shake the considerable dust of Zakros so rapidly off our feet? And was this impeccable front quite the way to ensure it?

I wasn't left in doubt for long. It might have worked in Stockholm or even London, but Cretans are different. They are a touchily proud people and not to be patronized. The lordling which they took Per for was allowed to make his offhand entrance while they stared in silence. The small office was full of uniformed men at, or on, desks. Gradually I became aware of a growing antagonism. It revealed itself in the way the officers slouched, dropped cigarette ash, vaguely shoved about untidy piles of papers, scratched, gazed out beyond us, through windows or regretfully into the sloppy dregs of their empty coffee cups. It was as if they chose to emphasize how different they were, how undisciplined and systemless, how essentially Mediterranean.

Scandinavians to them were overbearing, oversized visitors who drank too much alcohol, bought expensive jewellery and furs, and of a March midnight would dive into hotel pools that had not yet been filled with water. We had heard such tourist tales, just as we'd heard the other funnies about Germans, Americans, British. They were all oddities and outsiders. The normal way of life, the only way that made sense at all, was how things were conducted here, in this small back office in the centre of Zakros Town.

The truth of it eventually got through to insensitive Per. I watched his eyes grow wary as he accepted that it would take longer than he'd budgeted for. He tried a new tack, boyishly diffident, the innocent bystander enmeshed in a matter of baffling complication.

They didn't change, took it all in with the same dark-eyed, staring silence. Then one of them detached himself with a sigh, slumped into a chair behind the main desk and nodded the others on their way. An overweight, crumpled man with a face like a dried walnut. He sighed again as if we were no more than the most recent of a long line of delinquents. For me it felt just like queuing for tickets at a Greek bus station.

He went slowly through every item of Per's statement, raising tired eyes to judge the truth of each confirmation, even as to date of birth and sex. I didn't dare to look at Per but fixed my eyes on the black-haired backs of the policeman's brown hands. He had not offered us his name: he was anonymous authority.

'And you, Mrs Wennberg,' he said in the same low voice without any shift of expression.

With a start I realized he had done with Per. It was my turn now. He wasn't checking any papers, but his gaze was resting on my cream leather purse with its initials SW.

'My name is Westbury,' I corrected him. 'It's on my statement. We're not married.'

'Not married,' he repeated woodenly. 'But together.'

'For the purpose of this trip,' I granted.

'Trip?'

'This tour of Crete,' I explained. 'I have less interest in archæology than my friend, who is an expert. My own subject is botany. I hunt for wild flowers and then paint them in watercolours.'

'Miss See-ann West-bury,' he pronounced, using no

21

prompt and clearly wishing us to notice that our details were imprinted on his mind forever.

I gave him the correct pronunciation of Siân, explaining it was Welsh. 'From Wales.'

'Ah, Wales. A separate country of the UK, with a Prince.' He relaxed so far as to smile wearily.

'Yes. Very beautiful. Mountainous. Rather like Crete in some ways but cooler, and not an island.'

'You are Welsh yourself?'

'Only half. Mother was Welsh. Daddy is a Londoner.'

He thought about this. 'He knows that you are here with your—friend?'

I must have boggled at him. 'Daddy? Well, yes. I told him I was coming. And I've sent him a couple of postcards since, but I don't know for sure that he's received them yet.'

'You have not telephoned home since your arrival?'

'No.' There had been no occasion to contact him. He would have assumed that everything was going according to plan. An efficient man, well able to take care of himself and his business, he would expect as much of me.

'You should keep in touch,' the policeman said gravely, every gross centimetre of him the father of a dependent family.

I tried not to smile, staring down at my ringless hands. 'Yes,' I agreed meekly, 'perhaps I should.'

If he had handled Per with disinfected tongs, he used a vastly different technique on me. It was meant to build up my faith in him, coax out the confidences. I had to remind myself of Per's brusque instruction, 'Least said, soonest mended.'

The policeman linked his fingers on the desktop. 'Miss Westbury, did you actually see the dead man's car leave the road?' And then the real interrogation began, with me in the hot seat. As driver, Per was expected to have been fully occupied by the hairpin bends. Which left me as observer.

I tried to be factual and precise, utterly truthful about the limited amount I'd seen. There were details I didn't want to mention and although he approached them closely

22

I made no free gifts of information. At the end, just as we were about to leave, I had questions of my own for him. 'Do you know who the dead man is? Has anyone identified him yet?'

The policeman looked at me full face, frowning as if I'd said something in poor taste and he was disappointed in me. 'Miss, you saw it. How recognize that? Not even his mother, his wife—'

I sensed Per's tension as he stood beside me, the door already open. His hand on my elbow warned me to go no further.

'I'm sorry,' I mumbled. 'I didn't think. It was all so— horrible. I suppose I didn't really see—'

The policeman nodded sympathetically but didn't offer his hand to be shaken. We went out like naughty children dismissed after a scolding.

Per didn't speak until we were back at the car. 'Well,' he demanded, unlocking his offside door, 'what did you make of that?'

'Uncomfortable,' I told him. 'But then anything to do with the police is always meant to be.' It was the accepted student attitude to take.

Per waited, but I'd finished my answer. *Least said,* as he'd insisted before. 'I could use a long, cool drink,' I complained. We'd drunk nothing since breakfast. At least I hadn't. I couldn't speak for Per.

'We'll get some lunch,' he promised, 'but not here. Sitia, I think.'

We had been bound for the south, Ierapetra, then the Minoan sites at Phaistos and Aghia Triadha, but it seemed our plans were changed again. Now we were to head north-west. Whether from whim or as a result of our interview, I couldn't tell. Sitia would suit me fine, however. The soil was dry and rocky there with the vivid discolorations of bauxite deposits and other minerals. I might well find some rarer species on the slopes above the town.

'No one mentioned an inquest,' I suddenly recollected. 'Is Sitia in the same Prefecture? Is that why—?'

'As it happens, it is,' Per said shortly. 'But there's no

reason why we should be needed again. Our depositions are enough for an accident like that.'

'If it was an accident.' I barely voiced the dark thought, but Per caught my words above the engine's growl in low gear.

'Of course it was an accident. Why should you think otherwise?'

I shrugged, turned in my mind which hint to give him. Just one anomaly of the several that clamoured in my mind for explanation. 'Remember the flashing light?' I asked. 'There was something shining on the mountain road, above where we stood but below where you'd left the Volvo. Something moved and reflected the sunlight.'

'It could have been another car.'

'But we never passed one anywhere, and there wasn't one later down at Kato Zakros, which is world's end. It could have been someone on foot carrying a shiny object. Or using field-glasses as you did. Down by the body I had this feeling of being watched. And no one else came forward to report the accident. Why keep silent when they might have helped to save a life?'

'You don't know no other eye-witness came forward. The police would hardly confide in us.'

He was right there. I shrugged again and was prepared to let the subject drop, but he glanced sideways at me, speculatively. 'What are you imagining now? That this non-existent walker had previously been a passenger in the car that went over the edge?'

I hadn't actually arrived at that idea, but it was intriguing. Chilling too. If it had really been so, why had the passenger got out, and how had he managed to survive? I wanted suddenly to have done with all these frightening surmises. 'No,' I said dogmatically, 'it would be someone on a bike or scooter. Even a donkey. But suppose this person had taken it wide at a corner, to avoid a dangerous overhang, causing the car to swing out too far in its turn . . .' I couldn't hide a shudder. 'It's a hideous road anyway. You had me terrified every inch of the way down.'

He crowed then at my craven spirit, remembered to be

magnanimous and laid an arm across my shoulders. 'I forget sometimes what a timid child you are. Poor little one. You should have told me my driving scared you.'

I resented giving him that satisfaction even now, but certainly the turn of our conversation seemed to have purged his ill-humour provoked by the police interview and my incautiously voiced suspicions. Suddenly he was relaxed, almost euphoric, just as he'd been when some unforeseen danger had threatened and then was swiftly past.

He turned again to his own thoughts and to the demands of driving. I was left to brood over other aspects of the incident on the mountain road, mention of which would have cancelled out any relief he might now be feeling. But these were matters I'd do better to keep to myself for the present. At least until I knew from just which direction the icy gust was blowing in on me. The chill wind of fear.

CHAPTER 3

I checked with the map under the dashboard and confirmed that we'd passed the turn-off that led directly to Sitia. 'Directly' being a relative term because it was another zigzag mountain road crossing two high ridges. Instead, Per was heading due north on the main road, so that eventually our route would take in two sides of a right-angled triangle.

'You're not serious about lunching at Sitia, I hope? Better be frank and call it supper,' I said drily.

Per grinned. 'I'll admit to a slight diversion. Palekastro for drinks and lunch. In deference to your poor head for heights we will keep on the new roads. Then I thought you might enjoy a swim at Vai.'

It was certainly a thought. Although I'd never been there, I had seen photographs. The sands of Vai Bay were fringed with palm trees. Unique in Europe, the date groves were reputedly grown centuries before from stones dropped by marauding Arabs as they feasted on arrival. Now they

25

flourished so wildly that film crews came there to shoot Hawaiian sequences.

'Does that appeal?' Per persisted. 'A chance for you to show yourself off in your bikini. The bottom half anyway.'

'Lovely, provided we find a taverna first.'

'Of course.' He was going out of his way to be obliging, and I felt briefly ashamed of doubting him earlier. Everyone has his off-days, patches of gloom and self-absorption, so why not this handsome Scandinavian giant? It was because his charm and physical impact had so overwhelmed me at first meeting that I'd been unwilling to accept any flaw at all. I'd admit it was inexperience that made me intolerant. Apart from my father, I'd had no really close relationship with any man before. I was conscious of being a late starter, with lost time to make up for, so when Per happened along I'd just lost my head. Sex was a seismic revelation and I was still in shock. It meant I didn't altogether trust my judgment any more.

Take a little, give a little, I decided. I'd watched my stepmother at that, quite an artist. I put out a hand and tenderly rubbed Per's knee through the smart silver slacks. I was rewarded with a flash of white teeth in the ebullient Viking beard. Things were all right again. Well, very nearly.

Over lunch—wine and *Kotopoulo Yemisto*, which I ordered in confident ignorance and discovered to be roast chicken stuffed with a spicy mixture of rice, giblets, pine kernels and currants—I ventured to mention the policeman at Zakros. In particular his fatherly concern. 'It made me realize I ought to phone home,' I admitted. 'So when we get to Sitia I'll do it from a hotel, and stay there overnight if there's a room available. Then I can let Daddy—er, my father— have that as an address, in case he ever needs to get in touch.'

Per looked at me bright-eyed, as though a favourite student was coming up correctly with second-hand knowledge he'd imparted himself. 'I was going to suggest something of the sort,' he said. 'We can arrange for the hotel to hold later mail until we come back the same way.'

It had been easier than I'd expected. At Sitia, while Per

looked for parking for the car I would get in ahead and register for a single room. A real bed all to myself would be luxury.

We continued for another eight kilometres towards the north-eastern extremity of Crete and reached Vai at three-fifteen. It was far more beautiful than any of the postcard views, idyllically Pacific. You could almost hear the guitars, picture hula girls gently gyrating in *leis* with fragrant blossom in their hair. Nothing, in fact, to warn me of any danger. It was the last place you would imagine as the final sight my eyes would close on. And yet it so nearly was.

Under the palm trees the temperature was a good ten degrees lower, and a delicious breeze off the sea set their fronds slapping and rattling above us. We couldn't wait to get stripped off and wade into the water. After an initial shock of chill it slid warmly over my shoulders. I struck out away from the shore and lay floating, face up to the flawless sky, weightless and tranquil. Lulled by sun and gently rocking waves I felt myself strangely distanced from the voices of other bathers, the laughter of children which was growing ever fainter. Time and motivation simply ceased. But then a new sound came, sibilant and whipping, which I was too sun-drugged to know the significance of. And next —I don't know even now quite what happened.

Afterwards, when I came to, I was on wet sand, still staring up but the sky seemed darker, shaded by moving forms. There was a confusion of mushy sounds. Faces came at me out of the blur and then disappeared. I was being roughly handled. Someone was shouting angrily in a foreign tongue and a man crouched over me with his face close as if he'd been kissing me. I tried to push him off and was violently sick.

A querulous voice cried out and I knew it was me because it hurt my throat. I ached all over, but mostly it was my head. I went to sit up and the whole scene turned round and then swung back again. Someone pushed me flat on warm, yielding sand.

It was Per, and I screamed because I was terrified of him. The man I had pushed away before put his face close again.

'I am doctor. Doctor,' he insisted. 'You lie still. Rest, please.'
I closed my eyes and did just that. It was not a nice
nightmare at all. I'd be glad to wake up.

They told me later—Per told me and the doctor confirmed
it—that I had very nearly drowned, run down by a windsurfer. Some part of his equipment must have struck my
head and momentarily stunned me. I'd gone under for quite
a while and would have ended there but for Per swimming
to my rescue, and the doctor—also windsurfing—arriving
at the same moment. What happened in the confusion to
the person who'd caused the accident no one seemed to
know, but it was generally agreed that it was a man and—
curious detail—he had worn dark glasses.

'He must have been an expert,' I said feelingly, 'to risk
his Varilux or whatever.'

'Too expert,' Per grunted. 'He managed to right himself
and make off while we were busy with you.'

'Not good enough to avoid a collision, though.' And then
I had to laugh, however weepily, because it was so crazy, a
hit-and-run windsurfer. No doubt as crimes went it ranked
quite a bit lower than piracy on the high seas

Our plans were modified again, to meet the doctor's
instructions. He was from the capital Iraklion and had
connections with the big hospital there, so he insisted that
was the place to have a second X-ray, just in case there was
a hairline crack in my skull which the examination at Sitia
hadn't picked up. But I wasn't to risk travelling the same
day. He personally arranged a Category A hotel for us in
Sitia where I was to forswear alcohol and hot showers, and
keep my feet up until noon next day when he would examine
me again. It was a lot of fuss, but it did fit in with my
personal preferences just then. I even phoned home as
intended and although Daddy wasn't there my stepmother
promised to deliver the discreet message that Crete was
wonderful and I had acquired a good tan. She made a note
that I would send a *poste restante* address from the hotel at
Iraklion and wished me a happy holiday.

Per seemed a little startled when I told him what I'd
done. 'How much did you tell them?' he asked.

'Very little. I don't want them worrying. I said I'd write in a day or two when we'd moved on.'

'Did you—mention me?'

It made me smile. He was so careful of his own reputation. It wouldn't do for him to become involved with any dubious person.

'In a general sort of way. Not by name,' I said. He had to be satisfied with that. There had been questions, of course. I'd breezily mentioned to my stepmother that 'we' had teamed up with some Swedish archæologists. As well as myself, Per too sounded less risky in the plural. She reminded me—as if I could possibly forget—that my Finals results were due in just over a fortnight. I swore I'd be home by then, sent my love, rang off and had misgivings about the phone bill.

Per was quite sweet to me that evening, went out for some flowers for my supper tray, dimmed the light and sat talking quietly until I felt like drowsing off. When he'd left for his own room—I'd turned down his offer of night-nursing me from a made-up bed on the floor—I began to regret my distancing of him. He'd shown a concern I hadn't expected, even seemed vulnerable. I've always been fonder of people once they've shown a few chinks in their armour. It must give away something about me, that I'm uncertain myself under the brash manner. Or is everyone the same in this, and we love because of human failings, not despite them? Anyway, snuggled between laundry-scented sheets, with the drumming in my head less as the pills took over, I could review the day without too much alarm. The accident receded until it mattered no more than the last chapter of a thriller I'd read before switching out the light. Someone else's adventure I'd happened to come across.

I seemed to see it unfolding in slow motion at some distance while I hovered over the water, an invisible voyeur. The palm trees were there, darkly moving under the hot wind. I heard their soughing, the sound of gravel under running feet, distant voices of the bathers.

And then suddenly it was happening over again—what I hadn't been able to recall clearly before—the hiss of the

29

windsurfer cutting through the water, a brief instant of instinctive fear, then white pain exploding inside my head. I was sinking, freely at first, then enmeshed. My chest flamed as I tried to hold my breath and fight against blackness. I went down *feet first*, with a brutal clamp on my ankles! I knew then that I was going to die, and my last thought was anger.

I came instantly awake, pouring sweat, and found that it wasn't Per I struggled with but the pillows. I switched on the light and explored my ankles with careful fingertips. Where they were most tender blue bruises were coming up like the marks of fingers. Whose?

The door to my balcony was open and I staggered out there to stand leaning on the rail while the night wind blew over me taking away the heat. But not my fear.

Fear had been breathing over my shoulder ever since the descent to Kato Zakros, the wind then, like now, slicking sweat from my skin. That had been the beginning of the horror sequence. And now it was being repeated. I felt trapped in a continuous loop of nightmare, with no way to break out.

I returned to bed, but despite the pills I slept badly, waking often to patches of half-consciousness when I drifted between horror and shame at my own suspicions. In those lonely hours of darkness I began to believe that everyone encountered in the past two days had threatened me. Even the doctor, windsurfing so close when I was struck. He could have been the one who 'disappeared'. Easy enough to drop his dark glasses in the sea. Or had that description been his invention, to divert suspicion?

This was paranoia. I knew it. A state of mind, but real for all that. Wasn't there anything I could fix my mind on that would give me back daytime courage?

When it started to get light I went out again to the balcony and watched the world wake up. Three lean dogs which had spent the night barking on and off on the hard-packed soil under my balcony, sat down to scratch at their fleas and then slunk off separately to find a place to sleep. Then half a dozen cats crept out. Finally, on the road beyond, the first

30

motor-scooters signalled the opening of the human day. I slept in the bamboo chair on the balcony until a waiter came with my breakfast.

When I had showered, in tepid water, leaving the bathroom door open at Per's insistence, I felt less of a wreck. I put on the ivory cheesecloth dress which I'd bought with Per's money at Zakros, and when I remembered Phyllia, the girl of my own age who had embroidered it, I knew everyone wasn't bad and the world not all black. I managed a weak grin for Per.

'Welcome back, soldier,' he said, kissing my forehead. 'You begin to look yourself again.'

Nevertheless I suggested that when we reached Iraklion he should continue on his tour of the Minoan sites and leave me there. As soon as I felt quite fit again I could catch him up by the bus network or, if I still felt under the weather, fly to Athens and transfer to an Airbus for Heathrow.

'Do you think I would run out on you?' he asked, visibly offended. 'We stay together. For today we make no plans. Tomorrow, when Dr Vassilakis has seen the new X-rays and okayed you, we will travel on.'

He didn't consider the possibility that my skull might actually show a crack and his schedule be further affected. Perhaps the omission was deliberate, to prevent my morale from sinking too low. Anyway he proved right.

The transfer to the capital with Dr Vassilakis went off without incident. Once there, the respect—almost reverence —shown him by the hospital nurses and radiologist would have dismissed any lingering doubts I'd had about his covering up his own part in my accident. By now I knew he was a serious-minded, caring person all through, and I was flattered that he invited Per and me to dine with him that night at an open-air taverna down by the harbour.

I realize now that I've never described Andreas Vassilakis. He is youngish, say twenty-seven or -eight, no Prince Charming although we did meet in a kiss of life. He is solid, strongly built, with a broad untroubled forehead under crisp, black, cropped hair; solemn eyes, the darkest of browns; and a rather heavy face that just escapes being

31

jowly. Grooves from nostrils to the corners of his wide, firm mouth give a false impression of self-parodying humour. At least, I guessed that it was false. I could be wrong. He is of only medium height for a man, our eyes being almost on a level. His body is muscled, barrel-chested, flat-bellied. His legs—as I remember from Vai—are straight, teaky brown and almost hairless. When he smiles he shows large, square teeth that are startlingly white. Perhaps they, and his well-tended hands, were what made me accept at once that he was a doctor. Apart from that distinction, he gives a comfortable, semi-comic impression: a nice cartoon dog, or a solemn teddy-bear. And then, as sheer contradiction, he has to wear gold-rimmed spectacles that look like academic disguise.

It was a perfect evening for our celebration. As my head-ache had lifted I was allowed one glass of wine with my *Bekatses Krasatas*. The restaurant was lovely. The tables, each lit by a fat candle flickering inside a crimson glass globe, were prettily set under a horizontally trellised vine. The main dish of woodcocks in red wine was *table d'hôte*, but we began with a choice of *Kakavia* or *Kalitsounia* and to end there was a sweet trolley to charm a harem.

At the next table they were having *crêpes flambées*, with brandy hissing in blue flames as a white-aproned acolyte conducted the ritual. When the diners were served I became aware of him staring, the brilliant dark eyes under the tall chef's hat fixed on me inquisitively. It wasn't my imagina-tion. Per too had noticed his interest and motioned him away when he approached with his trolley with spirit heater and liqueurs.

'But wouldn't you enjoy a *crêpe suzette*?' Dr Vassilakis inquired. 'It is quite a favourite of the ladies here.'

I accepted, and now when the little Greek chef was occupied I could take a frank look at him.

He was vivacious. His mouth curved with unspoken mis-chief; a compact, bright face with sharp chin and cheek-bones, topped by glossy black curls that tumbled wantonly towards his eyes. His movements were all swift and exagger-ated, like a conjuror's. I noticed particularly his hands which although deft were square with short fingers which he splayed as he waved them, compelling, as if he was going to produce a live rabbit out of a tophat. He pranced between us, leaning in to serve, sure-footed, sure-fingered. Small and fine—he was little more than five feet three tall—he was a doll. No, a doll is static. He was a mechanical monkey-on-a-stick, gaily grimacing. A child's toy, with the same direct appeal.

He was half way through serving us before I realized, mainly from Dr Vassilakis's gestures, why he was hyperactive. It wasn't clowning, but speech. The little man was a deaf mute.

He was clearly a favourite with his customers, who nodded and smiled just as energetically back, mouthing their words carefully, full-faced, so that he might lip-read. I couldn't tell how many languages he understood but everyone spoke his own to him with confidence. Whatever they wanted he seemed able to provide. All Greeks in catering seem to be natural linguists, but it must have been a triumph for him to pick up even his own language. Perhaps his real tongue was intuition.

I found myself joining in the body language, rounding my mouth and closing my eyes to tell him how delicious the sweet was that he prepared. Later, as he stood back against the wall, waiting between customers, I saw he was alertly watching every movement of our lips, an eavesdropper from across the terrace.

After dinner we strolled through the Parco El Greco and down again to the Venetian harbour. Iraklion, a vital town by day, really rockets at nightfall. The streets were thronged with local people in family groups. Many shops were still doing business, with tourists turning over the handicrafts and bric-à-brac. There were the embroidered tablecloths, blouses and dresses of any Cretan town, but I never saw one as simply beautiful as mine from Zakros. Probably it was the embroidered dress that the little dumb chef had been admiring and not myself at all.

Dr Vassilakis let us give him coffee at a terrace in the *Plateia Eleftherias*, then he said goodbye, warning me still to keep early nights. And it was already eleven-twenty.

Per had shown a barely concealed interest in two discos we'd passed, so when he'd waved a taxi down I closed the door smartly after myself and left him in the road. 'Enjoy yourself,' I said through the window. 'I'll see you tomorrow morning, lateish.'

His face had such a curious expression: pleasure, sheepishness and utter astonishment. But he took his dismissal.

I slept wonderfully through to half past eight and heard nothing of his return next door in the early hours. There was still no sign of him after breakfast when Reception told me of a note left with them. The note was typed and signed with a flourish, M. Dritsas. In rather stilted but elliptical English it requested a few moments' conversation in the front lounge at my convenience between ten and eleven a.m.

It was after ten already so I'd need to make up my mind quickly what to do about the mystery summons. A pick-up just wasn't on.

'Do you happen to know of a Mr, or it could be Miss, Dritsas?' I asked the front desk clerk. She shook her head.

'There was this note left for me,' I explained.

Her face lit up. 'Ah, you mean Manolakis? He is here somewhere. I just saw him. Yes, over there behind the newspaper stands.'

He looked so anxious, wearing a crisp linen suit and crushing a straw hat with both hands against his chest, brown eyes pleading with me for recognition, that I had to go across and offer my hand in greeting. The little *crêpes* chef of last night. But how had he come to know my name?

He waved towards the lounge and we found a settee near an open window. He pulled a glass-topped table towards us, produced a jotter from a pocket and began to write on it.

'Forgive please. I am Manolis Dritsas.' He sat back, seeming to think it should explain all. I nodded, then raised my shoulders. Facing him I mimed the words, 'Did you follow me here last night?' And I gave a discouraging frown.

He shook his head, scandalized, began to talk with his hands and then realized that I couldn't follow what he said.

He wrote again and pushed the jotter across. 'I visited Dr Vassilakis to know your hotel.'

I shook my head vigorously. 'No. He would never give you my name.'

'But I knew your name.' He frowned at me, holding the jotter under my eyes, and puzzled by my lack of comprehension. Then he gave his bright, wide smile, ducked his head and added, 'The Manolis of Phyllia. She speak of you. I know she make dress. She go later to London and meet you again. I fear much. Phyllia so innocent.' He put down his pen and looked anxiously at me, to see if I was offended.

I was nodding like crazy and smiling. Phyllia at Zakros, of course. The receptionist had spoken of 'Manolakis', using the familiar diminutive. Phyllia and her "dear Manolis" were to be married next year. Meanwhile she would go to help her sister in London and "come back rich".

'She spoke of you too,' I said. At last we had our connections clear and could tackle the purpose of his visit. But still Manolis felt the need to confirm his *bona fides*. Every evening, it seemed, he wrote to Phyllia and she to him, exchanging all their news. He was a Zakros man himself, and his family had taken Phyllia into itself for her protection, she and her brother being refugees from Cyprus, orphans, who had lost everything to the Turks. There was the older married sister in London who invited Phyllia to come and help in her taverna. On this she and Manolis were not of one mind. He found it unseemly, unnecessary and dangerous. At the same time he admitted that Phyllia had rights, and might wish to consult her sister regarding the married state. One had to remember she had no mother. But he was afraid for her, London being so distant and—if I would forgive the criticism—known to be a wicked city.

'Do you intend to stop her?' I asked.

He wrote, then tilted his lively little face to watch mine. 'When I am husband I am master. Now she choose. She say she go. So I ask you take care.'

He was perfectly serious. Life to him was that simple. Just as his family had absorbed the two unknown orphans from Cyprus, so now I was to accept Phyllia. Involving my

35

family too. I tried to imagine Daddy feeling responsible for a strange foreign female. He would simply send for some college prospectus and suggest she fix something up herself. My stepmother might inveigle her into au-pairing, but with a distinctly downstairs bias.

'She will live with her sister?' I mouthed.

'In Soho, London. But she need a friend. She admire you. I too have much respect.'

'You don't know me. London is, as you say, distant and wicked. It's very big too.' I didn't know how to continue.

His eyebrows met in a crumpled line over the soulful brown eyes. He bent over his jotter. 'You give Phyllia phone number.'

Yes, I had done, but never expecting anything to come of it. What had I meant by that over-generous gesture? Just that I responded to her, girl to girl. Nothing more? Had I intended, back in grey old London, trying to recapture something of this burning Cretan summer?

'I will go to her in Soho,' I found myself promising. 'And if she needs me I will help her.'

'You are her friend,' he wrote, then threw down his pen, reached for me with both hands and kissed each of my cheeks. Beaming, he gestured to his heart. I was his dear friend too. Something told me that I'd let myself in for no small thing. All because he was the observant type of lover who actually notices what his beloved is working on. I tried to make this observation to Manolis in sign language.

He nodded and put his finger on the most intricate part of the embroidery at my shoulder, pursing his lips in approval. Then he laughed and stared at my hair, touched his own eyes. Of course there was that too. During their recent postal courtship Phyllia had described the English girl with dark red hair. A thatch like mine is uncommon enough in England, let alone here. Once described I could hardly be missed, and in the capital fate had made me walk straight into the restaurant where he worked, in the company of a customer he knew well enough to question.

He wrote out for me the address of the sister in Soho, and for a while we continued in conversation, he reading my lips

36

as I patched my imperfect Greek with English, and putting his own remarks on paper. I told him a little of my reasons for coming to Crete and of the wild flower study I was making.

Eventually he wrote that he must go and supervise the kitchen at the taverna. Respectfully he took my hands in his own and kissed their backs. 'I will look out for Phyllia,' I promised again.

He went off radiant, having no doubt at all that his love would now be perfectly safe in London, however distant.

I made another acquaintance that day, though a less pleasant one. I had gone out to the hospital by bus for my last check-up from Dr Vassilakis, and waiting at the stop for the return one from Knossos, I stood alongside a shapeless beanbag of a woman in faded slate-blue cotton and scuffed sandals. Eight or nine years older than me, she had a fleshy, loose-mouthed face, with staring eyes and a triangle of acne at one corner of her mouth. In a Midlands English accent she told me she'd been 'for treatment' which, because of her size, I took to be for some kind of thyroid trouble. Since she was uncomfortable and perspiring I suggested we share a taxi. In it she poured out the sad tale of her marriage to a Greek grocer who had died two years back leaving her his business and a rapacious female-dominated family. She could not afford to go back to Birmingham and life here made her feel suicidal.

I dropped a load of drachmas in her hands for my share of the ride and got out as Per came loping down the hotel steps to swing me round in expansive greeting. My head felt quite wonky again as he set me down.

Per didn't notice, staring after the receding taxi. 'Who's that?'

The overweight woman had her face pressed flat against the rear window, like some grotesque white fish in an aquarium tank. For some reason she frightened me and the hair bristled on the back of my neck. 'I don't know,' I said, and the taxi turned a corner, taking her out of my life. But I was left uneasy.

CHAPTER 4

Per was in the same jaunty mood when we set out next morning on the road south. 'So much for High Life,' he said, 'such as it is on the islands. Now for the reverse of the coin. Of the earth, earthy.' There was an ill-concealed sneer in the last words.

'I like Cretan country ways,' I said defensively. 'I prefer the islands to Athens any day.'

Per gave me a pitying glance. 'I have an eccentric aunt who lives out here all the year round, on Rhodes.'

'Does that make her eccentric?' He'd never volunteered anything about his family before and I was curious to draw him out.

'Not in itself. She just happens to be crazy, a real pain to the rest of us. A sort of "remittance aunt". You know how once they used to pension off delinquent sons to live in the colonies? It's that sort of arrangement. She was in an asylum not so many years back.' His tone had changed from one of flippancy to disdain.

I tried for a more general slant. 'I can understand any Scandinavian settling in the Med, just to escape the snow.'

'Oh, she's not a Swede. My mother's sister, English as they come. Look, I've marked our route here,' and he passed me the map fitted inside a plastic cover on which a blue line meandered like a vein.

I studied it, thinking: That accounts for his English being so good. He's Anglo-Swedish, probably schooled in the UK. 'Yes,' I said, 'I see. Iraklion's like Rome. All roads lead there, and we're going out by the south, across the Messara Plain to Phaistos.'

While I'd been to-ing and fro-ing between hotel and hospital he must have restocked with provisions and fuel. They were ready loaded, and when I swung in beside him he slapped a bill on the dashboard in front of me. 'Fifty-fifty, I think we agreed?'

I picked up the paper. 'That's right.'

'Twelve thousand then, to make it a round figure.'

I had just changed a £50 traveller's cheque and tucked the notes away separately from my remaining cash. I pulled the bundle out now and passed it across without a word. I had certainly offered to pay my half-share of all expenses, but should have liked to help make the shopping-list, especially since the cooking fell almost invariably to me.

Per pocketed the notes without counting them. He may have thought such casualness gave the appearance of non-chalant generosity, but I guessed he'd read my transaction upside down on the hotel's exchange currency sheet when he'd cashed a cheque of his own before leaving. He'd know I hadn't had time since to spend any drachmas. The bill was made out in his own neat handwriting and merely stated, 'Half supplies and fuel—12,000 drx.'

Well, I wasn't going to argue. In fact I found nothing at all to say until we were well on the way. Then it was Per who needled me into speech by sneering down his nose, 'I didn't realize it was catching.'

'What was?' I asked, caught out.

He flicked a sideways glance at me and although his teeth showed briefly between beard and moustache his eyes were coldly antagonistic. 'You've been stricken, like your little dumbo chef. Wasted no time in picking him up, did you? What turned you on—the hand movements?'

If he hadn't been driving so fast, and on yet another winding mountain road as we dropped towards the Messara Plain, I'd have jumped out and hiked back to Iraklion.

But duck out leaving the main part of my money with him?—my cautionary conscience challenged. Just as well that retreat was out of the question. I had to grow up there and then, learn to employ a little acid when the Pers of this world got under my skin.

'How you do judge others by your own standards,' I threw at him. It came out as scornful as I'd intended. Per was delighted.

'I don't, I assure you. My standards are way above a tramp like you. But keep your eyes open and you may learn

39

technique in time.' He spoke from an enormous imagined height, and I let him think what he chose. He didn't deserve any explanations. People like Manolis and Phyllia were beyond his appreciation. If I told him the whole story he would most likely crow at my naïvety, say they'd conned me into obligations which no mature person of even average sanity would allow laid on them.

And how had he known that Manolis had been in touch with me? He must have observed us the previous morning when the little Greek sought me out at the hotel. The idea of Per keeping watch without revealing his presence disturbed me. I began to wish again that he'd gone on ahead to Phaistos leaving me free to decide whether I followed or went elsewhere.

'The doctor was better, if you fancied a Greek. At least you know he washed properly.'

He was unspeakable. 'Don't you ever think of anything but sex?'

'What else is there?' Per was enjoying himself.

'Archæology?'

The taunt went instantly home. His whole demeanour changed, he retreated inside himself and left me in peace for the next half-hour at least. I was free to marvel at the country we were passing through, at the polka-dotted precision of tiny olive trees measuring out the dry earth hundreds of feet below, at the carefully engineered curved terraces sloping right up to the last thrust of volcanic rock.

So much evidence of human labour, but where were the people? Only at very scattered intervals could you pick out a single habitation half hidden by riotous wild vines. Later we passed through, or near, several small villages each with its toylike white church topped with dumpy tower and pantiled dome. As we descended, the plain stretched widely open from the Ida range on our right to the Dikti mountains on our left, rich with long grass starred with daisies and stained with poppies. I longed to walk in the cool lushness, part the green stems and see what hidden flowers grew deeper down.

We stopped for a lunch of ice-cold beer from the freezer-box and toasted buns with hamburgers cooked over the butane gas burner which Per always packed close to hand. I'd nothing to complain of there in the supplies, unless it was the barbecue relish which Per packed too liberally in the burgers I'd cooked, so that they burned my tongue and made me double up on the beer. By the time I'd cleared up and we'd gone on another quarter hour of our way I was more ready for sleep than for Gortys, which stretched vast and shimmering under the afternoon sun.

There is always that awed awareness of half-sensed disasters at a site with such evidence of vanished generations. At Gortys you face not just one great civilization gone forever but three: the Minoan, the Roman and the Byzantine, each period building over the previous site and using many of the original materials. And now—no city, no law-giving centre, no great vehicle of Christian instruction, but a wilderness to which strangers are bussed in air-conditioned coaches, to wander bored by ancient site after ancient site and made irritable by heat and mosquitoes. You feel they are glad to leave because the place demands too much of their modern minds, and so they return gratefully to concrete-stacked hotels with balconies, ice cubes and 'international cuisine'.

I saw few flowers in that part of the stony hollow. Perhaps I should have started on the long climb up the rocky shelves, but there wasn't time. Even Per was impatient to be gone. It was probably the superimposing of Roman on the prehistoric past which made him feel cheated of centuries. I don't know. I never quite made out the exact appeal of his sites to him, but I know it was the Minoan strata that were the great magnet.

We trudged back to the Volvo against an incoming tide of tourists with reddened flesh, unsuitable shoes and some with knotted handkerchiefs covering their hair. 'Phaistos next?' I asked.

He nodded. 'Phaistos will be better. But we'll find somewhere just this side of it to camp.'

First we lay on the bleached grass to the shady side of the car to drink more beer. Finally we piled back into the hell-hot interior and resumed our journey.

There was no pleasant riverside camping ground. No water, in fact. Phaistos had been touristically equipped with a 'pavilion' dispensing twentieth-century comforts, and when we inquired they warned us that vagrancy was discouraged there. If we intended to stay in the vicinity longer than the half-hour which the coaches averaged, and if we scorned to find lodgings in the nearest town, we should haggle at some outlying farm for parking and tent-space. Per was pretty disgusted, and when I'd stocked up with a few cans of soft drinks we set off again to look for such a place.

We stopped at a dim, dusty little farm off the main road with outbuildings and a couple of trailers abandoned in the corral behind. 'Okay for a night,' Per said indifferently, and I didn't demur. If I had known then how long it would be before I could be free of the place and its memories I would have started to run and never looked back. Yet then it was welcome enough because I felt exhausted and my head seemed to expand and contract with the beat of a Heavy Metal disco. I sat under the sagging vine of the terrace, put my face on my arms on the table and was asleep before Per had finished haggling with the farmer's wife over our accommodation.

When I awoke, in the dusk, I was told she had insisted I sleep in the house. Per had meanwhile pitched the tent for himself. During our meal, which was *souvlaki*, quite passably cooked, with salad and followed by delicious fresh fruit, it became obvious why this arrangement had been made. Per was smugly at pains to let me see that in 'picking up' he could run rings round me. The lean and long-toothed lady of the farm was little short of moaning with desire as she served at our table. Well, Per could please himself; it made no difference to me. Or so I thought then.

It was a two-storey building with a surprising number of rooms, and had once been an inn, used as a stopover for archæologists. For quite a while however it had been supplanted by alternatives. The luxury German and Netherlands coaches purred past the lane end, barely stirring up the sandy dust that coated the sparse furniture of the uninhabited rooms.

Next morning I didn't wait for Per but started straight in on breakfast as soon as Kyria Kostantinou brought in the coffee. She seemed in a new mood of sleek satisfaction, flicking me glances while she fiddled with the table as if inviting me to speak, but I'd no desire to be expansive, especially as I was sure Per would have given her more than enough details about me in the course of the night, and none of them flattering. Nor was I in the least curious about her.

Eventually she gave up, went away, and I heard her in the kitchen talking Greek loudly with a male voice whose interruptions were short and little more than a surly grunt. After a while a man came clumping along the passage and stared in at me from the doorway. I wished him '*Kalimera*,' and after blinking his ox-like eyes once or twice he passed a hand over his mouth and managed an answering '-*mera*.'

He was massive and paunchy, the dark, scowling brows and brigandish moustache merely cosmetic, I was sure, to cover a slack and lethargic nature. I heard him climb some wooden stairs and then, directly overhead, there came the complaint of old bedsprings followed by the double thump of boots thrown to the floor.

'He sleep now. My husband work at night.' Kyria Kostantinou had returned and was leaning in the doorway, grinning fiercely.

I stared coolly back. 'That's all right. I shan't disturb him.'

She must have read into it more than I'd meant, because she started to laugh, a rough yowling like a stray cat makes at night. She bent and hugged herself, she found it so funny, and just then Per came up behind and slapped her familiarly on the rump. She went taut and expectant. I thought she was going to take him on the spot.

'Uh-uh,' Per warned, wagging a finger. 'Food first.'

The woman gave another wail of laughter and disappeared down the passage.

'Sleep well?' Per inquired, scratching at an armpit.

'Surprisingly well, considering the circumstances.'

43

'You spent too long with the fleshpots of Iraklion.'

'I prefer stars to a canopy of cobwebs.' Even to myself my voice sounded bitchy. Our morning hadn't started well. I counted silently to three while Per spread honey on his bread. 'What's the programme?' I then asked as neutrally as possible.

'We'll be staying on here a few days. I want to do a circuit round Phaistos, see if there's been any recent digging in the neighbourhood. Official or clandestine.' His voice was affectedly casual.

'Why should there be?' I asked.

'Oh, prospectors, you know. People get hunches about places, poke about and sometimes turn up odd treasures, pass the word that they're open for a bid.'

'But would you buy from someone like that? It's illegal to export such finds, isn't it?'

'Buy, no!' He sounded cocky. 'But who knows, I might be lucky enough to make a strike myself. Then I'd know it was genuine. I wouldn't risk being rooked. You see, there's no reason to suppose we've already uncovered all the Minoan palaces that existed. Nor all the buildings of the known sites.'

I nodded. 'There must have been Minoan cities too, where ordinary people lived, the ones who dug and toiled and spun and did all the craftwork, certainly.'

'Ah,' he said, and he levelled his knife thoughtfully at me, 'there you have something, perhaps. Craftsmen, yes. Workshops, forges. Places with too much noise, and nasty smells not fit for royal ears and noses. So they'd be at some distance from the palace chambers. Well, that's what I need to find; that sort of site.'

'Will you be on foot most of the time?' I pursued. 'Because if so I'll take the Volvo into the next town and try to find a launderette.'

He considered this. 'I'll drop you in Timbaki. When you've done, get a bus back to Phaistos. I'll pick you up there this afternoon sometime, by the gate where the man sells reed flutes.'

Well, why not? The alternative was to wash all the stuff

myself and peg it out here, wasting time I could spend on my painting. It meant lugging a sack of clothes around all day as well as my paints and block, but that wouldn't break my back. The Volvo was Per's after all, even if he didn't need it so badly.

'I'll look out my dirty stuff,' he offered. 'I meant to get it washed at Iraklion, then forgot until we'd moved off.'

There were a lot of his clothes and two pairs of my cotton slacks. I'd rinsed out my small things and the precious new dress at our hotel and they'd dried overnight on the balcony. As I put the bundle together the khaki bush shirt reminded me of Per wearing it on the mountainside above Kato Zakros. I could see him again bending over the dead man as I turned away, and when I'd looked back he'd been slipping something into the breast pocket. It had been whatever had been clamped in the dead man's hand. When I'd asked him about it later Per had hesitated, then said, 'Nothing. It was just a tinny piece of metal.'

Now I could feel it still there under the flap, and it made me curious. I pulled it out. Metal it certainly was, and I'd thought Per had been lying. It was a corner torn from a nameplate stamped with the two final letters -IS. Not much of an identification in a language where almost all surnames ended in -os, -ou or -is. I wondered idly what the tag had come off and how the young man had come to grip it so desperately in his final spasm. Perhaps it had been attached to the car dashboard, though it was more like the nameplates some Cretans fixed to their pushbikes or motor scooters. It seemed unimportant and I tossed it through the open window, there being no refinement such as a WPB.

I turned back to see Per watching me from the doorway, with such a curious, secret smile. 'That the lot?' I asked shortly. It was, and it was load enough.

I didn't notice the name of the town where he dropped me. I was too busy digging out of him the sum I thought we'd need for the washing and my bus fare. I had to remind him he'd taken the whole of my previous traveller's cheque and I couldn't be sure of finding the right kind of bank open.

In the single long sunbaked street I was lucky to discover

a laundress who cheerfully tackled the lot while I drank coffee and swatted flies at a bar on the edge of the cratered pavement. When I went to pay she wouldn't hear of me lumping the bag back by bus. She demanded to know where I was staying and insisted on making delivery when the clothes were properly pressed. Maria should bring them that evening by donkey on her way home to Kalivia. She was so eager to be helpful that I had to trust her.

I waited almost another half-hour for a bus to Phaistos, joined by a group of young people who'd been at the same bar. They were a mixed lot, some speaking German, some French, but uniformly dirty and dressed half way between gipsies and Red Indians. Dropouts from other countries, I supposed, who'd come here to go native, the 'vagrants' we had been taken for at Phaistos. It seemed that some had unofficial jobs in the little town and earned enough for the others to live off, a sort of post-hippy commune. One strong-looking girl with hands stained black with engine grease stank of diesel fuel, but she was the one with bank-notes and sent others scurrying for bread, *feta*, water melons and other provisions. I bought some fruit myself and some of that bread that looks like varnished corn dollies. Per would have had lunch before he came to pick me up. Reinforced so, I could hunt up a few flowers and do some sketching before we met again.

I asked Per, when eventually he turned up at our rendezvous, whether he'd had any success. He paid no attention but sat at the wheel cracking the joints of his hands. His face was shuttered, but I sensed behind it some intense activity. His driving was on auto-pilot, as unconsidered as my own presence. He was quite daunting in that kind of mood, so I stayed quiet and kept out of his way. .

Before dinner he went into Kyria's private room to use her phone, and half way through our meal there was an incoming call for him. He volunteered no explanation for either.

He had partly unpacked our supplies, brought some perishables into the farm and dumped other articles in a stone storehouse where Kostantinou kept bags of fertilizer, old farm machinery and his fuel store. I went out to that dim and spidery place myself that evening to fetch a new can of camping gas to make our coffee out by the tent. Per had damned Kyria's brew as concocted from cigar ash and pencil shavings.

She didn't understand what he said and sat rubbing herself against his shoulder, catlike with her personal bowl of cream. I excused myself, said good night and took my coffee indoors.

Because I rose early and left before they appeared next morning, that was the last time I saw Per alive, seated in the half-dark, blond hair haloed by the lantern light that slanted down his handsome, bearded cheeks. A lean, strong young Viking, his white teeth gleaming as he laughed at something the woman was whispering in his ear.

CHAPTER 5

At the time, that day seemed the watershed of my life. The only ordered thought I was capable of, shattered by what had happened, was that nothing could ever be the same again. Everything taken for granted until then became suddenly, hideously, suspect. There was no security, nothing wholesome left. I was right over the precipice I'd blindly moved towards since Kato Zakros.

Or since encountering Per.

Per, of course, was the core of the whole disaster. Per alive, and then Per dead.

Why did I think: *His own fault?* He was reckless, yes, up to the very limits of his ability to extract himself, but how could he have done the *stupid* thing they thought of him? Per was many unpleasant things, as I'd learned in a few days, but he wasn't that kind of stupid.

I wasn't sorry for him yet. Appalled and even angry with him, certainly, but at first there was no personal blow. Even when I saw what remained of his beautiful body it didn't sadden. It was a horror scene. Only much later did I know

47

that I'd lost the tall Nordic god I'd met at Iraklion just a week before, the man I thought I'd loved at first sight.

Too much had happened and my mind was in a turmoil. Even the instinctive parts weren't getting their messages through. I am still muddled. I have to make a conscious effort to sort out what actually happened, and in what order.

I must have heard Per killed. It was the evening of the day after the laundry one.

I had intentionally stayed out since early morning, pleasing myself what I did and carrying my own meals in my back-pack. The work I got through was even better than I'd hoped. To start with, I'd come across a patch of tawny spikes, *Urginea maritima*, some three feet high with narrow bands of tiny off-white florets just starting to open. The single clump was backed by weathered sandstone and sun-bleached grasses—a subtle harmony of tapestry shades which I had to get into colour straight away.

As I began to climb I found other specimens I'd been looking for, and two I'd never hoped to happen on. Of these the *Pancratium maritimum* was the more spectacular, a sweet-scented, pure white amaryllis which usually grew nearer the sea and was badly preyed on by tourists. Its arrival up here was encouraging for its survival, and surely meant that a smallish bulb must have been carried up by some egg-besotted bird. What else could explain its presence?

I used a soft pencil to outline the graceful umbel and left it uncoloured, mixed a dark, plummy shadow and splashed in a background of dramatic contrast. Then I photographed the plant from ground level to get in the Ida mountain range as backdrop, just in case my story was ever challenged.

The nearly incredible find came in mid-afternoon at the highest point I reached. To look at, nothing special, and I nearly passed it over. Just a little tight lump of stiff green leaves with tiny stars of white tucked in it. I couldn't believe it was *Minuartia* because to my knowledge it has never been recorded for Crete. My botanical list gives it as a native of Epirus, Thessalia, the central mainland and Peloponnese. Yet the plant scored positives on every check I made. Some freak condition of the alpine-type crevasse where I found it had coincided with stray seed windblown perhaps for hundreds of miles, or accidentally embedded in some sack of imported supplies.

It is one of the wonders of the living world how survival occurs in alien surroundings. And at the time that I recorded that unassuming little plant Per was a part of the surviving world too.

I was coming back down the lower slopes, still a good half-hour off base, when I saw a flash below in a smudge of greenery. A second or two later the sound reached me, but by then there was a flowering of scarlet and orange where the foliage had been. I wasn't sure of the exact location because the track, such as it was, wound to accommodate itself to the contours, but it was over to the right, at two o'clock as I faced the distant sea. It could have been on the main road, but there was no village in that direction. It could even be near the farm we'd put up at.

The fire continued to burn fiercely as I went on down, and as I came closer the road was discernible here and there with traffic on it showing headlights as dusk crept over the lower ground. And some of the lights were turning now into a lane that seemed familiar. I lost sight of the place as I lost height and by then I had started to run, smelling burning varnish and paintwork, seeing the orange boiling of flames reflected in a pall of black smoke.

I came on the farm from the rear and was instantly among all the spraying water and acrid fumes. The front of the barn was obscured by dark billowings of smoke, the yard slopped with puddles. And dragged to one side, a blackened, steaming bundle of sodden rags. I ran forward and before they could stop me knelt to look.

I shall never forget. It was like one of those hideous newsreels of terrorist bombings. He had no face, no proper chest, and one shoulder was torn loose. How I knew I couldn't say, but I did know. It was Per.

Somebody forced me indoors. There was a lot of loud talking, and all the spoken Greek I ever knew deserted me. I put my hands over my head and they seemed to understand because it went deadly quiet except for the hissing of fire hoses and the drip-drip from the frame of the kitchen door.

I wanted them to tell me, quietly and slowly, what had happened, but I couldn't find the words to ask. Finally, '*Then katalaveno*,' came to mind. 'I do not understand.'

Kyria Kostantinou was pushed forward. She looked awful, hair bedraggled, her face grey under the streaks of ash, and with staring, bloodshot eyes. 'Is the place we put stores,' she said 'Go up—*pouf*!' She waved her arms wildly. 'He is there. He—he is dead, *Vespinis*. Your man is dead.'

I didn't faint, I wasn't sick, but everything simply stopped. Except the damn water raining back uselessly on to the lifeless thing in the yard. I sat, not believing, until one of the men shook me gently by the shoulder. 'I am police,' he said. 'I talk you now.'

He was patient, very kind. He took me up to my room, put his arms round me at just the right moment, let me hold on and cry all over his soaked uniform. He stank of smoke and it made me retch. That was the first feeling I had as reality began to reassemble. So good to me, and I couldn't stand his smell.

He extracted from me as much as I knew of Per's background. His home address and any correspondence with family would be with his passport probably, and that was in the Volvo. I was almost sure he'd said his parents were in Rome, his father a senior diplomat at the Swedish Embassy. The more details I gave the more serious the policeman seemed to get. 'You come,' he ordered, 'find papers, value-things.'

'Valuables.'

'Yes. Before someone touch. Please, now.'

We searched through the car, made up one package which I initialled, then did the same for the tent. It didn't strike me at the time how little money there had been in the cashbox. If I'd thought, I might have assumed that Per had it all on him and so the fire destroyed it. Actually I ought to have recalled his locking away my 12,000 drax along with his own bundle last night.

There weren't many valuables: some links recovered from

the gold neck chain he'd worn; his wristwatch, still going despite the explosion and the water; a gold lighter. Later someone brought in another item and rinsed it under the tap: the signet ring off his severed hand.

It was then I started to scream. Someone slapped my face, and later I was given an injection in one arm. It must have been the local medic. Before I went to sleep I managed to focus on him and whisper, 'Dr Vassilakis. At Iraklion. Tell him.'

He looked surprised, then nodded. When I awoke next morning dear Andreas was there.

So it was Andreas Vassilakis who told me the full story of the accident, or what we thought then was the whole truth. It had been the busy time of evening for Kyria Kostantinou. She had been alone in the house, preparing the meal. Per, she had thought, was out by the tent, which was pitched on the blind side of the house. The first she had known was the explosion, which shook the windows and rattled the shutters in their wall latches. The fire had been instant, garishly lighting up the yard. At once she remembered the fertilizers and gas drums in the store, so she went straight to the phone and dialled the emergency services.

It took over twelve minutes before anyone arrived and by then she had gone to see what could be saved. She saw Per lying some ten yards in front of the open barn, on his back where he'd been blown by the force of the explosion. There was an aureole of flames round him and she'd thrown a bucket of water over before it reached her that he couldn't be alive. All the same she had tried to beat out the flames outside while the barn roared like a fireball.

'I was away up the mountain,' I told Andreas.

'Yes, Kostantinou nearly fell over your sketching things in the dark. He came rushing back when he heard about the fire.'

'I must have dropped everything when I started to run.'

'Siân, your friend's parents are flying in from Rome this morning. They will come straight from Iraklion airport by

51

hired car. That is arranged, but they cannot stay here, nor should you. Shall I book a room for you in Vori? Or can I take you back with me today?'

I sat up. 'I shall have to see them, shan't I? They would never understand if I went without—not that I can do any good. It's going to be terrible for them. Oh Andreas, please don't go away until I've got through that!'

'I will stay until you feel safe again.'

I didn't believe that would ever happen, but was ashamed to say it aloud. Instead I kissed his rough cheek and he seemed to glow.

'I think I should stay on here,' I said after a while. 'That is, if the Kostantinous don't mind. All our baggage is here. Someone has to keep an eye on it, help sort out what was Per's and so on.'

'If you really wish that, then I will take a room here too. For a day or two. After that—' He shrugged.

'It was good of you to come, Andreas. I didn't give a thought to your work. I'm really sorry. Was it dreadfully inconvenient?'

'I have good colleagues. Don't worry. We are always—' He made a little balancing movement with his hands which made me smile, remembering Manolis.

'You Box and Cox,' I suggested. The expression delighted him and I explained what it meant. We had reached a level of normality. With Andreas close I could almost believe that little was wrong, but we were both still wary. When we went out for a walk we used the front entrance, avoiding the yard, and we talked about Phaistos, the Minoan legends, the flowers I had found on the mountain. And even that last was almost a subject to avoid, because of what came after. Perhaps tomorrow I should be able to talk about Per with him.

Around six that evening my policeman called again to tell me that Per's mother and father had arrived in Timbaki and were taking the tragedy with great dignity. I supposed that meant that they weren't weeping openly as Greeks do when they mourn.

When the policeman had left I asked Andreas to drive

me to Timbaki. 'I want to get it over,' I insisted. 'I must call on them or I'll never sleep tonight.'

Mr Wennberg was not at the hotel, having accompanied the local doctor on some business connected with the *post mortem*. He had already identified the body as Per's. I don't know how.

Per's mother sent down a message that she would see me if I would wait. I waited over half an hour in the hallway of the modest but clean little hotel which offered the only accommodation, and then she came reluctantly down the stairs, a cold, upper-class Englishwoman with all her defences raised against me. Coming down not to be comforted, but to do battle.

I went forward to offer my hand. I wished now I hadn't sent Andreas off to get a coffee. Two women together, I'd thought; linked by Per, no outsider was needed. But what I hadn't expected was a flesh and blood person with feelings. And animosity.

In the shadowed hall I had no impression of her features, but her stance said everything. Mrs Wennberg ignored my outstretched hand, standing stiffly with her own on the banister rail. But perhaps she needed its support.

'I'm Siân Westbury,' I said. My words came out like a hushed confession. 'I was with your son on his tour.'

'Ah yes.' Her voice was clear and high-pitched. I heard an echo of Per's arrogance in it. 'He has told me about you.' Dismissive.

I felt my hackles start to rise. 'He never mentioned you.'

She stared at me with shadowed, pale eyes, Per's eyes, and her mouth was a hard, straight line. 'Why should he? Why tell you anything important? You were not a lasting part of his life.'

Lasting longer than Per himself, though. I trembled with anger but still I couldn't say that aloud, not in such circumstances, however much we clashed in instinctive antipathy. She was a mother who had lost her son. It would be impossible even to share with her my fears, suspicions which might imply a greater horror than accident. To speak of that I must wait to meet Per's father.

'I wanted to say—' I began. But say what? That I was sorry? Didn't that sound like an apology?

'Yes?' She was waiting.

'To express my deepest sympathy,' I ended, knowing how hollow the cliché must sound.

'I will mention to my husband that you called,' she said coldly. The interview was over, and she hadn't come down that last step into the hall.

'Goodbye, Mrs Wennberg. I shall be at the farm if your husband should wish to contact me.'

It seemed at first that there was no likelihood of this. I should have to take the initiative again, risking a second rebuff.

'Must you?' Andreas asked gently.

'Yes, I must. I have to talk to him, tell him things.' I wouldn't admit to Andreas then the horrors that lurked in the dark part of my mind.

That night I woke screaming from a nightmare where I was sliding again down the scree above Kato Zakros pursued by a fireball. Even as I slipped and scrambled I knew that inside that fireball was Per and he wanted to kill me. I reached the dead man and as I bent over him he became Per too, reaching up to him, just as he turned to red dust under my eyes.

I heard my own scream and a hand touched my face. Andreas hushed me and rocked me close against his chest. It was his arms that had reached into my dreams, him I clung to, not the destroyed body of the young Viking. He stayed on with me till morning, and in stages I told him about the long nightmare of my waking, how it had started with fire before my near-drowning, and now there was fire again, destroying Per. The craggy brown face grew severe as he listened. 'You fear you are in danger,' he said at last. 'But perhaps what danger there was is over now. If it threatened your friend, not you.'

It sounded reasonable enough as he said it, but I was still afraid. There had to be some explanation of what had gone before if I was to accept that the run of disasters was complete. 'I just wish I knew what it was about,' I told

54

Andreas. 'Maybe if I tell all this to Per's father he may explain why I have this awful feeling that Per was caught up in some mysterious dealings.'

'I'm not convinced that that would be wise,' he cautioned. 'If he knows nothing himself you may be betraying your friend's secrets. And if the father does know something of this, then he may be involved himself and not wish you to interfere. Go slowly. You do not know the man. Give no facts, just indicate you are—uneasy.'

'Sound him out? Play it by ear? You may be right.' It was certainly true that I'd no idea what kind of man Per's father was. It could be as humiliating an experience as my approach to the man's wife. If the occasion arose I would do as my wise friend advised and watch my step.

The policeman who called after breakfast was one I'd not seen before, young and what in London we'd call a wide boy. His pale linen suit was a little too sharp. He spent quite a time with Andreas in the yard examining the ground near the fire, the tent and the Volvo. He had also brought a note for me. It was from Mr Wennberg, a formal summons, almost curt in its brevity. If Miss Westbury would call at his hotel that morning between eleven and eleven-thirty Mr Sven Wennberg would be obliged.

He did not appear obliged. It was a totally neutral gaze he turned on me, indicating a chair that faced the light. I deliberately turned it so that he must either change his own position or watch me in profile. Instead he walked right past and planted himself squarely in the window, facing out, his long hands loosely clasped behind his back.

A bad beginning. The silence between us unnerved me. I almost despaired of being able to talk freely at all. 'I don't believe it was an accident,' I blurted out suddenly, desperate to have it said and be on my way.

He turned abruptly, brought a chair over and sat facing me, close. 'I never for a moment,' he said flatly, 'thought it was. What do you know?'

It chilled me, and I remembered Andreas's warning. The man's eyes weren't blue but grey, slaty. And his skin was grey, grey and opaque as if it concealed some secret sickness

55

not yet diagnosed. He had a long, narrow face with a 'thirties moustache, the Niven sort. His appearance so preoccupied me that I lost the thread of what we were saying.

'You see,' he prompted, 'I know my son. *Knew* him. Very well.' The voice was not neutral now. I almost heard a following sentence which he never uttered: *Knew him and disliked him.*

Such a baleful face; perhaps another enemy before we ever met. And yet in his case the animosity wasn't so much directed at me as at Per. And Per was dead. It was myself for whom the mother had shown instinctive dislike. Resentment, because I had been with Per, and she loved her son. Two parents, quite different. An ill-assorted marriage.

'What do you know?' the man repeated softly.

'Know? Nothing really known. Just a feeling,' I said warily. I had my thoughts better controlled now. There was no need to voice my suspicions if this man was already alerted. He must have his reasons. He would pursue any inquiry implacably. He had power and money, all that was needed to stir up a full investigation.

He went on facing me and I could feel his displeasure. 'If you have any clue, any specific evidence—'

'Just a feeling.' The words hung in the air between us and neither of us was deceived. 'There was something on his mind,' I added lamely. 'Worrying him.'

'Since when?'

I haven't much experience at lying but this time I concentrated on recall, eyes long-focused, not making the mistake of bold confrontation. 'Since we reached Phaistos, I think. He was strangely silent.'

The man's lips twisted in the grey, sardonic face. 'He was not talkative, and so you think his death was not an accident?'

It was obvious I'd have to give him more, but nothing about that burnt-out car at Kato Zakros. Not the windsurfer riding me down at Vai. It was too dangerous somehow. Perhaps I'd been at risk because I'd known too much. I couldn't give him the same power over me. I hesitated.

Every lie should contain a nucleus of truth, shouldn't it?

56

And there *had* been something odd about Per at the time I'd randomly picked on. Then I remembered. 'He went off to phone before dinner the night before. I don't know who to, but he came back on edge, or perhaps excited. His hand shook when he poured our wine and he spilled some. Then there was an incoming call for him before we finished the meal. Afterwards he snapped at me and we had a silly argument. Nothing important, but we were both quite unpleasant. He went off to sleep in the tent.' No need to say with whom.

He was waiting for more. At length he sighed. 'Am I to accept feminine intuition as the whole basis of your belief that my son was engaged in some secret negotiation?'

'Why not?' Now that he had put it into words, that was just how I should have interpreted his actions if I'd bothered to question them.

'Feelings.' His tone was contemptuous.

'I was uneasy before then. A sort of premonition.' Now he would be convinced of my stupidity, a girl who blurted out ideas she couldn't back up, who had to be asked every question twice because she didn't listen properly. A promiscuous girl who picked up his son so casually that she didn't notice what, if anything, he was secretly engaged in behind that archæological *Wanderlust* façade.

He stood up to indicate that he had finished with me. Almost finished, because he was a diplomat after all, and the last throwaway question was always the one that counted.

'Miss Westbury, are you pregnant by any chance?'

I felt my face flame. 'Not by any chance, and certainly not by your son,' I told him furiously.

'And would you have any objection to a medical test to confirm that?'

I couldn't believe it. There wasn't an answer bad enough. I blundered from the room and ran out of the hotel.

I walked for half an hour along the dusty road before I turned and came back to face Andreas. Even then, when I had cooled somewhat, he gave me one worried glance and knew better than to ask how things had gone. Instead he waited until we were in open country and told me what the *post mortem* had revealed. Embedded in the trachea were small traces of tobacco, mostly unburnt. Per had smoked one of his cigarillos when he went for a fresh can of gas. As he went in, a build-up of gas from leaking drums by the door had ignited and blown him out again. Per, in fact, had killed himself, from carelessness.

CHAPTER 6

He wasn't that kind of stupid, I kept on insisting to myself, but every time I thought of Per his father supplanted him in my mind, that bitter, cynical old man who had wanted to know the worst about his dead son in order to cover it up. And, if I'd been a part of it, presumably I was to be bought off.

It had been a great mistake to stay on and meet Per's family. I should have gone off once the police were satisfied it had been an accident. But there was still the question of our shared belongings in the Volvo. I told Andreas now that as soon as I had my things packed I would go back with him to the capital.

Since the money had disappeared it seemed best that I should extract its value in provisions. The camping stores would be useless to the Wennbergs, whereas I had almost another fortnight to go before returning to England, and the main part of my work remained to be done. I couldn't see myself pushing on alone now that Per had been removed, but what alternative was there? Pointless to go home with my project unfinished. I'd counted on it to get me launched on some kind of career.

I explained this to Andreas and he offered to make an inventory with me of what remained of the stores. It was when we were checking them over that I realized someone had been there before us. The goods were not significantly rearranged, but they weren't stacked just how I'd left them. The salt, for instance, had moved so that I'd have to unload a whole box of canned foods before preparing the simplest meal.

'The police, perhaps,' Andreas suggested. But why should they be interested in our provisions? What had they expected to find among them?

The difficulty, as I saw it, was that Per had made the last purchases, a large quantity to judge by what he'd charged me as my half share, although that also covered fuel for the car. I had no list of items. I would never know if something was now missing. Nevertheless, I had to check, writing down everything that remained. When we'd finished with the car we went on to the damaged tent.

I was conscious of a great reluctance to be there, because this was the place from which Per had suddenly gone off, cigar in mouth, to his death. Fetching gas to boil water for coffee.

And that was all wrong.

Only the evening before I had fetched a fresh can myself and fitted it to the burner. It had been full. I could tell by the weight of it. I'd thrown the used can in the trash bin.

To prove to myself that I hadn't made some absent-minded mistake I went there now and hunted through the gruesome rubbish of the farm's past few meals. There was no gas can at all, empty or full. I returned to the tent and sat on the box where I normally ate my meals. It didn't make sense. There was the single-burner heater in front of me, and when I checked the can I could tell at once it was used up. So Per *had* needed to go for fresh fuel. But where was the full can I'd fitted on earlier? It couldn't have been used up in a single day.

'Siân, what is the matter?' Andreas asked. So I told him. 'Look,' I said at the end of it all, 'there's the heater, the pan of water, the pot of coffee granules, the sugar. He's even spooned Nescafé ready in our mugs. All that's missing is the gas, so he had to go and fetch some. If he hadn't been smoking when he went in the barn he'd have smelled the gas leak—' I stopped. 'Andreas, have you ever known camping gas leak like that before?'

He was silent a moment, sombrely watching me. 'No.

59

And that is what the police do not like. That so much escaped, to make so great an explosion. I think they are crucifying Kostantinou because of this.'

Fear gripped me like a physical pain, under the ribs. 'Andreas, do you think—perhaps—?'

'I do not know what to think. But tell me, did your friend take sugar in his coffee?'

'Never. But half a spoonful in tea.'

'And you?'

'Milk, when there is any. No sugar. You know that.'

'Yes. But you see, one of these mugs has sugar in it, with the coffee granules. The tent canopy protected it from water when they fought the fire, so you can still see the crystals. Dirty grey, but sugar just the same. If not for you or for him —who then?'

'He had someone here with him. Perhaps Kyria Kostantinou. She slept here with him the previous night. Maybe she wasn't as busy in the kitchen as she claims. Or her husband. Suppose he came back early—'

'And sat down to drink coffee with his wife's seducer?' Andreas's face was dark and lowering. 'Who saw you throw the empty can away the evening before?'

'No one. At least, I never saw anyone. It was quite dark so I took the lamp off the bracket there and went across to the bins. I *know* it was the empty one I threw away, Andreas.'

'Yes, yes. I'm sure you did. But someone took it out again and changed the cans over. When? And was it the person who takes sugar in coffee, or someone else who didn't need to show himself at all?'

'To make Per go to the barn.'

'Or merely to make him go away for a moment. You say things had been moved about in the car. Has anyone searched the tent too, do you think?'

I looked around and it was clear there was little enough to turn over: the boxes we used as seats, the lamp on its bracket, some sweaters. Per's sleeping-bag spread open along one side, the things left ready for coffee outside. They looked the same as when I'd looked them over with the first policeman. I shook my head.

'We have done enough here,' Andreas said quietly. 'Let us go back inside.'

Our entry by the kitchen door coincided with a car drawing up outside the front of the farm. 'A hire car from Iraklion,' Andreas whispered and we crept upstairs before Kyria Kostantinou could usher the newcomers in.

There were two of them, the first a man of medium height, solid and muscular, with a hard, flat face, wide-spaced eyes and well-marked brows. His chin was square with a cleft in it that made a blue shadow. His cropped hair fitted close to his weathered skin like a bristly black cap. He looked physically powerful, with an impression of watchful stillness. Not relaxed, but having a controlled tautness, like some spring-loaded gadget that flies into instant action at a touch. It was remarkable how vividly and instantly I was aware of him, and I knew he was someone who made things happen, whose impact couldn't be disregarded.

The other was a woman, tall and distinguished, with an athletic, confident stride. She could have been a model or a dramatic actress. I couldn't make out her features as she backed on to the light, but when she spoke I recognized her as the woman I'd dimly seen on the stairs of the hotel at Timbaki.

'Per's mother,' I whispered to Andreas as we watched from the landing.

Mrs Wennberg did all the talking although I didn't catch the words. Both Kostantinous stood dumbly and listened, then there was a general move towards the door again. They all went out by the front and round the side of the house to the yard.

'What do you suppose—?'

'Shh!' Andreas ordered. He drew me into his room which overlooked the rear. The two visitors were being shown the tent, the car, the blasted corner of the blackened stone barn. I shivered, finding it gruesome, but Andreas seemed to understand. 'Sometimes,' he said, 'it is the only way to make yourself accept something. To go and see, and then suffer.'

Mrs Wennberg gave no outer sign of suffering, but as I

61

watched I began to feel that perhaps the man wasn't uniquely under tight control. The woman's poise was surely overdone, flamboyant display to cover something else. Distress? She had confronted me with arrant resentment, and now the scene of Per's death with defiance. Sometime or other the hard exterior would crack. So much passion under too tight a rein could be dangerous to her.

The man was different. He stood and looked. Then he approached nearer and without touching examined each detail of the scene, head tilted, as if he were a surveyor making a valuation. Or an investigator assessing a crime?

What would a man like that make of my part in the tragedy? Would he write me off as a fool or a villain? Or jump to the same conclusion as Per's father?

The woman had gone up to the entrance to the tent and bent now to pick up an object from on top of the sleeping-bag. She pulled it close to her and began to back out. Per's sweater which he wore at night, purplish with a pattern of two white stags across the front.

I thought she was going to bury her face in it, but suddenly she went rigid and called out shrilly, 'Hooper! Mr Hooper, take me home!'

Home must be Stockholm, or some place in England where she'd been raised as a child. Diplomats' wives don't have any easy haven to run back to. All she had now was the little hotel at Timbaki, an anonymous room. Her cry was an instinctive plea for security.

I think that was the moment I began to mourn Per, because of the awful, irreversible *waste*, and the pain that must fill the space he left empty.

As I stood at the open window transfixed, the man below looked up and saw me. Neither of us moved for some seconds, and then he slowly went across to the woman and led her away, clamping a hand on her upper arm as if she was being arrested.

The two visitors left without asking for me, but they had brought a note. It was from Per's father and quite different from the frigid earlier one. He hoped that I would allow him an opportunity to apologize for his unpardonable

62

foolishness. Per's family would be honoured if I would spend the evening with them.

'Andreas, I must,' I told him, facing up to the stubborn set of his jaw. I had never seen him look so determined. Even his gold-rimmed spectacles gave off an angry glint.

'You will regret it.'

'I can't go running away and leaving so much unsaid. They misjudged me at first, but they misjudged Per too. I can at least put that right, reassure them that everything was all right between us.' But it hadn't been, of course. I'd been on the brink of walking out on him. Only the practical considerations of transport and finances had prevented it earlier. Although I'd not said as much to Andreas he'd picked up the atmosphere. Now, as I assured him of the opposite, he sensed my dishonesty and possibly resented my claim to have been happy with the other man. It was obvious to us both that between Andreas and me some genuine fondness was growing, but it wasn't so far advanced that either would start giving in on a matter of principle.

'I will drive you, then,' he said bleakly. I thanked him and felt guilty. He should be back at work with his X-rays and splints, not acting chauffeur to me.

'Tomorrow,' I reminded him, 'we go back to Iraklion.'

He looked at me, fiercely doubting. 'We shall see.'

I spent the rest of the afternoon working out that Per had left me badly out of pocket. Basic foodstuffs are cheap enough on Crete, and our total supplies barely topped fifteen pounds in value. The Volvo had been hired in his name, no concern of mine, though I could use it till its time ran out. My driving licence was very new, but I'd practised on the car and had the hang of it. As an alternative, once back in Iraklion I could exchange it for a more economical model. Either way it meant stretching my remaining travellers' cheques or drawing on my home account. Sharing with Per, we'd had too many moments of living up to a ritzy standard.

Mr Wennberg's invitation had mentioned no specific time. I decided to arrive about seven, reckoning that when they saw I had a friend to drive me he'd be welcomed too. There would be a meal of some sort to help iron out any awkwardness; they would ask a few discreet questions about our holiday; I'd supply answers; we'd part on civil terms.

It wasn't to be quite like that.

'No,' Andreas said firmly when I expected him to follow me in. 'I shall go back to the farm. When you are ready to leave, phone.'

I walked in through the open door of the hotel to find a hand-written card propped up on the reception desk. It said 'Shut' in four languages, except English which broke the news more gently with 'No Vacancies'. It brought back to me the lost world of South Coast landladies, sand between my childish toes, bucket and spade, a softer kind of sunshine.

The plump little Greek lady who popped her head out of the office nodded to me. 'Miss Wes'bry? You are expected.' She saw me glance again at the card and explained quickly, 'Mr Wennberg takes all the rooms, for three days.'

Of course, a diplomat. How civilized: the closed family front, private grief. No foreign journalists intruding by bar or dining-room.

'They are upstairs.'

The room I was shown into looked westward, and evening sunlight entered in horizontal slices through venetian blinds. A tallish, lean woman stood by the central table fingering the embroidery of its cloth. She looked up with bright eyes of a quite startling blue and put a hand to her breast.

'Mrs Wennberg?'

'Oh, it's Vanessa you want. I'm her sister, Alison Markham. And you must be Per's friend. I'm so pleased to meet you, my dear.' She came stiffly forward, almost limping. Certainly not the athletic lope of Per's mother, but there was a marked similarity which had deceived me for an instant.

I was aware of someone coming up behind me and turned to find the other sister there. I felt at a disadvantage between them, particularly as Mrs Wennberg made no welcoming gesture, just looked at me blankly.

'I can see the family likeness,' I said, to fill the silence. It was true. They had the same tall, lean frame although Per's aunt was angular and a little twisted. (Later I was to learn that she had suffered for years from arthritis which threatened to cripple her.) Their eyes were equally blue, their hair straight, fine and buttermilk blonde. Where Vanessa's was stylishly cut and flicked upwards to enhance the angles of her tanned, sportswoman's face, Alison wore hers long and softly swathed into a vertical roll behind her head. The real difference lay in the ravages of time.

'Yes,' Miss Markham said, uncannily guessing my thoughts, 'I am the elder. By how much do you think?'

It would be fifteen years at least. I ventured to suggest eight, to the great delight of Miss Markham who clapped her hands like a child. 'You mean to be tactful, child, but you are a long way out. Eight minutes, not years, is nearer. Vanessa and I are twins. But—' and she flicked her sister a glance of calculated derision—'the importance lies not in the extent but in the fact of seniority. The fact that I am the elder, by however slim a margin.'

There was some special significance here that I missed completely. Mrs Wennberg had flushed with anger at the taunt which was harmless enough in its wording. 'Sven is still out,' she said to a point six inches above my head. 'I shall wait for him in my room.'

'Let us go down to the garden then, you and I,' Miss Markham said comfortably. I followed the stiffly moving woman downstairs and out on the rear terrace. We walked slowly, Miss Markham pausing after every few steps to smile around as if admiring the view. It was a technique, I realized, to cover up her disability. I made the expected remarks about the oleanders which had been allowed almost to fill the little space that wasn't beaten pathway, but I didn't get a great response. She was waiting for me to launch out on some more personal topic and I didn't feel ready.

'I do like the Cretans, don't you?' I offered. 'They're so simple and direct.'

She laughed, like a short bark. 'Direct? They can be devious in the extreme, like all peasants. At least, they are on Rhodes where I live, so I suppose that here they go on much the same. No, their simplicity lies in their distinction between good and evil. They do recognize a bad soul when they meet one.' She stood leaning on an ebony stick which she'd collected from beside the terrace door, and seemed lost in private thoughts. That they were unpleasant ones was clear from the harassed lines which now transformed the formerly gentle face. 'We city-bred people from the North have fudged the outlines, made too many compromises with the Devil.'

She startled me. The last two words came out with such baleful force. The woman had not used the term figuratively. It was as though devils and angels were her familiars. Now, with the white face distorted in a rictus of pain, she looked like a witch. Hadn't Per once spoken of an 'eccentric aunt', how his family found her a pain? And that she was pensioned off to stay away from them, on a Greek island?

'Have you been long on Rhodes?' I asked hurriedly, to restore normality.

Miss Markham's mind seemed to be swimming wearily back. After a short silence she looked at me vaguely. 'On Rhodes? Oh, years and years. The climate suits me there. In England I could scarcely get about at all, with arthritis. I have a villa outside Lindos, far enough out to avoid the holiday crowds. And a car. When I need to travel Theo drives me. His wife is a superlative cook. I have taught her enough French and Italian for her to master the classical recipes. She could make a fortune in an Athens hotel but she was born on Rhodes and has no wish ever to leave it. Of course, I pay her relatively.'

Relative to her being a superlative cook or a rooted islander, I wondered. Miss Markham was obviously a well-heeled lady, wore fantastic clothes, very Mayfair Establishment. Some pension the Wennbergs must pay her! *If* it was true, as Per said, that they financed the lady to keep her distance. But if they did, why permit her coming now, on such a devastating occasion? Was Per's violent end to break down family barriers at last?

'I don't suppose you have seen your sister for some time?' I asked curiously.

'Vanessa?' Unreadable emotion passed over the patrician features. 'Not since the other funeral, no.'

'Oh, I'm so sorry.' I was appalled at having resurrected past miseries to double with the present. But I needn't have worried. Miss Markham smiled calmly. 'And that,' she said, nodding, 'was five years, three months and two days ago.'

She spoke with a special sort of satisfied wonder, shook out the folds of her full skirt and started walking on again. When I caught up with her she put a hand through my arm and gently squeezed it. 'You're a kind girl. Tell me, my dear, were you very fond of my nephew? Is it unbearably sad for you that he's gone?'

The switch of subject was too sudden. I couldn't reply. Would I ever know quite what Per had meant to me? And if I did, how could I ever express it in words to this socially correct, obviously maiden English aunt? 'I hadn't known him very long,' I admitted.

'You were fortunate,' said Miss Markham simply. 'In time either you would have discovered what he was and gone your own way, or he would have broken your heart and gone his. Per was his own awful creation, you know. Whatever it pleased him to do was, to his mind, entirely justified. What he became—what befell him—was all of his own making too. We shall find he called down his own death, I am sure.'

Forthrightly and without any hint of pity she had dealt with his case and dismissed him. Yet she didn't appear to be a heartless woman. She turned to me now and her blue eyes softened. 'We must try and make it up to you, my dear. You must not be allowed to suffer because of him.'

Mrs Wennberg appeared on the balcony above the terrace. 'My husband has arrived,' she called down, 'and would like to speak with you, Miss Westbury.'

'Then I shall stay here for a while,' said Miss Markham, planting herself firmly on the stump of an old pine. 'My brother-in-law is a deeply injured man, and suffering has made him cynical. But he is not bitter. You must not think that.'

I went up to see him for the second time, with a distinct feeling that the scene had been specially laid on; his absence, his wife's silence, the aunt's homily in the garden. To what purpose? I didn't care much for the idea of being manipulated.

CHAPTER 7

On the landing I paused while a man emerged from the sitting-room. He stood back to allow me in. It was the one who had driven Per's mother out to the farm. He showed no sign of recognition, passing out wooden-faced. Sven Wennberg turned from the window and came forward to greet me. This evening he looked older. For some reason I connected this with the man Hooper's visit. 'Miss Westbury, thank you for giving me this opportunity to make amends. I must apologize to you.'

He looked at me with troubled eyes from a face so like Per's that my heart seemed to turn inside me. So I did love Per a little, I thought with relief. Maybe I really did.

I let him place a chair for me and refused the offer of a drink. He remained on his feet, uncertain how to begin 'I made,' he said at last, 'an unpardonable assumption at our previous meeting. It was—insulting. My only excuse, however insufficient, is that of apparent precedent.'

He had been staring at the backs of his long, fine hands as he leaned over a small desk. Now he swung a chair round to face me and sat, fixing his disconcerting eyes on mine. They were haunted, empty of hope. 'As I told you, I knew my son very well, had few illusions left about him. Per was accustomed to take what he fancied. When he could not pay for it he expected someone else to pick up the bill. It was not necessarily a matter of money, you understand. Mistakes, indiscretions which could not be concealed, I had to deal with. It has always been so. And since he entered the Foreign Service for our country I have known little peace of mind, for fear what scandal he would next bring down on us.'

'But wasn't it your wish that he followed you in your

profession?' I asked, startled. 'I understood from him that it was a family tradition.

'We have a tradition of service.' His lips twisted as he controlled his emotion. 'A tradition which his mother and some of my less informed colleagues made capital of to overcome my opposition. Unfortunately, as it proved; because we have high standards in the Service which it was not in Per's ability to meet.'

He was physically reckless,' I granted, 'but careful to avoid personal clashes—'

'Becoming more adept at covering his tracks,' Wennberg corrected me, 'except that with women he was sometimes rashly blind to the outcome of his impetuous fancies. As a result, demands have been made on him, threats even. Twice before I have been obliged to rescue him from adventuresses.'

It sounded so old-world, as though girls hadn't accepted that they were at least as responsible as men for their own actions. But 'adventuress' might well be an acceptable myth in a society where any breath of scandal could bring instant disgrace. And I'd thought the Swedes such a sexually liberated nation! Poor Per, to have been raised against such an unbounded background and then to have Victorian restrictions imposed as career regulations. There were all the ingredients for disaster in the situation: the novice diplomat a victim of his own libido and of the unscrupulous wiles of blackmailing trollops. But it still sounded like melodrama to me.

I looked levelly back at Per's father. 'And you thought I was like that. But I was fond of him, dazzled. Swept off my feet.' It was important that he should believe me.

'I understand now. He had developed a finer appreciation of women than I knew. I insulted you. I do apologize, abjectly.'

'There's no need. I was angry only for a moment. It's over. And you've lost your son, which is terrible for you. I keep asking myself if there was anything I did which made it more likely to happen. And I don't know. Per had stored the burner fuel himself in the barn, because it was cool, and the farmer kept his own there, the big drums of gas. And I had fitted a new can on the burner the evening before. It hadn't been used at all. You can always tell from the weight. I can't understand how it came to be empty. I threw the old can away *before* I went for the new one, so there was no accidental mix-up.'

'They could have been exchanged.'

I stared at him. So already he had considered the possibility. 'Who?' I whispered.

'Someone who knew that to get a new can Per must go again to the barn. Someone who had already arranged some kind of bomb there.'

I could feel my own heartbeat up in my throat. 'You do really believe it was deliberate. *Per murdered*. In cold blood.'

'With premeditation, yes.' He sat with his head sunk on his chest. 'It suggests a long-held hate, don't you think?'

'But he'd been on Crete only eight days. His first visit, he told me. And I was the only person who'd been with him for any time at all. We met the second evening after he arrived. You don't imagine that *I*—?'

'No, no. I am sure of that.'

'But it could have been an accident?' I pleaded, although I'd been the first to voice suspicion to him, passing my reasons off as intuition. 'Even if the cans were switched, for a joke or as petty theft, couldn't the gas have leaked accidentally in the barn?'

'But why should it explode instantly as Per entered the barn? Someone had to engineer that. When the debris has been carefully sifted we will know how it was done.'

'Perhaps he was smoking. When he relaxed he used to light up one of those thin *cigarillos*.' It seemed that the police hadn't released the *post mortem* findings to Sven yet. Andreas had read them through as a privileged person, being a doctor with some forensic experience.

'Smoking, he went for fuel?' For the first time Wennberg sounded foreign. His brows flickered up and then met in a frown of denial. 'Even for Per that is too stupid.'

'He wasn't stupid, no. But he was a little stingy. He would drop his *cigarillo* and put a heel on it if it was half smoked, but not if he'd only just lit up. He must have started on one when he'd fetched the water for coffee, then found the gas can empty—which I'd said I'd renewed. He'd have been furious with me, and that made him overlook—'

I stopped suddenly, and despite myself my eyes brimmed with tears. '*He died angry with me!*'

Immediately Wennberg was out of his chair, his hands on my shoulders. 'Dear child, what does it matter? He was mistaken. And why is the final moment to cancel out any happiness you had given him before? I have been clumsy and insensitive, when I meant only to make amends. Some diplomat, you will be thinking!' He drew back and nodded encouragement. 'That's better, you have a lovely smile.

'Listen, I will ask my sister-in-law to come and you shall comfort each other. Or go for another little walk with her round the garden. You will find she has a great gift for soothing injuries, like no one else can. Then after a while we will all meet for dinner.'

'I'll go and find her myself,' I offered. 'I'm all right, truly, and I do thank you for seeing me again. It can't have been easy.'

I found Miss Markham sitting on the terrace. There was no sign of her sister. 'Would you care for another turn round the garden?' I asked, smiling because it sounded like something out of Jane Austen. We had already exhausted the delights of the little hotel's oleander alleys and a packed earth square of sparse shrubs and pecking chicken. 'Your brother-in-law suggested we might comfort each other,' I excused myself.

She gave a little lopsided smile while her eyebrows managed still to look bemused. 'Have you noticed, Siân, how we women are expected to be obliging? Men aren't, for the most part, and then only for a consideration.' She put on her hat which lay on the table and took my arm.

We strolled in silence a while before I suggested, 'Isn't the old order changing? Aren't modern women withholding the favours?'

'M'm. Do you think the trend will last? Perhaps it's no more than a phase while they jostle for more notice. Poor dears, so confused. They haven't even found a satisfactory name to go under. "Feminists": it makes them sound soft and fluffy. "Femalists" is suitably harsh, but I think it's their genetic function they so resent, although some seem quite keen on bearing children. It is complete relationships they can't seem to cope with. Relationships can, of course, be very complicated.'

'It's different here on Crete,' I offered, relieved for the moment to be spared discussion of the tragedy that hung so blackly over us. 'Their family life is positively Victorian, with women hovering respectfully in the background. But they have enormous influence over their individual men, I think.'

'Real women always had, my hear. My grandmother was a fragile wisp, but she invariably gained any point she put her mind to.'

'Wicked wiles,' I said and laughed.

'Why not? A little more guile in my dealings when I was your age and I might have spared us all this sad business. So much would have come out differently.'

I waited, puzzled, but Miss Markham's mood had changed; her face had taken on the ravaged look again. She moved her lips silently, but I hadn't Manolis's skill to read what she said.

How could anything she did or didn't do at my age make any difference to the tragedy of Per's death? She was surely being fanciful. Did she perhaps blame Per's lifestyle on Vanessa's marriage to Sven? And her own failure to prevent it? Certainly, with a different husband Vanessa would have had a different son, and he a different upbringing. Was that what Miss Markham meant? But with only eight minutes' seniority she could scarcely have hoped to put pressure on her sister once Vanessa had made up her mind about the man she loved. If she loved him.

'What were you like at my age?' I couldn't help asking.

'You are—what, nineteen?'

'I was twenty at Easter.'

'Nineteen fifty-six,' Alison Markham said thoughtfully, staring into the distance. But that made her only fifty-one!

She looked at least ten years older. Vanessa, on the other hand, looked younger.

'You must have heard about the Suez fiasco,' she said, turning back to me. 'It didn't last long but it was unpleasant at the time. I was caught in Egypt, with an older woman companion, when being British wasn't the safest thing to be. I had met Sven at a reception at the Swedish Embassy and he took us under his wing. A few months later he visited us in Cumberland. My brother was alive then, so there was no likelihood of my inheriting the estate. Sven and I became engaged just a few days before Christmas.'

Sven! Sven had been engaged to marry *Alison*!

She gave me the quick, bright smile of someone who glosses over an inescapable sorrow. 'You asked what I was like then. A little like you. Less worldly-wise than I imagined, and incurably honest. When so much happened at once I needed time to adjust. It happened that my father and my only brother died within six weeks of each other, Douglas out hunting. He hadn't married, and my father had left an awkward will, a trust so that everything went to the eldest child, and then the eldest child of that beneficiary or, failing one, to the next child, and the eldest issue of the next child and so on. Because he stipulated a stay of three months before the trust should become effective, I was the sole first beneficiary.

'As I said, too much happened at once, and I was quite overcome. The only way I could endure was to withdraw into my shell. I was incurably responsible, so I couldn't shrug off what I saw as a path destiny had forced me into. Our family home is an ancient one, and so many people's lives are bound up with it. People I had known and respected from childhood up. I couldn't hand everything over to an agent and go with Sven to his new posting in Teheran as he wanted. So I asked him to release me from our engagement, which reluctantly he did. I believed he understood that I meant it merely to give me time, and to leave him free while I regained my stability. I knew I loved him more than anything, but I was too immature to go selfishly for what I wanted.'

And Sven had married her sister! How ironic. All because of that eight minutes' difference which made Alison the one to inherit. Small wonder that there were undercurrents when the sisters came face to face. How could Sven bear to be in the centre of such explosive material? And he had sent me to Alison for comfort, not to his wife. It was Alison he said had this very special gift of understanding. What tragic secrets were concealed by this family of surface harmony.

She was watching me with her sad little smile. 'So you see what I mean about guile? When I saw what was happening it was in my power then to take back what was being stolen from me, and by the same means. But I was too proud.'

I shook my head, hardly believing. 'I was sent down here,' I said, 'so that we could comfort each other. And instead I've made you go over all this unhappy time again.'

'Strangely enough, it has comforted me. Just to talk of it. I have never confided it before. There is something about you, Siân, that made me want you to know. I hope it hasn't depressed you.'

I shook my head again, vigorously. 'No, it helps.' It had done, if only because I knew someone had been through a worse experience than mine.

'Shall we go and tidy ourselves for dinner?' Miss Markham asked. 'Perhaps you would like to borrow my shower?'

So we went up to her room and she admired the ivory cheesecloth dress I had on, which I could truthfully say Per had bought for me and Phyllia had embroidered. Which meant that I told her about the young Cypriot refugee girl who was going to spend the winter in London with her sister, and how I'd been inveigled into keeping an eye on her. She laughed and we went on to swapping experiences we'd had with Greek islanders, calling to each other between dressing-table and shower-room. By the time we were ready for the rest of the company we were in a much happier mood.

The meal, served by the hotel-keeper himself, was delicious, and convinced me that Sven Wennberg had given as much attention to the menu as he did to orchestrating the conversation. Each dish was first brought to him for

74

approval before serving, while his wife showed total indifference.

It wasn't an easy group for him to dovetail, or did I notice it more because of the background I'd just been made aware of? We were three badly matched women, my age setting me rather apart, and we didn't always behave as well as he expected of us. If he diverted one away from what seemed like dangerous ground, another was likely to start off at once on a tangent towards other emotional minefields. I didn't understand many of the references and so I was at risk of making unintentional gaffes. With the other two I was almost sure the lapses were sometimes deliberate and aimed in each other's direction. The Swedish diplomat needed all his professional skills.

Gradually I began to appreciate the surface pattern, its overall design being to convince me of a liberal-minded family of varying interests drawn together by grief at loss of one of their number. The jagged edges occurred because of their vastly different attitudes towards the dead Per which, if Sven could pull it off, were to be submerged in deference to what they supposed my own attitude to be. If I had rather overdone my fondness for Per I didn't feel so guilty now, because all round the table hypocrisy was the name of the game.

To begin with they were fishing, and I was wary what I permitted on their hooks. I talked of the practicalities of the shared tour with Per, explained the partnership arrangements, and even extracted approval for taking over the remaining supplies. I was crisply offhand about finances and we agreed a fair amount of cash compensation without my feeling beholden for charity.

When that was cleared without embarrassment I felt relaxed enough to talk about my flower paintings.

'Such enthusiasm,' Mrs Wennberg marvelled daintily, as though anything of the sort denoted a coarse nature.

'Yes,' agreed Alison amiably. 'Like Roland's for animals.'

'Roland?' I questioned, falling right in the pit.

There was a barbed silence. Then Sven Wennberg looked up from his plate. 'Roland was Per's older brother.' He spoke gently, as though the question was quite acceptable, but he had paused too long first. I couldn't miss the tense he'd used.

'He took a B.Sc. in Zoology,' Miss Markham said proudly. 'And then he went to work in a bird sanctuary in Gloucestershire until—' Her brightness faltered.

Wennberg moved in on his cue more promptly this time. 'Roland died tragically in a fire, just over five years ago,' he said.

Tragically. In a fire. A violent death, like Per's. Hadn't Miss Markham mentioned another funeral five years three months and two days before?

My throat dried up and I rushed at my wine, spilling some as my hand shook. Mrs Wennberg let out her pent breath in a hiss. She leaned over the table, glaring at her sister. It looked for a moment as though the two would break into open warfare, but help came from an unlikely source. The hotel-keeper reappeared at the door, anxiously hovering. There was, he said, a representative of the Prefecture Police below who wished to speak to the family and Miss Wes'bry.

'All of us?' Per's mother queried sharply.

'So he say. Do I say him wait?'

Sven dabbed at his mouth with a napkin, smoothing the Niven moustache. 'I think it would be more civil to invite him up, if that meets with everyone's approval. Yes, and another bottle of the same wine.'

'With a glass for the Captain?'

'Naturally with a glass for the Captain.'

The uniformed man who came in, cap under arm, gave the impression of being hewn from a solid block of grainy brown wood, and without great care paid to detail. Neckless, he moved all of a piece, and either pivoted his whole body as he regarded each of us in turn or, once seated, moved little more than his eyes in their slots. He wouldn't have been much good, I felt, in a physical chase, the sort a TV police series specializes in, so perhaps he was deskbound and that accounted for the solidity.

Sven Wennberg, however, hadn't been equally distracted

76

by the man's physique and was leaning forward intent on what he had to say. I brought my mind to it rather late and so missed the opening sentences. It appeared that he was here for a double purpose, to inform us of certain findings, and as a result of them to ask our assurance that we would stay in the locality until given official permission to leave.

'But I don't understand,' Mrs Wennberg said on a rising note of hysteria. 'What has this to do with us? We have come to make arrangements for transport of the—the—'

Sven's face had tightened into a rigid mask. 'The circumstances have changed,' he said tersely. 'It is now a question of a murder investigation. That is what he meant by the details of the gas leaks. That so many drums should become faulty at once is no coincidence. Am I correct, Captain?'

The policeman blinked assent. 'That is so.'

'And we are to be kept *here*?' Per's mother was enraged.

'We require that you stay until certain inquiries are complete,' the Captain said, swivelling his eyes. 'And, Miss Westbury, it will not be possible to have you continue at the farm. Please find another place.'

'She must come here,' Miss Markham said quickly.

'But I'm going to Iraklion tomorrow,' I protested, 'then westward, as soon as I've hired a car. I have to cover the whole island.'

'No,' the policeman stonewalled. 'In a few days, then we say okay, you can go.'

'We shall be very happy to have you stay here as our guest,' Sven Wennberg said with finality. 'We shall not be a nuisance to you. In fact we can probably help you with transport.' He turned to the policeman. 'Will you show us on a map how far you think we may reasonably move from the hotel by day?'

And so it stood. I rang Andreas at the end of our meal, not to ask for a lift back but to explain the change of plan. He sounded crestfallen and had obviously heard the news before we did. 'I have to leave the farm too. They are looking for clues all over the house and grounds. God knows what they expect to find.'

'Have they been through my things?'

77

'I am sorry. Yes. I objected, but—' I could imagine his hopeless expression as he shrugged. 'Siân, they insist the Volvo is examined further. I will bring your luggage, the food boxes, everything, to you now at Timbaki. I have repacked them in my car. It is best, I think.'

'Thank you, Andreas. What about you?'

'I must go back to Iraklion tomorrow morning as planned. They need me at the hospital.'

'I'm glad the police haven't restricted you too.'

'That is because I have an alibi, and the Medical Superintendent confirms it.'

'You mean they questioned you? That's ridiculous!'

He laughed quietly. 'I could have killed your lover to get you, they think. We are a primitive people, after all. Officials, pah! They just want to look busy.'

I went back to the sitting-room where they were having coffee. 'Dr Vassilakis is bringing my baggage across,' I said briefly.

'Vassilakis?' Miss Markham queried.

Sven Wennberg barely looked up from the tray of liqueurs he was examining. 'Is that the doctor who helped you after Vai?' His mind seemed partly elsewhere.

'Yes, he's been very kind.' I left it at that although both women were looking at me expectantly. It seemed that only Sven had heard of my near-drowning experience. And that was curious in itself. Who could have told him? Didn't it mean he'd had it from Per or Andreas himself?

'Have you ever met Dr Vassilakis?' I asked, curious.

His mind switched itself on properly again. 'No, but I look forward to it.'

Funny. Funny-odd. If when Andreas arrived he greeted the Swede as a stranger it must mean that Per and his father had been in touch much more recently than Sven had given us to think. He had certainly mentioned, with some bitterness, that he'd not seen Per since Christmas, nor heard from him for several months.

And yet he knew about Vai.

CHAPTER 8

Inevitably, I suppose, Andreas was invited to stay overnight in one of the empty rooms commandeered by the
Wennbergs. Before accepting he gave me a rapid, inquiring
glance. I nodded my agreement and even then he hesitated,
slow to accept a favour but eventually opting for extended
time to issue me nanny-like warnings.

He was decidedly on edge since meeting Per's family. It
was partly, I was sure, because he had picked up the phoney
atmosphere and felt the strong undertow.

Before we retired for the night he brought my gear up
and stacked it in a corner of my room. I was a bit offhand
with him because although I could see where things were
heading between us I was uncomfortable, being pushed into
too many roles all at once. I couldn't take it if he came too
close. I wasn't ready, with all this horror hanging over me.
The Per connection and its sudden severance had rocked
me back on my heels. I had a horror of rebound. More and
more I wanted to get free, stand on my own two feet (or,
even better, sit on my own four wheels), take the odd risk
alone.

At the same time I was scared. I needed somebody, almost
anybody. And that wasn't fair to Andreas, who wasn't just
anybody. He was special. We should have had a scene of
our own. In another time and another place I knew it could
have been wonderful. As it stood, his being seven or eight
years older than me, and a doctor, he might, if I wasn't
careful, slide into being a father-figure. It would be shaming
if he saw me that way. To escape that I'd turn my back on
him and hang on to Sven Wennberg who was already
handing out the 'dear child' treatment.

I waited awkwardly for Andreas to leave, but he had
something on his mind and was in no hurry. He laid my
sketching-block carefully on top of a suitcase. His face was
grave. 'I looked at your flower paintings,' he confessed.

'They're very sensitive. I'm sure they'll be a success.'

'Thank you, Andreas.'

'But I wondered—'

'Yes?'

'About the other two sketches. The dead man. This was the one you told me of, at Kato Zakros?'

I had forgotten. Not the incident—that was unforgettable —but forgotten how I'd purged my shock by drawing. Settling down to sketch the *Anacamptis*, I'd found my pencil tracing out the guesome scene on the mountainside, and then the dead, staring face. Strangely relieved, I'd pushed the loose pages into the back of the block, where anyone might come across them later. Now I had to explain my actions to Andreas, that they were drawings from memory. I hadn't settled down cosily at a death scene to commit it to paper.

'Of course it's the same dead man,' I agreed wretchedly. 'The only one I've seen, ever.' Andreas listened intently, asking no questions but seeming, if anything, more disturbed than ever as the details came out.

'Such awful things have been happening lately,' I ended lamely.

'Round you, yes. I wish you could go home right now. It would be sad for me not to see you any more, but you would be safer. These people are not good for you.'

So already he was deciding what I should and should not do. Part of me had also decided I wanted to get up and go, but I wasn't having him make my decisions. I shrugged, put on a sophisticated face. 'They intrigue me. I get very curious the more I find out about them. Per must have had a strange upbringing between them all.' Despite my pretence of detachment, I shivered, covering it up by asking brightly, 'What do you make of Sven?'

'I make nothing of him.' Abruptly Andreas had reached the limits of his patience. 'I do not know why you must be involved with these people.' He laid a proprietary hand on mine.

I pulled my hand away. 'These people, as you call them, are Per's family, and I was his friend, even if briefly. I can't

80

move off as though they had the plague. Who among them is so dangerous, do you think? They weren't here when Per was killed. Do you suspect the Wennbergs of doing away with their own son? They would need long arms to do it from Rome! Or the aunt—yes, Per did warn me she was crazy and had to be locked away once. I suppose you think she flew over from Rhodes to plant a bomb or something?' I was tired and infected with Andreas's impatience. It made my voice come out loud and scornful. 'You've met her. You're a doctor. Do you think she's mad?'

'I'm no psychiatrist.' He shrugged, neutral again. 'Of course, certain forms of madness can conceal themselves for long periods, but—not, I think, in her case. She *was* in hospital for some time, a few years ago. She has just been telling me about it, because I was curious enough to ask questions about her stiffness. She was quite frank. She is used to discussions with doctors.'

So in his eyes Alison Markham was as sweet as she seemed. And yet, face to face with Vanessa, she could show a dangerous edge. I made a face. 'Then I guess what Per said was all lies. He made out too that his family paid her to stay at a distance, but *she* turns out to be the wealthy one. It seems that Alison got the inheritance and Vanessa settled for Alison's fiancé.'

I stopped suddenly. Had it really been so crude—tit for tat? Simple sisterly spite, and not actual rivalry in love? Had the sisters only been scoring off each other? Doing a *Dynasty*? And were still hard at it! How far would they be prepared to go? If Alison had really been borderline insane as Per said—

Now I was back to accepting the wildest improbabilities. And fears. It didn't promise me a quiet night. Andreas caught the drift of my mind and comforted me in his arms. He pushed up his gold-rimmed spectacles into his hair before kissing me. 'Shall I stay with you tonight?'

'Better not. I'll be all right.' Perhaps he guessed I wasn't ready for what must have followed if he'd stayed.

*

It was just as well in the event that I refused his offer, because the minor drama played out overnight could have been aimed at demolishing my credibility.

As it was, Andreas crushed me to his barrel chest, contented himself with kissing me warmly on forehead and lips, then whispered, 'Fill your mind with pleasant thoughts,' before slipping away.

A little before eight next morning someone knocked lightly on my door. I had just finished dressing. When I called out, 'Come in,' Miss Markham appeared with a cup of coffee. 'Oh, you're up. Did you sleep well, my dear?'

'Like a log. I must have been more tired than I knew.'

'So you missed our little excitement.'

'Why, what happened?'

'We were awakened about one-twenty by Vanessa, shouting hysterically in the passage and hammering on a door. Not mine, needless to say. She had swallowed an overdose of sleeping pills, or so she claimed, and then suddenly recovered her will to live.' Miss Markham waved a hand airily. There was no hint of sympathy for her sister. She smiled wryly as she went on: 'So Vanessa called on your friend Dr Vassilakis, who promptly made her vomit them up. Not quite the high-powered melodrama she'd intended. You see, she found him asleep in his own room. Quite alone. Naturally.' And Miss Markham laughed a genteel, social laugh while her eyes danced with mischief. I couldn't possibly miss her meaning.

'How is she now?' I asked.

'Barely discomfited. Vanessa is as tough as the proverbial old boot. And quite conscienceless.'

'And Mr Wennberg?'

Alison's face grew sombre. 'What do you expect? It can only distress him further.'

Yes, awful for him, whether his wife had seriously meant to kill herself or not. It wasn't easy to guess how much sympathy there was between them, nor how unstable Vanessa would be in normal circumstances. But were there any normal circumstances in that family? The more I was with them the more they seemed some monstrous Gothic horror presented under respectable covers.

'I'm going for my little totter now,' Miss Markham said, rising from the corner of my bed where she had perched. 'It's a self-prescribed remedy. Not quite "every hour on the hour" but something akin. Your friend has just gone down to breakfast. The others are staying in their rooms. That is really what I came to tell you. Let me pour that coffee away. You will find some hotter and fresher in the dining-room.'

Whatever the truth about her mental health, Miss Markham was certainly shrewd and derived a lot of sardonic amusement from observing the human scene. She often spoke as if detached from it, but I believed it was a defensive technique. The suffering her face showed wasn't all physical. And I wondered how deep the injury had gone. She and her sister seemed to be playing the same cruel game. The game, which she regretted not playing when my age, was alive and well and thriving on Crete.

Andreas scanned my face as I came in, started to rise and let me force him down with a spanking kiss on his forehead. 'I heard about your night visitor,' I said briskly. 'I'm quite sure professional etiquette forbids your mentioning it.'

'Quite,' he said with overdone niceness, and he grinned wide enough to split any less rugged face. He nodded towards my plate which was covered by a square envelope addressed to me in cramped handwriting. 'Will you be as secretive over that?'

I opened it and read quickly through. It was from Miss Markham. I'd forgotten her words about 'making it up' to me over the loss of Per, but now the scene rushed back. Apparently she too wanted to buy me off with money, but hers was so different from the way Sven Wennberg had offered that I ended moved. The cheque, which I unfolded first, was enormous enough to anger me—partly, I suppose, at the suggestion that money can cancel out grief, but also against myself for not being able to grieve more.

What I felt *for* Per was still indefinite. What I felt *about* him was a mixture of horror, shock and a sense of mutilation. Our relationship had begun for our common convenience, and then there had been an almost instant sexual kindling. Wildfire for me. For him, as I knew him now, it must have been familiar, perhaps commonplace. It would have burned out before long, leaving him quite unchanged. That seemed incredible to me, when I'd been through the furnace. First love was wonderful, was abysmal, was chaos. And perhaps what at last I wept for now was the lost experience and not the man who had given it.

It was in this numb state of amputation that I began to re-read Alison's letter. It made my eyes blur with tears. She wrote of loss of life and loss of love, not academically but as if she had known and suffered every step of the doleful way.

Silently I pushed the letter and cheque across to Andreas. How, I asked him when he'd read it, was I to refuse the offer without wounding this sad woman further?

He shook his head. 'You really do not need the money?'

'I have a reasonable allowance from my father, and anyway I hope soon to be independent now I'm through college. I'd never want to be as rich as Miss Markham must be.'

'You could thank her and explain this. Then suggest a suitable way to spend some of her money—as a memorial perhaps. It may help her grief, to feel she has made a costly gesture.'

Yes, Miss Markham was probably old-fashioned enough to find some form of memorial acceptable: a statue, a church window, or a public park. Perhaps even some endowment of learning. I could go out to her now in the garden where she was waiting and put it to her.

When I tentatively suggested it Miss Markham sat silent, her bright birdlike eyes fixed on mine. Suddenly her face lit with delight. 'Oh, perfect! A perpetual reminder. A monument to the two noble brothers. Like the *Adelphi*. Why not? One of them was more than good enough to compensate for the other. I think I may know the right sculptor. Then it is a question of finding the right site.' She placed both hands together and bowed her head as if in a Hindu greeting. Her eyes closed and I thought it tactful then to steal away. But Miss Markham was aware of my movement. A clawlike hand shot out and locked on my arm. 'But I haven't offended you? You will let me give you some small gift just the same? Not money. For friendship?' She seemed uncertain that I would understand.

I reassured her. 'If it's really small, just a memento.'

She squeezed my arm gently, quite recollected now and calm. 'Good. I think your friend Dr Vassilakis is waiting for you. He has been hovering behind the oleanders as if afraid I might offer you some injury. Go and put his fears at rest.'

I was careful not to hurry away. It would have been tactless as well as over-eager. In any case I had a lot to think about. *Two noble brothers*. Per and—Roland, was it? Both destroyed in fires, with this lapse of five years three months and two days between the separate disasters. And how weird, almost sinister, the precision with which Miss Markham calculated it. That was how long since she'd seen her sister Vanessa. Vanessa, her twin; and twins were supposed to be close. What had Miss Markham done at that earlier funeral to set her so apart from the rest of the family?

'Andreas,' I called softly, when I reached the hotel end of the garden. He appeared from behind the overgrown vine lodge. 'I didn't think I could be seen here.'

'Miss Markham has sharp eyes. She teased me—that you were afraid she'd harm me.'

He frowned. 'I was keeping an eye on you both. I shall be glad when you have left this place.'

I considered him. 'It isn't the place that worries you. If we all return to Iraklion the danger's still with us, isn't it?'

'I *am* worried, Siân. I do not believe in coincidences. First the accident at Vai, to you, and now your companion killed. I wish you would go home at once, except that then I should not have your company any more.'

'But Vai wasn't the beginning, Andreas. Remember the previous day, when a car went off the road above Kato Zakros and a man was killed. That was no accident either, I am sure of it. So many things about it were—wrong somehow. And what happened in the sea at Vai—I was

85

deliberately run down. Afterwards my ankles were sore. I found blue bruises coming up where thumbs and fingers had gripped me, pulling me down. I know I went unconscious, but I must have half-felt myself dragged under. It came back to me when I fell asleep the next night. I was too scared to tell anyone. I wore tights for the next few days to cover up the marks. Oh God, what a relief to tell someone about it at last!'

He looked at me with horror. 'You never said anything to me about that. About the bruises. I never examined your legs. You didn't trust me either.'

'I couldn't be sure at first. You were there, you see. You were one of those who might have pulled me down. I even thought it could be Per, but now I know it wasn't, because he's been attacked too. We know now that his death was no accident. Someone planned it, someone who's been going round picking off people like—like flies. How many more do you suppose they'll kill? What is their reason for it?'

Andreas took my hands between his own. 'Siân, will you come back with me to Iraklion now? It is imperative I return to the hospital, but I cannot leave you here unguarded. We must make the police understand. Please come. Too much has already happened, and you are there at the centre. You have suspicions and perhaps—if you recall every detail— real evidence against whoever is doing these things, these accidents that are not accidents. It is unsafe for you to stay among these people.'

His hand was on my shoulder and he watched my eyes. A muscle twitched faintly under my thin blouse and betrayed my tension. 'No, you do not entirely trust me yet. So it is as well that you will not come with me as I ask. But who will you trust, then? Someone should be here to guard you.'

'Manolis,' I decided suddenly. 'Manolis Dritsas, who says he's my friend because of Phyllia. You know him. Do you think he would come? I'm so sorry about all this. Yes, I'm scared, I admit it. I do trust you, Andreas, and you've been so kind, but—'

'But I was there when you nearly drowned, and so you

cannot be utterly sure. I understand,' he said sadly. 'Suspect me, and be sure you go on suspecting everyone else as well. Except Manolis. You have chosen well. I will telephone his taverna now and stay until he comes.'

'Perhaps he can't get away. No. It was stupid of me, selfish. I wasn't thinking about his work. I don't want him to risk his job.'

'Oh, it's time he gave himself a holiday. He does everyone else's work, like a "*Figaro here, Figaro there!*" He is actually the taverna owner, with his partner Giorgios. They will fix it between them.'

Andreas was away some minutes. When he returned, he nodded and showed me the keys to his car. 'I spoke to Giorgios. Manolis comes in their van, so I am leaving you my car and returning the van to the taverna. Oh, and never use the car until Manolis has taken a good look at it. Just to be safe.'

'I don't know why you are so good to me when I've been so awful.'

'Don't you? Really?' He was laughing at me and I felt the colour rising in my cheeks.

'I shall be very careful, as you said. I'm going to write down everything significant that has happened to me since that day at Kato Zakros, and all the little incidents that made me feel something was very wrong.'

'Good. It will help you to feel in control of events. But there is one doubt I can eliminate for you.' He offered his arm with a quizzical flick of his eyebrows and walked slowly out on to the road, turning in the direction of Phaistos. When we were quite safely out of any unseen person's hearing, he confided, 'It concerns Miss Markham, or what your friend Per told you about her. It was not a charitable account.'

We walked on steadily while he thought about what he would tell me. 'I am not *her* doctor,' he explained, 'but what I shall say now she only told me because of my profession. So I need to be discreet. As I said before, she was for some considerable time in hospital, but not for mental trouble. Sudden sorrow and shock affect people differently. Perhaps you don't know, but she brought up Per's older brother as if he were her own son. He was premature and her sister was ill during most of the pregnancy. The birth took place in Iran under terrible conditions. The baby was born blue and Vanessa was nephritic. She would have nothing to do with the poor little creature.'

'So Sven sent him to her in England?'

'Where he grew up robust despite his bad beginning.' Andreas nodded. 'By the time Per was born Roland was established there, and Vanessa had recovered enough to take an interest in the new arrival. In fact she seems to have doted on the second child. Her husband was working in Bern by then and conditions were very different.'

'Did they leave Roland with Miss Markham?'

'Yes. He was schooled in England and actually found Swedish too hard to study. He became, to all appearances, Miss Markham's son. When he was killed, five years ago, she did have a breakdown, but it was physical, a chemical change that left her stricken with arthritis almost overnight. As a doctor I accept this. She is a sensitive lady and has suffered much, but she is not crazy and has never been.'

'Per wasn't always truthful. He'd exaggerate happily if it made a better story.'

'Or shed a more favourable light on himself. Remember, I met him too and spent some time in his company.'

'So I suppose he had tales to tell about me too?'

'Which I was well able to extract the truth from. I am not quite a fool, you know.'

'I think I've been one. About Per. I accepted him at his own valuation. And the same with most of the things he said—at the time. Since then I've wondered. When he called Miss Markham his "remittance aunt" paid by his family to stay away, he seemed to despise her. The Miss Markham we've met is almost the exact opposite of his picture.'

'Because it is really she who despised him, and he found this unacceptable?'

'Perhaps. They must have heartily disliked each other, but I find her kind and understanding. Which her sister certainly isn't. It's their antipathy that disturbs me most.

You can feel it crackling in the air, like static before a thunderstorm.'

'This is a time of great stress for them all, which is why I wish you hadn't to be with them. But in a few hours Manolis will be here, so things will be easier.'

But they weren't to be, because Andreas's departure must have coincided with the police tiring of grilling the Kostantinous. They had tried every enticement, every threat, to obtain a confession, either that the woman killed her seducer or that her husband took revenge on the man who ravished his wife. But the couple stayed adamant: they'd had no part in the crime, wouldn't have risked life and good name, let alone a valuable barn, on spiting a stranger. Local people were of the same opinion, knowing the woman's promiscuous habits, and they hadn't far to look for someone with a surer motive.

Scandal and rumour were rife in the tavernas and farms. I should have guessed how suspicion would veer when the hotel-keeper's plump little wife gave me such a strange look as she served at lunch. And when I went out to watch Manolis practise on Andreas's car, accompanying the van back for a few kilometres, both she and her husband followed out, to stare silently after us, shielding their eyes against the sun.

I watched both cars pull away and went back indoors thinking nothing of it.

CHAPTER 9

There was a little clump of *Saponaria* on a bare patch beside the stony path. Not one of the rarer magenta ones from Albania, but a pale pink *officinalis*, a perennial similar in appearance to the soapwort found in south-west England, and widely used by herbalists. In past times it was famous as a purgative, an appetizer and a treatment for rheumatism. Not a cure, I warned Miss Markham when I pointed it out to her. She stood leaning on her stick, beaming at the neat

89

little clusters like a sponsor proudly glowing at sight of a sleeping godchild.

'I might try that,' she decided. 'I haven't liked to mention it before, but since I've been on Crete I've felt so much better, more mobile certainly. Perhaps it's something in the soil or the water.'

'I wouldn't know,' I said, 'whether the plant really does any good. Botany's one discipline, herbalism quite another.'

'You should look into it,' she said dogmatically. 'Behind this art interest there could be a second. And as we don't know how to prepare the plant itself, can I commission its portrait? I'll hang it where I can see it every day. It may exercise a healing influence in that way. I sometimes believe my arthritis is psychosomatic. I know, in any case, there has been a steady remission since Per's been gone. If there's a connection, isn't it horrendous?'

'It's hotter here than on Rhodes,' I said quickly, before she became too morbid or self-analytical.

'Tomorrow I think I shall abandon my cane,' she decided suddenly. 'Trust my legs more and give my hands a holiday. The crooked joints won't straighten, but you've no idea how wonderful it is to wake up without pain.'

I watched her moving away among the shrubs. She did seem different, brighter and more confident. But wasn't this due less to Per's disappearance than to her being with Sven again after all those bitter years when Vanessa seemed to have won?

'Get your paints,' she called back to me. 'Would it bother you to have me watch?'

So I did a little square watercolour of the *Saponaria officinalis* and wished I could paint some magic cure into it. While I was at work Sven Wennberg came down briefly to watch, paid me some pleasing compliments and then returned to the terrace. Miss Markham stayed seated on her favourite pine stump, staring after him.

I'd finished the flower picture so I left it to dry and went with her on her next stint of gentle exercise. 'I don't understand,' I said, following the direction of her gaze, 'why he should be so kind to me now. At first, freezing me off,

90

that made sense: the suspicious father of an only son. But now he's so different, almost protective. He seems to be just stopping short of offering some kind of confidence or apology, as though he sees himself to blame for everything.'

'Everything?'

'Well, no. Per's death,' I admitted. 'My involvement anyway.'

Miss Markham lowered her head again, using the wide-brimmed hat to hide her expression. We walked on a few steps, then she stopped, leaned with both hands on her stick and looked sideways at me. Her eyes, although pink-rimmed, were quite dry. 'Perhaps he *is* partly to blame. We all are, to varying degrees: his mother, whose doting built Per into a monster; his father, who was too clear-eyed to avoid eventually recognizing the truth about him, then found that interfering only served to estrange him further; I who watched the whole battle from a distance but could find no room for pity in my grief. I wanted him punished, and to the full—but without wounding anyone else.'

She meant Sven. It didn't matter to her if Vanessa suffered along with her son. To her, Vanessa had been the main-spring of the mischief, raising Per the way she had, so much the opposite of how Alison had raised 'her' boy, the older brother. And Alison had remained in love with Sven, con-stantly since their broken engagement all those years before when Sven, believing himself supplanted by a Derwent estate, had allowed Vanessa to console him. Not so clear-eyed then in his misery. I could imagine how Vanessa had gone to work to achieve the double success of a socially distinguished marriage and revenge on her sister for those few minutes of seniority.

'What are you thinking, Siân?'

'Oh—Per, his father, all that.'

'What Sven just stops short of confiding,' she said gently, 'is how well he understands the way you were deceived by the fair face and the hollow within. But he hesitates to put it into words, because it might seem to slight your intelligence.'

I felt my face flame. 'Per was the first man I was ever

91

really attracted to. There was something about him, not just his physical beauty—that Nordic-god, blond-Viking thing —but his overwhelming confidence. Being larger than life. The sense of Superman.'

'He did it well,' she agreed drily. 'He wanted so much to dazzle, to outshine everyone else. One of Nietzsche's *Übermenschen* from a Master-race of geniuses. It was Lucifer's sin too, you know, if you recall the story of the great archangel's fall.' She sighed. '"*Hubris*," the Greeks say.'

Her voice took on a new, steely tone. "But Superman was a fake, and he knew it. Even after Roland was dead Per couldn't escape knowing himself to be second-best. So he had to keep striving to impress others with how wonderful he was, forever striking heroic and intellectual poses, resorting to trickery when he couldn't achieve it straight. Which is what he was up to when he was destroyed. Just think, both brothers died by fire, but their deaths couldn't have been more different, one in an act of courage, the other involved in shoddy deceit.'

She was nodding into the distance. When she resumed, her voice was even and low as though she uttered her private thoughts. 'Yes. Although we all contributed, Per played the principal part in causing his own death. Unless we accept the Ancients' concept of Nemesis, the avenging goddess— punishing him for killing his brother.'

I was appalled. She didn't seem to know she had said anything startling. We had come to the garden end and her eyes were still focused on the distant Ida range, a faded heather blue smudging into the gentian blue of the sky. I had a moment to cover up my shock at her disclosure. Per *killing* Roland? And how was she so sure what Per had been involved in at the time he was killed himself? She had knowledge unavailable to me. My mind was racing distractedly ahead trying to piece together snippets of earlier conversations. They started gelling now like dying blood corpuscles feebly jostling on a microscope's slide.

I didn't trust myself to go on talking with her. 'It's later than I thought,' I said, wildly improvising, 'and there's a letter I have to write. Will you excuse me, Miss Markham?'

I had to speak twice, her mind was so far away. She returned with a start, looked hard at me, then smiled her social smile, paper-fine cheeks looped up under pastel-rouged cheekbones. 'Of course, my dear. I've monopolized your time shamefully. It's very sweet of you to be so patient.' She had returned to her gentle-invalid role. It took an effort of mind to recall that she was little more than fifty, a contemporary of the athletic and vitally attractive Vanessa.

But the Vanessa I encountered at the stairhead of the hotel when I went up was altered too. She was wearing her bathrobe and had been drinking. Livid without the warm-toned make-up, her face was haggard, the flesh seeming to have become detached from the framework of bone underneath. It looked bloodless as parchment, her eyes swimming vaguely in grey shadows, her mouth slackly open.

She became aware of me standing back waiting for her to pass, and her whole body grew taut with hostility. I thought she would spit out some vitriolic insult or go for me with her nails. But when she lifted her trembling arm all she did was point with a long forefinger in my direction. Bad enough, it was an accusation and a curse all in one.

I turned and ran downstairs again, to the front of the hotel and out into the wholesome sunshine. As I emerged I was in time to see Andreas's little blue saloon pull up in a space nearby with Manolis Dritsas at the wheel, his elfin face transformed by a look of earnest concern.

I went straight across and climbed in by the door he held open. 'Drive anywhere,' I begged. 'Anywhere away from here. Just so that I get a chance to think.'

Whether he lip-read the words or not, he responded at once to my urgency. As he let in the clutch he flashed a quick glance over my shoulder at Vanessa who had pursued me out. Then he applied himself to manœuvring round a truck piled with tractor tyres which had stopped in mid-road.

Manolis could ask no questions while driving, and I never paused to wonder how much Andreas would have told him. When we stopped to enjoy a distant view of the Messara Bay he started busily writing in basic Greek on his notepad.

He had read about Per's death in the local newspaper and was sorry, he told me. Then Dr Vassilakis had asked him to come and help me in my need. He was very sad that I was sad. How could he make me happy?

I had forgotten how reassuringly childlike his presence was because of his primitive communication. I faced him and mouthed carefully, 'You are here, so I am better already.'

He gave his brilliant smile, reached for me, hesitated a moment reading my eyes, then kissed me soundly on both cheeks, clasping my shoulders as a comrade. I managed not to burst into tears.

In the event we didn't communicate a lot. I got out on the road and he sensed I wanted to walk alone, staying on his seat bolt upright like a uniformed chauffeur while I trudged the open grassland, my sandals whistling against the steely stems. There were no flowers to distract me, only hummocky turf and scattered golden rocks that led on to slaty scree which burned through to my toes. To the south the land flowed liquid with shimmering horizons, all heat haze and mirages. When I turned to go back the scene was kinder, cooler, pooled with shadows, the distant mountains laid back and familiar. Gradually I was able to give in to the torpor of mid-afternoon. Even fear, it seemed, requires its siesta.

Because I never asked myself then just what the fear was about, it went underground. I should have examined it logically, as dispassionately as I was able. Then either I would have known for sure where—or in whom—the danger lay, or it might have dispersed. But I didn't, and possibly because of that I find myself where I now am, writing this, doubly confused and resentful and quite unconvinced that any way will ever be found to extricate me from this awful hole.

But that was yet to come when Manolis drove me back to the hotel at Timbaki. 'Where will you stay?' I asked him. 'Would you like a room here? I could ask Mr Wennberg.'

He shook his head and made contented shruggings followed by calming movements of the hands. I understood he'd prefer to make his own arrangements. Then he laid a

94

finger on my wrist to delay me while he wrote on his pad again. 'The woman there. I see her once in Iraklion, three weeks ago.'

He meant Vanessa. But she'd come here directly from Rome. He was mistaken. Yet Manolis was particularly good about faces. He read disbelief in mine then and shook his head. 'That one certainly. Once I watch her a long time. She is strange. Dangerous. That woman does not forgive.'

I didn't need unsettling any more, however well-intentioned his warning. I said goodbye rather abruptly, asking him to inform the hotel where he would be lodging.

'I stay most time near here,' he wrote. 'In garden or car, or taverna across road.'

I thanked him, knowing I didn't deserve such loyal care.

Later that evening, after dinner, I looked from the window and caught the glow of his white shirt as he waited out in the car, and ashamed at my earlier curtness took my sketchbook out to show him. We drove out on the Phaistos road towards Matala, and over a bottle of local wine on a taverna terrace he looked admiringly through my flower paintings. I had decided in any case to tell him all about the burning car incident, so I left him to find the two sketches tucked in the back of the block. Just before he reached them I asked, 'Did Andreas Vassilakis tell you what frightened me on the road down to Kato Zakros?'

He looked steadily back without smiling and bobbed his head, calmly confirming it. So I was utterly unprepared for his reaction when he came on the first of the drawings, the staring face of the dead young man from the burning car.

He made a gurgling groan and started up from his chair, keeping tight hold on the little iron table. I hadn't known he could produce any sound at all, and it scared me even more because he'd been startled into making it. All his warm colour was gone, leaving his face drawn and olive-skinned. I pushed the ballpoint pen towards him and he wrote fiercely, 'This face I know. Is young brother of my Phyllia. His name Spiros.'

It was a shock even to me. I touched his hand gently and shook my head. '*Was*, Manolis. The poor boy is dead.'

He made up his mind instantly. I agreed that Phyllia's need of him was greater then than mine. For all we knew the dead boy was still unidentified, and Manolis might need to break the terrible news to the girl.

I could admit now that I was badly at fault in not showing my sketches to the police at Zakros, when they had insisted the body was unrecognizable. Presumably the fire had spread later and damaged his dead face. I'd left it at that just to satisfy Per's need to be on his way and, as ever, to avoid anything distasteful. *Mea maxima culpa.* But at least it was going to be put right now.

He was taking the two sketches with him to assist the coroner at Zakros. He wrote that if I ran him to the bus station he might catch the last connection that night, and I could keep the car for my own use.

But that would be wasteful of time. There was no direct bus to Zakros from here. I insisted he take the car and return as soon as the police had checked his story. Doubtless they would want to interview me too.

I was getting farther and farther drawn into difficulties through my connection with Per, but at least I'd started at last on extricating myself. Or so I thought at the time.

Manolis refilled with petrol and dropped me at the hotel. I waited for the dust to settle after the car had gone, then went upstairs. In the sitting-room they were all waiting for me; Sven, Alison, Vanessa and no less than four policemen.

The Kostantinous had been released from interrogation. Now it was to be my turn.

CHAPTER 10

Sven was white-faced and stiff with anger. 'I shall contact the British Vice-Consul in Iraklion. Immediately. Meanwhile tell them nothing at all. Keep demanding that they free you. That and no more. It is a preposterous mistake.'

He had made the policemen wait in the hall while I packed a bag and said goodbye. His concern was genuine, no empty diplomatic gesture. Grateful and touched, I could only nod my thanks, astonished that he should allow himself to be personally affected.

'Have courage,' he urged me, sounding old-fashioned and momentarily foreign. I looked at him, so kindly now, his handsome face scored with distress. This was the sort of man Per might have become, if he hadn't been hollow inside. How awful that now he would never catch up on what was missing. *That* was the tragedy, Per cut off in mid soaring flight; not my present little mishap, due to local police misreading the circumstances.

'I'm all right,' I assured them. 'They'll get it sorted out soon.'

'Is there any message we can pass on?' Miss Markham asked sharply.

'Just let Manolis know when he gets back, would you?'

'Your driver? Of course. But your friend—Dr Vassilakis?'

'Manolis will tell him.' I would have explained Manolis but it didn't seem appropriate then and there with the police impatiently waiting downstairs. 'I'll be back soon,' I promised again, smiled at their stricken faces, picked up my overnight bag and went, less certain than I sounded, out to my fate.

The senior officers got into the second car. I was led to the other, a small saloon which smelled strongly of stale cigarette smoke. There were two policemen, neither in the mood to talk; one to drive, the other presumably to restrain me if I went berserk. I didn't, but when we reached our destination I panicked silently inside.

The room they took me into was an office of sorts. There were notices on the walls, enigmas without any pictures to give a clue to the Greek text. In that state of shock my Greek had deserted me again. All that came to mind was '*Evkharisto*' and '*Endakhsi*', but I'd nothing to thank them for and things were anything but all right.

Well, there was always the negative. '*Then endakhsi*,' I said, meaning to sound indignant, but I choked on the words. The uniformed man left on guard looked doubtfully at me.

I went on choking, managed to gasp, '*Nero, nero!*'

He decided then that it was no trick because next I was aware of thick china clinking against my teeth and I swallowed the water greedily down. When my breathing returned to normal I at last had something to say '*Evkharisto*' for, and it seemed frantically funny. My eyes, clearing from the tears of my choking fit, filled again as I started laughing.

The policeman looked affronted, very inadequate in charge of this mad young foreign female. He didn't slap me to stem the hysteria. It was his face that suddenly sobered me.

'*Poo,*' I demanded, '*—poo ine o Kapetan?*' but he shook his head, under orders to tell me nothing. I was to wait. Wait and wait and be reduced to a state of quaking surrender. But they'd misjudged me, once as their criminal and again on my reactions. The crisis of nerves had passed; now I was gaining time to get myself together. And if the gap yawned long enough it might even allow the cavalry to arrive.

When the police captain returned with a shorthand writer he wanted to know about my early relations with Per. I did exactly as his father had advised and clammed, apart from a demand for consular representation. After a number of abortive attempts the policeman proved less stiff-necked than his spondylosis suggested. For the moment he gave in. A dumpy little woman in black cotton arrived to conduct me across the back courtyard and to this upstairs room with bed, chair, mirror and table.

The door is not locked, but all the time there is the nonstop rumble of voices from the room at the bottom of the stairs. The window has no bars, doesn't need any. The glazed casement has been removed and the outer shutters, loosely closed to admit air, are secured by a padlocked chain. A small child or a dog might wriggle through the triangular space they form against the sill, but not me, and never with a twelve-foot drop to the stone-flagged court below.

This house seems to be built at right angles to the police post. Peering between the shutters' flaking wooden slats, I can see the two cars parked in the shade of a wall. There is a desultory coming and going of uniformed men below. I catch snatches of casual conversation, the smell of roasting lamb and Greek cigarettes. No one seems to care that I am shut away up here.

When I tired of watching I explored the little room. Clean but shabby, it couldn't be barer. In a drawer of the pinewood table I found an assortment of religious literature, amateurishly printed on a single side like handbills. It struck me then that I might get in touch with someone outside, or at least start to prepare some kind of defence. Some unknown person's Orthodox convictions could serve to prevent my own for murder.

Murder. Per viciously killed. And it was believed that *I* could have done that. I scrabbled in my handbag for a ballpoint pen and started to write, hunched up on the bed with my back to the door, ready to cover up the papers at the first sound of footsteps on the stairs.

It seemed there was a connection between the first death and the second. The link had to be Per himself. What was it about him that disturbed me when we saw that blazing car?

He had hunkered beside me, staring down the precipitous edge. Through field-glasses he had been the first to pick out the body, and he'd grunted, 'Poor bugaroo.'

Was it up there that he'd said that, or later when we'd clambered down? He hadn't touched the body then as I had, and I never let on to him the strangeness of what I noticed. Why hadn't I cried out, 'The body's cold!'? Surely it was because already I didn't trust him with my fears.

Scorched hair on the young man's forearms, and scorched clothing; so he'd been in the burning car at some point, probably fell out as it rolled down the mountain. But cold. Because he was dead some time before.

I wished I knew more about *rigor mortis*. The arm had been fairly limp. Was that entirely due to broken bones or had *rigor* had time to set in and withdraw? I had a vague idea that death should have occurred less than three or more than twelve hours before. Neither way fitted the crashed car scenario.

And then the fingers of his right hand crimped about the metal object, tight although the rest of his body was slack. As he met his violent death he had convulsively seized the thing and hung on into eternity.

There had been no mention of any such state or of any such object at the Zakros police bureau next day. No experienced pathologist could overlook it. So either the body's state had changed or the police thought it no concern of strangers such as Per and me.

Perhaps that was a mistake. Mightn't Per have been able to help them there? Momentarily we had been distracted by a moving point of light above us on the road. When I looked back Per had had his hand to his breast pocket. Putting something away? Later I'd asked him what that object was, and he'd mentioned a tinny bit of metal. When I took his shirt for the laundry the pocket had contained a twisted scrap of metal plate with some embossed letters, like part of an identity tag used on bikes and motor-scooters. Could that have been what Per took from the dead boy's hand, and couldn't it have been a clue of some kind?

Per had concealed it. Was that more or less suspicious than my not arguing about the corpse being unrecognizable? If Per was at fault, I was just as much so. We had both shrugged off responsibility towards him because he was a stranger. Now, when it seemed he was the younger brother of Phyllia, I was ashamed of walking away. Per, however, was past remorse, because Per too was dead.

Two young men destroyed by fire within a few days. Three, if you counted that other death five years before. Roland, Spiros, Per. What else had they had in common?

I made several attempts to list chronologically the things which had most alarmed me and the stages of my own involvement in both the recent deaths, but my mind wasn't up to analysis. So I began again, with a simple narrative, recalling it all just as it happened, and starting with Per's reckless driving down from Zakros, sighting the sudden sheet of flame that was a car on fire. Ending in this place little short of a prison, trying to come to terms with myself about Per, about what he's done to my life, what I've done

100

to myself through meeting up with him. What he was, what I am.

Can he really have been the monster his aunt and father see him as? I never knew him long enough to judge. He let me down repeatedly in little things. More; he slept with that Greek farmer's wife right after making love to me, and so I'd thought him a first-class shit. But what standards do you go by? I'm new to all this. Is that how you bring someone to heel in this world, by humiliation? I hadn't thought so, but how am I to tell what goes on between lovers? Is anyone ever true?

Love, sex. Not the same thing. I knew that in theory before. But I thought that with Per they had come together, and that a miracle like that lifted human behaviour on to a different, higher plane. How long before I know which it was I had with Per, before I can learn to take what I want and walk away from the rest—be like Per, in fact?

Vanessa doesn't condemn him, but then she's his mother. A frightening person, Vanessa. Neurotic, ruthless. Sometimes she ignores me, and then there are times when I know she detests me for what I had with Per. Now that's love too, of a kind. Possessive, and it used to be called unnatural. With incestuous undertones. So she despises me as her son's poor plaything and hates me as a rival. Unstable from the beginning—that awful scoring off against her sister; then turning against the first little baby; the clearly strained relations with Sven. She goes round punishing everyone for the things she feels too keenly. Still, how can she be rational, grieving over Per? What is left to her to live for now, except to hurt whoever she considers to blame?

This gets me nowhere. Vanessa doesn't matter. What about me? There has been too much sudden passion, too much fear, too many deaths. All I want now is to get away from here, walk right off and never look back. I want to be ten years older and have it all safe in perspective.

I just want out.

Part Two

FAMILY FRONT

CHAPTER 11

'*Who* killed the Swede?' the neckless Captain repeated, batting smoke away with his box of matches. 'It doesn't tell us.' The *cigarillo* glowed red at the tip as he drew on it. He removed it from his lips, observed it approvingly as if it were a Havana, replaced it centrally between his teeth and growled round its side. 'Put the papers back under her carpet. See she has plenty more tracts in the drawer, but I do not think she will write more. Her account seems to come to some sort of end. Inconclusively.'

'What did you expect?' The slim young lieutenant in the sharply-cut linen suit mocked him. 'A full confession with precise circumstantial evidence? Watertight proof of guilt?'

The Captain was unperturbed: you paid a price for having bright assistants, and there would be occasion to put Papadopoulou flat on his arse soon enough. 'Mind,' he said modestly, 'I am not dissatisfied with our little ploy.' He shook the bundle of papers. 'Inconclusive, but full of beginnings. We have plenty to work on here, inconsistencies to examine, points to check which will tell us how reliable her judgment may be. So much verbiage produced under pressure while she cheated herself of sleep is more likely to be the truth as she saw it than a complicated tissue of lies. (Yet we must admit the possibility of deceit.) And *if* the truth as she saw it, how distorted was her view?'

'Tangled strings,' Papadopoulou said, grinning. 'Which loose end do we tweak first?' He looked down from the window to where the English girl was being exercised in the courtyard. He folded his own set of photocopies and slid it in an inner pocket of his Italian-style jacket.

'Connections. Is the girl truly unknown to the Swede's family? Is her version of meeting up with the young Cypriot refugees what actually happened? Or had she seen the boy Spiros alive on some occasion and so remembered him well enough to make the sketch from memory? Then the deaf mute: is his connection with the English Miss truly a matter of recognizing her dress and the red hair as described to him in small-gossip correspondence from his beloved? The beloved herself, this little innocent Phyllia—whose brother merits, apparently, being savagely done to death—how blameless is she?'

'The Zakros end—' the young lieutenant prompted, still somewhat in the dark.

'Ah yes. Forewarned as I was by this account, I was able to contact our colleagues there before they phoned me. Dritsas did deliver the young man's portrait to them, but there can be no positive identification of the body until dental records are traced. They are in Occupied Cyprus, and the Turks are not likely to cooperate, even if such records survived the fighting. But the girl Phyllia is convinced it must be her brother, who has been missing now for almost a week, an easily led young man, without regular employment and having some questionable friends. It is possible such a young waster might have crossed professional smugglers or drug-traffickers and required quick removal. There are plenty of possibilities outside any connection with the dead Swede. Yet both suffer similar deaths within a matter of days.'

He coughed ash off the end of his *cigarillo*. 'I do not like coincidence. Whatever the truth, Zakros is sending an officer here. I shall warn the girl of visitors from the North after siesta. She will expect her Consul and be disappointed, of course, but I shall contrive to keep him away until our colleague has spoken with her. So, get those papers back where she hid them and let the child get some sleep. She can barely have closed her eyes last night with all this writing. We can't have her looking ill-treated.'

104

'I'll send her up to you, then,' Papadopoulou smirked. 'With Old Agatha alongside?'

The Captain did not raise his eyes from the desktop. 'Of course. We must be very proper.'

When Siân Westbury was shown in, her face betrayed the frantic industry of the previous night's outpourings. The Captain observed her gravely. Let a prisoner resist your questions as stubbornly and as long as he can, he thought; then supply a means of relief—a fellow-sufferer to confide in, or—as in the case of this educated young foreigner— materials for writing a secret testimony. Nine times out of twenty the effort won't be wasted.

She faced him with weary stubbornness, eyes ringed with shadows, shoulders stiffly hunched. This morning the magnificent red of her hair seemed darkened to chestnut. She had sweated at her self-imposed labours through the night.

'You may expect visitors today,' he told her abruptly. 'In the late afternoon.'

'The British Vice-Consul?'

He hesitated. 'Possibly. In any case there will be more questions and you would be advised to answer helpfully.' Glancing up as she stood before his desk, he moved his whole torso, neckless as ever, head rigid on massive shoulders. 'This does not surprise you?'

'Nothing surprises me any more.'

He pursed his lips as if satisfied. 'Ah. Well, rest until then. Is there anything you require?'

She stared at the unexpected offer. 'Shampoo?'

'I will see that some is supplied. Do you wish to make a statement?'

She shook her head and started to move away. At the door she turned back, chin defiantly raised. 'Only that the soap has an offensive smell.'

The hint of a gleam showed in the man's eyes but he replied with owlish gravity. 'Then we must be more selective when choosing the shampoo.'

From a habit of politeness she almost said thank-you, but bit it off in time. He had done her no favour. She would be lodging a strong complaint through the consular office.

There had been no reason to hold her for questioning. They had no case against her at all.

When the policeman from Zakros interviewed her, accompanied by the young officer in the sharply-cut suit, she was not so sure. Having had so little to do with the earlier death, she had been willing to tell all she knew. But the officer from Zakros was set on going deep. He kept on, flat-voiced, hard-eyed, slowly hammering away at why she had deceived him before.

It wasn't deceit exactly, just failure to inform completely, because under Per's influence she had been persuaded not to delay their departure. Why, the man pressed, had she been so easily persuaded? Was a fellow-creature's death of so little importance? Had she, he implied, no proper feelings? —all the time acting like an automaton himself. The effect was to have her teetering between shame and a scalding sense of injustice.

'This man Wennberg,' said the younger policeman, 'he was not your husband.'

'Not my husband, no. We hadn't long met, but—' If she admitted emotional involvement she could get in too deeply when they came to consider his death. Locally, wasn't her supposed motive for killing Per jealousy at being scorned for the farmer's wife?

'Go on, miss. You said "but—".'

'But he had a strong personality. He was used to having his own way.' She scanned their noncommittal faces. Was that the wrong thing to admit? Would they accept her as a wide-eyed innocent, which she wasn't really, or would they assume she might have had cause for passionate rebellion? The trouble was their foreignness, or her own: a great gulf fixed between women of one culture and another. How would Phyllia have reacted in the circumstances? Surely she would have wrung her hands now and poured out the whole tale, would have had the local policeman pressing coffee and paternal comfort on her. This awareness served only to widen the gulf.

'I was uneasy,' she admitted in a rush. 'There were things that disturbed me at the time but I didn't say as much to

Per because I didn't entirely trust him.' She saw the quick glance exchanged between the two men and dashed recklessly on. 'Not that I suspected him of anything bad. I knew he couldn't have been involved. No, nothing like that. But he—'

How could she explain his lordly disregard for others' authority, his intellectual dishonesty? Oh, damn Per, it didn't matter what he was. It was herself in the hot seat, her own emotions and inaction that they were taking to pieces. Worse than that, because now they were impassively watching her disassemble herself. And she was appalled at the shabbiness of what came to light.

'He made me feel a fool sometimes,' she admitted. 'So I gave up being frank with him.'

'These things that made you—uneasy,' the older man said at last after a small sigh. 'We take them now. One by one. First a light on the road above where you find the dead man. A reflection on something that moves.'

'Yes. I thought perhaps another car, or a motorbike, coasting down. There was no sound of an engine.'

'Or a scooter,' the young one suggested.

She remembered then the torn scrap of metal tag in the dead boy's hand. Which could have been part of an identity plate from a scooter. More concealed evidence, more testimony to the deceits going on between Per and herself. If only she'd been more open at the time. She tried to make up for it now. The younger policeman made notes, including Per's mention of 'a tinny piece of metal' and her finding it in his shirt pocket when she sorted his clothes for the launderette. Where it was now? She couldn't say. Maybe among their things in the Volvo. Perhaps thrown away.

'Are you sure it was the same object taken from the dead young man's hand?'

She couldn't swear to it. She had only Per's version. He wasn't beyond substituting something else in his pocket to keep her off the right track. That would be in line with his arrogance. He was a devious person.

The older man gave another of his small sighs. Perhaps he had been listening so intently that he'd forgotten to breathe in properly. Siân began to feel some slight sympathy for him, coping in a foreign tongue, patently worried by the case and the time lost in getting on its trail. 'We go back to the sketches,' he said patiently. 'You make them later that same day, down at Kato Zakros.'

Of course, Manolis had explained all this to them. 'Yes. It was like a photograph printed on my mind. A haunting. Drawing the man seemed to release me.'

'The face you draw is very like photographs the sister has. She did not show you these? You had not seen the young man before?'

'No. I didn't even meet Phyllia until the following day. In the hour before you took my statement at Zakros. At that time the sketches were in the back of my drawing block.

'And you did not show them to us.'

However she tried to excuse herself it would sound lame, enough. Siân merely shook her head.

'Although I said then that the dead man was unrecognizable?' The senior man's voice was funereal.

'Although that, yes.' Under curt instructions to say nothing and get on their way; but there had been enough of blaming Per. Ultimately it had been her own choice. Withholding evidence, the men's silence seemed to say. But was her memory, her ability to catch a likeness and reproduce it on paper, truly evidence in the legal sense?

'How did you explain to yourself the difference?'

'Difference?'

'That you saw him plainly, but the police did not.'

'I supposed the fire had broken out again, after we left, and—and burned his face.'

'Was that likely?'

'It must have been like that. How else?'

'Tell me how.'

She was frightened now. 'I don't know anything about fires, but the mountainside was tinder-dry. The car was still burning. There was quite a wind off the sea up there.'

'The car twenty metres below the ledge he lay on and among bare rocks.'

'There were one or two bushes, I'm almost sure. Yes, one

about eight feet from the body, a withered old broom.'

Her voice died away but its desperate note of appeal seemed to reverberate while the older policeman looked through some papers clipped in his file. 'Broom. *Spartium junceum*, yes? As a botanist you like to be precise. Our pathologist too. The body lay with its face down, directly over burnt-out roots of *Spartium junceum*. The rest of the bush was ashes.'

He looked at her sadly. 'Perhaps the dead man crawled to that position after you had left. And set fire to it himself.'

She sat transfixed while they observed her, and then she began to shake, cornered. *Someone* had done it. When she'd left, the body—Phyllia's young brother—had quite definitely been dead, dark eyes wide-staring up at the sky. *Who* then? 'Someone up on the road,' she said in a rush. 'They must have seen us looking at him, came down and tried to cover up—'

'*Disfigure*,' the senior man said heavily. 'I found the word in my Greek-English dictionary. There was no need for it before. Not since the German troops were here.'

'Why disfigure an accident victim?' the other policeman demanded of the ceiling.

'Accident? Who called it that?' They were working together like a pair of sheepdogs, rounding her up to pen her in.

'Murder,' purred the younger.

'Decidedly,' the other agreed. 'So we are looking now for a murderer; the person who caused the car to leave the road.'

'I know nothing about that,' Siân said vehemently. 'I've told you everything now.'

'Begin again,' said the man from Zakros persuasively. 'Start at the point of the reckless drive down the mountain, how the Volvo began to go out of control, forcing the other car off the road. And be sure to mention—' his voice was silkily menacing—'which of you was behind the wheel!'

CHAPTER 12

With narrowed eyes Miss Markham watched her brother-in-law's precise movements as he checked the contents of his jacket pockets. 'You are going to Iraklion straight away?'

'I must. The girl has to be properly represented.'

'You don't believe she could have—?'

'Not for one moment. Do you?'

Miss Markham shifted her weight from one foot to the other and took a firmer grip on the silver head of her ebony cane. 'I don't wish to. Not that the other options are particularly attractive.'

He glanced at her sharply. 'For instance?'

She shrugged angular shoulders. 'Not one of us, of course, beause we weren't anywhere near. But who else knew him long enough to find it necessary—?'

'You believe Per was involved in some dishonest business, and one of his—'

'Associates.' Miss Markham offered the word almost absently. 'What else can we think? Would you prefer to suspect the Greek couple at the farm? Their account appears to have satisfied the local police. Which leaves us that hoary alternative of a passing tramp.'

Sven looked at her sadly. 'You have become very cynical, Alison.'

'No more than you, my dear. Even apart as we've been, it is still essentially the same world we live in.' Her mouth became less severe. 'And not the same one as when we were young.'

'Neither of us retains many illusions about Per, certainly. I have no confidence that his—death—that his death will prove any less shameful than his recent life. But I can console myself that whatever comes to light now must be the final scandal.' The man's voice was bitter; his mouth, twisted with pain, looked almost cruel.

Miss Markham swayed, putting out a hand to the wall.

110

Her brother-in-law pulled up a chair and tenderly helped her to it.

'Sven, can't you make arrangements with the British authorities by telephone? I won't be held responsible for Vanessa's actions while you're gone.'

'No one can be, my dear, but I do not intend taking her with me. Hooper will keep an eye on her. That at least he should manage to get right.' The tone of censure was not lost on Alison.

They eyed each other steadily a moment. Miss Markham was the first to turn away, a sad little smile tugging at the corner of her mouth. 'Don't be gone too long, my dear. I shall stay close until Dr Vassilakis or his driver returns, then try to see Siân myself. Do you think if I wrote a little note they would allow her to have it?'

'Insist. They can only demand to read it first. Keep it innocuous.'

'You can depend on that. But do go now, and hurry back. I'll explain your absence to Vanessa when she wakes from her rest.'

Lindsay Harrison, the British Vice-Consul, was a non-career FO man, a lanky, relaxed East Anglian with an unlikely background in the banana fields of the West Indies. His expertise had been called on when cultivation was first started in Crete, and succumbing to the blandishments of the climate and social tempo, he had elected to stay on in the capital. There were few consultations now that the industry was established, so he was able to use the empty hours dealing with such uncomplicated matters as lost passports, drunken tourists and the odd Distressed British Subject. Redirected from the consular office, Sven ran him to earth in a taverna on Dedalos Way, among a group of locals bemoaning the follies of European Community regulations.

The prospect of acting Galahad to a teenage suspected-murderess had sufficient novelty to stimulate Harrison to action beyond his normal practice. The personal involvement of a senior Swedish diplomat was added inducement, and whatever the outcome of his own part in the affair—which past experience taught him was likely to be negligible —it would ensure that he had top gossip ratings on his return to the capital.

It was not until he was well on the way south that Harrison properly realized his driver was more than an intermediary for the defence, being also the victim's father. It struck him then that the case might be one of unusual ramifications and himself marooned among aliens.

Access to the girl was not immediately granted. Permitted to send in his card, Harrison informally scrawled, 'Pleased to see you as soon as possible,' in large drop-stitch script on the reverse side. No need for any warnings: the Swede had already told the girl to say nothing until represented. But instructions were more easily given than conformed with. Police, wherever and whoever, could be overwhelmingly persuasive.

He had to content himself for the present with listening to a second recitation of events leading to Per's death, as offered by Wennberg *père*, unemotional, unbiased, and weirdly detached as though the subject were diplomatic trivia concerned with strangers. Behind and beneath the frigid façade there must surely be more active emotions. Harrison began to look forward with morbid curiosity to meeting other members of the dead man's family.

At three-thirty, lingering after an indifferent taverna meal of greasy *stifado*, they were approached by a young man in a pale linen suit and led to the Captain's office, a large, square, ground-floor room made cooler-looking with cocoa-brown walls and translucent cream curtains. A table-top fan revolved through ninety degrees in one corner and a jug of iced coffee awaited them on a tray. There were four thick tumblers, and only the three of them including the Captain. The girl came in from an opposite doorway, escorted by a dumpy middle-aged woman in black who was waved away. The Captain made the introductions. His own name was Fotiadis. Everyone sat down.

'Miss Westbury has been helping my colleague from Zakros,' Fotiadis said cheerfully. 'Concerning an accident there last week. Which turns out not to be an accident at all.'

'Now they're saying that I did that too,' Siân burst out wretchedly. Her eyes went to Sven in desperate appeal. She looked terrible, young, tense and hunched, her face blotched with colour.

'Do you wish to lodge a complaint about your treatment?' Harrison put in quickly, trying to sound dependable, and knowing himself to be total jelly inside.

She seemed to see him for the first time, shook her head and turned back to Wennberg. 'I know you told me to say nothing, but that was about the other matter. About Per. I didn't think there was any harm in telling them all I knew about finding the dead man at Zakros. Because there was no connection.'

'Because you weren't involved, whereas in the second case you are—as you English say—up to your ears in it?' The Captain's voice was deceptively sympathetic. Siân mistrusted all policemen by now and she rounded angrily on him.

'You had as good as accused me of murdering Per, and that's why I'm being held.'

'Isolated from undesirable contacts,' the Captain purred. 'Have we insisted on your answering our questions? Have we not patiently waited for your friends to be present?'

'What is all this about Zakros?' Sven Wennberg asked.

'I am not entirely clear on this myself,' the Captain said and lifted a phone. He exchanged a few sentences in Greek with a female voice. 'Good,' he told them afterwards. 'An English transcript of Miss Westbury's statement will be available in half an hour. Meanwhile let me pour you some iced coffee. Then perhaps we can begin sorting out some of the facts concerning the tragic explosion at the Kostantinou farm.'

Siân took her tumbler in a trembling hand and before drinking laid its coolness against her eyelids. 'What do you want to know?' she asked wearily.

Fotiadis smiled. 'Everything. Just tell us in your own words how it all began, your meeting with the young man,

113

your arrangements over the shared research. Where you went, what you did, who you met.'

Siân looked towards Wennberg for his approval. He nodded. Harrison cleared his throat. 'Is this interview to be recorded? Has any charge been read?'

Captain Fotiadis looked mildly offended. 'Nothing of that sort. I wish to clarify my own impressions, that is all. This is not, you understand, a common type of crime for us down here. I have to take every necessary precaution.'

'Including the detention of my countrywoman as a suspect?'

Fotiadis regarded the part-time official reproachfully. 'A protective precaution. Once Miss Westbury has told us all she knows, I believe she will no longer be at risk from anyone her information might—unknowingly—implicate.'

Harrison blinked watery Anglo-Saxon eyes at the reproving brown ones. His period of protest clocked off. This Captain was neither the bumpkin he'd expected nor a lotus-eater. With such perfect command of English he had to have an Athenian background, procedural experience gained in the metropolis, perhaps even with Interpol. Certainly he'd no Cretan accent. Well, he himself had made the right consular noises, and it would be no disgrace to go down for the count against a security heavyweight.

Siân recognized that the final flabby protest had been made. There was a certain truth about what the Captain said. All the time she clutched the information to herself she was a potential threat to whoever had killed Per. Complete openness, even if at first it seemed to count against her, must eventually lead to the guilty person. And the threat she represented would be discharged. So, where to begin? —with meeting Per, the casual link-up; leave out the Zakros business because the account of that would be provided, as the Captain had ordered, within a half-hour. Right then, a précis of the route they had taken and its purpose; omit the Iraklion details which were irrelevant; pick up the story again with coming south to Phaistos.

There wasn't a lot to tell and she'd sorted it already in her mind as she wrote last night, but there were details the

114

Captain picked up from her story along the way, searching queries, little promptings when he suspected she was short-circuiting events. He had an uncannily probing mind, like a Customs Officer's. Faced with such persistence, she began to concentrate totally now on what words she used, seeing the account from an outsider's angle. Without prompting, she volunteered the point about sugar in the second mug of instant coffee left at the tent when Per went to his death. The observation seemed important to her.

'It wasn't for Per and it wasn't for me,' she stressed. 'Somebody called on him while I was away, somebody he found interesting enough to offer hospitality to. That's why Per needed hot water, and camping gas to heat it. If that person hadn't come we'd have needed the gas later ourselves. I expect it would have been my place to go and fetch it. And I don't smoke. Then the leaked gas in the barn wouldn't have exploded. I'd have smelled it the instant I opened the door.'

'We don't know of any other person there that evening,' Fotiadis said heavily.

'Surely there must be fingerprints. On the sugar spoon?'

'Mugs and spoons had been properly washed and dried beforehand. They had only the dead man's prints. The sugar jar was overprinted with many smudges from at least two people's hands. We know that one was yourself. Much the same for the can of gas, but fewer and clearer prints, a firmer grip being used to attach and remove the can from the burner. The uppermost set was Per Wennberg's as he removed the can to test the weight. Beneath it, a little smudged, was yours.'

'I left that can in the rubbish bin. And I put a new, full one on the night before. Whoever changed it back could have used gloves, or a cloth.'

There was a short silence.

'The sugar,' Siân insisted.

'Who uses it in coffee?' the Captain demanded of the ceiling. 'Not your friend Per, not yourself, not Mr Wennberg here, neither of the Kostantinous. Only the ladies in your party, mother and aunt of the dead young man. And they were not here at the time. Could the sugar have been intended to deceive us, do you think?—in case we suspected the death was not the accident it was meant to appear?'

'Per put the sugar in,' Siân said, frowning. 'The fingerprints prove it.'

'Perhaps he simply forgot you do not take it. Perhaps he had everything ready for your return, a reconciliation in mind.'

'I doubt it. We were finished with each other. He must have known that as surely as I did.'

'But perhaps he was not prepared to accept that. Perhaps he had an exaggerated belief in his own charm—or in his ability to overcome your resistance by force if necessary?'

Siân suffered a brief flashback to that disagreeable last night at Kato Zakros when she hadn't wanted Per. And he'd forced her. She'd fought him silently because she was too proud to call out for help, but he'd been too strong. It was uncanny how the Captain seemed able to sum up a man he'd never known in life. Or perhaps he was like that himself and assumed that all men took what they wanted when they wanted.

'Is this really a profitable line of inquiry?' Sven Wennberg asked with distaste.

'I find no evidence of a third person having been present,' the Captain said mildly, 'so I must prepare a scenario with the characters already provided.' He sighed. 'You say, Miss Westbury, that you were finished with the young man. So what did you propose as an alternative?'

'I hadn't decided.'

'After a whole day spent on your own, thinking, you had still reached no conclusion?'

'There were so many things to consider: money, resources, transport. If I couldn't manage to continue on my own I should have to go home with my work unfinished. Anyway, I didn't spend the day thinking, as you suppose. I worked quite hard, and enjoyed it. There are sketches and paintings I did. And photographs in the camera, taken up on the hillside. They should at least prove that I wasn't near the farm all day.'

116

'Maybe. They will be carefully examined, but lacking proven times or dates—' His out-turned palms expressed what his unmoving shoulders failed to do.

'Your painting things,' he said, suddenly cheerful, as though delighted to find one item on which they could agree, 'were found in the right direction, from where you ran on first seeing the fire. Kyrios Kostantinou came across them later. The camera too. If there had been no death for us to investigate he would most likely have taken it to Mires to sell, such a valuable piece of property.'

'We are not concerned with a missed opportunity for petty theft,' Harrison reminded him waspishly.

The Captain swivelled his body to survey the Englishman with exasperated amusement. 'That would certainly not justify your troubling to visit us, it's true. So, agreed, we are investigating a violent death. Murder, in fact.'

'Well, I didn't kill Per,' Siân said doggedly, 'and I don't know who did.'

'You had motive, opportunity and means.'

She considered the policeman, frowning. 'No motive to *kill* him. You're thinking of hell having no fury like a woman scorned. Maybe it's not just a convenient male quote. It could be true, sometimes. But not in my case. I don't feel *scorned*. I think knowing Per has left me wiser, and a bit ashamed. I was thinking of moving on myself, not removing him.'

'Moving on. In the Volvo perhaps, as you're now free to do? I understand Mr Wennberg has agreed that you take over all the provisions and equipment. The car hire was paid in advance and there remain over two weeks to run, with an option to extend.'

Siân flushed. 'I don't know who told you that but it's materially true. Mr Wennberg has been very generous, and I'd paid Per more than my half share anyway.'

'The insinuation is infamous,' Sven Wennberg broke in coldly.

Fotiadis was not easily put off. 'Every possibility, every facet of the case, must be examined. Even revenge exacerbated by hope of gain. It is a solid motive which would stand up well in court.' The policeman sounded smug.

'It wasn't me,' Siân said with a sort of hopelessness. 'The Kostantinous had just as much against them circumstantially, and you let them go.'

Fotiadis stood, pushing himself up from his desk with scarred, brown hands. Siân sat staring at them, horridly fascinated. She hadn't noticed the scars before. He had managed somehow to keep them out of sight. They frightened her now, proof that he'd lived in a different world, one of grim suffering. How could he ever understand a person like herself? He needed to fix guilt on someone and he'd do just that. Even if it had to be her.

She raised glazed eyes to find he was smiling. He offered her one of his mutilated hands. 'Goodbye, Miss Westbury, and thank you for your help. I do not think we need to trouble you for a day or two. Feel free to continue your work, but please telephone my office every evening from your hotel in Timbaki. By eleven o'clock, shall we say?'

The others were rising too. Siân found that she was still clutching her tumbler of chilled coffee. She put it unsteadily down and held out her hand. The man's touch was warm and scaly.

She thought: *Now he will strike, just as I think I'm going free.*

Sven Wennberg held the door open for her. Harrison was making consular gobblings behind them. She walked out into the brilliant afternoon and stood, sickly bemused.

'Are you feeling unwell, Siân?' Wennberg was bending over her, anxious-eyed.

She looked past him, across the courtyard, to the closed shutters of the room she'd been held in. And remembered the papers hidden under the carpet.

'I'm all right, thanks.'

They had already brought down her overnight bag. She made an excuse to go back to her room: there was a handkerchief she'd mislaid, a specially nice one. And anyway she needed to fix her make-up.

They let her go up without Old Agatha this time, and she retrieved the papers. There were too many to go into her shoulder-bag and there was nothing in it she could jettison,

118

so she re-distributed the rest round her body just above waist level, where they pricked her flesh. She tightened her belt and surveyed herself in the mirror. The effect was rather lumpy, but she might get by so long as the tracts didn't crackle, and there was less likelihood by the minute because of the sweat pouring out of her.

She put on lipstick, gazed round the room, took her final look from the window, saw the Captain emerge from his office and encounter someone in the courtyard below.

They embraced, one in uniform, the other civilian, clapping each other on the upper arms like old friends. Siân recoiled at the same moment that the policeman snatched the other man out of the angle of her sight. Heart pounding, she craned to see the empty space where the two had stood.

What could it mean, their meeting like old friends, their hiding from sight like conspirators—the neckless Captain and Andreas Vassilakis?

CHAPTER 13

Back at the hotel Siân looked out fresh clothes and began to run a bath. Someone had been in her room doing more than tidying it. She remembered how the stores had been moved about inside the Volvo. So they were still searching. For something specific, or for anything that could pin the murder on her?

Out on the landing there were voices: Sven greeting Vanessa as she came in from a drive with the man Hooper. Siân thought she heard Alison's lower-pitched murmur as the sitting-room door opened. When the bathwater was turned off, in the steamy silence there came the tapping of fingernails on the door.

Surprisingly, it was Vanessa—looking quite recovered, even radiant, with crisply lacquered hair and immaculate tan make-up, once more the confident, health-conscious Swedish-by-adoption Lib woman. 'I heard you were back.

What an experience!' She sounded faintly amused, quite without rancour.

Siân was at a loss how to respond. 'Your husband has been very kind. The Vice-Consul too.'

'Sticking together, the diplomatic brotherhood. Men are good at things like that. Look, are you fixed up properly for clothes? Shoes, dresses, that sort of thing? Better let Hooper drive you to Mires tomorrow, set yourself up.'

'Thank you for the offer, but I guess my shirts and jeans will have to do. I must catch up on my work, you see.'

'Really?' She moved her shoulders elegantly, to show how incomprehensible she found the girl: it was nothing so ordinary as a shrug. 'But one must want pretty things sometimes. What a strange girl you are. Per set great store by dressing well, as I'm sure you know.' Still the cool put-down act, but no venom. 'Well, I did offer.' She ran a sensuous hand down one bare arm and a scent of freesias came off her. 'See you at dinner, then?'

Siân agreed, shut the door on her visitor and leaned a moment with her back against its panels. Vanessa was more than strange. It was surely some kind of sickness that made her so changeable. Siân had known a girl at school who alternated without warning between affection and spite, but she had been diabetic. With her it was a problem of chemical imbalance. In Vanessa's case Siân suspected something more sinister. There were schizoid personalities, she knew, who teetered between reality and a fantasy existence where nothing corresponded to how others saw it.

When Per spoke of a 'dotty aunt' had he really been thinking of his mother, setting the defect at one remove because he would not admit any taint of heredity? And her behaviour was definitely abnormal, displaying much the same two opposed faces as Alison said her sons had had.

But Roland and Per had been raised apart, one by each sister, so their differences could be due to environment. And how had that curious arrangement come about? Someone —Sven or Andreas—had mentioned that Vanessa was ill when Roland was born, but she'd managed to rear Per a few years later. And still the brothers were kept apart.

120

Then there had been that awful disclosure which Alison had made, seeming to be thinking aloud; that Per had *killed* his older brother. And again, that each had died by fire, one heroically, the other involved in a 'shoddy deceit'. How could Miss Markham have discovered such a thing about Per unless she'd kept watch on him in some way? But from all those hundreds of miles away, on Rhodes? There was no way she could have done.

Siân sat on the side of her bed holding between tensed hands the ivory cheesecloth dress she was to wear at dinner. Looking down at it she thought of Phyllia, her brother, her 'dear Manolis'. There was something about Manolis too that was disturbing, but she couldn't remember what it was. Something he'd done just before he took off for Zakros, still sitting in the car. Wrote down something as a warning to her. After he'd glimpsed Vanessa. Yes; he'd claimed that he'd seen her once before, three weeks back in Iraklion, and she was dangerous. That would have been before Per himself arrived on Crete. Probably Manolis was mistaken, but he had seemed so sure.

If only there were just one person she could take all these worries to. The Wennbergs and Miss Markham were too personally involved. Manolis had gone. There had been Andreas before, but since that scene in the police courtyard she couldn't be sure of him any more. It was clear he was on the Captain's side and in a position to trap her. 'Don't trust anyone at all,' he'd told her, 'not even myself.' How right. And since he'd come south again from Iraklion, where was he now? What was he hatching with his friends, this secret police spy she had been so mistaken about?

Andreas Vassilakis took his time reading through the two transcripts; first the photocopy of Siân's minute writing, then the typed account of her interview with the officer from Zakros. Alternately drinking *ouzo* and black coffee, he and Captain Fotiadis pulled out points to discuss.

'You will need to exercise some caution,' the policeman warned, 'because now you know more than she has told you. She could catch you out. She is shrewd enough.'

'Intelligent,' the doctor allowed, 'but an innocent. I feel like a *voyeur*, reading this.'

'She's fond of you, my friend.'

'As I am of her. But there is no future in it. Her roots are in England, and I belong here.'

'As a botanist, she might surprise you by transplanting her roots. Or yours.'

Vassilakis grimaced, darted a glance at his watch. 'I have thirty-six hours' leave. Had. Less now. I must be back by eight tomorrow evening. Manolis has his hands full with his girl in Zakros, so it will be up to your men after that.'

'To protect her? There is less need now that she's told us all she knows.'

'All she thinks she knows. Suppose there is a face only she can identify?'

'Seen where? Doing what? I should be glad to have just one link between those two deaths, apart from the girl herself. There is nothing. We have been unable to find the piece of metal tag which the first victim was clutching when he died. Photographs of the dead Wennberg are being circulated here and at Zakros. Some good may come of that, but nothing yet. There was that whole hour before his questioning about the burnt-out car. We know how the girl spent her time, but who was the man with and where did he go to get his new clothes? What windsurfer ran the girl down (if it wasn't your clumsy self)? And then the phone calls down here, at the Kostantinou farm: who was Per Wennberg in contact with, and what was he up to on the quiet?'

'While you solve all that,' Andreas grunted, 'I must go and see Siân.'

'Press your suit,' the Captain said, suddenly switching to English.

The doctor made ineffectual flicks with one hand at the creases in his pale grey jacket, then stopped. 'Ah yes, press my suit. A curious expression.'

'Curious people, the British. Well, go safely, my friend. I shall not be far away.'

*

They had finished dinner when the hotel-keeper announced Dr Vassilakis. Andreas found the group at coffee and had an instant impression of startled interest, except for Siân who was not taken unawares but seemed smouldering with something other than fondness. He entered the general conversation aware of a vibrant silence from her quarter of the room.

'You will stay here overnight, of course,' Wennberg assumed.

'If I may. I'm most grateful. There are things I need to discuss . . .'

They understood at once, and since Siân made no move to withdraw they started to get up themselves.

'Oh, please,' he demurred. It was embarrassing.

'All right,' Siân said suddenly in a brittle voice. Her chin was set stubbornly. She went across to the door, said good night to the others. On the landing there was no making for her own room. She started down towards the hotel's front door.

'Car or walk?' Andreas asked, equally curt.

'I could do with some exercise.' When they reached the end of the main street he asked, 'May I know what I've done wrong?'

She walked on into the increasing gloom, stumbling now and again over stones on the rough path. After a few moments she stopped and turned on him. 'You never told me you were such friends with that awful policeman, the one without a neck.'

Her anger startled him. Then it was his turn to walk on in silence, hunched and frowning, until he realized she was left behind. He swung round and went back. 'Siân, let us go back into the light where we can see each other.'

'I don't want people staring at me. Everyone knows where I spent last night. I'm sure they all think I killed Per just because he slept with the Kostantinou woman.'

'Does it matter? Do they matter? Let them see you are free and have friends. Then they'll know the police accept you are innocent.'

'You haven't explained yet about the Captain. I saw you together in the courtyard.'

'I shall do so, over a coffee. Or something stronger.'

He led her to the brightest taverna which spilled out of the main street into a narrow alley overhung with a wild vine haphazardly strung with fairy lights. When the brandies he ordered had arrived he put both hands flat on the table and stared into her eyes opposite. 'That "awful" policeman is my friend. And his having no neck, as it appeared to you, may be partly due to my professional incompetence. There was a great deal to remove. Splintered bone, soft tissue and steel fragments. He is a very brave man indeed. You may know that there have been terrorist activities in Athens from time to time. He was a metropolitan police officer on duty when a hand grenade was thrown into a crowd of tourists. He threw it back, but still it burst in the air and so he was badly injured. We thought at first he would be paralysed for life, but God has been good to him. He is now even able to continue his career, in this quiet backwater.'

'And you were his surgeon.'

'One of three. The most junior registrar. But during his recovery I grew to admire and love him as a brother. It was his decision alone to call you in for questioning. He did so, I am sure, because he knew I was afraid for your safety and you were unprotected.'

'I should have guessed some of this when I saw his hands. Andreas, I am sorry.'

'You were afraid of him, and so you made him your enemy. We forget that enemies are people too.'

'And he wasn't awful at all. In fact he was so reasonable that I kept expecting trickery. Every time he eased up I was waiting for the final blow to fall.'

'My poor Siân. You look exhausted.'

'I am. I didn't sleep last night. I did something you suggested before you went back to Iraklion.'

'What was that?'

'I wrote out all I could remember about Zakros and Vai and what happened to Per. And I sneaked it out when I was released. It's upstairs in my room and I want you to read it. Will you, please, Andreas?'

'Very well, but you must get a good sleep tonight. I will stay with you, if you wish, and read what you've written. I haven't long. They expect me back on duty tomorrow evening.'

'Just the one night,' Siân said in a small voice. 'And I have sleep to catch up on.' He didn't miss the smile that teased the corner of her mouth.

They did as he proposed. Andreas read through her account as if for the first time, and when he laid down the last page he found her eyes were open again and on him. 'What do you think?'

Deliberately he turned the manuscript over and read the print on the reverse side of one sheet. 'So many religious tracts! I think that you must be a very devout young lady. It would not surprise me if you became a nun!'

Andreas was gone from her room before morning light. They met again at breakfast, which Sven had just finished. He was looking through mail directed from Rome. He looked grey and drawn, stood up at Siân's entrance, exchanged a few brief phrases and returned to his reading, his mouth a grim, tight line under the falsely bland moustache. There were no other places set at table; the ladies were breakfasting in their rooms.

'Today,' Andreas announced to Siân, 'you can work while I watch. Tell me where I should drive you.'

'Westward, I think. If you're feeling energetic we could tackle the Samaria Gorge. I could paint and take a specimen box to bring back other flowers to work on later.'

'Good. Can I use your camera?'

'The film's nearly finished. We'll need another. Shall I order two packed lunches?'

'No. We'll make up our own from the market. Much better.'

Siân poured more coffee for them both. 'The marvellous thing here is that you don't have to wait for the right weather: it's guaranteed fine.'

He looked doubtful. 'Year in, year out, you could get tired

125

of it. You would feel nostalgia for your English uncertainty, opening the curtains each day to a surprise.'

'Perhaps, but I'm here for such a short time, and summer should be really summer, not the snivelling version we get at home.'

'Persephone.' Sven glanced up briefly from the papers in his hand. 'You could be like her: half the year in sunshine and half in the Underworld.' He had this gift of sharing his attention between two matters of interest. As on some previous occasion, his words had unconsciously given away a level of thought no one else had yet arrived at.

It left Andreas slightly embarrassed, with the sense of being rushed. Siân's eyebrows were puckered as she tried to recapture an elusive memory: the other occasion when Sven, distrait, had spoken in the same absent fashion. It had been in this room, as he selected bottles for their drinks, and she had just mentioned Andreas by name for the first time. Then Sven had said something like, 'The doctor who helped you at Vai?' and the two sisters had looked up expectantly but were never given an explanation. And Siân herself never learned how Sven got to hear of the incident, never having met Andreas, nor been in touch with Per for months.

She looked at him now from the corner of her eyes and he seemed quite unaware of her scrutiny, concentrating on things of greater moment.

Andreas and the girl left early before the ladies appeared. They took the Volvo and as it pulled away another car eased in before the hotel. In it were Captain Fotiadis and the young man in the sharp suit. Getting out, the Captain bowed distantly, solid and teaky as ever in his grey-green uniform. Siân ventured a small, uncertain wave and received in return a half-salute from a large, white-gloved hand. Reconciliation. Andreas grinned.

The day went well but too fast. Siân was careful to take the minimum of sprigs to paint from later, scrupulous not to disturb any roots. There were seven specimens of real interest which she threaded through foil lids on her water jars, packing the arrangement inside her box with moistened wadding, then she settled down opposite an exciting accident of nature. Backed by a brilliant show of flowering Spanish broom was a clump of *Daphne oleoides* bearing long-tubed white flowers and simultaneous clusters of fruit like cherries, the whole set off by dense foliage of vivid green.

'No one will believe this is true,' she told Andreas. 'Would you like to photograph it for me as proof?'

He unpacked the camera and took several close-ups, then three with Siân in the foreground busily at work. She was completely absorbed and for a while neither spoke.

When her painting was well under way and Andreas had gone back to sprawl on the grass nearby, Siân sounded him out about Sven Wennberg. The young doctor lay back, scowling at the sky, hands clasped under his head. 'Kind? M'mm. Going for your Vice-Consul was a diplomatic reaction, but it's true he does seem concerned for you. A complicated man. There are layers, and layers within layers, in a person like him. Reticence and concealment are born into him, out of so many generations of authority.'

'I thought Sweden was a socialist democracy. Do you mean they still have aristos?'

'They are relics from Bernadotte's retinue.'

'Bernadotte? Wasn't he the United Nations chief who was assassinated?'

'I mean an ancestor of his, a successful general in Bonaparte's army. The Swedes admired him so much that they elected him their king.'

'That does sound vaguely familiar. But unlikely just the same.'

'It's perfectly true. The original Bernadotte was a plain man of the people, but with time his family have acquired a certain grandeur. So did the other French families who went with him to Sweden. Many have Swedish names now, through marriage on the female side, or by a change of pronunciation. This Wennberg is a professional diplomat from that ruling class. In Athens my father has a number of patients from the diplomatic corps, so I know a little about them.'

Siân considered this, rinsing her brush in clear water before mixing a clean, sharp yellow. 'Per must have been a terrible disappointment to him.'

'Yes, to a man with such a marked sense of what is honourable. Of course, I know nothing really against the son. It is an impression of—' He frowned, searching for the right word.

'Hubris,' Siân said quietly. 'That is how Miss Markham sees it.'

Andreas waved the word away. 'Oh, the anarchy of being young! Fortunately one usually grows out of it, learns to fit in.'

'Per expected the world to fit in with him. With so much charm he managed to hide for a while what a self-centred creep he was, and so dependent on others' admiration. Do you suppose Per minded that his father despised him? He must have known. Sven had faced him out a number of times.'

Andreas sat up, looking troubled. 'Are you sure?'

'Oh yes, Sven told me. There have been rows over girls, and Sven felt responsible, because Per didn't.'

'So they had reached a state of declared war?'

Siân looked at him, puzzled. 'They had discussed it together. I suppose it must have been acrimonious.'

'*Acrimonious?* A matter of principle to a man like the father; and the son who thought himself above reproach? What kind of "discussion" would that be? How would it leave each of them afterwards?'

Siân hadn't considered this. Of course, Per would have been consumed by acid anger, outraged, determined to do something, anything, to prove himself above the scorn poured on him. How, though, could he hope to buy himself back and score over his contemptuous father? Some magnificent, outstanding achievement was needed—but what would be within the scope of an inexperienced, very junior member of the diplomatic corps? Nothing professional, then. It would have to be found in a quite different sphere. Some kind of extraordinary distinction . . .

'I do not think,' Andreas was saying rather ponderously,

'that a proud man like Sven Wennberg could bear to leave the situation like that. His anger is as dangerous as dry tinder. It would take only a spark—'

Fire, Siân thought. Per killed by fire. As the words passed through her mind she saw the shock in Andreas's eyes as the same thought struck him. *Sven, kill his own son?* Impossible, surely. That would be taking pride and family honour to an insane degree.

Her hand was shaking. She had to lay the camelhair brush down and wipe her fingers on the paint rag. 'No, Andreas, there was no spark. Not like that. Sven was in Rome. Whatever happened—happened in time to prevent anything so awful.'

'But Per is dead, Siân. He's dead just the same. However much Sven Wennberg grieves, he must also feel some relief.'

CHAPTER 14

For lunch Andreas spread coarse pâté and goats'-milk cheese on fresh rolls; mixed chopped tomatoes, parsley, onions, olives and cucumber chunks in a spicy dressing. They finished with almond honey-cakes and fruit, kissing over the last of the wine. This feast had almost chased away their earlier dismay.

'To think that I have to go back,' Andreas said regretfully.

'It's good to know one's needed.'

He stared at her mournfully, eyes doggily reproachful.

She smiled. 'Oh yes, you're needed here too, I admit it.'

'You heard what Mr Wennberg said. About Persephone. Could you do that?'

She had a sudden vision of the beanbag Englishwoman she'd shared a taxi with from the hospital, rootless and wretched, widowed in a strange land, with hostile in-laws. Not that the same would happen in her case, but it was a risky business. She hadn't seen the risks in advance when she'd teamed up with Per, and look where she'd landed!

129

'I don't know. Persephone didn't have the necessity of choosing.'

He stroked her hair gently back and nibbled with his lips at her ear. 'Is the choice so difficult?' Abruptly he became more practical, prosaic. 'Siân, have you informed your parents of what happened, that you were in danger? I know how much you value independence, but they too have rights.'

'I rang home from Sitia that once, then sent my address from Iraklion. There could be a letter waiting at the hotel.'

'Ring again. Now that Harrison has seen you he will report to London. The English newspapers could get to hear of it. You must warn your family.'

'I could tell them I'd been questioned. And cleared, do you think?'

'But still required as a witness.'

'That might bring my father out here.'

'I shall be happy to meet him.' Andreas grimaced comically. 'So I tell myself.'

'He'll like you. No question of that.'

'When he comes, I meet his plane. You agree?'

'If that's what you'd like, Andreas. *If* he comes.'

Back at the hotel at Timbaki they found a telephone message for Siân. It was from Phyllia. The hotel-keeper had written it out in careful, misspelt English.

The Cypriot girl had wanted to say goodbye because she was leaving that night by air for Athens with Manolis's father. There he would put her on a flight for London. It was better to go right away for a while as everyone advised. It was so sad now in Zakros. She was desolate to be parted from her dear Manolis, but happy he would return to be with Siân who suffered grief even as she did herself. She hoped to see Siân a second time, in London, soon.

'When does Manolis get here?' Andreas demanded.

'She doesn't say. If he sees her first plane off tonight, the earliest he could arrive is tomorrow morning. But he may need to do things in Iraklion first. There's the taverna and his partner—'

'They've plenty of alternative labour. I'm glad he's coming. I shall sleep better for knowing you're not alone.'

'I'll ask him to help me write to Phyllia in Greek. I wish I'd been able to tell her how sorry I am, and now it's too late.'

A yellow taxi arrived to take Andreas on the two-hour journey back to the capital. He kissed Siân tenderly, no longer troubling to push the gold-rimmed spectacles out of his way. Practice was giving him confidence. 'Take great care of yourself.'

'You too. I'll be fine, between your Captain and Manolis.'

The evening fell flat after he'd gone. There was no sign of the Wennbergs, and Miss Markham was seated on her favourite pine stump in the overgrown garden, lost in reverie.

Siân unpacked her wild flowers and set them out in the coolest part of her room before changing for dinner. When she went along for drinks, there were only the two sisters there.

'Sven has gone back to Rome,' Vanessa said indifferently. 'For consultation with his chief, it seems.' She watched Alison removing the cutlery from Sven's place-setting and her eyes hardened. 'No, leave it, Alison. We can't be three women on our own. Hooper must take Sven's place.' There was a tinge of malicious irony in her voice. Siân saw Alison stiffen, then relax. She shrugged delicately.

'Why not?' and she started replacing the knives and forks.

'Did Captain Fotiadis call today?' Siân asked, to fill the embarrassing silence. 'I caught sight of him in the street this morning.'

'Not to my knowledge,' Vanessa said languidly. 'Did he come to grill *you*, Alison?'

'No. He spent about half an hour with Sven in here after breakfast. I think that was all.'

'He'll be looking for a new suspect.' Vanessa's tone was scathing. 'He's no good at all. Why don't they get someone out from Scotland Yard?'

'I don't imagine you can pick detectives like Harley Street specialists,' Alison said mildly, examining the *hors d'œuvre* of

131

fish salad. 'And Captain Fotiadis must have some good ideas. He didn't take long to clear Siân.'

'Shall I go for Hooper?' Siân asked quickly, to stem the undercurrent of bickering.

'Shout over the stairwell,' Vanessa ordered. 'His name's Warwick.'

Siân went out on the landing and called, 'Mr Hooper, Mrs Wennberg would like you to come up for dinner.' Almost immediately she heard soft footsteps on the hall tiles and a door closed quietly below. Hooper started up the stairway, prompt on his cue. He must have been sitting with his door ajar, awaiting orders.

Now Siân met the man face to face, and it was as disturbing as her first glimpse at the farm when he brought Vanessa there to see where her son had died.

There was a passionless discipline about him that frightened her, as if he were an automaton. His smoothness wasn't that of a townie. Just the reverse, he was weathered and muscled, his movements controlled, his hair cropped too short, the planes of his gleaming face too clean-shaven, the eyes too hard and glittery. Like an SAS man on leave from Northern Ireland, briefly back in civilian dress.

If the invitation to join them astonished him he gave no sign of it, silently taking Sven's seat when Vanessa indicated it. Her attitude towards him was a curious one, half disdainful, half provocative. Siân found herself wondering whether he would as unemotionally take over Sven's place in her bed if Vanessa required it.

Alison was watching him, birdlike and bright. Over their meal it was she who elicited something of his background, but Siân had the impression that Hooper would answer as it pleased him, irrespective of what the truth was.

He had worked for Mr Wennberg in Rome, he said, and Vanessa didn't contradict this. His role was a confidential and personal one.

'As a bodyguard,' Miss Markham defined it more precisely, nodding.

'That, among other duties,' he agreed. Rome could be a dangerous place. There had been too many kidnap and

132

murder attempts for anyone of importance to feel one hundred per cent safe.

'And before that?' Miss Markham probed.

He'd been in the armed forces. Unspecifically.

Where? Siân wondered. His voice was flat and rather nasal, the accent in the grey area between Australian, South African and London East Ender. Not a gentleman, Miss Markham was probably deciding. If an army man, not commissioned. A Warrant Officer, seasoned and experienced; inflexible; a fit minder for Sven Wennberg to leave in charge of his wife and sister-in-law while he was recalled to Sweden.

'Is there an international crisis on?' Siân asked, and Vanessa's eyes widened at this apparent *non sequitur*.

Miss Markham, however, seized on it. 'Yes, one wonders. So singular that Sven should be recalled just now, at such a—such an inconsiderate moment.'

Vanessa threw the question brusquely at Hooper. 'Well, *is* there a crisis? I haven't seen a newspaper since I arrived, nor television. There must be airmail copies of English papers on Crete, but I suppose they all get snapped up in Iraklion.'

'Andreas had a Greek paper today,' Siân remembered. 'It didn't seem to excite him at all. He just grumbled about the wine surplus in Europe. Nothing else.'

'Perhaps Stockholm is upset about Per,' Vanessa said. She sounded uncertain. 'They hate publicity. The Foreign Office is so—well, they'll insist it has to remain an accident.'

'Even if it wasn't?' Siân had meant to keep off the subject, but now they were knee-deep in it. 'The Captain didn't release me because he thinks it's an accident. It was because he knew he'd got the wrong person. They'll go on looking until they find who it was, publicity or no.'

Vanessa threw down her table napkin. 'This lamb's disgusting! I can't stomach it. You'll have to excuse me.' She rose, abruptly pushing her chair back so that it fell over backwards, trapping her with its legs. She seemed instantly to go to pieces, batting at it wildly with one open hand, the other clutching her handbag to her chest. 'Warwick, get me out! Don't just stand there!'

He moved swiftly round the table, righting the heavy chair in one fist, grasping her elbow with the other. In a couple of strides he had her at the door, through it, the door shut to cut off her panicky yelping.

The change of tempo had been so rapid, so unexpected, that the other two were struck silent with shock. And then Siân recognized what else Hooper reminded her of: a hospital orderly, white-uniformed, aseptic, emotionlessly plunging in a hypodermic needle.

Miss Markham stood up and walked across to the sideboard. 'I think I need something stronger than Greek wine tonight. Brandy, Siân?'

'I'm not sure it wouldn't make things worse. Oh well, perhaps.'

'Sometimes there is just no point in thinking too clearly.'

'You're right. And I need some Dutch courage to make a phone call. Andreas has reminded me that my father isn't in the picture about what happened out here, and with the Vice-Consul becoming involved it may get through to the English newspapers.'

'Oh my dear, what will you tell them at home?'

'That my travel partner's been accidentally killed, I think. Anything worse they might put down to Press exaggeration. But I don't feel ready to tackle my father yet. I need my mind damped down a little. My imagination, anyway. It's been suggesting such awful possibilities.'

Miss Markham looked at her strangely. 'What sort of possibilities, Siân?' She sounded apprehensive.

The girl gestured vaguely. 'About Per. It's ridiculous. I mean, we've all been talking as though he was a really evil person, someone we might even want to kill—when truly we're not much more than disappointed in him.'

'Evil.' Miss Markham's voice had a faraway sound. 'I don't think I've ever heard evil defined. But I suppose it is the state of mind when someone is so self-obsessed that he's no longer aware of any necessity but his own gratification; no love, no pity, no remorse, no basic rules of behaviour, no ambition beyond getting his own way. And that is how Per was. I watched him from a small child, learning to take whatever he wanted, later manipulating others into offering him his desires—without consideration of cost, or pain, or his own overweening awfulness.

'He used to come to us for Christmas when he was a schoolboy in England. Sometimes at Easter too, and by the time he left he had us all at each other's throats; even Roland and me; our guests; the servants; my best people on the estate. Complete disharmony, and all for sheer devilment. Sometimes he brought about these clashes deliberately, sometimes they seemed to follow naturally in his wake. There were cases when I couldn't decide exactly which it was. As on the night of the fire.'

'The fire?'

'The fire when Roland was killed.'

'You said once that Per killed him.'

'Did I? Well, it's true. That last April, they went fell-walking and were to be gone five or six days, taking camping things and provisions, and putting up overnight at Youth Hostels. It was at one of these that the fire broke out, unaccountably, at two in the morning. There were separate dormitories for boys and girls, and awkward corridors. The smoke was so dense that they couldn't be sure everyone was safely out. They called the roll afterwards and Per was missing. No one remembered seeing him when Roland was helping the others to escape. He went back in, although the upper floor was already falling away. It was certain death, but he wouldn't be held back. He died in there, searching for his brother.'

'And Per?'

'Per turned up at midday, when the house was steaming ash. He swore he couldn't remember where he'd been all night because he went drinking with some local men. Later the police came to my home to question him. They'd been up to the old cockpit on the moor above the hostel and found hastily dug graves. They dug themselves and found—along with the mauled remains of four dogs—a lot of bloody rags and crumpled tally sheets for the betting. These showed that Per had won over fifty pounds that night, and the money was still in his trouser pocket. Once he was faced with this he admitted he'd been at the dog fights and said wasn't it lucky, or he could have been burnt in the hostel himself.'

Alison Markham's voice had faded to a whisper. Siân barely caught her final words before she turned away and hid her face in her hands. 'He said, "Like—that—poor fool —my brother"!'

A tricky little breeze had sprung up when Siân stepped out of the hotel doorway. It whipped up the skirt of the Phyllia dress and sent her hair snaking across her cheeks, stinging her eyes. Turning to face upwind, she began to walk the length of the main street, willing herself to find something to crowd out the appalling story Alison had told.

It was as vivid as if she had been there herself, seen the aureole of flames and the dark shape of Roland stumbling back into the blaze in his search for the missing schoolboy. And she saw Per's face, flushed, rebellious, self-righteous in his discovered guilt, facing the bereaved woman with contemptuous bravado. A younger Per than she had known. Some five years, three months and two days younger.

Unconsciously she'd been making for the taverna where she'd been with Andreas the night before. The vine of its terrace was shaking with the wind, loose tendrils tossing, and the white paper cloths clipped to the tables were flapping like pelicans' wings. The mixture of wine and brandy was providing her with a dream-sequence, slow-motion world.

She ordered coffee, sitting uncaring whether she was pointed at or not, and after a while was conscious that attention had turned away. Between moves of backgammon, items of gossip, capping of longwinded jokes, the drinkers had another interest now. Their eyes went always back to the windows of the little hotel, as if waiting for action to begin, the High Noon confrontation or some equal cliché from melodrama. Significantly she had now joined the audience, no longer one of the cast.

She picked out the lighted windows on the street side.

There was the room she'd recently had dinner in, and farther along was Vanessa's bedroom. No other light showed on that level, but several above it, where the hotel-keeper's family lived. On the ground floor no light at all except in the entrance hall and a reflected glow from the staircase. So where was Hooper? The answer needed no effort of imagination.

The hotel was like a dolls' house with the front lifted off. In her mind she could see exposed all the miniature tragedies inside. In the dining-room a distraught woman sitting over her brandy, passing in review a life that was a succession of radiant promises withered away to nothing: a fortune and a home that she was exiled from; a sister, a lover, an almost-son wrested away from her. And a few boxlike dolls-house rooms farther along, a scene enacted by a man and a woman. Again a bereaved woman whose sweet things had grown sour, now being controlled or consoled by a man whom her husband paid for 'personal and confidential service'. What a sick, sick world. It had been more wholesome in that prison room the Captain had held her in.

But tomorrow things would surely improve. Tomorrow Manolis would come.

A third light came on at first floor level, showing that Alison had retired to her own room. It was time for Siân to return to make her two disagreeable phone calls, the first reporting in to the Captain's office and the second to her home number.

Andreas had made the local call for her last night and she had marvelled at the rumblings and chuckles at his end of the Greek conversation. Speaking to Fotiadis would be less easy for her, forced into a false position by his protective move which at first had seemed such a threat. Even now she felt him capable of further deviousness, and not necessarily to her advantage.

When she dialled a strange voice answered her in Greek, then changed to halting English. She left a message that she was where she was supposed to be and wished Captain Fotiadis good night. The voice informed her that the message would be passed on. So far, so good.

Her luck still held with the second call because her father was giving a dinner-party—(the time was two hours back in London)—and couldn't leave his guests. Her stepmother accepted the news of Per's death in her customary unflappable manner, only inquiring, 'Wasn't that rather upsetting, dear?'

Siân agreed that the 'accident' had been quite a shock one way and another, but she'd spoken to the British Vice-Consul, and her friend's parents had arrived to take over the more grisly arrangements. What with formalities and covering the rest of the island's summer flora, she would be pretty hard pressed for the next week or so. Rosemary took it well. 'Let us know if there's anything you need. Hugh forwarded some extra cash yesterday, care of the hotel in Iraklion. We thought it would come in handy.'

'Thanks, Rosemary, it certainly will. Love to Daddy.'

'I'll tell him. 'Bye.'

There was a five-second interval during which she reached the foot of the stairs, then the telephone rang. Andreas this time, speaking from the hospital in Iraklion, with a message from Manolis. Could she meet him off the morning bus due in at Phaistos at nine-thirty? If she drove out there she could have more privacy than at the hotel in Timbaki. Good idea, she agreed: all that exaggerated miming and notes on his jotter could attract unwelcome attention. And beyond Phaistos she could go either north to the lush Messara Plain or east along the coast. Both were areas she hadn't yet covered. She hoped that Manolis would as patiently watch her painting as he'd watched Phyllia embroider.

On arrival he seemed subdued and ready to fit in with her plans. Phyllia had sent her a gift, wrapped in white tissue paper tied with gold streamers. Siân undid it to find a simple tunic dress in aquamarine cheesecloth with a silver braided belt. And Manolis insisted that Siân wasn't to offer any payment this time; Phyllia would be offended. 'She remember your sizes,' he printed on his jotter, and grinned.

He was good at spotting the right kind of habitat for wild flowers, and even knew some of their local Greek names. On the coastal strip they found a late variety of *Cistus incanus*

138

(which he called Ladania), its soft rosy-magenta flowers having orange pin-cushion centres; and higher up were patches of slender *Scabiosa crenata*, of harebell-blue and lilac-pink.

While she painted, Manolis sat cross-legged some distance away, lost in his own sad thoughts. After we've eaten, Siân promised herself, I will ask him all about Phyllia's brother. Now is too soon.

When she had suggested buying provisions for a picnic Manolis opposed it. 'Taverna,' he wrote down for her. 'We go to Ierapetra. I know best chef.' Well, being a restaurateur, of course he would. There was probably some Cretan free-masonry of chefs, and he would be well known to their circle.

It was after one o'clock when she packed her painting things away. Manolis took the wheel of the Volvo and drove them down to the town. Last night's wind was still buffeting the sea, smacking sheets of grey water against the promenade wall to spill over the road like any rough sea at Hastings or Brighton in the off-season winter months. But it was still hot down here, gritty and unwelcoming. The windsurfers and small boats had all withdrawn until the squall blew itself out. Date palms on the terraces rattled and fanned grimly. Siân was glad they had a table indoors close to the cheerful bar.

When they had finished their *Kakavia* and a main course of *Arni Kapama*, she mouthed to the little Greek, 'Tell me about Phyllia's brother. Is she very shocked at his death?'

'Spiros,' Manolis wrote in Greek, 'only sixteen but look older. Angry person, hate Turks, for Cyprus. Blame English also. Wanting money quick, but not work. A man already, very proud. Not liking rules but exciting things.'

Siân nodded. There were young men like that everywhere. 'At risk. Was he a criminal?'

Manolis had to think about that. He hunched his shoulders, spread his hands, palms up, before bending again over his notebook. '*With* criminals perhaps. Phyllia always worry. Spiros has bad friends, one she thinks English, but perhaps Spiros ride him.'

139

'Ride? Do you mean Spiros *was taking him for a ride?*'

'That, yes. Perhaps.'

'So if he upset the Englishman, there may have been a quarrel?'

'She think.'

'Who was he, this Englishman?'

Again the hunched shoulders, the hopeless expression with his hands. He wrote, 'Many English come in summer. Spiros talk with some, sell things, act guide. All sorts. Nobody know. Police ask all the time. And they find he has money, a lot of drax.'

'Poor Phyllia.'

'Is bad in Zakros now. Good she go to her sister, then soon we marry. Nobody ever say Kyria Dritsas have bad blood.' Fiercely he underlined 'nobody'.

So people had turned against Phyllia because her brother was suspect, when she needed sympathy because he was dead. And the two of them were Cypriot, not Cretan. 'Has she no family at all in Greece?'

'Phyllia have *my* family.' In his anger and pride he was impressive. You forgot he was small, pixie, disabled.

'Thank God she has, Manolis. I wish I could do something for her myself. I will as soon as I get back to London, I promise.'

He nodded, taking from his discarded jacket a large envelope, and unfolding from it Siân's original sketches of the dead young man. 'First,' Manolis wrote, 'I show to police. They question Phyllia: where is brother? Then they take us see dead boy and she say yes, Spiros. Is Spiros because Spiros break foot here.' He tapped his own leg low down.

'His ankle. Spiros had once broken his ankle, and so had the dead young man?'

'Has lump. So Phyllia know now Spiros is dead, but she not see face. Police show sketch again and she say, "Yes, yes. Is my brother. I tell you already." And police say, "No accident. Somebody kill him. Is deliberate."'

Siân nodded. 'One of them came down to question me about what we saw on the mountain road, about the burning

140

car and how we found Spiros dead but not badly burnt. So they knew that he'd been moved afterwards and—and disfigured, to delay recognition. But who would have done a thing like that? It's horrible.'

Manolis hesitated, looking doubtfully at Siân, then wrote again. 'This is secret. I have cousin is policeman and he tell me. Police think your friend Mr Per.'

CHAPTER 15

Per could have done it.

Siân sat with her back against a rock, paintbrush in hand, idle. Slowly she went back over the scene above Kato Zakros, relived her own movements and calculated what Per might have done.

Physically he'd had the opportunity, while she climbed back to the road at the lower loop to sit there until he brought the Volvo down. Her route had been easier and more direct than his, but there was a jutting cliff that cut off the scene of the tragedy after the first hundred yards. The point where she waited offered no view of his return to the car, nor of any new outbreak of fire near where they'd left the body.

She shuddered. But admitting that he could have interfered didn't supply any reason why he should. Per had had no part in the initial accident—well, incident—because he'd been with her in the Volvo, fully occupied with holding it to the road. She had been the first to see the bright burst of flame as the other car struck the rocks below. And why should Per want to disfigure the dead boy, a perfect stranger?

Unless he wasn't a stranger. Suppose . . . Could Per have been the 'Englishman' Spiros was supposed to have been involved with? He was tall, very fair: to a Greek he might well seem English, and that was the language he always spoke out here. But, as Manolis said, Crete was full of British in the summer, and Per had arrived only a few days earlier.

141

Could Spiros have picked on him as a potential victim for some con trick, which Per had at first fallen for and then been furious about when he realized he'd been gulled? Surely not furious enough to disfigure a dead man, a mere boy, because of it? No, she could dismiss Per's involvement entirely. The Zakros police were wildly guessing. They had nothing concrete that connected with Per—except his own murder within a matter of days.

She closed her eyes and the sun's white disc was printed in black on the backs of her eyelids. Her head had begun to throb again as it did after the accident at Vai. She should get out of the heat and take a siesta. Manolis was already asleep in the shade of the Volvo, coiled neat and compact, his crisp blue shirt steadily rising and falling with each breath, perspiration faintly misting his forehead.

She observed him at leisure for the first time. Without the animation of his visual speech he looked older and more male. When he was prancing, bright-eyed and faunlike, you didn't notice the resolute chin, the strong neck and muscled shoulders. She appreciated now that he was a perfect athletic type in miniature. Phyllia was a lucky girl.

Poor Phyllia, less lucky in her brother. Siân remembered the defenceless dead face, dark eyes staring at the burning sky, defiant in death, fingers crimped about the piece of metal tag.

About something, anyway. Less and less could she be sure of that detail, because it seemed likely that Per had meant her to find it later in his bush-shirt pocket. It would be so like him to have substituted the tag, to hide whatever the real object had been. He was normally secretive, emptied his pockets carefully and transferred their contents before he put anything in the washbag. Did that possibility of deceit reinforce the suspicion that he'd interfered more positively with the corpse? (The suspicion the police held; which she herself refuted, but could not entirely dismiss for all that.)

Her thoughts made circles and led back to where they'd begun. She seemed physically to see them, like the disturbance when a pebble is thrown into a pond, and as her

142

eyelids grew heavy the concentric circles spread slowly ever wider, flattening in their outer rings until the water was smooth again, smooth as glass under the relentless sun, and the only sound was the whisper of date palms. The stretch before her was rocking as she floated. It had become the sea off the shore of Vai. It was going to happen over again! From the corner of her eyes she saw the straining brown figure skimming towards her, the coloured sail like a monster shark-tail. She started up, awake and trembling, just a split second before the windsurfer struck her.

Vai, she thought, her heart drumming. I have to make up my mind about Vai. *If* Per set light to that dead bush and put Spiros face down on it, and *if* he had got to know the boy in the short time he'd been on Crete—*if* I accept all that, then am I going to blame him in some way for what happened to me at Vai? An attempt on my life because I'd seen the boy's face, or noticed something dangerous, such as the object taken from the boy's dead hand? And as Per hadn't run me down himself—which was impossible—do I believe he arranged for it to happen, either while he was free for that hour at Zakros or by a phone call when we stopped for lunch? If—so many ifs!—if I believe that too, I must accept that someone else was involved, that Per had *two* shady friends on Crete, at Zakros, the three of them possibly associated together. So, where did number three of the trio come into the story? Would he be the killer of Spiros and Per? And my would-be killer at Vai?

She saw Manolis come suddenly, neatly, awake. Being deaf, he wouldn't have been startled by any sound into instant consciousness. She followed the direction of his gaze and saw gauzy wings fluttering on the back of his left hand. An exquisite silver-blue butterfly had landed, and its light touch alerted him. He made no movement now while Siân reached for pencil and sketchblock. The butterfly seemed content to stay still.

'I'll never get the colours before it goes,' Siân wailed quietly.

Manolis had read her lips and made urgent gestures with his free hand towards the plastic bag she used to protect her sketches. She saw at once what he wanted, pierced holes in it with her pencil point and put the bag in his hand. Gently he inverted it over the butterfly and enclosed it together with his fingers. The creature fluttered wildly for a moment until Manolis reached in the bush behind him for a leafy twig to insert beside it. The butterfly clung on and began to preen itself. Manolis plucked the bag's corners out to their farthest extent and secured the opening.

'It won't be for long,' Siân told the butterfly. She renewed the water in her flask and washed it precisely over the drawn outline, dropping in dilute colours to mix as they met on the paper. When they had half dried in the sunshine she used a fresh, fine brush to wipe out the paler veining of the wings.

In less than ten minutes she was satisfied and Manolis released the captive. Siân had no idea what species it belonged to, but it had been too beautiful to pass by. With artistic licence she would reproduce it poised in flight over some suitable flower.

It seemed a good point at which to finish work for the day. She fetched the Thermos flask of coffee which she had prepared that morning, two mugs, and the sugar. This would be her first use of these things since Per had started to make coffee just before he was killed: as pleasant a way as any of exorcizing his grisly ghost.

She poured out, and handed the first mug to Manolis. He set it down beside his feet and unscrewed the sugar jar. Digging the plastic spoon in for an ample helping, he made a distinct scraping sound, but this was not what caught his attention. He had felt a resistance as some object was caught between spoon and side of jar. He dug deeper and twisted upwards. A serpentine piece of metal showed above the surface of the sugar, giving off a dull gold gleam in the sunshine.

'Manolis, what is it?'

In answer he picked it out and held it up for her to see. It was a flattish piece of zigzag metal with a lump at one end. As she took it in her hand she recognized it was meant to represent a barbed snake with a horrendously open

144

mouth. The whole thing was little more than two inches overall and surprisingly heavy for its size. The thin tail end of the serpent appeared to have been broken off.

Manolis thrust his jotter under her eyes. 'Is very old,' she read. 'Is also of gold.'

The two facts together implied an archæological find, something that the ambitious Per might have given his back teeth for. She stared at it in amazement. Because it was hidden in Per's sugar jar there was a possibility he had actually found it at one of the sites he'd visited. On the other hand—and the idea was anything but reassuring—wasn't this a 'scrap of metal' such as Per had said he'd prised from the dead boy's fingers? Could this be the missing object she'd intuitively known Per had substituted the metal tag for?

And it had been hidden in the sugar, presumably by Per. Unless someone else intended it to be found and so incriminate the Swede. There were strict rules about arte-facts over a certain age. Siân couldn't remember if they were automatically the property of the state, but there was certainly a code of conduct preventing speculative digging without licence. Disputes over the marble figures off the Parthenon, which Elgin once acquired from the Turks, had ensured that more recently discovered treasures remained in Greek hands. So what had Per intended doing with this find? Or, alternatively, what had someone intended it to be thought that Per was doing?

Undoubtedly the thing was of some value, and equally clearly no one could publicly claim it without the question of provenance being challenged. Experts could establish its age by assay alone, and its probable locality from the craftsmanship. Owning it would be like holding the *Mona Lisa* after a raid on the Louvre—pointless, except to satisfy a need for secret gloating. If it was really ancient, say Minoan, it would be almost pure gold. They hadn't learned about alloys then. Would Per have been philistine enough to have melted it down for its basic value? She was sure not. He liked money, but fame mattered more. Perhaps he had hidden the find while he decided what to do.

Had he ever shown it to anyone? Could the person who was to have drunk coffee with him (and presumably killed him)—could that person have been there specifically to discuss the disposal of the gold serpent?

She looked up to find Manolis's brooding gaze on her. 'What should I do with it?' she asked.

He didn't reach for his jotter but mouthed one word she couldn't mistake. 'Police.'

Yes, well. That had to be right. She would take it this very afternoon to Captain Fotiadis. And he would be rightly livid because his forensic experts had taken fingerprints off the screwtop jar without checking through its contents.

And someone else had missed it. Twice she'd been aware of a search having been made through her own and Per's belongings. It seemed likely that someone knew about the piece of worked gold and had tried to get hold of it. She turned it now in the palm of her hand and marvelled that anything so ancient—if it really was Minoan it could be between three and four thousand years old—could still arouse passion and greed to the level of a motive for murder.

It had a strange, almost repellent beauty, and reminded her of the snake goddess figurine found in a trunk in the sacred pit of Knossos Palace, but whatever whole this had once formed a part of was different from that statue. This snake was too tightly curved to allow a handhold midway, and there was no sign of any attachment there. The broken end was at the tail, so the snake must have been rearing off some other object. It was difficult to imagine what the entire thing had represented.

'Let's go now,' she said, 'and find the Captain.'

Manolis put his head on one side and mimed telephoning.

'All right, if you think that's better.' She packed everything away in the rear of the car and sat in the passenger seat beside the little Greek. She phoned from the next town they went through, and discovered that Fotiadis was not at his office. He had left instructions, however, for the police post to pass on any communication from Siân. The sergeant on duty demanded the number she was phoning from, asked her to ring off and wait for a call.

146

In less than seven minutes the telephone rang. Fotiadis sounded alert, almost eager. 'There is some development?'

Siân told him she believed she'd discovered what Spiros had really held in his hand.

'Not a scooter's identity tag?'

'No, a serpent. Of solid gold, we think, and probably very ancient.'

'Ah!' There was a short silence. 'Miss Westbury, I am at home. Will you bring it to me? Meanwhile I will summon a friend who knows about these things. Let me tell you how to get here. It is only a matter of eight miles or so.'

It would have seemed curious to Siân that the Captain should take daytime hours off duty at the start of a murder case, except that what Andreas had told her about the man's medical history made it reasonable. When the Volvo turned off the main road on to a long, straight lane between orange groves she understood even better. Fotiadis, meaning to retire, had bought a Cretan farm far from the hurly-burly and politics of Athens. Then he had recovered sufficiently to miss involvement in his life's work of criminal investigation. Perhaps to qualify for a better pension, or from habit, he had accepted a part-time posting to supervise the local force. This was one of his farming days.

He came out on the verandah to meet them, in khaki drill slacks and open-necked cream shirt, the sleeves rolled up to reveal that the pitted marks and white scars continued up beyond his wrists. Behind him a tall, drooping figure blinked at the newcomers through thick-pebbled spectacles. Fotiadis waved a big hand. 'Miss Westbury, my friend Professor Tsallas is very interested in your find. We are fortunate that he lives so close. Shall we go indoors?'

Siân had brought the sugar jar, resealed and wrapped in two paper napkins. Fotiadis clucked when she unpacked it, annoyed as she knew he'd be. 'Inside this?'

'Yes. See? I'm afraid we've both handled it.' She passed over the little serpent in a handkerchief and watched the academic carefully unwrap it. The man's immediate excitement was obvious although he made no remark. Eventually he murmured to Fotiadis in Greek. It meant nothing to Siân but she noticed Manolis lip-reading from across the room, and smiled.

'Will you trust us with it?' Fotiadis asked. 'Apparently it could be of great value. I will give you a receipt.'

'If you think that's necessary. I'm not the owner. It is really gold, then? And Minoan?'

'Almost certainly, he says. It is the most important find for over a decade. Is it Kato Zakros it came from?'

'Who knows?' She explained her theory about Per's substitution of the valueless metal tag to ward off her curiosity. He seemed warily ready to accept the possibility.

'But if it came from Kato Zakros,' Siân said doubtfully, 'why should Per be so willing to leave such a rich site? He must have guessed there were other treasures nearby. Yet we went wandering off to Vai, and Sitia, Iraklion. Phaistos was the first archæological site he visited afterwards, apart from a cursory glance at Gournia on the way.'

Fotiadis stared at her with unblinking eyes. 'Perhaps I would not remain long myself where I was involved in a violent death.'

'But Per wasn't. He couldn't have been. He was driving the Volvo when that other car went over the edge. There must have been half a mile of twisting road between.'

'Ah yes, someone else would have sent the car over, but it is the body we are discussing. There have been further pathological tests made, and some interesting facts have emerged.'

'What facts?' She was conscious of a terrible constriction in her throat. Her voice came out strangely hoarse.

'Changes in the state of certain body cells. Unusual absence of signs of vital reaction. Evidence of some measure of refrigeration prior to the burning.'

'What does that mean?' She could barely get the question out.

'Simply that the death must have taken place some time before the apparent accident. The body was preserved by chilling, to gain time to arrange a spectacular exodus—and provide the killer with an alibi.'

148

'And you think that *Per*—? Because he's dead and can't defend himself!' She was shaking with anger, or it might have been fear. All the suspicions she had mentally levelled at Per struggled against the outrage of such an abominable suggestion. 'He wasn't like that! I won't believe it.' This must be another of the devious Captain's tricks to force her into accepting some other alternative.

'Look,' she said, fighting off her own near-hysteria, 'if Per killed Spiros, who killed Per? Do you think there are two killers loose?'

Fotiadis sighed. 'It was just an idea I had. Of course, anyone could have killed young Spiros. Anyone at all. Even yourself.'

He had gone back to attacking her, as if everyone had to take a turn at being suspect. It was like some kind of petulant children's game, but she wasn't going to let it get to her this time.

'Or you, Captain Fotiadis,' she accused.

He was caught with his mouth slightly open. It spread into a beatific smile. 'I think I can prove I was fully occupied elsewhere over the probable period,' he claimed modestly. 'But you do well to suggest it. We must suspect everyone, including your silent friend here, who is to marry the dead boy's sister. If Spiros can be proved the owner of so valuable a trinket, it would be to your friend's advantage that she inherits an interest in it, as well as compensation eventually due to the family for their losses in Cyprus.'

'But the serpent was probably illegally acquired. Phyllia might have to share some of the blame.' Siân seemed to have joined in the irresponsible spot-the-suspect game.

'Ah, so you know that with ancient artefacts it is not a case of "finders keepers". But Mr Dritsas might have been trying to get it back from your late Swedish friend just the same, for melting down in secret.'

'Then he wouldn't have let me bring it to you. He could have taken it from me before I phoned.'

'And then there would have had to be another "accident", to ensure that you never told about it. But I agree, it is far-fetched; you have exonerated Manolis Dritsas. Which leaves as suspects the remaining population of Crete plus several thousand foreign visitors.'

He had taken on the tone of a jolly uncle talking down to the kiddies. Suddenly he relented, gave up the humour. 'But you have brought me the first real clue to link the two deaths, and I thank you.' He was leading her out again to the Volvo. She climbed in beside the offended Manolis.

Fotiadis offered her his scarred hand. 'You need not report in any more by telephone. Unless, of course, you make some other spectacular discovery. You are quite safe now this little snake has reappeared. Be sure to tell everyone what has occurred. Then there will be no more searching.'

So he had known what was going on. 'Have you any idea who—?'

'Someone at your hotel, obviously. Think about it.'

She thought all the way back to Timbaki, while Manolis ground the gears and looked as though he ground his teeth too. 'The Captain is always like that,' she told him. 'He doesn't need anyone to like him.' But Manolis glared ahead and wouldn't bother to see what she said. Siân shrugged and settled again to her thoughts. Fleetingly she remembered that Andreas Vassilakis did like the Captain. Perhaps she did herself, a little. He was so fascinatingly awful. She thought perhaps he could grow on one.

Manolis still had to find somewhere to stay in Timbaki. It would be a taverna, Siân imagined. He parked the car in front of the hotel and she asked him to come back for her in an hour. That would allow her time to bath, change, and start to circulate the story of what had turned up in the sugar jar.

As it happened, neither of the sisters was in, so she left a note for them on the sitting-room table and went down to join Manolis. They had strolled less than fifty feet down the main street when Hooper drove the Wennbergs' hired car up to the hotel steps and helped the ladies out. First came Vanessa in a cotton sheath of burnt orange, and after her Alison a little stiff after the drive and uncertain without her ebony cane.

Siân felt Manolis's fingers tighten on her arm. He was

150

staring in the direction of Per's mother and aunt. She realized that he had not properly met them, had only glimpsed Vanessa earlier when he'd claimed she was 'dangerous'. He said he'd seen her in Iraklion some weeks before, when actually she was in Rome.

The three disappeared up the shallow steps into the hotel and Siân nodded Manolis on. He appeared confused, so when they were seated at the taverna she explained who the sisters were. He nodded slowly and took out his jotter to write. Now he seemed frankly worried.

'Not the first one. It is other I see three weeks back in Iraklion. The one walking bad.'

CHAPTER 16

Manolis had been so sure. But if he'd been mistaken the first time, wasn't it likely he was wrong the second, identifying Alison?

Siân lay on her bed staring at the ceiling, examining in retrospect each detail of what she had learned from the little Greek. Was there any reason, she puzzled, for him to make the whole story up? Not unless he was diverting suspicion from himself, which was necessary only if you took seriously the Captain's irresponsible slur on his connection with Phyllia. Nobody could make of that a serious motive for murder, and she had been convinced herself that Manolis was genuinely disturbed at first sight of Vanessa, then Alison.

But how could anyone so observant have taken one sister for the other? They represented two different kinds of women, two widely opposite ways of life. But then she knew them quite well by now. What were the things a stranger noticed?

The bone structure was the same. (She reached almost absently for a pencil and her sketchblock.) To draw either face she would begin with a simple hexagon, one point downwards for the chin, then add long curves under the cheekbones, the same short, straight nose, wide-spaced luminous eyes. The brows not alike. Vanessa's winged away from above the nose, upward-tilted. Alison's were little colourless dashes dabbed on crookedly just under the hairline, giving her a slightly astonished, quizzical look. It was the hair that distinguished them most at a distance. The almost identical shade of buttermilk blonde, Vanessa's sprang vigorously out and swept up, cut short, while Alison's was long and fine, looped or coiled or knotted according to whim. And the complexions were utterly different, Vanessa made up as the sun-tanned Swedish sportswoman, her sister pale, protected from the sun, powdered, and with sweet-pea pastels as her chosen make-up. If Manolis ever mistook one for the other it was because the woman he'd watched in Iraklion had had her head covered by a hat. One of those wide-brimmed Ascot specials Alison affected?

Siân had sketched the two faces side by side as she considered them. One basic face for both, because they must be identical twins after all, even if time and vastly different lives had made them a contrast too.

There remained a space in each sketch for the mouth. Mouths are so mobile they can change the character of a face within seconds. She thought a moment before she added the last feature: for Alison a little, lopsided triangular smile; on Vanessa's face the confident 'cheese' grimace of the professional model. Now she softened the hexagons' outer angles and the portrait sketches were complete.

Even as she compared the finished faces on paper, she heard their voices out in the corridor, one almost strident, the other low and unemphatic. Manolis hadn't that clue to the difference. Their voices had probably coloured her own opinion of the sisters considerably. Subtract that and she would admit that a stranger could momentarily attribute the witnessed scene to the wrong one—until he'd seen them both together.

And the scene itself, the lip-read conversation and the papers passed between the two persons, which Manolis had observed and described to her this afternoon—what did it add up to? Appearances implied some kind of sinister consultation; more precisely a contract offered by the woman which concerned a third person. And not to that person's advantage.

Could she really accept that Miss Markham was setting up someone, out of spite? Was that seemingly genteel lady actually plotting against some man who'd wronged her? Who would she need to take revenge on? Sven, for that failure of love nearly thirty years ago? Not unless her present evident affection for him was a brilliant piece of acting.

The only other man in the picture was Per. And Per, she'd said, was responsible for Roland's death, whom Alison had loved like a son.

The truth was, Siân admitted, that she didn't want to believe it had been Alison at all. Far better believe such a thing of Vanessa, except that then there would have to be an alternative victim for the vicious set-up. Vanessa was too besotted with her wonderful son to aim her spite at him.

Siân sat up straight and swung her legs to the floor. This was impossible. She would never get to sleep with such horrific ideas going through her mind. It was the ready-made stuff of nightmares. She had even been on the brink of imagining Vanessa planning an attempt on her husband's life. That sort of thing belonged to wildly romantic fiction and the Sunday newspapers. And in any case nothing terrible had happened to Sven. It was Per who was dead. And that, dear God, *must* be only coincidence!

She wished Manolis had never spoken of what he'd seen, because now she felt obliged to do something about it. Yet, do what? It wasn't direct evidence, only hearsay—on the other hand she'd withheld the sketches of Spiros and that had delayed his identification. Whatever the value of what Manolis claimed he had seen, she would have to pass it on. Tomorrow she would phone Captain Fotiadis. Let him find out which of the sisters it had been, what the conversation referred to, and who the mystery man was who had received the instructions.

Sleep was out of the question while so much hung in the balance. Siân stepped out into the corridor and barefooted made for the sitting-room. She opened the door on to unexpected brilliance. The two sisters were there, caught in the

153

act of pouring drinks. 'Welcome to our midnight feast,' said Vanessa with heavy irony. 'It seems we all have uneasy consciences. Isn't that what keeps sleep at bay?'

'Is it? I think in my case I've not had enough exercise.' Siân's voice sounded brusque even to herself. 'But I could do with a nightcap,' she conceded.

They gathered round the table where they customarily took their meals, and Siân wondered what had become of Hooper. Did he insist on hours off-duty, even from Vanessa's bed? And was his absence the reason she couldn't settle to sleep?

'We read your note. That was a strange business with the snake,' Vanessa said. 'Have you still got it? I'd like to see it.' She sounded as if she'd made several trips to the decanter.

'I left it with Captain Fotiadis.'

'So the police have it now?' Alison put in quickly.

'It seemed important. I thought it might help to explain what Per had been doing.'

'Well, obviously he found it at a dig,' Vanessa said sharply. 'Didn't he say anything to indicate which site it had come from? There must be other things at the same site, and he should get the credit for making the discovery. Now somebody else will claim it as theirs.'

Siân was thinking. 'He did say something once, but I didn't take much notice at the time. It was after we reached the Kostantinou farm. Something about wanting to see if there'd been any recent digging near Phaistos, official or clandestine. He said prospectors sometimes had hunches about places, turned up odd items and passed on the word they were open for a bid. Then we went on to discuss the possibility of workshops existing at some distance from the actual palaces. That was the sort of buried building he hoped he might just happen on.'

'So where exactly did he look that day?' Vanessa was pressing her.

'Oh, leave it, Vanessa. Does it matter now?' her sister pleaded.

'In any case, I don't know,' Siân answered. 'We weren't together. I took the washing over to Timbaki, to find a

154

launderette. Per dropped me off early and I caught the afternoon bus back towards Phaistos. He had the Volvo all day and I've no idea what mileage he covered. He wasn't very communicative that evening. Not to me anyway. And that was the last time I saw him alive. I got up early next morning and went up the mountains on foot, looking for flowers. Per was still in the tent.'

'You say he didn't say much to *you*,' Alison intervened. 'Who did he talk to?'

'The Kostantinou woman for a while. He used the phone before dinner, and while we were eating there was an incoming call too. I don't know who made it and I didn't ask. Per had his shuttered look on, as though there was a lot on his mind and he couldn't be bothered with anyone.'

'You should have talked him round,' Vanessa said waspishly. 'You young girls have no finesse, no imagination.' She reached for a cigarette and began flicking her lighter with little savage jerks. To no effect.

'Light?' suggested Hooper, leaning forward over their shoulders and striking a match. He startled them all with his sudden appearance. Intent on the questions and answers, no one had heard his silent approach. He could have been standing behind them for minutes, listening. Unlike the three of them, he was still in day clothes.

Conscious of her flimsy pyjamas, Siân turned away and was at once confronted by the puzzlement on Alison's face. 'Where did you get that?' she demanded of her sister, like an accusation.

'Get what? This lighter? It was Per's, so I have every right to it. It was among the—the *effects* which that useless policeman handed back.'

Hooper reached down and took it from her fingers. Now that attention was drawn to it Siân felt it was vaguely familiar. 'But I never saw Per use it,' she said. 'He always carried matches, because they could be used for the gas burner as well.' All the same, she had seen it before. If the police had packaged it with Per's ring and watch it must have been on him, or—'I remember now. I saw it without registering it properly at the time. It was with the coffee things by the tent after the fire. If it wasn't Per's then it belonged to the person who was with him just before.'

'The last to see him alive,' Hooper said softly. 'The one who needed water heated and sent him off to the gas-filled store. And made sure he lit up before he went off.' He weighed the gold lighter lightly in his hand. 'Would you all agree this belonged to the killer?'

'No!' Alison's denial was shrill. 'It was nothing like that. That is my lighter, and I can prove it. Look, my cigarette case has the same design. They were a set from Cartier. How could it possibly have been at that farm? I was nowhere near Crete. I lost the lighter about a month ago. Someone has planted it to incriminate me.'

Siân regarded her with horror. Of course the lighter seemed familiar, because she'd so often watched Alison help herself to a cigarette from the Cartier *étui*. Both had the same elongated lily design embossed on the gold. There might be similar sets elsewhere in the world, but surely not now on Crete.

'You,' Vanessa whispered. 'You hated him enough for that! You she-devil!' She sprang, panting, hands clawing for her sister's face, but Hooper was between them. Chairs went over and Alison backed to the window, groping in the curtains for some protection.

'Don't, don't!' Siân pleaded, pulling at her convulsive hands. 'They'll see in from the street.' She felt naked as if exposed on a floodlit stage. Miss Markham let go of the curtains and put out her hands beseechingly. 'Siân, you don't think that of me?'

'Oh, of course not.' She put her arms round the frail body. The woman was all soft bones, like a fledgeling bird. 'Come away to my room.' They moved round the other two who stood locked together in the centre of the room. Hooper was bending over Vanessa's face talking monotonously in a low, urgent voice, and the woman looked transfixed.

'That was terrible,' Siân said. 'How could she possibly believe—' And then the memory rushed back of what she herself had been considering only some half-hour before— that Alison might have plotted what happened to Per.

156

Miss Markham sat down suddenly on Siân's bed. 'We couldn't sleep before. What chance have we now? I suppose we could both take some of my pain-killers. I was trying to give them up.'

'Let's go out,' Siân said abruptly. 'Put something over your nightie. Here, take the quilt. I'll drive you somewhere and we'll wait and watch the sun rise. Maybe that will tire us enough. Then we'll sleep when we get back.'

'It would be good to get out of this place, after that scene.'

Siân pulled on a tracksuit and stepped into her sandals. Then she found her purse and the car keys. 'Ready? What about your cane?'

'I don't use it any more. I told you I wouldn't.' Alison was regaining her composure, proud now of her own strong-mindedness. Her mouth twisted with wry humour. 'After tonight I shall probably give up smoking too!'

Siân missed the sunrise, but when she awoke in the car just before seven, with one end of the quilt tucked cosily round her, Miss Markham was serenely smiling. 'It came up. Just as it always did at home. So beautiful. Strange to think it's the selfsame sun, and the same me watching. It's a steadying thought when other things seem so hideously distorted.'

'Are you feeling better?'

'A little stiff, but much better able to face things. Even Vanessa.'

'Shall we make for a taverna or go straight back to the hotel?'

'Let's find some real Greek coffee and some fresh bread in the next village. We'll sniff it out. I don't mind being seen in my nightdress.' She gave a faint smile. 'It's rather an achievement for someone of my settled years.'

'Just as you like, but we have to phone the police straight afterwards. We'll ask them to meet us at the hotel, shall we?'

'Siân, you are talking to me as if I were a little simple. I'm no different from how I was yesterday, you know. But I think your view of me has shifted. It's that wretched lighter. Listen, my dear, I wasn't with Per at that farmhouse.

157

I didn't kill him, however much he deserved the end that overtook him.'

'Of course you didn't.' Siân reached for the ignition. 'I'm sorry to sound so stupid, but I'm barely awake yet. So, coffee first, then phone, and back to get dressed. Agreed?'

Miss Markham nodded, tucking loose strands of the fine blonde hair back behind her ears. The day which she had watched dawn would be a harrowing one, but not the worst she'd known. She would survive it, survive her sister's hostility and the Captain's interrogation. She was quite ready now to answer his questions. She only hoped he wouldn't dig too deep.

They found their Greek coffee in a village taverna where they sent a boy out for fresh bread. It arrived warm and smelled wonderful spread with honey and soft goatsmilk cheese. While Siân went to phone, Alison sat in the sunlight and silently rehearsed what she would say about the lost gold lighter.

'Well, what do you think?' The Captain rolled the dead *cigarillo* damply over his lower lip, grimaced and mashed it in the tin he kept for the purpose. It overflowed among the clutter of used coffee-cups. The eight men packed into his office looked at each other, then at the floor, waiting for him to give them the direction to move in.

'She knew someone would recognize it as hers.' That was young Papadopoulou in the sharp suit taking the bait. 'So she is relying on her alibi. It stood up to examination at a precautionary level. Now we tear it to shreds.'

'You do that,' ordered the Captain. 'Inform our colleagues at Lindos that National Honour is at stake. Our youngest additions to Greece have the fervour of converts. No one is Greeker, they believe, than an islander of Rhodes.'

Papadopoulou rose to his feet. 'Now?' He was unwilling to miss the general briefing.

'Run along.' They waited in silence until the door sighed shut behind him. 'Now,' the Captain said, 'we are left with the woman herself. I think she will tell us all we need to know, perhaps without knowing that she does.'

'We hound her?' one officer asked with wolfish glee.

'Not too crudely. Two of you take a radio car. Park near the hotel, follow whenever she goes out, allow yourselves to be seen. You others, on a roster, turn up singly, quite by chance, wherever the lady appears. Give her a hard, long look and disappear. Soon she will feel your presence even when you are elsewhere. Then we shall see which way the goat leaps. That's all.'

'What of the girl?' asked a small, wizened man.

'It is always the girls with you, Aris. You must restrain yourself. But seriously, she will feel sympathy because once she was under pressure too. She will defend Miss Markham. If the association appears to be more than that, advise me at once. Any more questions? No? Then on your way. Appear and disappear, but do not accost.'

Miss Markham had opted to brave the heat of midday and accompany Siân on her botanical quest. They sat together in the rear of the Volvo, with the collapsible easel, a large sunshade and the art materials piled beside Manolis as he drove east, then north on to the fertile plain.

Alison had seen Dr Vassilakis's driver before. He had a way of coming and going, leaving Siân stranded for days at a time, but the young man had a pleasantly earnest air about him. A quiet, unfussy person, even if, twenty minutes away from the hotel, he began to display symptoms of nervousness, fiddling with the driving mirror and flapping one hand as if a wasp were worrying him. Siân, lightly asleep again, awoke suddenly at a sharp bend taken too fast and leaned forward to stare at him.

She laid a reassuring hand on Miss Markham's arm. 'Manolis thinks we're being followed.'

'Well, why didn't he say so?'

'He can't. He's dumb. Deaf too.'

'Oh, poor boy. I didn't understand.' But even as she sympathized a different kind of unease assailed her. A deaf mute; why should that disturb her? Because she'd encountered one before, very briefly, almost a month ago, in Iraklion. He wasn't a quiet, sad-eyed boy like this one, but a prancing clown of a young man making a carnival out of his misfortune.

That had been the day she met Jerry Paine, by appointment, at the Akti Zeus Hotel. An agony of fear seized her suddenly. Perhaps too that was the last time she'd used the gold lighter. It was low on gas and she'd accepted the match Paine had struck for her. She'd laid the useless lighter on the table. It must have remained there between the coffee-cups when she got up to leave.

So which of the two men had pocketed it?

Siân was looking back over her shoulder. 'I believe they're police,' she announced in disgust. 'They seem to have decided to shadow us.'

They were over-reacting, she thought bitterly. If they behaved like this over the story of the lighter's reappearance, what would they have done if she'd passed on what Manolis had told her? She didn't really know why she'd kept it back, but in the event she had to. Perhaps the cards seemed stacked too heavily already against Miss Markham without added doubts. It couldn't do any harm to wait a little longer. Maybe some innocent explanation would come to mind and then she would be glad she hadn't interpreted the scene as a sinister conspiracy.

CHAPTER 17

While Manolis concentrated on his driving, Siân explained to Miss Markham how the doctor had come into her life when he'd saved her in a swimming accident. It had happened at Vai, and now Alison remembered her brother-in-law making some remark once about Dr Vassilakis in connection with Vai. So, obviously, Sven had heard about this incident before.

At a later point Siân had met Manolis in the capital when she had been with the doctor. (The girl had an unusual faculty for making friends, some fortunately more reliable than the one she'd elected to travel with.) And Manolis was the doctor's friend, not his chauffeur.

It seemed that Siân already knew this young man's fiancée, a Cypriot refugee who boarded with his family at Zakros. Which was less of a coincidence than it sounded at first, because Manolis only approached Siân when he recognized her dress which the fiancée had made and embroidered.

How typical of Greek islanders, this close inter-family network, so foreign to the more fragmented society of northern Europeans. She could imagine her Theo and Mina creating just such intricate relationships and persisting in them with the same dogged loyalty that Andreas and Manolis had shown to Siân.

Alison darted another look at the young man driving them. Clearly he was the same one who had crossed her path briefly when she gave Paine his instructions. And she had not seen Paine since, not even to complete payment. Somewhere, at some unwelcome moment, he would reappear and present his account. It was disturbing to know that Manolis might glimpse and remember him. It was, after all, only three weeks ago.

It had been very hot, she recalled; more so than in Rhodes. She had gone by taxi from the airport to the Akti Zeus Hotel, and Paine had been there waiting. She recognized him from the description Theo's friend had given: a long sheep-face with the eyes set high; a small, nibbly mouth. He was a con-man without respect for anyone except a greater rogue than himself, but the carroty hair, freckles and thick sandy lashes gave a deceptive air of being only recently corrupted. He should match up well to Per's notion of a middleman in shady business, the sort whose own involvement would ensure silence about Per's part. Above all he had no aura of officialdom—which would have put Per on his guard.

The interview went as planned, except for an unexpected nervousness which she had some difficulty in controlling. Her fingers were stiff and she had trouble extracting a cigarette from the gold *étui*. One dropped to the terrace flags

161

and rolled away. The young man seemed about to stoop and pick it up, but she made an impatient gesture forbidding him. The disdainful look reached him in mid-movement. He froze, then deliberately put out his heel and ground the neat white cylinder to shreds.

She did not miss the implied brutality, and winced. To accompany the expression a spasm of arthritis cramped the hand that had gone out towards her lighter. The young man put two fingers into the breast pocket of his bush shirt and extracted a book of matches. He held the light close while she drew nervously on the tobacco.

And he stared, the small mouth fixed in a sly smile. Silently he was assessing, pricing, despising. He found her style laughable, but his eyes returned to the worked silver of her ebony cane and to the gold cigarette case.

She acknowledged his interest by turning the cane for his closer inspection. Arthritis, she explained, was why she had recourse to a walking-stick. He should understand at once the limits of her need for him; that she was not of a mind or a condition to require a gigolo. She watched the calculation in his eyes change to a more rapacious interest.

She had sent him a first class return ticket out of Heathrow and generous expenses, was offering a set fee, thirty per cent in advance and the rest in two stages on delivery of his part. Any pretence midway that he would complete only for a higher fee would mean she washed her hands of him. 'The detailed requirements are in this envelope,' she had said. 'Don't open it now. Study it and if you accept come here tomorrow at the same time. You can drive me somewhere quiet while we discuss the first stage of what I propose.'

She started stiffly to rise, using the cane. He let her struggle just long enough to emphasize her frailty before he too stood, chest out, stomach muscles taut, displaying his own macho superiority. Then, rattling coffee-cups, he lifted the iron table away bodily as if it were made of paper, and let her flap herself to her feet.

She had laughed then. He really was a loathsome person, so exactly what she required. When she offered her swollen knuckles to be shaken he exerted more pressure than her masklike face was allowed to betray. 'Tomorrow then, Mr *Paine*.' She heard, herself, the stifled wry laughter in her own voice.

She had chosen a far table for privacy, but it meant a long walk back to the hotel lounge. She endured this purgatory straight-backed, pausing where a delivery van barred her in a service lane. A young Greek leaning on the vehicle's side threw her a brilliant smile and held up a finger to beg her patience. He drove off, leaving her ample space, just as a chef emerged from the kitchens, roaring to call him back.

Alison stood a moment to watch the little comedy. The driver hung out and waved his arms histrionically before reversing.

'Ah, it's you, then!' shouted the chef in Greek. His scowls turned to smiles. 'He cannot speak,' he explained to Miss Markham, pointing to his own mouth and ears.

Alison waved her thanks and the young Greek jumped down, to give a monkeylike skipping bow, smiling delightedly.

'Miss Markham!' Siân said, louder and more insistent than the first time. Alison wasn't asleep but stared unblinkingly ahead as if mesmerized. Now she came back to the present, apologizing for her absence. 'Your friend—reminded me of something. I wonder if I've come across him somewhere before.'

Siân considered her. 'He wondered the same about you.'

'Did he?' She sounded thoughtful, decided that there was no need to go into the circumstances. Better to leave it vague.

But Siân was persistent. 'Yes. In Iraklion, just over three weeks ago. Could that have been you?'

Now it was out in the open and Alison Markham could say neither yes nor no. Her throat had become stiff, there was no cavity for the sound to come through, and her mind was crammed with felty wadding. She turned to Siân and saw the girl's slow realization of her state. She couldn't scream, she couldn't faint, and the question still hung there, like a noose over her head.

Siân started talking, rapidly, about something else, anything, giving the older woman time. At some point the car stopped. Manolis came round to open the rear door, offering an arm to support her, but Alison shook her head. She felt her throat unblock, her jaws came free again. 'I think I'll stay here a while, inside.'

'The car will get unbearably hot standing still,' Siân urged.

'I suppose you're right.'

'There's a big old olive tree. Shall we put your cushion there, in the shade?'

'Just as you like.' She seemed incapable of making up her mind. The little Greek helped her to the shady place, kicked the loose stones clear and set her cushion at the base of the black, gnarled trunk. She eased herself down. Looking up through an intricate lacework of foliage at a burning sky unsoftened by cloud, she felt her eyes swimming with tears. It was the harsh whiteness of the light. Or perhaps she was weeping; she wasn't sure. Was it for herself, or dead Per, or Roland gone so much longer? Perhaps it was for all the losses of her life, all the sadness and wastage of the world.

'Is it all right to leave her?' Siân mouthed to Manolis. He nodded, indicated himself and another tree nearby. He would stay close. Alison would be safe enough, and at present she seemed not to need company, nor even to be aware of anyone else.

Siân deeply regretted putting the question to her. It had demoralized her. While she was so off balance, in shock or whatever, it was unthinkable to draw police attention to her. The Captain's men must have stopped some way behind and would be watching from an unseen vantage point. That was more than enough aggravation. Tonight she would phone the police post and complain of harassment, but she didn't think it would carry as much punch as if she did it in England. Meanwhile, with Manolis left to watch over Alison she would unpack her easel and set it up in the longer grasses where there was a rich assortment of flowers. Painting was, after all, what she'd come for.

*

At the police post there had been great activity by telephone, long-distance calls put through to Rome, Lindos, Athens; all followed after varying intervals by incoming information. Now Fotiadis was ingesting it, counter-checking and confirming details with Papadopoulou, ticking them off like beads on an abacus.

'Six days,' the Captain recapitulated, 'between the boy Spiros killed at Zakros and the Swede blown up here. And the only person with a solid alibi for the whole period is yesterday's favourite suspect! Miss Markham is vouched for by no less a person than the chief of the National Bank of Greece on Rhodes. She was dining at his home when the news came through of her nephew's death. Her brother-in-law called her from Rome as soon as he was notified.'

'Why?'

'To tell her, of course. She doesn't have a crystal ball.'

'But why tell *her*? I have no son, but if I had and he suffered an accident I shouldn't straightaway inform my sister-in-law.'

Fotiadis pushed out his lips. 'There is a certain—empathy there. He needed her to know, perhaps, for his own comfort. The young man's mother is less helpful. She has fallen apart.'

'So how long was that phone call after the death? She might just have arrived back. It's only half an hour between the islands by air.'

'But flying is the negligible part of the journey. From here it would take two hours to get to the plane, before boarding, then at the far end it is a considerable journey by car from Rhodes airport to Lindos. She couldn't have done it. Her housekeeper says she rested all afternoon before so important a dinner engagement. One would not expect her to be James Bonding about the Mediterranean.'

'So the lighter was a plant.'

'Not a very intelligent one, since it's so easily proved a red herring.'

Papadopoulou preened himself. 'But whoever left it at the scene of the crime had to get it off her first. She is quite sure it is the one she lost.'

165

'About three weeks or a month ago. So what have we got on her whereabouts then?'

'Ah!' Papadopoulou grinned like a slice of melon. 'That we shall need to ask *her*. For a fortnight she was not at Lindos. The house was being redecorated and the staff were on leave. Her chauffeur drove her to Rhodes Town. She was booked in at the Chevalier's Palace, but she was there only six days. The room was kept on while she was "touring".'

The Captain nodded. 'So perhaps she came to Crete.'

'Olympic Airways have no record of her on their lists. And on an internal flight she would not need to show a passport.'

'So perhaps she booked under an assumed name.'

Papadopoulou made a hopeless gesture with his hands. 'We have proved she couldn't have killed her nephew, however much she detested him. Why should she go to such lengths to conceal an innocent visit? He hadn't arrived here then.'

'"Innocent"?' The Captain grunted. 'How much of what we do is entirely innocent? She may have her own reasons for desiring privacy. Travelling *incognito* is not necessarily fraudulent; we have done it ourselves. But she did not have to come here. The killer could have obtained the lighter from her elsewhere. Who of the others cannot be accounted for over the same period?'

'Wennberg *père* was back in Stockholm. He does a lot of travelling. They must pay high taxes in Sweden to support their diplomats.'

'Where else has he been recently?'

'To London. He was there for four days, up to the date his son was killed. Arrived back in Rome two hours after our message reached the Embassy there.'

'Not a happy return.' Fotiadis played with the crumpled stub of a *cigarillo*. 'A father frequently shamed by his son. And the son suddenly dead. We shall have to make sure he did return directly to Rome from London. Do we know what his business was there?'

Papadopoulou looked offended. 'Diplomatic matters. How can we penetrate . . .?'

'Nevertheless, it must be done. With his cooperation preferably. If not . . .' He shrugged.

Papadopoulou shook his head regretfully. 'I still prefer to go for the girl. Menstrual instability. A lovers' quarrel. And some connection, unspecific as yet, with the business at Zakros. I haven't much faith in her story about Vai. My opinion is that she faked that accident, to gain attention or to irk the Swede.'

Fotiadis was flipping through the paperwork with some alerted purpose. 'I thought there was some previous mention —Yes, here it is. *London,* in young Wennberg's dossier. His first and only posting outside Sweden, very junior. Is that merely coincidence, do you think? Terminated after only seven months. Then at the beginning of this year, he returned to Stockholm for a course in Statistics. Statistics, my God; do we all have to suffer the same?'

'Perhaps there was a scandal,' Papadopoulou with relish. 'Do we send a man across to sniff it out?'

'Among diplomats? They would wrap our man up in protocol and file him in the Thames. Nor do we burn drachmae.' Fotiadis smiled bleakly. 'No. "Set a thief to catch a thief" is better.' He laid a finger alongside his nose. 'We rely on whispers from their kind on our own side. We will inquire of Athens who is at our Embassy in London.'

Papadopoulou had saved his most titillating item for last. 'There was another absentee from public sight at the same time,' he said slyly. 'As soon as Wennberg left Rome for London, his wife also disappeared, driven off by the body-guard, Hooper. Nobody seems to know where, but they freely speculate for what purpose. The lady was picked up by her husband en route for Crete when he came out to identify the body.'

'And Hooper?'

'Joined Mr Wennberg here the day they arrived.'

'Interesting,' Fotiadis granted mildly. 'Somewhere in all that research of yours is a detail which will hammer nails into someone's coffin.'

'So what about the gold snake?' Papadopoulou demanded. 'Has the Professor come to any decision about it?'

'Purest gold, as we thought. And the craftsmanship shows every sign of being Minoan. Not a land snake, he thinks, because of the barbs or rudimentary fins along the body. Some kind of sea creature; which raises all sorts of interesting conjecture among the learned diggers. Theories about a pre-Poseidon sea god, who was also identified as a bull, thundering and snorting to produce tidal waves and earth tremors.'

'Which eventually destroyed the Minoan civilization?'

'Exactly. A real best-seller of archæological theory, which could prove as spectacular as the Linear B Texts. And that is why Professor Tsallas is eager to locate where the serpent was obtained. It is a part of a larger artefact, he thinks. And that, if they can find it, could be the most valuable find yet, indisputably dating the links between Minoan and Mainland cultures.'

'This is going to make some splash,' Papadopoulou appreciated. 'Either the young Swede was an incredibly lucky amateur, or a man ready to gamble that somebody else was.'

'According,' Fotiadis said weightily, 'to whether he made a strike or a purchase. Or whether, indeed, he stole it from a dead man's hand.'

CHAPTER 18

Returning home, Miss Markham seemed to have fallen quietly asleep in her rear corner of the car. Siân regretted more than ever Manolis's inability to converse while he drove. There had been no opportunity for them to discuss Alison's strange reaction to her question, nor whether it was wise to say nothing about the scene he had eavesdropped on at Iraklion.

Whatever they did depended, of course, on what they thought lay behind Alison's interview with the unknown man. (But not quite unknown, because Manolis had lip-read his name, *Paine*, when Miss Markham was saying goodbye.)

Although Siân had been given an account of the conversation, she would have liked to hear the tone of their voices. Going by facial expression alone, Manolis had claimed that they fenced: Miss Markham was offering a well-paid job with cautionary strings attached to it, and didn't expect to like the man as a person. She'd almost welcomed his nastiness. And the man in turn appeared as sneering as his dependence allowed. So Manolis had assumed it was a job of some deliberate unpleasantness. Against someone Miss Markham felt had waited too long for vengeance to catch up with.

There was only one person Siân believed could merit such antipathy. *Per*. But it was unthinkable that someone she felt such intuitive affection for should put out a contract on her own nephew's life. Yet the police would accept it, since her gold lighter had turned up at the scene of the killing. They would take it as proof of Alison's presence, or count it a clever piece of double bluff, which she had volunteered in order to appear innocent.

Siân wasn't sure how far Manolis trusted Miss Markham. His impression of her at first meeting had been *anti*, although he'd amiably aped about while removing the van from blocking her way, just to get a closer look at so disturbing a lady. Indulging a lively curiosity was one of his main compensations for being cut off from normal talk.

How his suspicions would be reinforced if Siân shared with him Miss Markham's confidences about Per's petted upbringing, his mean and heartless tricks, the growing antipathy between them, his resentment of his steady older brother! It was clear that Alison had seen the boys' relationship as a second-generation development of her own warfare with her sister. And as a final culmination of that vicious rivalry, Per had perversely caused Roland's death, *her* Roland whom she regarded as a son.

Per had been the ultimate waster, the evil catalyst, destroying by leeching on to the other's generous and heroic impulses. While Roland suffocated or burned to death in a vain rescue attempt, Per was swigging spirits with the local riffraff, goading dogs on to tear each other savagely to bloody shreds. It was abominable. And making money from such calculated suffering.

But Miss Markham had not punished the callous boy at the time. Had she hoped that in the knowledge of what he'd caused to happen he might reform? But with the passing of time he grew instead more horrific. The adult Per had academic successes, grew strikingly handsome, made conquests, cut a magnificent swathe through whatever he set his sights on. And had respect for no one.

'*Hubris*', Miss Markham had spoken of, and unavoidable *Nemesis*. Could she, after all those years of silent agony alone, have detached herself from reality sufficiently to plot his destruction and blame it on Fate?

Certainly her present state seemed to be abnormal. Her usual rather astringent intelligence was clouded. It was as thought she'd quite forgotten Siân's alarming question and the circumstances that went before those few minutes of being struck speechless. When they were over she had picked up further back in time, and went mildly on from there at some less conscious level. Watching her, Siân was deeply uneasy.

When the Volvo pulled up in front of the hotel Miss Markham was total sweet lady, preoccupied with observing the social niceties. She let Manolis come round and open her door while Siân unloaded her equipment. 'Thank you. It was a delightful outing,' she said, enunciating carefully full-face. So she was observant enough to know how Manolis picked up their conversations. 'You will come and have dinner with us, won't you? We don't make any fuss. In two hours, say, for drinks?'

He looked first at Siân, who smiled, then bobbed his head, giving a bright, gamin display of white teeth.

Perhaps this struck a chord with that scene she'd pushed to the back of her mind, because Miss Markham seemed momentarily less certain of herself, looking round for Siân's support.

The girl dumped her painting things on the hotel steps and offered her arm. Manolis hovered, waited until they had gone inside, then lifted the paraphernalia in behind

170

them. By the time they reached the staircase he had gone.

It was true what Alison claimed. Since giving up the ebony cane she was walking better. Which was cause and which effect, Siân wouldn't guess at, but determination came into it. Miss Markham's will-power plus, perhaps, the Cretan summer. It was marvellous how she stood up to the heat, while Siân felt herself almost permanently dehydrated.

As if she was conscious of Siân's thought the woman said, 'I'll get them to send up some iced orange juice. It should be ready by the time you've had your shower.'

There was no sign of Vanessa or Hooper, though the hired car was standing out front. Upstairs, shutters were closed over all the windows on the south side and all doors stood ajar to circulate the air. Under the fine jets Siân shuddered at the shock of what seemed icy water, although she knew it had warmed in the cistern all afternoon. She dried off and wound her red hair in a dripping coil on top of her head. When she went through to her bedroom Alison was sitting on the bed sipping from a long tumbler that clinked enticingly with ice cubes. 'Limes,' she announced. 'It makes a pleasant change.'

She still wore the same peach-coloured lawn tunic she'd had on all day. She had some reason for not seeking her own room, and Siân waited for her to reveal it. For a long while she sat there just doing nothing, seeming lost in unhappy thought, then abruptly she rose to go. 'We'll meet at dinner. I imagine you'll want to catch up on your lost siesta.' At the door she turned back uneasily. 'Your friend Manolis. I find him rather—disturbing, Siân.' And as if ashamed of the admission, she made a grimace and slipped out.

Why? Siân demanded of herself. At least Alison could have given some reason for that fear. Now she wouldn't sleep for trying to work out what was behind the remark. She didn't think it was the young Greek's disability, because Alison had been quick to cope with that without any embarrassment. So it could be because of their first encounter, and Alison guessed he had a good idea what she'd been up to.

So perhaps it would worry her enough to bring it out in the open. At the moment she was alternating alarmingly between encouraging Manolis socially and trying to overlook that he was there. It didn't augur well for a very comfortable dinner-party. And there was Vanessa too. You could toss a coin for the mood she'd be in. Siân poured herself another glass of fresh limes, lay back with her hair spread over a towel and composed herself for sleep.

To please Manolis she put on the new aquamarine dress for dinner. It hung loose and simple, caught in at the waist with the silver belt. Vanessa noticed it the moment she walked into their sitting-room. 'There, I said you ought to go shopping in Mires. I wish you'd told me you were going, and I'd have gone with you.'

'I didn't buy it,' Siân said shortly. 'A friend made it for me.'

It looked as though Vanessa was drinking vodka. Hooper had a tumbler of milky-looking *ouzo* and water, Alison a glass of white wine. Siân indicated the same bottle and Hooper poured it for her. As she took it there was a knock at the door and Manolis was shown in. He looked crisp and fresh in a cream slub-cotton suit, matching shirt and blue bow tie.

'Oh, I like the pussycat,' Vanessa said and stretched out a hand to him. Siân wondered if Alison had warned her he was deaf and dumb. But no need to worry: with a smile like that, Manolis could say all that Vanessa required to understand. He'd been that way all his life and used his disability like a special kind of gift.

'Yes,' Alison said, coming to life, 'we're all very smart tonight.' She smoothed down her own wide-skirted grey silk and nodded towards Vanessa's emerald sheath. 'Two gentlemen to dress up for. Let's see how we'd better sit at table. When Sven gets back we shall balance properly.'

Did she expect Hooper to remain one of their number, then? Siân wondered.

'Perish the thought,' sighed Vanessa. 'If he doesn't come back for weeks it will be soon enough.'

Alison flushed as if she'd received a slap in the face. If

172

Sven walked in now, Siân thought, it's true: we should balance. Vanessa with Hooper, Manolis with me, Alison and Sven.

'Ah yes,' Hooper said drily, 'I had something to tell you all. Mr Wennberg will be landing in Athens about now and will take the night plane out.'

'How do you know?' Vanessa sounded indignant.

'He left me a number to ring in Athens, and they passed me his message.'

'But why give *you* the number? Why not me?' Her voice was rising shrilly. 'There's something wrong, isn't there? He's trying to upset me!'

'Well, don't let him, then!' Alison's tone was one of familiar astringency. The rivalry had returned. She couldn't pass up the chance to reproach her sister.

Siân looked round the table. Manolis's eyes were darting from face to face, following their lips, as he frowned in concentration.

'Warwick!' Vanessa beat on the table with her fist, making the cutlery ring. 'What is he up to? Tell me that! *What has be found out now?*'

Coolly he removed the frenzied grip on his arm. 'Mrs Wennberg, there is no need to get excited. You knew he would be returning sometime. Why not now? He will arrive here during the night if he's driven down from the airport straight away. He knows you like to sleep right through to morning. So it was left to me to make arrangements.'

'I shall stay up.'

'You must do as you wish.'

'Or shall I take some sleeping pills? All of them! Do you hear me?' She was shrieking now, turned towards him, both hands gripping his lapels as he sat beside her.

Siân saw the man's empty face go suddenly taut and the eyes snap. He broke the woman's grasp, was out of his chair and had her tipped back in hers, helplessly struggling. 'You need to take something,' he said grimly, 'and calm down.'

No, they weren't a couple, as she'd supposed. Siân felt herself trembling at the threat in the man. He was a gaoler, or a mental nurse; Vanessa his prisoner, undergoing some cure. Manolis had grasped this and was standing up ready to help handle her if she became more violent.

'Is her handbag anywhere about?' Hooper asked generally. Siân groped on the floor and produced it.

'Right. Off we go, then.' He had Vanessa's wrist behind her back. It looked uncomfortable and she wasn't resisting. They all looked away except Alison as her sister was marched to the door.

'That man—' Alison faltered, when they had gone. 'What will he do to my sister?'

'Give her a tranquillizer,' Siân assured her. 'My sister', Alison had said, almost protectively. It was unexpected.

'Are you sure? Tranquillizers. Is that what she takes? I thought, perhaps—something else—'

'Oh God,' Siân said aloud. 'I wish Andreas was here.'

Siân awoke to the sound of urgent screams. They came from the corridor in short intense bursts like a steam whistle. *Vanessa*, she thought, and scrambled from bed in pitch dark, pulled open her door. Down the pasageway light streamed from the sitting-room. She heard a sharp slap, a moan, and then Sven's voice steely with pent anger. 'I have had enough. I do not care any more who hears you. Scream and scream, *but it will not wake the dead*!' Vanessa's moans turned to sobs.

'Oh, this is horrible, horrible!' Alison said low, somewhere behind them. 'What have we all turned into? What will become of us?'

Sven Wennberg came slowly out into the corridor, dishevelled, his jacket slung over one shoulder. His thin face was dark with fatigue, eyes bloodshot from lack of sleep. He stopped short on seeing Siân. 'My dear child. We have disturbed you. I do apologize.'

'Can I do anything?'

He smiled wearily. 'Make me some coffee if you would be so kind, while I take a shower?'

'Coffee? Shouldn't you sleep?'

'It won't stop me. I could sleep for ever.'

'He has been travelling for days,' Alison put in. 'And now this at the end of it.'

174

'End?' Sven asked with quiet bitterness. 'Does it ever end?' He went off towards his room, pulling his shirt free of his waistband.

There was no sign of life from the service part of the hotel, although no one could have slept through Vanessa's hysterical outburst. More and more the foreigners were being isolated by the local people, like lepers. Perhaps soon their food would be left outside the door and spyholes bored in the plaster wall. Siân shook her head and stole down to the kitchen to prepare a tray. When the coffee was ready she carried it to the dining-room. Alison was rearranging the chairs, but the imposed order seemed false. Through the drawn curtains Siân could imagine the people of Timbaki, alerted by the screaming, massed and looking up, counting the lit windows as she'd once done, picturing the drama within. 'Your sister?' she asked.

'In her room. Sedated.' Alison sat down, staring at the backs of her own hands. 'This is more of Per's mischief, which lives on after him. It was as I feared—cocaine. She had started on it with him, to make her sparkle, to have fun and stay young. Pathetic. And now she has gone on to heroin. Sven just confirmed it.'

'How long has he known?'

'About a month. Their doctor found out and felt bound to warn him.' She lifted her shoulders and let them drop. 'That is something I would not wish for anyone. And she is *my sister.*'

'I'm so sorry.' Siân looked round the room. 'Is Sven coming here, or shall I take his coffee . . .'

'I am here,' he said quietly behind her. 'Thank you, Siân, for being so understanding. You must be very eager to see the last of my family. I must talk with the Captain as soon as it's daylight and insist I get my wife away from here. Unfortunately there are still things to clear up, and I seem to have done more harm than good by trying to speed the process. Every stone I turn over I find some new loathsome creature wriggling underneath.'

'Where have you been turning stones now?' Alison asked.

Sven considered the question with eyes downcast, and it

seemed he would block the intrusion on his private grief. Then he looked levelly at them both. 'There is no reason why you shouldn't know. Very shortly I may have to get used to unwanted publicity. At least now I can choose to tell you.

'I went to Rome and received confirmation of something I had not wished to believe. As executor, I had asked for details of my late son's financial dealings. I found that two large sums of money had been credited to him from my own current account. The only way this could have been done was by cashing cheques drawn on my forged signature. I was ready to believe that this too was Per's doing, but the dates suggested someone else, and the cheques were correctly numbered from my own book which I always keep with me.

'I charged Vanessa with this tonight on my return, with the result that you heard. All she will tell me is, "I couldn't refuse him. He made me." Whether it was payment for her drugs or blackmail about something else, I do not know. I do not ever want to know.

'That he should use *his mother* so! That he should drag her down to this level! I am glad that he is dead. *He should never have been born!*'

Sven turned stiffly away and stood for a moment with his back to them. Then he offered a chair to his sister-in-law and sat beside her at the table. 'That is not all. There was a letter waiting for me in Rome. Alison, my dear, this will grieve you, I know. It concerns your father's old friend Professor Duffield who was once out here with the British School of Archæology in Athens.'

'He is dead then, at last?'

'So you knew he was ill?'

'It was a stroke that paralysed him back in November. Yes, I knew. He wrote to me the evening before it happened. A very unhappy letter.'

Sven looked at her with a new dismay. 'So you also knew what brought it on?'

Alison put a comforting hand on his. 'Doctors say they can't attribute strokes to definite causes. If it is going to

176

happen, then it will. Anywhere, at any time of its own choosing.

'But his wife is quite sure. She makes specific accusations, blaming Per.'

'Ah. All this time that Alex has been hanging on, unable to move or speak, she has kept quiet. So why does she want to cause a scandal now? It was the missing artefacts, wasn't it? I didn't think it would have bothered Dinah so much. Alex said in his letter that she thought he'd mislaid them —an old man's muddle-headedness. It's true that the small things weren't properly catalogued, but he had a phenomenal memory for his darling souvenirs, even such ordinary items as shards and carved seals. Per was their guest in London and after he left there were eight objects missing. I thought Alex meant to warn you at the same time he wrote to me.'

'He did.' Sven's face was grim. 'He tried to excuse it, saying he understood how dishonest an enthusiast can become over such attractive objects, just as some bibliophiles can't bear to return a book they've borrowed. But he insisted that I should know of it. And he was right. I was able to get Per recalled from the London posting, but by then Alex had been struck down and we couldn't communicate. I am ashamed now, but I took the coward's way out, Alison, to prevent a scandal which could have done no one any good. I did not even confront Per, but from then on I have tried to believe I had no son.'

'So now Alex has finally passed away. When did it happen?'

'A fortnight ago. His will was read and Dina found that her stepchildren were left everything except the house and the incomplete manuscript for his planned great book. She has money of her own, and Alex hoped that she would surmount her grief by working hard on his papers.'

'How wise of him. Yes, the responsibility will make her very proud.'

Sven's face grew tight with suppressed anger. '*Would have made.* The manuscript is not where it was locked away before Alex fell ill. In fact, Dinah now accepts that it left with Per when he knew there was no chance of Alex recovering. Just one more item he casually helped himself to, expecting to escape discovery. He could have had no conscience at all.'

'He was sick, Sven. Sick with over-importance. For him, no one else mattered.'

'I went across immediately Dinah wrote. It was true. The papers weren't in the house. I returned to Rome to hear that Per was dead, so as executor I ordered a search in Stockholm. My attorney found them in an old briefcase at Per's apartment. It was this news that I found waiting for me yesterday in Rome.'

'And Dinah?'

'She is almost out of her mind, poor woman. It has been like losing Alex a second time.'

'Thank God you can satisfy her now. Of course Per would have kept the manuscript safe. It must touch on so many digs and discoveries he was interested in. When Dinah has it in her hands again she will be overjoyed, and that will be an end to it all.' She leaned towards him, reaching out to stroke his tumbled hair.

Siân, forgotten by both of them, moved backwards to the darkened doorway and made her escape. In her room she sat rigid on the side of her bed, appalled. Was there to be no end to the distress Per had created about him? But yes, of course there was an end. Someone had killed him and so prevented new outrages. Some as yet unknown person had chosen to act God.

She thought of Vanessa, led into addiction through a casual social fashion, falling apart and estranged from her family, perhaps even blackmailed by her own son, shamelessly reliant on a hired attendant; Sven, his proud name dishonoured, presented with betrayal after betrayal; Alison, already having lost a lover, a sister, an almost-son, confronted by the destruction of a respected one-time friend of her father's. Was that final revelation the straw that broke her passivity and moved her to find a hit-man to stop the flow of evil?

No, not Alison. Please, not her. Not any of them. It was unthinkable. Yet who else was there? Only herself and that

178

Greek couple at the farm—all of them exonerated.

Back then to considering the same familiar faces, this time more crucially.

This last incident, from the outcome of which Sven had just returned, could as easily have driven him to violence as Alison. More easily, because there was a quick and terrible anger under his calm, while Alison was gentle, could surely resort to killing only if her mind was deranged. Both had known of Per's pilfering back in November, which had distressed the old professor and possibly led to his stroke. Long enough ago for either to prepare some form of retribution. Either, or both together.

Somehow a joint plan would be much worse, implying cold-blooded conspiracy. Siân wouldn't admit the possibility. The long-enforced distance between those two was surely real, because over the past few days she had seen it lessen under the impact of their emotions. And the scene she had just crept away from was more than a sharing of knowledge kept private until then. It had been for them a discovery that they were coming back together.

But if only one of them had been guilty of Per's death, where was the sense of shame? And there was no sign that either suspected the other. *Could* both be innocent? She wanted so much to believe that.

Yet the only way was by fixing suspicion on someone else.

CHAPTER 19

Morning came too soon for Siân, with light lancing between the shutters and a blaring of horns in the street below as a truck piled high with melons struck a baker's hand-barrow and careened off into a stack of chairs on the pavement. Fruit and bread were everywhere. The ensuing traffic block accompanied by voluble cross-accusations at full volume made it a widely enjoyed local occasion. Siân, forced suddenly wake, sat up and at once remembered the disastrous evening before. Out of all the doubts and suspicions one

179

stood foremost in her mind. She had a vivid recall of Alison hesitant at her bedroom door admitting, 'Siân, your friend Manolis—he disturbs me.'

That was surely because the sharp little Greek had seen her with the mystery applicant for her commission in Iraklion. Or was there another reason? Could Alison have an intuitive mistrust of someone Siân herself had readily accepted from externals; the bright smile, the ingenuous approach, his undeniable charm? Could all these be a cover for something sinister, the malevolence of the deprived confronted by such physical beauty and easy arrogance as Per's? And could Manolis have known a great deal more about Phyllia's brother than he cared to admit?

And where was Manolis? She had barely seen his departure after Hooper took Vanessa from the dinner table. No one had been able to finish the meal. The little Greek had simply faded after thanking Alison. Whether he fled from discretion or embarrassment she couldn't guess. It all seemed an age ago.

Siân went to the window and looked down on the riot of spilled fruit and gesticulating Cretans. The road was effectively choked with cars, agricultural trucks and milling pedestrians. It would have been worse if the Volvo had still been parked there, but someone had removed it. Since Manolis had driven it yesterday he must still have the keys. So where had he taken it without asking her? And when?

She didn't need to have doubts now about Manolis. The others all had sinister sides to them, had suffered such appalling harshness that she looked to Manolis as the one sane, unscarred person here that she could rely on. Yet just now as she awoke, Alison's fear of him was uppermost in her mind; so was it because the little Greek had been witness to her meeting with the man Paine? No, there was more to it than that. *Fear.* Alison must believe that one of those two men had taken her lighter, leaving it to incriminate her in Per's killing. And would Paine have done so when it might link the incident so readily to him?

But Manolis had been quite open to Siân about how he encountered Miss Markham, and there was no reason to think him a petty thief. Also he could almost certainly count on an alibi for when Per died, because of his 'Figaro-here, Figaro-there' activities in the capital.

So, not Manolis. It was this unknown Paine of whom Miss Markham should be afraid, the unpleasant man chosen for an unpleasant job. If he hadn't left the lighter deliberately, then it must have been overlooked. He'd been using the stolen piece of finery, could even have used it as a vital instrument in Per's killing. First he'd tampered with the gas drums in the store, then changed the empty can for full on the little burner, finally ensured that Per lit up his *cigarillo* before he tried to heat the water. Offered him the light himself! All that cold-blooded plotting; so much to think of; a second's loss of concentration and the lighter left behind, a *real* clue and not a red herring, leading eventually back to the one who had given him his instructions. Miss Markham. It was the logical explanation, but Siân couldn't make herself accept it. There had to be an alternative. Miss Markham must be made to explain who Paine was and what she had really intended him to do.

And then what about Sven and Vanessa? Better not to dwell on the misery of their lives. But both had strong enough motives to kill Per in a fit of uncontrolled anger. Whether they also had opportunity was the Captain's business to discover, but the means were there to hand for anyone to use. It took just a certain inventiveness of mind. And evil intent.

Her thoughts were interrupted by Miss Markham rapping at her door and sliding into the room with a tray of tea. Only one cup, Siân noticed. So she wasn't planning to stay. Her face still showed lines of tiredness but she was quite composed. And why not? Sven had returned, her sun was in the sky, God's in his heaven and all that.

'I thought you should know,' she started in without preamble after greeting the girl, 'that Sven has asked the police Captain to call this morning. He'll be here about eleven. It is time things were straightened out.'

Yes. With so much public scandal about to break on the family because of Per's actions, what point was there now

181

in reticence? Except for the person responsible for the killing.

Siân waited. There was something else Alison had to add, but she was searching for the right words. 'You won't need me here,' Siân suggested.

'That is what I was going to ask you. Whether you needed to see Captain Fotiadis or not. Sven thought, since your own transport seems not to be available, you might care to have Hooper drive you wherever you intend painting today.'

'How about Vanessa? Won't she need Hooper?'

'Sven and I can manage. Until the Captain comes.'

Siân stared at her. Did she mean that they'd decided Vanessa was the killer? That once the Captain came their own responsibility would end? How could Alison be so calm if that was the case? As she'd said last night: 'my own sister'.

'We all have a lot of explaining to do,' Miss Markham added. She almost smiled. 'It will be such a relief to be finally free of all secrecy.'

'Of course I'll go,' Siân said slowly. She would rather have driven herself, although she'd never handled the Japanese model the others used. Nor was Hooper the company she would have chosen. She didn't like the man, but clearly Sven wanted both of them out of the way when he put his case to the police.

'We thought of ordering a light lunch about two o'clock,' Miss Markham continued, as if it were a normal house party and herself the hostess. 'Do come back then if you're ready. It isn't good to stay out all day in such intense heat. It can be debilitating.' She smiled, nodded and withdrew.

So, by two in the afternoon it could all be over. Perhaps then the Captain would release the body for burial and herself to go home. And somebody would have been arrested to face trial for murder.

She wasn't certain what was intended for Per's final disposal. Surely now they wouldn't have him transported back to Sweden? If the Press there were already alerted to the scandal of the Duffield papers, it would be anything but a hero's return.

And what of her own disposal? Suddenly she felt drained of any future. A mere month ago everything had been self-evident. Once her Finals results were published she would arm herself with a CV and her portfolio of flower paintings ready to storm the job market on two fronts. But since then she'd aged immeasurably, metamorphosed. Life after Per would never be the same self-absorbed floating through scenes with distant figures. From now on she was right in the human crush, one of the struggling millions, hurting and being hurt.

So, what lay ahead? First she would get free of this Anglo-Swedish nightmare. Andreas had been right: the family were horrendous. But they had become part of her life by now and she would always need to know how their story ended. And Crete itself had got to her, forever a special place with a claim on her emotions. And then Manolis and Phyllia. Andreas. How could she bear simply to get up and go?

She went through the motions of showering and dressing. Breakfast had been set for two in the sitting-room and Hooper was seated across from her. He didn't rise as she went in and it amused her that she'd grown accustomed to expect it, because of the other men here observing etiquette. 'Good morning,' she said, ironically polite. She smiled at the village girl who was hovering, ready to pour coffee. '*Kalimera.*'

'*'mera, Vespinis.*'

Hooper nodded, raised a quirky eyebrow. 'You've received your instructions too? That we're straightway to lead our donkeys off-stage?'

'Donkeys?'

'A translation from the original American.'

Donkeys—asses. Yes, very droll. Hooper as a humorist was a new line. She hoped he wouldn't feel obliged to keep it up. 'Another working day for me,' she said flatly, 'and I haven't decided yet which direction to head in.'

'Try Matala,' he said, blank-faced, 'and enjoy yourself on the beach. Take your swimsuit.'

'There are no flowers at Matala. Not at this time of year anyway. And there are crowds.' All the same, a swim would be pleasant after so much exposure to the sun. 'Maybe we'll go on there later if the work goes well. I think we should head inland first. If you have a map I'll show you.'

The route they took passed the end of the lane to Captain Fotiadis's farm. For miles after that there were orange groves alternating with vineyards, at first with bare sandy soil under them, then with roughly scythed grass; later, meadow grass under olive trees, and where the uplands began there were steep terraces of them where the grass grew coarse and wiry with interesting ground-hugging plants at their base.

Siân had to scrabble among the tough roots to uncover them and identify the many forms of *compositæ*. It was hot work but they were rewarding flowers to work on. She had always had a special fondness for daisies; they made such satisfactory patterns against their rocky backgrounds or the deep blue of the Cretan sky.

Her spirits rose and she forgot Hooper's presence. In fact he seemed absent, having found some concealed place to stretch himself out, shirtless in the sunshine. She almost trod on him once as she trudged up to a new position, arms full of gear, and he sat up exposing a mahogany torso which set her wondering again about his origins.

'Watch it, Blue,' he warned, and she couldn't quite suppress a smile.

'You're not really Australian.'

'Nuh. Spent some time in Southern Africa. Lots of people confuse the accents.' That was all he was going to give away. He hadn't said 'South' but 'Southern'. So he meant one of the other states. Mozambique? Angola? And what would he have been doing there? Fighting, perhaps.

She moved on, but now as she sketched and painted she was conscious of him not far off, lying on his back in the grass, eyes narrowed slit-like against the light, chewing on a grass stem. His face was expressionless, his thoughts elsewhere—perhaps, like hers, back at the hotel, where the police must be dragging out the truth. Long before noon she put the painting things together and trudged down again to the car. 'Okay, Matala then,' she told him in passing.

Although parked under the trees, the car was intensely hot. Hooper drove fast to cool the air inside but, facing south now, there was little respite. Her one thought, on arriving where the road gave suddenly on to sand and sea, was to fling herself straight into the water. It sparkled, turquoise and diamonds, dimming away to a hazy skyline, and over the bay on one side hung the golden honeycombed cliffs with their neolithic, square cave openings.

'You can strip off in the car,' Siân offered. 'I'm going to that taverna.' She scuffed through blown sand to reach the door. Grit lay thick on the floor where it had been tramped in, and it powdered the flat surfaces of the room. The place was crowded with foreign tourists. Siân queued at the counter for a can of lemonade, then slid into the primitive toilet to change into her swimsuit.

There was no sign of Hooper when she came out. He would probably hang back until she'd chosen a place to settle, then join her. At least she could be free of him in the water. She went to its edge before dropping her beachbag, and started wading in. She had tied her red hair up in a chiffon scarf, which made identifying her difficult. Striking out towards a large group of bobbing heads she duck-dived down into the delicious cool. The sun struck at her harshly as she surfaced. Mad dogs and Englishmen, she thought; none of the locals would swim at midday.

She splashed about avoiding collisions, observed gratefully that windsurfers used a different part of the bay. The long honeycombed cliff loomed over the water but she resisted the lure of its underwater caverns. After the incident at Vai it was enough to be swimming in the open without fear.

Leaving the water, she pulled off the headband and shook out her damp hair. Sharp grey grains, not quite fine enough to be sand, stuck to her wet feet and pricked between her toes. She bent to brush them off and heard her name called. Striding towards her from the cliff end of the beach was a familiar stocky figure, spectacles glinting in the sunlight.

'Andreas!' She flung herself into his arms and felt the warm bear-hug of the man. 'Oh Andreas, where have you been? I needed you.'

Silly thing to ask. He'd been about his work. Although

185

the question had been purely rhetorical his eyes took on a wounded look. *Stunned bear.* She hugged him back and saw his face light with fondness. She suddenly knew what it felt like to be Andreas. This was a new dimension: entering him, his goodness and concern for others. Something strange was happening, because she didn't see him any more from the outside. She stood back and really looked at him, feeling him anxiously doing the same to her.

'I think maybe I love you,' she said slowly, and saw—felt it too—the immense rush of relief through him. And then there was no longer any 'maybe', no doubt about it at all.

After a few moments she withdrew her wet arms from him and stared ruefully around, at the body-strewn beach, the crude touristic, catch-penny structures. 'We should be somewhere more romantic. Vai, under the palm trees, if we could get it all to ourselves.'

'Vai,' he repeated. 'That reminds me. I brought your photographs. The roll of film I finished for you the other day, remember? There are some good ones of you, and the rest are mostly flowers, but six or seven of your Swedish friend with various backgrounds.'

They found a place to sit and he dealt out the prints over her spread towel. 'Thirty-seven,' she counted. 'That's lucky, getting an extra one in. Yes, they are good, especially the flowers. I'll have to get more practice at long shots.'

'We could go back to Vai if you find it so romantic. I thought it might still be rather frightening for you.'

'We met there, if you remember. Some kiss of life!'

'I remember very well.'

'Andreas!' She looked puzzled. 'How did you find me here today? Did we have a police tail? Are you and the Captain—?'

'In league against you? No. Quite simply, Manolis came for me late last night, because he can't phone. I had a theatre list to clear; everyone in Iraklion is breaking bones just now. When I was through at the hospital I snatched some sleep and brought the Volvo back. Manolis had written me out a report, so I knew things were getting worse here.

186

When I arrived you had already left, but the girl who served you breakfast remembered the one Greek word you discussed with Hooper. Matala. I've been here over two hours now, waiting for you to turn up.'

'And worrying.'

'That too.'

'I was all right. Hooper's in charge of me. The body-guard with the hypodermic needle. Did Manolis mention that?'

'Yes, and I had guessed something of the sort.'

'Andreas, I think he's been a mercenary.' She shuddered.

'Well, he can take himself off now. I'm taking over.'

She stood up and brushed grit from her limbs. As they walked together towards the road Hooper appeared standing in their path.

Andreas nodded. 'Have a good swim?' He ran his eyes over the other man, noted the muscle, the tan and the way his weight was distributed. It must be a healthy life, the mercenary's. If you survived. 'We are leaving now,' Andreas said mildly. 'See you sometime?'

Hooper stood aside, gave Siân a mean look as she went by. 'It's a pleasure,' he murmured, just as if she'd thanked him.

CHAPTER 20

Andreas drew up at the hotel and came in with Siân. In the sitting-room a side table was laid with a cold buffet. Sven and Alison were in armchairs with plates balanced on their knees but neither seemed to be eating.

Siân hesitated on the threshold, and seeing her embarrass-ment Sven stood up, giving his weary smile. 'Do come in, Siân. It is good to see you again, Doctor. Please help yourselves to some lunch. There has been a change of plan. The police rang to put off their visit until the afternoon, so we are having a scratch meal first. Let me pour you some wine.'

187

'I thought it would all be over. I'm so sorry. We can go away again,' Siân offered hurriedly.

'No. Captain Fotiadis sent a message that we should all be here. That includes you both. It will help to clarify any points we aren't familiar with.'

Siân looked quickly across at Alison, who nodded encouragingly. 'There's plenty of chicken and salad. Vanessa won't eat anything. She's resting in her room until we're all ready.'

'I don't think I could eat either,' Siân began.

'In any case the police are just arriving,' Andreas told her, glancing from the window. 'Two carloads.'

There were two when they'd taken her into custody, Siân remembered. She looked at the others, wondering who was the most likely to be threatened today. She wished she hadn't to be here to find out. She could have stayed on at Matala with Andreas, but she'd been anxious to know the outcome.

There was a quick rush to clear the dishes and glasses before the visitors came upstairs. Siân loaded a tray while Alison slipped away to fetch her sister. In the delay while Vanessa was collected, Fotiadis appeared, solemn and wearing a crumpled uniform, followed by two officers the girl hadn't seen before.

The two women came in arm in arm, but there was no sense of closeness. Alison looked away from her sister, spots of high colour on her usually pale cheeks. Vanessa stared rather wildly round the room and then headed unsteadily for an empty chair. Sven kept his gaze on the carpet.

Giving Siân's hand a little squeeze as he passed, Andreas lowered himself into another chair and patted the padded arm for her to join him. She sat, facing Sven and sideways on to the sisters. No one spoke, each locked inside a private dismay. With the entry of the police the room had suddenly become too small. There was no escaping others' eyes. When Siân felt Andreas's fingers lace into her own it was warmly reassuring; they at least were together.

Fotiadis stood at ease, solid and sturdy, with his back to the wall where the food had been displayed. He seemed passive, but his dark eyes missed nothing, moving in their slots to compensate for the suppleness his neck had lost. Again Siân was made aware of menace in the man, as if she were once more the one he would pit himself against. She wondered what had caused his change of plan, delaying him. Further evidence discovered? Some new witness come forward to implicate one of them?

The policeman started talking dates. It was the old stuff over again: when Per arrived on Crete; when and where they met; all that about hiring the car, arranging the route; the mad drive down that awful road towards Kato Zakros, and how she'd first seen fire down the mountainside. He told it choronologically, only stopping occasionally to cock an eyebrow, waiting for her confirmation.

To Siân it was almost pedestrian by now, but she was aware of others hanging on the details. They hadn't known how she'd suppressed the fact that she'd seen the dead boy's face, unrecognizable by the time the Zakros police came on the scene. They hadn't known either about the way Per had concealed the little gold serpent, substituting a metal tag to fool her.

Fotiadis continued his narrative; to Vai, the near-drowning and her meeting with Andreas; then on to Sitia, to Iraklion and Manolis; finally the journey south. He dwelt significantly on the date when they'd reached the Kostantinous' farm, where Per was to die in a fire of his own making.

Fire, Siân thought, and fancifully saw its trail all the way from the hostel in Cumbria, through the burning car at Kato Zakros to the farm explosion. Suddenly it wasn't fanciful. The pattern was one of cause and effect, with a single thread drawn through. Five years, three months and two days from beginning to end. And didn't that lead back directly to Alison Markham?

Siân looked sideways at her. The woman's eyes were closed, her face drawn as if in pain. Deep vertical lines were chiselled between her brows, and she held one hand tightly clenched across her breasts.

As if Fotiadis sensed the direction of Siân's suspicion,

he began checking on Alison's movements at that time, examining her alibi, pronouncing it 'impeccable' with such an ironic twist of his thick lips that it sounded extremely dubious. Could it be false? That depended on how well she knew the people who vouched for her presence. Was it beyond belief that the Rhodes chief of the Greek National Bank might lie to oblige a very good client?

But Fotiadis had passed on by now to Sven, extracting a confusing list of comings and goings, Sven stiffly embarrassed at having to account for all his journeys and absences. He'd left London the morning of Per's death and received the news at Rome on his return to duty late that evening. Between-times he had slept at his flat. Fotiadis, pressing him on this, seemed to imply that he'd had time to reach Crete between London and Rome.

London, Siân thought. Of course, he'd been there searching for Professor Duffield's lost papers. Furious at not finding them and goaded by the distraught widow, mightn't he have decided finally to confront his son and demand the manuscript's return? So he came to Crete. Couldn't there have been an almighty quarrel during which he struck Per, accidentally killing him? Then he might have set up the explosion to cover what he'd done.

Nothing but fatigue and distaste showed on Sven's controlled features, but there was no knowing how far he might go if that self-control snapped. In observing him, Siân lost the Captain's next words. She turned back and started to listen again.

He was talking to Vanessa. No, *about* her, because Vanessa had gone right out of touch. Her head was thrown back against the cushions of her chair and she stared wide-eyed at the ceiling as though all the action was up there. Siân could see only the corded muscles of her neck and one sharp angle of her jawline up to a bulbous gold earring. Fotiadis was going on about her supposedly being in an Italian clinic for some time before her son's death, but confirmation had not yet been supplied to the Greek authorities. Discretion, it seemed, was taken to unreasonable lengths by this institution.

There was a little pause then as Fotiadis produced a small object from his pocket. Siân's heart beat faster as she leaned forward to look. Not the little Minoan serpent but the gold lighter found by the tent after Per's death.

Vanessa managed to focus on it. 'Mine,' she said loudly. 'It was my son's.'

'What do you say to that, Miss Markham?'

Rapidly Alison claimed it as her own, matching the gold *étui* from Cartier. She thought she remembered losing it at a hotel in Iraklion almost a month back, when interviewing a man for a job. She'd been clumsy and couldn't make the thing work. While the man offered her a light she'd laid the lighter on the table between them. She must have left it behind when she left the hotel terrace. He or another man she'd spoken to might have picked it up. Or, indeed, almost anyone passing by.

'Per's,' Vanessa insisted again. She sounded drunk. 'S'with his things.'

'Listed with his effects,' the Captain purred, 'and identified by Miss Westbury as being beside the coffee mugs at the tent after Mr Wennberg's death. But she had never seen him with it, so we think it came with his visitor.'

'We need to know where it was in the time between,' Sven said thoughtfully. 'Almost a month ago, I think you said.' He turned to his sister-in-law. 'Who were those two men you spoke of, Alison? Can you give us their names?'

Miss Markham moistened her lips, mumbled, then said clearly, 'One was Manolis. I don't know his surname. He is a friend of Siân and Dr Vassilakis here. The other one's name I have forgotten. He wanted a job, but really didn't seem at all suitable.'

'Why not, Miss Markham?' the Captain put in smoothly.

'A shifty sort, I felt. And he had no Greek. It wouldn't suit a man like that to be a house servant buried in the country all year round.'

'How did you contact him, Miss Markham? Was it by letter?'

She seemed to consider before replying, and Siân moved restlessly on her chair arm. 'His name was Paine,' she interrupted. 'Manolis told me. He was lip-reading their conversation just then. He often does it. It's not really eavesdropping, but because he's missing what the others all pick up by ear.'

'Paine,' the Captain repeated patiently. 'Perhaps you will remember more about him now, Miss Markham. His forename, for instance.'

'Jerry,' she admitted. 'That's what he called himself. A shortened form of Jeremy, I assumed. And I did write to him initially. It was some contact of Theo's, my chauffeur-handyman on Rhodes. A friend of a friend recommended him.'

'But if he took your lighter,' Sven pursued, 'and it turned up here later, on the day Per died—'

'—There has to be some connection between this man and your son,' Fotiadis finished for him. He turned again to Alison. 'Did you happen to discuss your nephew with him?'

Miss Markham thought about this carefully. 'I had no occasion to.'

Siân frowned. Perhaps this was literally the truth. The information would have been in the papers the man took away with him. Should she mention this to the Captain? Miss Markham was very reluctant to give a frank explanation. In fact it was a downright lie that she hadn't given Paine the job, unless she'd later withdrawn her offer. Manolis had been quite sure of this.

Andreas suddenly sat forward in his chair. 'All we need now is to find this Jerry Paine,' he almost roared in relief. 'Then it is all settled. We shall have our man.'

Captain Fotiadis swivelled, looking from face to face. His smile was not pleasant. 'Oh, we have him already,' he claimed.

There was an amazed silence. No one moved. Miss Markham looked stunned.

'You have him,' Sven repeated encouragingly, since the Captain seemed disinclined to go further.

'In cold storage.' Fotiadis sounded grimmer now. 'But having him settles nothing. We are no nearer finding out

192

who killed Per Wennberg. You see, this other body dates from the evening *before* your son was killed.'

It should all have been over by now, the body released, one of them in custody, the others free to leave. But the meeting that was to have provided all the answers ended in even more questions. The fiasco of Alison's interrogation was broken up by Vanessa quietly keeling over and slipping to the floor. It was no stagey trick; she looked like death. Because normally she liked making demands and complaining, no one had paid her much attention until then, but she must have been feeling ill when she came in, possibly even before that.

Andreas went across at once, examined her eyes, made everyone keep clear, and carried her to her room. He was there for about twenty minutes with Sven and one of Fotiadis's lieutenants who had earlier trained as a male nurse. When the doctor came back he spent some time at the telephone ordering an emergency medical team and supplies from a pharmacy. Sven volunteered to drive out to fetch the prescriptions, because Hooper wasn't there.

No one else knew what to do: it was chaotic. Alison fell back on the English expedient of ordering tea, but again the hotel staff seemed to have deserted them and the kitchen was empty. Siân and she ended by making it themselves with tea-bags, and for the non-English added a large jug of coffee and a bottle of *ouzo*.

Then, when order seemed on the point of returning, there was a phone call for the Captain. He took it there among them and it was clearly unnerving. Afterwards he spoke in Greek to Andreas who became equally grave. Fotiadis looked round the silent faces. 'We must leave it there for today. I am needed elsewhere. The lieutenant will stay with Mrs Wennberg until a nurse relieves him. There will also be a duty man left in the hall.'

'We'd better go with him,' Andreas murmured to Siân. 'Maybe I can help, and everything's quiet here for the present.'

'Yes, but what has happened?' They were running down

193

the stairs after the Captain. He slammed into his police car and called through the open window, 'It is my Maria. She has fallen and broken her leg.' Then the engine was revved and he shot away from the kerb.

Incredible, Siân thought. Awful for him, of course, but he was surely a policeman first and a husband second. Would a British manhunt be instantly called off because of an accident to the chief investigator's wife? She put this to Andreas and he seemed to find it funny. Siân began to feel foreign, which made her angry. 'And Vanessa?' she demanded. 'What about her? Was it an overdose?'

'Ah.' He darted a glance at the girl. 'What do you know about that?'

'I know that she started on cocaine, with Per, for kicks. Then recently she went on to heroin. Alison told me last night. Sven had known about it for a month. Then there was this terrible row when he returned during the night. I suppose today she felt desperate and tried to end it all.'

The doctor's face was grim. 'She didn't give herself the needle. I saw the bruise marks on her arm. She may have wanted it, but someone else held her and gave the injection.'

'Who, then? Someone in the hotel. One of us? *When*, Andreas?'

'About the time we got back, I think. A sizeable dose, and the grains left in the envelope seemed barely cut.'

'Cut?'

'Mixed down with innocuous powder.'

'Is she safe to leave like that?'

'The emergency team are with her. They have drugs experts and all the proper equipment. They will pull her through if anyone can.'

'It's as serious as that? Someone meant her to *die*?'

'Who can tell? Would you know what a syringe contained if you hadn't filled it yourself?'

'Perhaps it was just meant to break up the questioning, to prevent it reaching a point that was dangerous for someone.'

Andreas considered this. 'Difficult to time that in advance, but it is possible. Where *did* we get? What point had the Captain just made?'

194

'It was Alison's lighter, and that reminded me of the gold snake. They sounded like Musical Parcels.'

'What do you mean?'

'It's a children's game played at parties. You pass a package round until the music stops.

'What made you think of that?'

'Well, take the lighter. It started with Miss Markham and ended with Vanessa. Somewhere in between it reached Per, but the man-in-the-middle, Jerry Paine, was already dead by then, so yet another person must have had it after him, to leave it where it was found. The missing link; the man, or woman, who probably killed Per.'

'Unless Per took it off Paine previously. And how did Paine die? That was one detail Fotiadis never got round to.'

'No, he didn't. But the gold snake was passed from hand to hand too. Someone had to dig it up originally, then Spiros got hold of it. One thing struck me: the way he grabbed it as he was killed—which was well before the car incident I witnessed, according to the police—he might have snapped it off the main piece which the Professor said it was joined to.'

'At the broken tail end, yes. Go on.'

'So what happened to the rest of the gold object? I think someone else was hanging on to it, there was a struggle and as Spiros was killed the serpent broke off. The other person never noticed it was missing or he'd have recovered it. We don't know why Per hid the snake as he did, after he prised it from the boy's fingers, but he may have been killed because of it. While it stayed safe in the sugar jar, Per's things were turned over twice that I noticed. I think someone was trying to get it back. The question is *who*?—and has this person got the main part our snake broke off?'

'What would Per have wanted with it?'

'To find more of the same himself, I'm sure. Which is why he kept quiet about it. As soon as he saw it he must have realized what a valuable find it was. It was enough to fire him to look for a great treasure underground. That's what he was talking about after we reached Phaistos: the possibility of happening on the remains of a Minoan crafts workshop, or on *someone who knew where such a place existed.*'

Andreas gripped the wheel tensely in concentration. 'And Spiros was involved in this at some level. Perhaps he was the contact putting out feelers for customers. That seems reasonable if the treasure was dug up anywhere near Zakros. A local boy, none too honest, a bit of a con-man already—'

'*Con-man.* Wait a minute. That's the connection. Wasn't Miss Markham's Jerry Paine a con-man too? Wasn't she setting Per up? Didn't she believe he would destroy himself by his own arrogance and ambition? Suppose it was Miss Markham who had actually acquired the treasure so that Per could make some underhand deal that put him on the wrong side of the law?'

'I think you have it, Siân. Or very nearly. She wanted him to trap himself, to go to the logical end of his awfulness, and be publicly found out. Found out doing what? Making false claims over somebody else's work? That's hardly scandal enough. There has to be something more.'

'A fake! A clever fake,' Siân sang out. 'One clever enough to deceive Per, even Professor Tsallas on first examination. And then, when all the claims are made and the fame rolls in—exposure! Per caught out in all his intellectual dishonesty. A phoney, made a laughing-stock by his own publicity!

'Don't you see, Andreas? That's what those papers were which Alison gave to Paine in Iraklion. Instructions how to trap Per, maybe photographs of the "treasures" and of the place where they were supposed to have been found. And Alison knew of Per's weakness for Minoan relics, because he'd stolen some from an old friend of her father's. Paine had three clear weeks to set it up, to find someone like Spiros and get him word-perfect in his part, which was to approach Per when he came into the area, maybe in Iraklion soon after he first arrived. That would be before I'd met him and we joined forces.'

'Yes. He would show the photographs first. Then later, when you both reached Zakros, he would have produced the gold object from which our piece later snapped off. If only we knew what that looked like. Obviously beaten gold, fairly flat. Perhaps an enthroned sea-god attended by his creatures.'

'Not genuine, though. We're agreed, aren't we, that it was a clever fake provided by Miss Markham as her ultimate revenge.'

'Of course, she lives on Rhodes. They are as skilled in Rhodes Old Town as the goldsmiths on Crete. She would have employed some local craftsman she trusted, even used purified gold beaten out in the Minoan manner and then weathered. She could have found expert advice on the period, and it would be welcome advertisement for a gold-smith, once the deception was admitted—such skill, and only intended as a hoax; no wish to defraud.'

'Like the Tom Keating art fakes which fooled the experts and made the counterfeiter a celebrity. Andreas, I believe we've guessed right. And Alison wasn't set on killing Per, only exposing him. Cruelty enough, but she'd suffered so much through him. They all have.'

'But who did kill him then, and why?' Andreas punched the horn to scatter a group of goats on the road ahead. 'For the treasure? But that would imply he had it in his possession.'

'Perhaps he did. Perhaps all that was left for him was to track down the place it was supposed to have come from. Once he had discovered that, he could make his find public, offer the artefacts to the Cretan authorities and claim the archæological fame he coveted.

'Just a moment.' Siân reined in her own enthusiasm for the theory, closed her eyes and tried to picture the sequences. 'The snake broke off and stayed in Spiros's hand. The main piece stayed with whoever was fighting him for it.'

Andreas glanced sideways at her and his face was grim. 'Which means Per, the dupe-customer. And it also means that Per killed Spiros to get the treasure, but without dis-covering where it was supposed to have been dug up.'

'And Paine knew who had it—Spiros's *only* customer. So he went after Per, to get the gold back or make sure he was paid for it. Or even to blackmail him over killing the boy.'

'So they did a deal,' Andreas continued the story. 'Paine

faked a different death scene to help Per out. He kept the body chilled a few hours until you could witness the car's plunge off the mountain road. But we don't have seat-belt rules like you, and the body was flung clear of the fire. Which was why your friend Per decided to humour you and climb down to the wreck. And make a more thorough job of hiding the boy's identity.'

'But why bother?'

'They may have been seen together at some point. Or he may have doubted whether the boy could drive a car. In any case it gave him time to move on.'

'And Per's payment for this deal?'

'I think he must have handed back the treasure, at least until he was ready to pay hard cash for it. But at that point Paine hadn't noticed the piece missing, and Per still had something to bargain with against learning the site's location. He would have known Paine wouldn't betray him, because of his own part as accessory. So he felt safe enough to summon Paine to the farm you were staying at, and there would have been a second deal made.'

'But Paine died before he got there, and before Per blew himself up with the gas! Look out, Andreas! The Captain's stopping.'

Andreas pulled on to the crown of the road and as they drew level Fotiadis put his head out and shouted. 'I have been thinking.'

Andreas braked alongside. 'So have we. Tell us now, what killed this Jerry Paine?'

'It was an accident, a genuine road accident, all over a damn donkey that ran berserk, charged the motor-scooter and sent Paine straight into a truck ahead of him. Among other things it was carrying steel scaffolding. Paine was impaled. He died almost instantly.'

'So he was identified from papers he was carrying?'

Fotiadis smiled. 'He had a passport, yes. He also had some interesting photographs.'

'Not of gold artefacts, by any chance?'

Now the Captain's face cracked in a huge grin. 'You certainly have been thinking. To some effect. Perhaps we

198

should pool our ideas now and see if the picture is complete.'
He reached under the dashboard and passed to Andreas a
mortuary photograph of a sheep-faced man, slight and pale
of complexion. 'Jerry Paine, deceased.'

'How about your wife?' Sian reminded Fotiadis, since he
seemed no longer so pressed.

'Yes, poor Maria,' Andreas put in quickly. 'We must see
to her first.'

Fotiadis grunted, put the car into gear and turned into
the lane that led between the orange trees. They followed,
past the house and on to a bumpy track. When they got out,
Fotiadis opened a barred gate and they were in an orchard
of nut trees. Two cows raised mildly inquisitive heads and
came across to nuzzle the policeman. They were small like
a Kerry cow but coloured a sandy brown. The Captain
rubbed each gently behind the ears. 'Aphrodite and
Ariadni,' he introduced them. 'Maria is just over there.'

'*Maria?*'

'Maria Callas, in full. She has a powerful moo.'

Siân swung round on Andreas. 'You let me think it was
his wife!'

'Oh, Maria is much more precious,' Fotiadis gloated with
a diabolical laugh. 'Where would I find another such? Wives
are commonplace things, but how often have you seen good
milch cows on Crete?'

'And you left the investigation for—'

'A creature in pain, Siân,' Andreas reminded her, trying
to look serious. 'Come on, there's work to do. Six hands are
better than four.'

Afterwards there was retsina and apricot ice-cream, with
an exchange of information. 'I was content to leave things
as they stood in Timbaki,' the Captain concluded, 'because
I had reached much the same opinion as yourselves. Spiros
killed by Per Wennberg, perhaps accidentally, in the course
of a fight, and the car event rigged by Paine to give
Wennberg an alibi. Our forensic men are in Zakros examining a cellar in the house Paine was staying at. There are
plastic sacks there, partly full of water—which may once
have contained ice—so that is probably where Spiros's body

199

was left until arrangements were complete, perhaps a day or two, perhaps less.'

'And when Per moved on, Paine followed,' Andreas prompted.

'Because Miss Markham's plan had not been completed, so he didn't qualify for payment,' Siân offered.

'Your friend was greedy,' Fotiadis said. 'He still wanted to believe in untold wealth and fame lying somewhere waiting to be dug up. You remember the phone calls at the farm? He was in touch with someone. Was it Paine? How do you like the idea of Paine, balked of trading with Wennberg, setting up the leaked gas in advance, out of spite? Then he met his death on his way to keep the appointment, but the gas claimed its victim just the same?'

'It doesn't quite fit,' Andreas decided. 'There's still the second coffee mug, with sugar in it.'

'And there's still the lighter to explain away,' Siân said sadly.

'Perhaps there never will be a satisfactory explanation for that. Of course, Wennberg could have taken it off Paine earlier, even fancied it and bought it.'

'Or someone else did, an unknown.' Andreas was still feeling his way in the story. 'There has to be someone else, if what happened to Siân at Vai was deliberate. Paine wasn't the windsurfer. His skin is too pale and he hasn't the body.'

'Perhaps Miss Markham can help us with that,' the Captain said without much hope. He rose. 'I am going now to put a little pressure on that lady. By this time she should be anxious to confess how she set in motion such a run of fatalities. I hope she may confirm that Paine had *two* assistants, even if she didn't know their names.'

He rang through to Timbaki and spoke to one of the men he had left there. 'They are working on Mrs Wennberg now,' he reported when he had finished. He made a balancing movement with one of the scarred hands. 'Fifty-fifty, it seems.'

'We should avoid Timbaki for the rest of the day,' Andreas declared. 'In fact, I think we should find an alternative hotel.'

'Why not?' Fotiadis shrugged. 'Go back to Iraklion if you wish. Andreas, once again I am in your debt for your skills. I shall name Maria's next bull calf after you.' His eyes almost closed with laughter as he turned to shake Siân by the hand. 'You see, I *am* a family man after all.'

'Well,' Andreas demanded as they came to the end of the lane of orange groves, 'what now?'

'I'm hungry,' Siân discovered. 'Let's find a taverna with a smell of good cooking.'

It was early for an evening meal, but neither had eaten since breakfast. They had the family's whole attention at the ancient little inn they stopped at. The other customers were all old, male and local, well able to replenish their own glasses when required. Every now and again one would stroke his extravagant moustache and, fixing Siân with unwinking eyes, raise his glass ritually in salute. When she did likewise and drank to them there was an appreciative throaty rumble and the brown faces would crease with pleasure. 'At this rate,' Andreas said, 'you'll require treatment for alcohol poisoning.'

Between courses Siân asked to see the flower photographs again. Andreas pulled them from his jacket pocket and spread them over the table. While Siân gloated quietly over the prints he re-examined the ones she had taken at Vai, looking for any figure in the background which might have resembled Paine's. 'No,' he said definitely, 'there's no one the least like . . .'

Siân looked up as the silence lengthened. Andreas had removed his spectacles and was moving them about slowly just above the level of the prints, peering through. He seemed to have grown quite pale under his usual tan.

'Oh my God,' he said faintly. 'It can't be. It couldn't.'

CHAPTER 21

'What have you seen?' Siân asked, watching him with growing disquiet.

'Someone—I thought I knew. But I can't be sure. No.'

He's lying, she thought leadenly. Probably for the first time, he's tried to deceive me, but he's too transparent. It *is* someone he recognizes, and he doesn't want me to be frightened. She looked across at the print he had been examining. 'Are you anywhere on this?'

'I don't think so, unless I'm the little blob there, out to sea. It's the right colour for my sail. Do you remember the colour of the one that ran you down?'

'Not really. It was just a blur—bluey-greeny-grey. I'm not even sure of that. I'm sorry; it's no help.' She stared at the photograph. The foreground was very distinct. She could even see the stones in the ring of a woman lying on the sand, and the teeth on the zip fastener of her beachbag. Even in the middle distance definition was good enough to show the wetness or otherwise of people's hair and skin. But there was no one there whom she knew. Not even Per, unless a round shape in the lower right-hand corner was his knee as he squatted beside her, ready to go into the water.

Siân shuddered. 'This could have been the last shot I ever took, if you hadn't come along in time. This was just before it happened. I put the camera in its case, walked down to the sea and waded in.'

She looked up at Andreas. He still had the sick expression. If I keep calm, she thought, he may come round to telling me what he's seen. One of the figures in that picture is someone he thinks tried to kill me. And it shocks him.

The daughter of the taverna keeper brought them a basket of fruit; purple figs, oranges, early grapes and apricots. Andreas started talking about places where he'd swum off the mainland and, listening carefully, she decided his mind wasn't on what he was saying. When he ran dry of information she told him about English beaches, the flinty pebbles of Brighton, memories of seaweedy rock-pools and tiny green crabs slicing into wet sand to escape the children's probing plastic spades.

Coffee arrived and while they drank it he led the conversation back to the Wennbergs. 'You've seen more of them than I,' he said. 'What do you think Sven really felt about his son?'

Siân shook her head. 'Terrible disappointment, anger, shame. Shame above all, I think.' Then she remembered the man's bitterness as he confronted the havoc Per had caused in his mother's life. 'No. *Anger* mostly. He said last night that Per should never have been born.'

Andreas brooded over this. 'Is that the same as wishing him dead?'

'Not quite. In a way it's worse, because it would wipe out any good Per had ever done. But wishing isn't doing. Sven isn't a violent man. He wouldn't kill anyone.'

'Not even as a point of honour?'

Siân recalled the fury with which he'd once spoken of how Per had brought shame on their name, stooping to steal from a paralysed old man, starting his mother on cocaine. 'I really don't know.' She watched Andreas for any reaction to this. There was none. But then there had been no one remotely like Sven on that photograph which had upset him.

Then Sven's voice came back to her, remarking absently on Dr Vassilakis helping her at Vai. It had struck her at the time that she had never told him about the incident. He hadn't yet met Andreas and he'd claimed not to have seen Per for months. So how . . .

'Do you think,' Andreas said heavily, 'he mistrusted his son enough to send someone to spy on him?'

It had to be that. They had both reached the same conclusion by different routes. She looked into Andreas's troubled eyes and nodded slowly.

'And how far do you imagine this person's instructions would go?'

'Not to killing me. Certainly not Per. Obstructing him,

maybe, if he was likely to do anything dishonourable.'

'Which he was.'

'No, Andreas. No instructions would stretch to making him blow himself up!'

Andreas pushed his cup away and leaned over his arms on the table. 'It depends on who was sent. What sort of man. How he interpreted his duties.'

For some reason Siân thought of Hooper. Sven did pick on toughies, it was true. If he'd selected one such to mind his drug-addicted wife he could have selected just such another to tail his delinquent son. To spy on Siân herself and report back that she was an 'adventuress'.

'Andreas,' she said, reaching out to touch his bare forearm, 'I'm sure you're right. Per and I must have been followed. Maybe this minder overstepped instructions and tried to get rid of me as a potential threat. I can accept that. Are you going to show me the person you recognized in the photograph?'

He held her eyes defiantly and she thought he would refuse. Then he picked out a print from the wallet where he'd stowed them. 'There,' he said, pointing.

She saw the three-quarters back view of a man in purple swimming trunks. He was well-built, compact, very brown, but there seemed a fault on the print, or a mark of some kind. She rubbed at it with one finger end.

'It won't come off. It's on the man.'

'A birthmark, or some kind of scar?'

'Some three or four years ago, I'd say, he was shot at. The bullet slanted across his ribcage and entered the fleshy part at his waistline, coming out at the back and leaving quite a sizeable exit hole. See the puckering where it healed? He was lucky. One degree of deflection and he could have been killed.'

'How can you tell that in a print of this size?'

'Because I have seen the scar in the flesh. It isn't obvious, but I have a special interest in scar tissue, because I cause quite a lot myself.'

'You mean that you have actually seen *this man*? You know him? When, Andreas? Where?'

He puckered his lips and frowned, so she thought he would clam up on her again, but he only took a fresh breath and said, 'Today, at Matala.'

Even then she didn't realize at once what he meant.

'But—*Hooper*? No, Andreas, he was with Vanessa all that time.'

'He didn't have to be. Sven was away from Rome, and at the same time Vanessa disappeared with Hooper, causing some scandal.'

'Do you mean they came here?'

'Not Vanessa. She was in the clinic, where she stayed until after Per's death. Her husband told me that today. Later she joined him to come out here, before the cure was properly under way. Hooper materialized a day later. From where, we don't know, but he wouldn't have been needed at that clinic because the staff would manage their own surveillance. So he was either on leave or on alternative duties for his boss. I believe he was here. His instructions were to see what Per was up to while Sven repaired his indiscretions elsewhere.'

In the silence after his voice died away Siân was remembering Hooper's insistence on Matala today, and swimming. If she had gone into the water with him, would he have completed what he just failed to do at Vai? Or was there no longer any need? Was he satisfied that she couldn't recognize him from that split-second view at near-drowning? To test her he had even stripped down again for swimming, and she had noticed nothing. As a man of violence, perhaps he had enjoyed dicing with the chance of recognition, not thinking twice of leaving her drowned in one of those convenient caves if he found it necessary. She shivered.

'I'm sorry, love,' Andreas apologized.

'But, Andreas, where is he now?'

'I don't know. Perhaps Fotiadis is questioning him with the others.'

'He wasn't there with the rest of us this afternoon. That's why Sven had to go himself to the pharmacy. And—Andreas, Sven took their car! Which means that Hooper must have returned with it from Matala.'

'So he could have been there when Vanessa received that overdose.' Andreas's mouth tightened. 'A trained killer, a pitiless man.'

'He wanted her dead too,' Siân whispered.

'It seems so. Perhaps she knew too much about his other interests. I didn't mention it before, but she had never used a needle until then. I examined her for marks and there were none. She hadn't reached that stage yet, which made me almost sure the dose was meant to kill.'

'We must warn the Captain. Can we phone from here?'

'I doubt it. There's no line. We ought to start driving back, and stop when we see one.'

She said goodbye to the drinkers and went out to stand beside the car while Andreas paid for the meal. When he came out she asked, 'What would you do now if you were Hooper?'

'Cut my losses and get out.'

'Is that what mercenaries do when they find they're on the losing side?'

'They must do, to survive. Not that he will be out of pocket. Wennberg will have paid him well, Vanessa too, possibly. And he might have acquired a collection of faked Minoan artefacts. Pure gold, even if not genuine.'

Siân nodded. 'So how would he get away? Not by hired car from Timbaki, because that could be traced. Maybe he'd just get on a bus and lose himself at the far end before anyone knew he was missing.'

'So where is "the far end"?'

The girl frowned. 'He needs to get off the island; that means by sea or air.'

'The police could warn the airport before he reached it. Iraklion harbour too,' Andreas assured her.

'But he could leave by some nearer point. He could cross to the North African coast, couldn't he? From Ierapetra.'

'Or from Matala, if he made a private arrangement with a caïque-owner. There are smugglers who go across. He would get a welcome in Libya if he told the right story. He might have fixed that escape route earlier today when he came here with you. I thought he'd meant to contact a drug pusher, but he could have had a second motive in coming.'

'If we made for Matala we just might pick up some trace of him, and we can still ring Timbaki to warn Fotiadis.'

Andreas scowled. 'I am not letting you go anywhere near that man, Siân. He's too dangerous. If he saw us back again he could guess we were suspicious of him.'

'So you waste time arguing and we could lose him. Andreas, this is *my* hired car. I'm going back to Matala in it. Are you coming?'

His face darkened with anger. He looked like a furious bull before the charge.

'I mean it, Andreas. I shall leave you here if you won't—'

'You are a terrible woman,' he roared. 'Get in. I am driving. To Matala then, but you are still an impossible person!'

He spent more than seven minutes on the phone in the next village, talking first in rapid Greek, then listening, with interspersed grunts and monosyllabic questions. 'Where?' and 'Why?' and 'Who?' were words she managed to follow. At the end Andreas nodded, gave a short '*Ya soo!*' and replaced the receiver.

'Well?'

'Vanessa is not so well. Sven has been talking.' Andreas got back in the Volvo, slamming his door. 'We were right about him sending Hooper over to spy on Per. Sven had opened a letter to Vanessa as she was packed off to the clinic. It was from Per, saying he would spend a few weeks' vacation in Crete and see what he could dig up. So Sven thought he should be watched, as a precaution. Hooper was here from day two of Per's holiday. If he did his work properly he could have witnessed much of what remains a mystery to us.'

'A witness?' Siân questioned. 'Don't you think any more that he's the killer himself?'

Andreas shrugged, started the car. 'Let's leave an open mind for the present. It is vital, in any case, that he shouldn't slip away before he's thoroughly questioned. Fotiadis agrees he might be in Matala, and we are needed there to identify him for the local arresting officer.'

'They'd have an impossible task without us—one sun-tanned foreigner among so many.'

He glared at her, then suddenly grinned, putting a big paw over her wrist. 'You are right, I'll admit it. We go on to Matala. And you are still a very stubborn woman.'

'So, don't forget it. What do we do when we get there?'

'We shall be expected. In twenty minutes Fotiadis can perform miracles.'

Matala was different with the sun gone down, its outlines altogether softer; the typical Greek Island mixture of dilapi-dation and brash innovation, but smudged together with a naïve charm. The locals had not troubled to remove piles of debris at the roadside or by shop doorways, but they had strung up coloured lights on cables along some of the terraces on the shore side, and not many of the bulbs had burned out. The general air was amiable, vague and slow, as the sun-drugged little town made half-hearted efforts to come socially alive with the cool of evening. It needed one or two Manolises to get its catering on its feet.

Strolling the length of the street of tavernas, they were conscious of being surreptitiously watched. When they picked a corner table to sit at they didn't remain alone long. Siân looked up to recognize the Captain's assistant with the sharp suit. '*Ya sas*,' she said, 'how did you get here from Timbaki so quickly?'

He pulled a face. 'It is my free day. I am with my young lady, Sofia here.' He pulled forward by the hand a plump, pretty girl with soulful eyes.

They wouldn't sit down. Papadopoulou suggested a res-taurant a few doors back along the street. 'Our man is there,' he said. 'I saw him once in Timbaki, when he did not see me. We can be your friends out with you for an evening meal.'

'We've eaten,' Siân confessed.

'There's always room for *souvlaki* and Greek salad,' An-dreas growled. 'Come on, act a little drunk, then we can greet the man more cheerfully when we meet him.'

Hooper wasn't alone. The four newcomers entered the restaurant noisily, merry and a little clumsy in their movements. Neither Siân nor Andreas appeared to notice Hooper in the ill-lit bar. By the time they had hung over the charcoal burner and chosen their spitted suppers the Greek who had been at the mercenary's table had slipped away.

Siân was weaving a passage between the tables, balancing her plate at shoulder height on the flat of her palm. She stopped and peered. 'Goo' gracious. You're not *still* here?'

Hooper regarded her with flat, half-hooded eyes. 'I make the most of a buckshee half-day. I thought you were both going back to Timbaki.'

'Oh, we did, but it all got a bit out of hand,' Siân said vaguely with a wide gesture. 'The Wennbergs, you know.'

Hooper sucked a lump of lamb off his skewer and swallowed it. 'What was it this time?' His voice was casually disrespectful, but the eyes stayed wary. He made no space for the others at his table and Andreas shrugged, pointed with his fork to the next one. At least he'd not be obliged to introduce the other couple, and he could still pick up the conversation with Hooper.

'Vanessa,' Siân said, dumping her plate opposite the man, 'went a bit odd again and collapsed. Luckily Andreas was around.'

Hooper glanced across at the next table and nodded coldly. 'Ah yes, *Dr* Vassilakis. Lucky Mrs Wennberg, as you say.'

'Oh, I don't know. She's pretty sick all the same. So we cleared out.' Siân looked round and flapped a hand helplessly. 'No drink. I'm awfully thirsty.'

'*Vespinis!*' Hooper called the girl who was clearing glasses, and ordered a local wine, insisting it should be cool.

'You've picked up the language quickly,' Siân said, recklessly admiring, 'and you've only been on the island as long as me.'

She felt the atmosphere drop several degrees. There was a marked pause before Hooper asked, 'How do you make that out?'

'What out?' Owlish bemusement and a barely suppressed burp.

'That I have been so long on the island.'

'Oh, Sven said. He wanted you to watch Per. Peeping Tom, that's you. Dirty old man.' She waved her fork matily. 'No harm done, though.' She leaned forward confidentially. 'Got a nicer boy now.' She managed a giggle. 'What did you tell Sven? He didn't like me one bit at first.'

Hooper considered her evenly, chewing on his *souvlaki*. 'This and that. Quite a bit of "that".' He wiped his fingers and took the wine bottle the waitress had presented. 'Have a drink.' He poured into their glasses, twisted and handed the bottle across to Andreas. 'Kill it. The lady's had enough.'

'Cheeky beggar,' Siân complained childishly. 'Tell me something. Were you following us on the day the car went over the cliff below Zakros?'

'Maybe.'

'Why are you so cagey?' She sounded petulant. 'I bet you only did a half-job and made up all the rest.'

'You could be right.'

They weren't getting any admissions. Siân decided to risk everything on a bold throw. She bent forward and whispered groggily, 'Bet you didn't see Per actually kill that boy!'

It seemed that at that moment the whole room went quiet. Then the babble and clatter of crockery resumed. Siân peered leerily up at Hooper. In some subtle way his appearance had changed, as though the skin was pulled tighter over the angled bones, the ears lying flatter against the skull. A dangerous face. He stared at her pretended muzziness and she knew he wasn't fooled. His eyes flicked sideways towards the other table and he started rising, 'I have to go and—'

'—see a man about a boat?' Papadopoulou was also on his feet, right hand darting under the opposite armpit.

Siân never saw the next action. Darkly the table rose and came over on her, spilling food, wine, plates, glasses and herself over the floor. She lay among struggling feet and overturned chairs. There was a confusion of voices and crashing china. A woman screamed, men shouted. She

210

rolled away into a corner, feeling glass shatter and pierce her limbs as she moved. Someone came crashing through the chairs and landed almost on her. It was Papadopoulou, his pale jacket reddening with a growing spread of bright blood. She screamed, 'Andreas!' and groped around to pull herself up.

The policeman's girl came stumbling across and moaned over his limp body. Her hands snatched up a table napkin, rolled it and pressed it against the open knife wound.

'Good girl,' Andreas muttered, lumbering across. One sleeve was ripped from the shoulder but he didn't seem to be bleeding. 'Keep the edges closed.' Then he realized he'd spoken in English and repeated it in his own language.

He was all right; that was all that mattered to Siân then. She got to her feet and started picking shards of glass from her forearms. 'Hooper?' she asked.

'Got away. He had a knife. But they'll get him. The local boys are waiting down the street. He won't make it to the boats.'

'My fault,' Siân muttered. 'I went in too fast.'

CHAPTER 22

There was nothing speedy about Captain Fotiadis when next they saw him. He was dispensing drinks in the solid, ochre farmhouse among the orange groves, and some of the faces round him were ones Siân had previously seen in uniform. The change of venue seemed to make them shy. Even Papadopoulou was there, sickly diminished and against doctor's orders, the lilac silk shirt bulky with padding over his wound.

'Welcome, welcome,' Fotiadis cried, kissing first Andreas and then Siân on both cheeks. 'We are having a small celebration and you are our guests of honour. Here's to your health!'

'Health!' shouted the others and drank.

'You had better catch up,' Fotiadis said drily. 'I under-

211

stand that the lady is a great drinker, and ended up under the table on one memorable occasion. And this is a special day. Crude crimes we have here in plenty, but to solve an intriguing murder mystery is a feather in all our caps.'

'How did the interrogation go?' Andreas inquired, pouring water on his *ouzo* and watching it turn milky.

'We traded a few details,' the Captain said blithely. 'Hooper was under no pressure, and he gave us a good account of young Wennberg's fight with Spiros for the mask. He wasn't an actual eyewitness because it took place in the cellar, but he had Paine's version of what he discovered when he returned; that Wennberg was quite demoralized with fear and confessed. Although he didn't admit it, Hooper obviously helped Paine stage the car accident on the road to Kato Zakros. We let him get away with that for the present. There are bigger breaks to make first.'

'Mask?' Siân queried. 'You said Per fought Spiros "for the mask". What was that?'

'Did you ever see the so-called Mask of Agamemnon?'

'In photographs of Mycenean treasures, yes. It's beaten gold, rather grim, but priceless because of its antiquity.'

'This one purported to be even older. Sad that it was a fake. Of hammered gold and representing Poseidon, or some earlier version of the sea-god. Your little serpent was one of the marine creatures that made up his hair and beard. The interesting feature for the experts, however, was the presence of horns, which seemed to confirm an already suspected connection between the sea and the bull-cult of Knossos. It was thought to prove that this pre-Poseidon was the one that roared beneath the waves and made the earth tremble. The Cretan god of earthquakes, in fact.'

'No wonder Per was so wild to get his hands on it.'

'Yes, and he underrated the strength of those hands, because when he knocked young Spiros down the boy's skull was fractured on the stone floor. He was left there, in a coma for some hours before he died, and then Paine made a pact with Per to fix a suitable accident for the body to be found at. You can guess how the timing was arranged, to give Wennberg an alibi and to provide you both as witnesses to the car's death plunge. And you know now how Per Wennberg added some final touches when the fire failed to consume the body.'

'We both saw with field-glasses that the body had been thrown clear. I suppose that is why he agreed to climb down and take a closer look. And when I'd seen the boy's face and was likely to mention the fact, I was a threat to them all.'

'Exactly. Hooper was at Paine's lodgings when Per went there and asked what could be done to keep you quiet. They told him to prevent you talking at the police interview and to ring back later that day when they would have something arranged. He did so and was told to proceed to Vai for swimming. Hooper will admit to giving you a "bit of a fright" in the water there, but no more.'

'I don't understand how Hooper came into all this.'

'Because, as you guessed, his job was to follow Per. He saw young Spiros make the contact and trailed him back to where Paine was. He recognized in him an old acquaintance from their early Service days in Cyprus. Paine had been a young aircraftsman and Hooper in the Royal Marines. They had been in trouble together in Limassol, so, meeting up again, they decided to join forces, with Per as their victim, and probably intending to get their fortunes made by Miss Markham later.

'But there was one important piece of information Paine kept back. Hooper believes the fakes are genuine and that the lady bought them illegally from site robbers.'

'So who had the mask after Spiros was killed?'

'Paine had it off Per, as part of the price for covering his killing of Spiros; but, for his own safety, he let Hooper think that Per still had it. That is what Hooper was after at Timbaki, whereas Paine went down to negotiate its sale to Wennberg.'

'Taking it with him?'

'No. He left it in a safe-box in Iraklion. The key was on him when he met his death in the road accident. Perhaps when Per paid him off they would have gone together to get the mask out. We can only guess at that. But it was necessary if he was to qualify for Miss Markham's final payment.'

'And Per's death? That *was* Hooper?'

'Oh yes. To keep him quiet and cover his own retreat. I think he left the gold lighter there to implicate Paine in case it wasn't accepted as an accident. It would at least have held Paine up while Hooper got away. But he didn't know that just as he'd taken it off Paine, so Paine had taken it off Miss Markham.'

'Did he admit to killing Per?'

'Oh no. You see, we omitted to mention that Paine was dead, and Hooper gave a very concise description of how the Englishman visited the Swede that evening after an earlier scout around when he had shown interest in the cooking equipment and the inside of the barn. Hooper even claimed to have been watching when Paine was offered coffee, lit Per's cigar and let him go off to get blown up. It was a terrible shock to him, he said, so he lay low until his boss sent for him. Then he claimed it was impossible to admit he'd been there and incapable of stopping it in time.'

'But we know it wasn't like that.'

'There was only one difference in the crime itself. That of the man cast as murderer. The movements Hooper claimed to have observed were his own. When he had written out the statement, signed and dated it, we told him exactly when Paine had died.' The Captain shook his head. 'He went insane with rage. I have seen some furies in my time, but nothing like that.'

The Wennbergs were driving Miss Markham back with them to the airport at Iraklion. From there they would go on by air ambulance to Rome, she to Rhodes, but she spoke of clearing up at the villa and returning to England. She seemed very quiet, as though it was she and not her sister who was barely alive.

'I shan't keep on the villa at Lindos,' she told Siân, 'so I have to make settlements for Theo and Mina. If ever I go back there, to escape the Cumbrian blizzards, I shall put up at an hotel. Nothing permanent.'

'How about your arthritis?'

'I hope the remission may continue. And there are alternative cures to try. No, I don't need to run away any more. I shall pick up where I left off when I lost Roland, take an interest again in my land and my neighbours, probably interfere abominably in running things which have been admirably organized for the past half-decade.' She laughed shortly. 'Would you come and visit sometimes, Siân? Give me something to look forward to?'

'Of course.' But she would need to live an idle life to fit in all these promised visits: Manolis and Phyllia, Alison, Andreas. Thank God she had no need to keep in touch with the Wennbergs. That would have been too painful for them all. Probably Alison would write and tell her what became of them. She knew that Sven had decided to retire whether Vanessa ever recovered consciousness or not. If she did— a slender hope—perhaps from habit they would go on together, grieving and resentful, each having suffered too much to dare look back on it alone.

And if Vanessa failed to pull through, Sven would be free. Perhaps to follow Alison to England, to take up their life together where they had lost it so long ago.

Siân had more immediate romantic plans of her own. She phoned London and her stepmother had a message for her. Daddy was at a conference in Vienna all week, and at its end would fly down to Athens to meet her.

She went off to find Andreas and warn him. 'More time off hospital needed,' she said, her eyes shining. 'I'm summoned at last to account for myself to the family. Will you come along to hold my hand?'

'To London?'

'Athens. My father's flying out at the end of the week.'

A slow grin threatened to split Andreas's face in two. 'I'll phone my own family. We'll make it an occasion. Then you will see a real Greek celebration!'